BLANCHE OF BRANDYWINE

BLANCHE OF BRANDYWINE

By

GEORGE LIPPARD

American Fiction Reprint Series

BOOKS FOR LIBRARIES PRESS
Freeport, New York

1969

First published 1846 & 1847 in Philadelphia by G. B. Zieber
& Co. and by T. B. Peterson [cop. 1846]

(Items # 1678, 1679, 1670; Wright's AMERICAN
FICTION 1774-1850)

Reprinted 1969 in American Fiction Reprint Series from the
1876 edition by T. B. Peterson & Brothers under title "Blanche
of Brandywine; or September the Eighth to Eleventh, 1777".

STANDARD BOOK NUMBER:
8369-7005-5

LIBRARY OF CONGRESS CATALOG CARD NUMBER:
77-76926

PRINTED IN THE UNITED STATES OF AMERICA

BLANCHE OF BRANDYWINE

OR,

SEPTEMBER THE EIGHTH TO ELEVENTH, 1777.

1483882

A ROMANCE OF THE AMERICAN REVOLUTION.

THE SCENES ARE LAID ON THE BATTLE-GROUND OF BRANDYWINE.

BY GEORGE LIPPARD.

AUTHOR OF "THE LEGENDS OF THE AMERICAN REVOLUTION, 1776; OR, WASHINGTON AND HIS GENERALS;" "THE QUAKER CITY; OR, THE MONKS OF MONK HALL;" "PAUL ARDENHEIM, THE MONK OF WISSAHIKON;" "WASHINGTON AND HIS MEN;" "THE MYSTERIES OF FLORENCE;" "THE MEMOIRS OF A PREACHER;" "THE EMPIRE CITY; OR, NEW YORK BY NIGHT AND DAY;" "THE BANK DIRECTOR'S SON;" "THE ENTRANCED; OR, THE WANDERER OF EIGHTEEN CENTURIES;" "THE NAZARENE;" "THE LEGENDS OF MEXICO," ETC., ETC.

"'Blanche of Brandywine' is a continuous Legend of the Revolution. Rather a group of Legends combined in the form of a Romance. The scene is laid on the battle-ground of Brandywine; the time from the eighth to the eleventh of September, 1777. Among the purely historical characters introduced will be found—Washington, La Fayette, Greene, Mad Anthony Wayne, Stirling, Sullivan, Howe, Cornwallis, Lord Percy, and Count Pulaski. The interest of the reader is kept up from the first page to the last. The following scenes have been noticed and praised by the Press everywhere for their interest and power: the Escape of Washington, the Charge of Pulaski, the Meeting of the Brothers in the Quaker Temple amid the Scenes of the Battle, the Revenge of the Blacksmith Hero, and the Charge of Captain Lee's Rangers."—COURIER.

PHILADELPHIA:
T. B. PETERSON & BROTHERS;
306 CHESTNUT STREET.

PROLOGUE.

A BEAUTIFUL girl—a white-haired old man!

A beautiful girl, her proud form, attired in robes of white, a single lily, gleaming from the midnight blackness of her hair—an old man, clad in almost royal robes, with a star, glittering over his breast, an old man, with a high brow, blue eyes, and snowy hair.

They stood alone in the centre of that lighted hall, admired by an hundred eyes, flattered by a chorus of voices, this lovely girl, and proud old man. Say as you gaze upon this festival scene, this lofty hall, blazing with a brightness like day, these gaudy hangings, floating from the painted ceiling to the bounding floor, these young forms, undulating in the graceful circles of the dance, say as this light, this beauty, this motion dazzles your eyes, as the music fills your ears, do you not envy that old man, the lord of this proud mansion; do you not long for the destiny of that beautiful girl, who with the lily in her glossy hair, stands there, alone amid the throng, her dark eye gleaming with the memory of one, now far away?

Gaze from yonder lofty window, and behold the wide park, shadowy with age-worn trees, the deep lake, that now reflects the stars on its motionless bosom, the distant hills, that now arise into the midnight sky. A magnificent domain, this Earldom of Monthermer; a proud old man, this white haired Earl; a beautiful lady, this orphan ward, who bethrothed to his son, now stands with the lily in her dark hair, the glare of festival lights, upon her brow.

And the music, swells on the air, and the lake gleams in one broad column of light, and the stars shine calmly down, upon the towers of Monthermer, embosomed among lofty trees.

An hour passes. All is music and dance and beauty, in the lighted hall, but the old man, has gone to his lovely room. Yes, in that dimly-lighted chamber, beside the narrow window, with the stars gleaming over his pale face, he stands, gazing over the broad extent of his domains. There is agony in his writhing face, doom upon his darkened brow, remorse in his glaring blue eye.

He turns and speaks to the aged servant, who grey-haired and withered, stands like a piece of old-time furniture, by his master's side.

" Bernard, it is the Seventeenth of July !"

The servant shudders, from head to foot. With trembling steps, he turns to the farther corner of the chamber and lifts the purple tapestry. Three doors, known only to the Earl and his servitor, are revealed, with a few strange words, written on their dark panels.

On the first door is written: " THE SEVENTEENTH OF JULY."

On the second: " THE ELEVENTH OF SEPTEMBER."

On the third: " THE FOURTEENTH OF NOVEMBER."

The servant shudders, for on the return of each of these days, his master, the proud Earl, enters one of these rooms, and passes long hours in unspeakable agony.

(vii)

So it has been for years. Into the first, old Bernard may enter with his lord; but the others, are sacred to the Earl. No form, but his, may pass their threshold; no voice but his, disturb the echo of their walls.

"It is the Seventeenth of July!" said the Earl, and the cold drops, started out from his forehead. He unlocked the door of the first room, and entered. Soon a lamp, suspended from the ceiling, was lit by the old servitor and its light, fell around a vaulted chamber, with roof and walls and floor of stone. In the centre arose a white altar, surmounted by a cross of iron.

The proud Earl laid off the jewelled robe, which enveloped his slender form. Nay even the vest, which encircled his sunken chest. With his aged form, bare to the waist, he knelt on the hard floor, beside the cross of iron. He knelt groaning with agony.

"The lash, Bernard, the lash!"

The old servant, with tears in his eyes, drew forth, from beneath the curtains of the altar, a thick cord, knotted at the ends.

"Strike, Bernard, and do not—spare," said the old Earl, in a choking voice.

Then Bernard, with tears raining down his aged face, wound one end of the cord around his wrist, and lashed his master on the shoulders and breast, until the blood ran down. His withered flesh, was all one mass of gore. As the servant struck him, with the dripping cord, he called on God for mercy, murmuring a terrible confession of broken vows, innocence betrayed, and holy rites profaned

Still as the blood ran down, in separate streams, he shrieked, "Strike, Bernard, strike!" The memory of this day is terrible, but, oh God—the Eleventh of September! The Eleventh of September, it will soon be here! I can endure the lash; that I have endured without a murmur, for twenty years! But that terrible Fourteenth of November, spare me, oh my God, spare a weak old man!"

At last he sank exhausted on the floor, his hands covered with the blood, that streamed from his breast and shoulders. Bernard, weeping like a child, wrapped the azure robe around his form, extinguished the lights, and bore him from the fatal room. He locked the door, and laid his master on his couch.

After a long while he unclosed his eyes.

"This seventeenth of July is terrible, but—ah! The Eleventh of September —the Fourteenth of November—my God, have mercy and crush me at once! This slow torture is worse than a thousand deaths!"

His words were interrupted, by a hurried footsteps, and a voice, shrieking in tones of horror—

"Woe for us, woe! The Lady Isidore—ah woe, woe! So young too and yet to die! Could none of ye save her? As she wandered by the lake, why did ye not warn her from the brink? Ye saw her, hurry from the hall, ye saw her white form, gleaming among the trees, ye heard the plunge, and now—woe, woe, woe! There is her scarf and the lily, that she wore in her dark hair!"

And with a shriek the aged woman, burst into the room, and flung herself at the feet of the Earl, placing in his hands, all that remained of the Lady Isidore.

The white scarf, which had been warmed by her bosom, the lily which had gleamed from her dark hair.

"This" shrieked the Earl. "This, is but the seventeenth of July, but the Eleventh of September, the Fourteenth of November—they are yet to come "

BLANCHE OF BRANDYWINE.

BOOK THE FIRST.

MONTHERMER.

CHAPTER FIRST.

THE DOOM OF A BLIGHTED HEART—THE PACQUET AND THE DREAM.

"I TELL you, Clarence Howard, that there is a—hell!" exclaimed the young lord, leaning over the oaken table, while his face glowed in the light of the lamp beams—" a dark, a fearful, and an eternal hell—far more dread, far more terrible, than the flames of a never-ending fire, imagined by priests, or taught by the dogmas of superstition! Aye—curl your lip with that incredulous smile, and laugh in my face, if it pleases you! But, Clarence, there is a hell—dark, fearful and terrible. That hell is here—*the hell of a blighted heart !*"

The young lord half raised himself from his seat, and leaning one clenched hand upon the oaken table, stood for a moment gazing fixedly in the face of his companion, while over his pale and expressive features, glowing in the light of the solitary lamp, there flashed one wild, one dread, and intense expression, which trembled along his lips, and brightened in his dark eyes, overarched by the darker brows, fixed in a settled frown.

"My lord, you really discompose me"—exclaimed his companion, glancing with his clear, blue eyes, around the dark and dismal apartment. "You are agitated, Monthermer—you are, by my soul. Now, I don't like this agitation, for—for—" he continued, with a faint and commisserating smile, as he quietly settled his nether limbs on the oaken planks of the table —" for it's in such bad taste! But, my lord, must you carry this valley beauty off for certain ?"

The complacent Clarence shifted his curiously carved German pipe from one side of his small mouth to the other, and while an expression of inimitable ease and *nonchalance* gathered over his features, he glanced across the table at the face of his companion, but as instantly withdrew his gaze, for the eyes of the young lord flashed with a clear and brilliant, yet strange expression, and his small and finely chisselled features were impressed with a calmness that was too fixed to be natural, too rigid to indicate aught but powerful, yet suppressed emotion.

"I have told you, Howard, it must be done!" said Monthermer, in a low and even voice. "It must be done; and, by my soul, it shall be done, ere another night has passed over this head!"

The scene was strange and solemn. The light of a dim and smoking lamp, standing upon the massive oaken table, fell in fitful gleams around the small apartment, with its closed window-pannels, its walls, confined and compressed, dark with smoke and tottering to decay, while the low ceiling, supported by awkward rafters, and hung with cobwebs, slanted irregularly to one side, completing the appearance of neglect and gloom, that hung like a cloud around the lonely room.

The handsome figure of Clarence, half veiled in a drooping military cloak, carelessly disposed along an armed chair, with the nether limbs defended by Hessian boots, resting on the oaken table, was also disclosed in the lamp beams, while his clear and ruddy face, relieved by a well-powdered wig, and marked by calm and vacant blue eyes, a prominent acquline nose, and thin and well formed, yet expressionless lips, looked the very picture of easy assurance and genteel selfishness.

His military cloak falling back over his shoulders, gave to view the gaudy coat, crimson in hue, and brilliant with gilded epaulettes and other ornaments of gold, with a slight ruffle protruding from an unfastened button near the throat, while the belt of snow-white buck skin encircling his slender waist, supported the trooper's sword depending from his side. In the delicate fingers of his right hand, he grasped a handsome German pipe, which ever and anon he puffed, sending thin light wreaths of smoke to the ceiling, and filling the air with the fragrance of the Indian weed.

His companion, who stood half raised from his seat, glancing across the table, was a young man, with a slight and well-proportioned figure, marked by a prominent chest, drooping into a long and slender waist, while his small and delicate hands, with thin and tapering fingers designated the descendant of a long line of Norman ancestors.

A military cloak of blue, thrown back on the oaken chair, disclosed the proportions of his figure, clad in a close fitting coat of dark rich green velvet, faced with gold, and bright with a jeweled star suspended along the breast, while over his prominent chest swept a belt of dark leather, from which depended a long, straight sword, with hilt of wrought gold, marking the Aid-de-camp of Lord Cornwallis, and the Lieutenant Colonel of the Hussar corps of the British army.

His face, standing out boldly in the glare of the lamp, with the back-ground of gloom and shadow, was one that might be looked upon but once and never forgotten. The features small and delicate, and pale and faded in hue, were relieved by luxuriant masses of jet black hair, sweeping aside from the calm and unwrinkled brow, and falling in glossy ringlets to the very shoulders, untouched by powder and untortured by the barber's art. His eyebrows were dark and arching, his eyes of intense and flashing blackness, his nose regular and Grecian in outline, the chin small and prominent, and the mouth, neither very small nor very large, was marked by thin, expressive lips, that trembled like things of seperate life, as he thus stood regarding the complacent individual who was seated opposite.

This was the general outline of his face, but there was a clear, wild, dreamy brilliancy in his eye, a vague and shadowy expression resting upon his pale yet youthful countenance, an expression that moulded the contour of his face, indented a solitary wrinkle between the eyebrows, and gave a character to his visage which seemed fraught with dark prophecy and shadowy omen.

"I tell you, Clarence Howard, that I have sworn a solemn vow that this proud girl shall be mine, and none other than mine! And, let me ask you, Clarence, did you ever know George Percy, of Monthermer, to break a vow, or fail in a single act he had sworn to accomplish?"

"Nev-er did," drawled out Howard, eyeing a volume of smoke wreathing upwards, with a calm, philosophical glance. "But then, my lord, this idea of falling in love with a—a—rustic beauty, and wishing to marry her at that! Curse me, my lord, but it's in such bad taste?"

"Captain Howard, I am in no mood for trifling!" exclaimed the young lord in a quiet, even voice, that came through his clenched teeth.

"Y-e-s, y-e-s, my lord," exclaimed the complacent soldier. "But just look at the case. Here is young Lord Percy, heir of the broad lands of Monthermer, renowned in the Court of Windsor, famed in the circles of Almacks—the envy of the one sex, the adoration of the other—the well known roue—the finished man of the world—all at once, in the full glow of London life, urged by some wild freak of fancy, or the devil knows what, suddenly accepts a commission in his Majesty's Huzzars, and sails for these cursed wilds of America, just the same as me, or any other miscreant of a—younger brother! And, for what, pray, does Lord Percy do all this? Why, for the very questionable purpose of falling in love with a country Phillis, daughter of some retired Provincial Colonel, who served in Braddock's time, and who lives in a sort of a wilderness, called Wild-wood Grange, situated on the banks of this stream they call the Brandywine, near this identical Cross-Road inn, in which we are now sitting, and within a stone's throw of a ford, called Chadd's Ford. And this Lord George Percy not only falls in love with the country Phillis, but, indeed, he wishes to marry her; and he, the beautiful boy, all the time betrothed, (that's th

word, isn't it?) to a proud Countess in merry England. Now, my lord
you must see all this is in bad taste, very, my lord."

"Clarence Howard," exclaimed the young lord, "let me whisper a word
in your ear. You speak of—you know not what. Clarence, gaze upon
me, and tell me, do I look like a man who would hesitate to use any means
to accomplish a vow, for the fulfilment of which he has sworn the safety of
his soul ?"

"Why, Monthermer," drawled the Captain, "to tell you the truth, your
face, just now, wears that strange, wild look, that I have often noticed pass
over your features in the gayest moments of the ball-room, or amid the most
jovial revellers of the mess-table. Now, my lord, I don't like such agitations
of the countenance. They are all of a piece—in such bad taste !"

"Clarence, I have been your friend in times of difficulty," exclaimed
Percy, resuming his seat, "and now I demand your aid—the aid of a true
heart and a stout arm. I will first tell you the whole story of my love for
this girl. It is not more than ten days gone since our troops, under the
gallant Howe and the brave Cornwallis, made a landing on the peninsula,
washed by the Chesapeake, near the mouth of the Susquehanna. No sooner
was the landing made, than, urged by some unknown, some indefinable
impulse—call it restlessness—call it a spirit of adventure—call it what you
will—I obtained leave of absence from our General for a few days, and,
with some ten gallant hussars in attendance, rode northward into the interior
of the smiling land, that opened like a pastoral Arcadia before me. A week
ago, on a fine, clear afternoon, I found myself riding near the entrance of
this valley—near this place they call Chadd's Ford—when we were suddenly
suprised by a skirmishing party of the rebel force—some of my men were
killed, and I was left insensible on the earth, while the remainder of my
gallant band made a stout fight over my body and drove back the rebel
skirmishers. I was laid, insensible, upon the road side. When I awoke
to consciousness—"

"Y-e-s," murmured Clarence, puffing at his German pipe, "that's just
like an old story. 'Left on the field for dead—when I awoke to consciousness.' Very good."

"When I awoke to consciousness," the young lord resumed in a warm
and impassioned tone, "the warm light of an afternoon sun was streaming
round a pleasant chamber, opening upon the west, with the breath of flowers
and balm of the autumnal air floating through the opened windows. The
chamber was a pleasant one, and the couch upon which I reposed afforded
ease and comfort to my wounded frame. I awoke, and—oh, God—the
vision that met my unclosing eyes ! A calm and lovely face—all youth—
all bloom—all innocence, was gazing upon mine. A calm and lovely face,
shaded by glossy locks of midnight hair, with dark eyes, of wild and
dreamy beauty, that were gazing all softly and sadly into mine, and seemed
melting with liquid light as they gazed ! And, while a fair white hand was

aid upon my throbbing brow, I looked upon that face, so wild, so dreamy in its beauty, and the thought flashed over my soul, that, for that fair face, with all its grandeur of hidden thought, with all its nameless charm, its weird and mystic fascination, I could dare death in any shape, and grapple with the terrors of the World Beyond—aye, grapple with a terror more dread, more terrible, than,—let me whisper it in your ear,—than this phantom form which glides by my side day by day; which startles sleep from me at night—aye, the phantom form which guided me across the wide Atlantic, which led me, step by step, to this lovely vale—this phantom form now with me, about me. around me, leading me onward to an unwept death—to a *nameless grave !*"

As he spoke, Lord Percy slowly arose from his seat, and while his chest heaved with a terrible emotion, with every feature of his pale countenance convulsed by a fearful expression that worked along his features like a death-spasm, with his dark eyes flashing with that strange, wild light, so often noticed in their glance of late, in a voice marked by no loud shout, no sudden burst of passion—in a voice solemn and deep-toned, he uttered the words that caused the complacent Clarence to start from his seat with a feeling of sudden horror.

"Clarence, Clarence !" he exclaimed, "I am a doomed—a fated man ! Doomed and fated ! One little week will measure out my life ! But in life or death, Blanche Walford must be mine !"

"Goodness me, Morthermer !" Clarence exclaimed, "you will really drive me mad. Tut, tut—this is all folly—all d——d nonsense. You are unwell, Percy, you are, positively. You quite frighten me—and it's in such bad taste to frighten one's friends."

"One word more, Clarence," Percy resumed. "As I gazed upon this lovely face, I marked that the form of the proud girl was that of a queen— each gesture was grace—each attitude was loveliness. I loved her—with my whole soul I loved her—without knowing who she was—scarce knowing her name. I looked upon her beaming countenance, where thought shone forth like a star, and for one kind word from her, I would have named her Lady Percy ; and for one soft smile, I would have throwm—oh ! how willingly thrown, the lands of Monthermer at her feet."

"Your uncle, the Duke of Northumberland," murmured Clarence, in a half-aside tone, "would say that was in shockingly bad taste."

" And thus, while my wound, which was more painful than alarming in its character, grew better, day by day, did I remain at the mansion of Colonel Frazier, which you may see from the door of this Cross-Road inn, standing upon a hill that arises, green and grassy, over the waters of the quiet stream—the Brandywine. Thus did I remain, day after day, content to sit unnoticed near the side of this proud girl : content to mark the bloom on her cheek, myself unmarked ; content to sit silently, listening to the on, soft music of her voice, whose lightest tone flows with the harmony of thought."

"Tolerably good taste, that, for George Percy, the lady-killer of the West end," murmured Clarence, taking an ardent puff at his meditative pipe.

"The very morning of this day, Clarence, I walked forth with Blanche Walford, along the brow of the hill, where arises the mansion of Colonel Frazier. Scarce knowing what I did, maddened by her beauty, I seized her hand. She repulsed me with a chilling look. I pressed that fair, white hand to my lips. I wound my arm around her waist. In an instant my kiss was upon her lip. She flung me from her with scorn. She taunted me with making dishonorable proposals to an innocent girl. I threw myself at her feet. I offered her my hand—I, George Percy, of Monthermer, offered this nameless niece of this Provincial Colonel, my hand. I laid Monthermer its towers and its castles, its broad lands and its revenues, at the feet of this nameless girl—this Blanche Walford! And what think you was her answer?"

"Did I not know otherwise," observed Clarence, "I should say she'd be cursed glad to take you at your 'bid.'"

"She drew her proud form to its full height," continued Percy, as a single red spot glowed in his pale cheek—"She waved her hand proudly to me—she bowed with a smile of keen and biting sarcasm—'The neice of a Provincial gentleman were not a fitting bride for the proud English lord, whose pleasure it is, to fight for the cause, that writes its title to justice and right in the blood of a happy and unoffending people!'—These were her words—proud and peerless as a queen she spoke them. By St. George! how her eyes blazed—how her cheek fired as she spoke!"

"That, my lord," murmured Clarence, "is certainly a very remarkable girl. In point of beauty she may be a phœnix, or anything else peculiarly rare, but in point of taste, she is, it strikes me, most especially deficient. Her taste is certainly d——d bad!"

"I have told you my story, Clarence—the rest you know."

"Oh, yes," drawled the exquisite—"How I met you this morning, riding pell-mell, with your seven hussars at your back,—bound for the Lord knows where!—How you joined me on a scouting party; how we returned in company to this neutral ground—the valley of the Brandywine—and how, after a hard day's ride, we put up at this 'Green Tree' Inn, at Chadd's Ford. And now, my lord, for our future operations."

Percy started from his seat, and traversed the apartment with a quick and hurried step, while his right hand clutched nervously at the hilt of his sword.

"Clarence!" he exclaimed, suddenly turning round, "how far from this valley are the British forces?"

"About ten or twelve miles to the south east," returned Captain Howard

" The Continentals, under *Mister* Washington, are supposed to be near the river Delaware, in the vicinity of a place they call Wilmington, about fifteen miles to the south west——"

" A battle must take place within a week?" inquired Montherner— " Is it so, Clarence? You nod your head. How long will it be ere the British troops arrive this far, on their path northward?"

" Not more than three days, my lord," answered Howard. " 'Tis now the seventh of September, Anno Domini, 1777, as the copy books say. By the tenth or eleventh, the banner of the red cross will float over the valley of the Brandiwine."

" To-morrow morning, Clarence," said Percy, as he drew near to his companion, " nay, this very night, you will return to the British camp. I must prolong my leave of absence. Three miles west of this place, looking out from among the depths of the forest, there is a lonely cabin, tenanted by a friend of the British cause. Meet at this cabin to-morrow night—meet me at sundown—meet me with twenty good stout dragoons, whose hands are sure, as their hearts are daring. Let them be armed to the teeth. Not a word to these dragoons of the object of their adventure. Only tell them, that it is an adventure that will try their mettle, and put the steel of their broadswords to the test. And as for the reward—hark ye, Clarence— promise each man of them a fortune, in case the affair of the night is crowned with success."

" T-wenty men!" slowly drawled Clarence, depositing his pipe upon the oaken table—" Y-es, my lord, it can be done. What with the aid of tories, refugees and, renegades from the American camp, it can be done. I must away to camp to-night. I will leave Sergeant Hamsdorff in the valley until to-morrow, with a band of five or six dragoons. He must scour the adjoin- ing country—collect information of the rebel movements—quarter traitors, arrest deserters, and hang spies. Quite comprehensive—eh, my lord? To- morrow night he will meet me at the wood-cabin—all in good taste."

" This Sergeant Hamsdorff is the man commonly called Hessian Dick— aye, Clarence? I had rather he were not here. He is a wild, reckless fellow, and may do much to mar my plot; however, let it pass. And now, Clarence, at sundown, twenty men armed to the teeth—ready for any fight —prepared for any adventure? This is our agreement. And now I must away to the wood cabin."

He slang his military cloak over his shoulders as he spoke, and turned to the door, when Clarence suddenly arose from his seat, and hurrying forward took Lord George by the hand.

" A word with you, Percy," he said, in a low, quick voice. " I am a fop, and you may think me a heartless fellow; but you have been my friend when I had not a friend on earth, and, by ***, I'll stick to you to the death. I want to ask you one question. Sit down for a moment, and hear me. There now—I never like professions of friendship—they're in such bad taste.

But, Percy, I know there is something preying upon your mind. You are
haunted by some horrible fear—some dreadful fancy. Had your voyage to
America no other object than the mere gratification of a devil-may-care
spirit of adventure?"

"A moment, Howard, and I will tell you all," said Monthermer, advan-
vancing to the door of the apartment, leading to the bar-room of the 'Green
Tree' Inn. "Can the revellers in the outer room of this hovel hear us?"

"I d-o-nt know; but supposing they did, it would be in very good taste
to cut their ears off."

" Well, Howard," exclaimed Percy, motioning his companion to a chair,
" I will entrust you with my secret. You know my father—the once gallant
and adventurous Earl of Monthermer—he is now aged and care worn, and
when last I saw him he trembled on the very edge of the grave. Every
day I expect—with fear and anxiety I expect—the arrival of the sad news
which will name me Earl of Monthermer."

" Now, M-o-n-ther-mer!" drawled Clarence, " you say you love this father. I don't doubt it, not I: but how came you to leave him when so near
death? I should say it was in bad taste."

" The Earl of Monthermer implored me as his son, to hasten to America
—to hasten to the wilds of Carolina, among the high hills of the Santee.
He entrusted me with the execution of a commission, which by the solemn
form of an oath, he bade me fulfil. This was the cause of my visit to
America—until that commission is fulfilled, the Earl of Monthermer will
know neither peace nor rest; and as for myself—ha! ha! those words have
been strange sounds for years!"

" And that commission?" inquired Clarence, starting forward, while his
clear blue eye shone with interest—" And that commission?"

" *Secret!*" said Percy, in that deep, even tone of voice which went to the
heart of his listener—" Secret from all eyes, secret from all ears but my
father's. I am but the blind instrument of its execution. Clarence!" he
continued, leaning suddenly forward, while his voice sank to a thrilling
whisper, " I may fall in battle—I may die suddenly in my bed—I may sink
to Night and Death in some nameless fight or broil. When I am dead, you
will find a pacquet resting upon my very heart. You will find its destination
and its object written upon the envelope. Swear to me, Clarence, by the
God that made you, by your hope of Heaven, swear, that whether I fall in
battle, or in some nameless fray—whether I meet death on the couch or in
the field—swear that you will take charge of this pacquet—that you will
make the execution of the commission named on its face, the sole object of
your life, and, if need be, the sole object of your death! Swear, Clarence!
by the God above us—by your hopes of Heaven, swear!"

" I swear!" exclaimed the man of the world, in a solemn and changed
tone of voice, as he laid one hand upon his sword hilt, while the other was
raised to Heaven.

" And now, Clarence, I have told you all. I have——"

" No, Monthermer," exclaimed Captain Howard, " you have not told me all. I know there is something more resting upon your mind—some dark presentiment of coming doom—some fearful forboding of overshadowing evil. It was of this you spoke some few minutes since."

" Ah, ha ! Clarence !" exclaimed Percy, with a ghastly smile. " So you wish to know all ? You wish me to bare to your gaze the secrets of a heart, which the world might term a madman's heart, and I will tell you Clarence. There is a dark presentiment of evil and of death—sudden evil and sudden death—with me ever, riding my soul like a nightmare, and gliding beside me by day, and hovering around me by night. I feel—I know—that I am a fated man !"

" Monthermer, tell me. How did this presentiment, this wild fancy, originate ?"

" It was a night of storm and terror, when we were crossing the wide Atlantic—you remember the night—dark, fearful, terrible !—lightning around —the thunder above—and death below ! When the lightning flashed most vividly—when the ship's timbers groaned and started—when the red thunderbolt came crashing down the mainmast—then, Clarence, then I had a dream——"

And drawing closer to his friend, in a low and whispering voice, that thrilled Clarence to the heart, Lord Percy of Monthermer, with a face all expression, and an eye all fire and brilliancy, murmured forth the story of his dream, while around, the gloom of the apartment, the faint flickering flashes of lamplight, and the silence of the hour, added awe and terror to the legend.

CHAPTER SECOND.

THE INN ROOM—THE HOST—THE FARMER'S MAN—THE BLACKSMITH AND THE SOLDIER.

WIDE and roomy, with a low ceiling and an oaken floor, two windows looking to the north and two toward the south, the bare and blackened walls on one side and the spacious fire-place on the other, the bar-room of the hostel of the Green Tree was dimly lighted by two large candles, standing in candlesticks of iron, and placed upon the large table made of roughest oak, fixed, with its massive legs all curiously fashioned and carved, in the centre of the inn room floor. Flickering gaily and merrily, a light hickory fire burned on the hearth, whizzing and streaming around a savory steak, while around the table were seated three individuals—a mechanic, a stout

3

farmer's man, and a soldier—with their faces and their attire all turned to glowing red by the light which ever and anon fell upon the slim and bending figure of mine host of the Green Tree, as pacing along the oaken floor, with a peevish, snarling voice, and an extravagant movement of his long, bony arms and talon-like fingers, he gave his own ideas and opinions on matters and things in general, with an independence of thought and action that was quite creditable and very worthy of general imitation.

"You needn't talk to me, Tom Davis,—Gotlieb Hoff, you needn't talk to me!" cried the slender, little man, as he shuffled along the floor, diving his hands in the spacious pockets of his breeches, which hung ungartered at the knee, "I tell ye I'm mad, regular, right down mad. Aye, aye, Tom—Blacksmith Tom—Iron Tom—any kind of Tom but sensible Tom—you may wink at Gotlieb there: and, Gotlieb, you make a face at that sleepin' red coat,—dang it, ain't his steak a burning?—but, I tell you, for all that, times hain't as they used to be. The world's gone wrong, I say—upside down—it wants winding up—and the Britishers are a-goin' to wind it up, and be hanged to 'em. And the Continentals are goin' to help 'em—may blue blazes take 'em. A purty time as Chadd's Ford's people shall have 'twixt two fires! Oh, *sich* a nice time!"

And, roused up to a pitch of irrepressible excitement, the host stopped suddenly before the oaken table, and, throwing his exaggerated features forward—the large, pale nose, tinted with red; the wide mouth, the sallow cheeks, and the wide oyster-like eyes, all shining in the light—he cast a sudden gaze at the portly soldier sleeping at one end of the oaken table, and very deliberately proceeded to make a face—and an expressive face it was—at the fat, round cheeks, and obese form of the unconscious trooper.

"There's scarlet for you, Iron Tom," he exclaimed in his quick, peevish way. "There's scarlet for you, Gotlieb Hoff! Scarlet on his shoulders—scarlet on his fat paunch—scarlet on his nose! Wonder how much brandy it tuk to paint that pictur? And he must eat my steak, must he?—hey? But he shall pay for it—by the lord, he shall. And these is fine times—all eat and all drink—dev'lish little pay. Tom Davis, it is my opinion that old sattin has broke loose of late, and taken the reins right into hand. Where's he drivin' us? Axe the Britishers—axe the Continentals." Here the little man made one of his superhumanly ugly faces, and then stooping for a moment to fix the loosened slippers on his shuffling feet, he raised his head with a sardonic grin. "Axe your grand-mother," he continued, "axe her—axe the old lady her own self. Pr'aps she'll tell you where old sattin' a drivin' us to!"

"Why Hirpley Hawson, you are in a ter'ble pucker," said the blacksmith, turning his rugged, yet honest face, with the broad forehead, the clear grey eye, the short, thick nose, the prominent chin and the stiff bristled hair that covered his head, towards the light of the fire. "I wonder if you ain't in a dreadful pucker," he continued in his low, drawling tone of voice as, raising the beaker of ale to his lips, he took a hearty draught, winking sidelong towards Gotlieb at the same time, with a glance that seemed to say, " now, see me give Hirpley a rostin'." " Now, Hirpley, I don't see why you should complain. You've plenty of customers here at Chadd's Ford— plenty. Yer house is always full. Why, man, you ought to be coining sov'reigns."

" Y-a-h—'besure he ought—by Saint Christuffel he ought," exclaimed a voice strongly spiced with Pennsylvania German, and the phlegmatic face of Gotlieb, with the clear skin, the blue eyes, and the encircling locks of bright, golden hair, was turned towards the growling host. " Why, I looks down from de hill up at Coonel Frazier's every day, and, mein Gott! what lots o' people I see here! *Thee* tav-ern, Hirpley," he continued, with a slight approach to the Quaker dialect, " ish run down mit custom—it ish, by Saint Christuffel, it ish."

" ' Y-a-h'—' thee and thou'—' by Saint Christuffel,' " whined Hirpley Hawson, suddenly wheeling round toward the phlegmatic Gotlieb. " Quarter Dutchman, quarter Englishman, quarter Quaker, and three quarters fool! Gotlieb Hoff—I wonder you hain't half Yankee like-*wise*. Who ever heard a feller talk in that quilted way—regular patch-work talk, as I'm a sinner."

The irritable host made another face, dived his hands yet deeper in the unfathomable breeches pocket, traversed the inn room twice, with his short pipe-stem legs shuffling about in a fashion somewhat circular, and then in his harsh, whining, whipt-child-sort of a voice, he commenced his angry soliloquy afresh.

" Plenty o' custom, did ye say ?" he exclaimed. " D—l bless sich custom, say I! To-day a party o' red coats! eat, drink, tear and swear—all of the best too! To-morrow, a party of blue coats! Lord, don't my rye whiskey go though? Don't the vittles fly—don't the steaks smoke on the h'arth. And, where's the pay, I'd like to know?—hey? Where's the first brass fa'thin'? The red coats, (may sattin burn 'em in their own lobster-jackets,) they pay me with 'cusses! The blue coats square off the account with a— ' oh, it's all for the good o' the country.' What care I for king or country. I'm my own king—I'm my own country. I am—(dang it, is that steak burning?) This Green Tree Tavern's my country—it is; I say it is. I'm king here. I cook my own vittles, do my own washin', churn my own butter, keep all woman-kind away from my doors—and don't care a tinker's 'cuss for nobody, I don't; no, I don't—hanged if I do!"

And as the little man stood in the centre of the table, with his ugly face turned to the hearth, a sudden blaze of the hickory fire flashed round the room and made a picture of the scene.

There were the warm flashes of light falling round the apartment, reddening the rafters and glowing along the smoky walls; there was the massive oaken table, with the light falling full and strongly on the muscular

form of the stout black smith, seated at one end, his burly chest protruding
in the light, his swarthy and black bearded features, topped by stiff, bristled
hair, all warming in the kindly beams ; while at the other end, resting on a
capacious chair, with one large gouty hand on his trooper's sword, slept and
snored the half drunken soldier, his gross and corpulent form, clad in buff
and scarlet, forming a substantial point of the picture, his bald pate, his low
forehead, the short nose, with wide nostrils, the large sensual mouth brist-
ling with a thick, grizzly mustachio that widened around his chin and
throat into a stiff black beard, intermingled with streaks of grey, were all
turned to a deep and blushing scarlet that would have made a frozen man
warm to look upon.

In the centre of the table, with his face to the fire, clad in the coarse attire
of a farmer's man—the linsey-woolsey coat with a diminished tail, the
brown vest, with lappels of tremendous facilities for spacious pockets, the
wide shirt collar, and the parti-colored neckerchief, in a position of great
self-complacency and ease—sat Gotlieb Hoff, his clear, ruddy face, with the
clustering locks of light golden hair, the large blue eyes, and the sand-hued
beard, all standing out boldly in the hearth light ; while, at his very shoulder, his long slender arms upraised, and his narrow chest thrown forward,
stood the irritable Hirpley Hawson, *the* figure of the picture, with his pale,
ague-ish face contorted into an expression of combined peevishness, ill-
humor, sarcasm, and misanthropy—the large, wide mouth, drawn half way
up the sallow cheek, the goggle-eyes starting from their sockets, the high,
narrow forehead, all intricate with wrinkles and with frowns ; and first and
foremost, beacon-like and prominent, twisted in an opposite direction from
his mouth, that large, pale nose, stared the fire out of countenance, while on
its very tip shone one brilliant and intense spot of carbuncled red.

"Why, Hirpley, somebody must a-been givin' you a bit o' somethin'
sweet," Iron Tom Davis observed, taking a fresh draught of the Green Tree
ale, "yer in sich a spankin' good humor about this time. Howsomever
Hirpley, or Growly Jake, as the valley people call you, you must allow
George Washington hain't sich a small figure in creation, arter all."

"Shortz Washington is a good man," observed Gotlieb Hoff, with a very
determined manner—"Y-a-h, by Saint Christuffel."

"Then, why don't ye go and sght for him ?—hey ?" cried Hirpley Hawson, wheeling from one face to the other. "Then, why don't ye go and
fight for him ?—hey ?—hey ? Yer a fine feller, Gotlieb Hoff—big-fisted,
bull-headed feller ! George Washington wants soldiers. There you sit,
smokin' your pipe, up at Curnel Frazier's—and ' George Washington's a
fine feller.' ' George Washington no small figur' in creation'—hey, Tom
Davis ? Then, why the d——l don't you put a naught to that figure ?
Why don't ye jine yourself to Washington ?—you might count ten. together.
You're very purty men, both o' you. You're worth considerable more that
'he market price. Baugh !"

" Why—why—Hirpley," exclaimed the blacksmith, somewhat confused by the pointed cross-examination, " you see I am a plain man ; and I've got my blacksmith-shop over at Dilworth-corner, 'bout two miles north-east o' this place, and I've got my wife to make a livin' for—and there's a baby crying about our house ; and the Britishers hain't trod on my toes as yet, and so—and so—I've kept myself at home. But—"

" Tat's jist te case mit me," observed Gotlieb with great emphasis, " tat is, mitout the wife and the baby."

" But," continued the stout-built smith, " in case the Britishers do come cuttin' shines along this way, why, then, Hirpley, d'ye see, there's a rifle hanging over my h'arth-side at home—my wife's the very woman to put it into my hands in case any thing goes wrong."

" ' In case !' " mimicked Hirpley with an ineffably ugly face. " ' In case any thing goes wrong ?'---Fiddle-faddle ! Look here, iron Tom---look here, Gotlieb Hoff—d'ye see this checker-board ? hey ? You do ? I'm glad you can see somethin' with your three-inch skull, Gotlieb. This checker-board is Brandiwine valley—them black checkers is General Howe and his men—the white checkers is George Washington and his fellers. D'ye see that pewter mug,—hey, thick head ?—that's 'Fildelfy, that's the city, its ownself. Well, now, what're you staring at ? In less than four days the black checkers and the white 'uns are 'goin' to play a game—a nice game of blood and smoke—and the game is to be played on this checker-board, and the stake is—the pewter mug ! Does that idea trouble you, Iron Tom ? ---does it make you feel easy, Sourcrout ?"

The blacksmith laid his clenched hand upon the oaken table, and a wild light shot from his clear grey eye.

" I must see to th' primin' o' my rifle," he said in a low voice, spoken through clenched teeth. " And then it may be jist as well to hunt up my bullet mould."

" Mein gott !" ejaculated Gotlieb Hoff, " if dat game ish to be playt, den I'll be a white checker, by Saint Christuffel !"

CHAPTER THIRD.

THE BRAVO TROOPER AND THE QUIET GILBERT GATES.

" You see, my name's Hessian Dick---be gaw !" the sleeping soldier murmured in his sleep, as his head rolled to and fro under the mingled influence of brandy and fatigue---" and my name's Hessian Dick !---be gaw ! Ride 'em down, the rebels ! Charge ! Ride—ride—down—in the dust—down !

I'm a sol-dier, and name's Hessian Dick—be gaw! Damme, d'ye con. tradict me?—I'll sliver your ears off. I'll chop your d——d head off. Ha, ha, ha!—Captain Howard's the boy. And so, Gilbert, you've an eye for this pretty girl—the daughter of the old school-master? have you? So has the Captain."

"Mein Gott!" exclaimed Gotlieb Hoff, slowly rising from his seat— "what's tat!—you taint stuffed, red petty-coat!—what say you, apout the shool-master's daughter?"

He sprang toward the sleeping soldier, and raised his hand to strike him on the carbuncled face, when Hirpley Hawson sprang between him, and the object of his indignation.

"What are you up to, Long Ears?" he cried, pushing Gotlieb from the soldier—"d'ye want to pick a fight with that bloodhound? Wait till some other time, then. Look! you've woke the porpoise!"

"Where's Captain Howard? Where's my beef-steak—be gaw!" cried the redoubtable Hessian Dick, unclosing his large, muddy eyes. "Hey? Why the —— don't you answer, lueface! Who am I? Hey? Say, you spider-legged Publican, who am I? Ain't I Hessian Dick?"

"Is it possible!" exclaimed Hirpley Hawson, with a face extravagantly solemn. "Is you that celebrated critter? Don't look so fierce—you quite make me afeerd. There's yer beef-steak—clean plate and all. As for yer Captain, he's in my sleepin' room, and been there since sundown, talkin' with that strange gentleman, all rigged out like a pine tree, or a box-bush, in green. Any thing more, please your worship? Would'nt you like a small leg of roasted child, jist done to a crisp? Maybe it could be got."

"Be gaw, I shouldn't much mind something o' that kind, just now," mumbled the trooper, either too much intoxicated or too stupid to understand the ridiculous irony of the host. "Be gaw, you know how to cook a beef-steak. Rare. Umph. See here, Ague-face, d'ye know this Colonel Frazier, as you call him, up on the hill yonder. Who made him a Colonel, I'd like to know?"

"He was out in Braddock's expedition," replied Hirpley Hawson, while Gotlieb Hoff was sternly eyeing the corpulent Hessian Dick. "I believe he came from Scotland to this country, somewhere about the year '46."

"Be gaw, you don't say so?" exclaimed the ruffian-like trooper. "Thirty years, man and boy, have I followed the red cross to battle or plunder; I have, be gaw. '46 did ye say, Publican? That was about the time of the outbreak of the pretender—confusion to him. We crushed the rebels of 45. In the same way, be gaw, we'll crush the rebels of '76. Here's a beaker of ale to't, anyhow. Ha, ha, ha!"

"Them rebels is reg'lar sarpents," observed Hirpley Hawson, filling the beaker afresh, and making a tremendous face at the blacksmith, who sat silently eyeing the trooper, while Gotlieb Hoff was clenching his large,

bony hands after a very significant fashion. "Them rebels is reg'lar sarpents, faith—snakes is kings to 'em."

The trooper muttered his favorite oath—' be gaw'—and then proceeded
to discuss the merits of his steak with a renewed appetite.

"Look here, Publican, why can't ye stand straight, and not be waggling
about there as tho' you had a pipe of brandy under your belt. My name's
Hessian Dick—damme, every body knows Hessian Dick. How far is't
from here to the house of this rebel spy—this school-master Mayland—be
gaw. How far d'ye call it ?"

"About a hundred yards—ye can't miss it," replied Hirpley Hawson,
casting a glance at Gotlieb, who was swearing between his teeth. "The
first little stone house standing in from the road, running northward, along
the Brandiwine meadow—it stands in from the road, and there's a hayrick
near it. Sure the one-arm'd school-master's a ribble spy ?"

"Sure as death, be gaw !" cried the trooper.—

"And then his daughter, Pretty Polly, —ah, ha !—The Captain's a sad
dog, and so is Gilbert—Gilbert—Here, fill me this beaker with ale, again."

"He wants a goot lambasting, by Saint Christuffel !" murmured Gotlieb
between his teeth.

"Rein in, Gotlieb, rein in," exclaimed Iron Tom, of Dilworth-corner,
"the feller's drunk, and rye whiskey speaks a great many curious secrets,
sometimes."

The valiant Sergeant Hamsdorff glanced around the company, rolling his
muddy eyes from side to side, while his mouth was filled with savoury
morsels of Hirpley's rarely cooked steak. He certainly looked the picture
of a human anaconda to great perfection.

"You don't know the Captain, do you, hey ?" he mumbled forth, with a
desperate attempt at good humor. "Devlish fine fellow, Captain Howard
be gaw—is, damme. Funny fellow—every thing's in good taste or in bad
taste with him. Deuced funny fellow—expected a fortune from his old
grand-aunt, in England. She cut him off with a shilling. What did the
Captain do ? Tear ? tramp ? swear ? No !—merely said that his aunt was
a fine old lady—but her will was in very bad taste, very. Ha, ha, ha !—
funny dog ! His uncle cut his throat, one day—' extremely bad taste, that,'
says the Captain, ' why couldn't he shoot himself ?' Crossing the Atlantic
—devil of a storm—every body crying ' ship sinking—woke the Captain—
leaned out of his hammock, and' cussed 'em for waking him. ' Why, the
ship's sinking,' cries the mate. ' Don't care for that,' says the Captain.
' ship sinking or not, it's in d——d bad taste to wake a man in the middle
of a nap !' Deuced funny fellow, the Captain—ha, ha, ha ! My name's
Hessian Dick, be gaw !"

As he spoke, the door of the adjoining room opened, and two figures,
muffled in long drooping military cloaks surmounted by trooper's caps, with
nodding plumes, advanced towards the table.

"Landlord, our horses, quick!" said the foremost of the troopers, as the face of Captain Clarence Howard appeared from amid the folds of his cloak, with every sign of life or color vanished from his features, while his voice was low and tremulous with emotion. "Our horses, landlord!" he continued flinging a purse upon the table, and then with unsteady steps, moved with his companion toward the door.

"By * * *, Monthermer!" he cried, as his hand was upon the latch of the door, "you will make me as mad as yourself! My brain burns like a coal of fire—let's into the open air!"

"Be gaw!" muttered Sergeant Hamsdorff, "the Captain might a spoke to me. Didn't say anything to me. D——d bad taste. Ha, ha, ha!"

"Friend Hamsdorff, a word with thee," exclaimed a mild, soft voice, as the door opened, and a man of some thirty-three winters came gliding with a cat-like pace toward the light. "Friend Hamsdorff, a word with thee!"*

"Gilbert Gates! as sure as my name's Hessian Dick!" cried the Sergeant, as, turning to one side, he surveyed the stranger with a drunken leer. "Why, Gilbert, what's broke loose?"

And as the light flashed over the face and form of the stranger, he nodded with an insinuating smile to Iron Tom and Gotlieb Hoff, but it was perceivable that neither the blacksmith or his companion regarded the new comer with feelings of the most favorable kind.

Tall and slim in figure, the gaunt form of the stranger was attired in the drab coat, the drab vest, and breeches of the Quaker faith; and his broad brimmed hat, half screened from the lamp beams, a long, thin visage, marked by a sharp, prominent nose, thick, bushy eyebrows over-arching a cold, grey eye, whose look had something of deep and cautious scheming in its slightest glance; a small mouth, with thin pinched lips, while, swept back from his low, broad forehead, his brown hair fell in curling locks behind his ears, giving a mild and saint-like expression to his solemn and peaceful countenance.

"Friend Hamsdorff," he exclaimed, with the calm, quiet voice of one desirous of conciliating the good opinion of all men, "I came to tell thee that thee friend Howe, can have the provisions he bargained for,—in truth can he. I am a plain man—a quiet man of peace, my friend, and would

---

* With regard to the character here introduced, a single word of comment may seem necessary. The unflinching integrity—the consistent patriotism, and the unvarying devotion of the great body of the brethren of William Penn, to the cause of freedom, is too well known to require mention at my hands. But that traitors and refugees, spies and tories, assumed the garb and speech of the Quaker faith for the purposes of deceit and wrong, is a fact which the history of the times insinuates, and legend and tradition amply attest and fully confirm. The illustration of that fact is attempted in the text. The author's opinion of the integrity and virtue of the Quaker patriots, may be gleaned from "Herbert Tracy," the first Revolutionary Novel of the series, where the character of "Joab Smiley" together with the contest between principle and feeling, in the heart of a strong, honest man, is endeavored to be delineated.

fain persuade friend Howe to refrain from bringing war into the land; therefore do I advise him to go away in peace and quiet; therefore do I sell him provisions, else might he rob my neighbors; in truth, it is so, my friend, Friend Hamsdorff," he continued, hissing a whisper in the ear of the trooper, with a voice sharp as a dagger'spoint, " have thy men ready at the midnight hour—have them ready in the meadow of the Brandywine.   Mayland is the spy—I will see him presently—should the fair maiden, Mary, his daughter, come to reason, well.   At all events, friend Hamsdorff, let thy men have their pieces loaded—thee knows thee orders! I, myself, will give the word!"

And, as he spoke, the smooth and insinuating Gilbert Gates glided out of the room with the same cat-like pace with which he had entered, and, at his heels, with steps unsteady from intoxication, followed the corpulent Hamsdorff, shaking the floor as he stumbled onward.

In a moment, the stout blacksmith stood in front of the fire, now faint and flickering, fixing his clear, grey eyes upon Gotlieb Hoff, who stood opposite, with a glance that expressed the dark and fearful thoughts that could not be told in words, while Hirpley Hawson, who had just entered, stepped between the twain, and, looking from one to the other, whispered their mutual suspicions to the ears of his listeners in his own peculiar and biting vein. " Iron Tom, what d'ye think o' it?" he exclaimed.   " Better look to the priming of your rifle!   Where Gilbert Gates goes, there follows mischief.   Gotlieb, what say you?   Hunt up your bullet mould now?"

CHAPTER FOURTH.

THE EXILE AND THE MAIDEN—NORMAN FRAZIER AND THE DESOLATE
HEARTH-SIDE.

"NAY, Blanche, neice of mine, never start thus suddenly, never frown thus darkly. I' faith, you were wrong—wrong, Blanche, wrong.   What! discredit the sincerity of the Englisher?   Ha, ha, Blanche, by the sword of old Simon Lovat, you are a sad girl.   Refuse an English Lord!   Tut, tut, girl, this lordling was sincere—I doubt it not a whit; not I.   Are not the English noted for their good faith?   Tell me, girl, when did an Englisher violate solemn oath, or perjure himself more than once a day?   I' faith, Blanche, I like that blush!   The spirit of my ancestors glows on thy cheek, and flashes from thy eye!"

" Name him not, my uncle, name not the proud English lordling.   He knelt to me—with proposals of dishonor he knelt to me; and, as he knelt,

4

the blood of my race throbbed in my temples and fired in my veins! He knelt to me as the proud lord, offering homage to the nameless girl."

" He crept from thee, as the thing of shame ever skulks from the face of a virtuous thought! Thou'rt a true Frazier! By the sword of old Lovat, but thou look'st the queen!"

" So should the neice of Norman Frazier look! A queen too proud for he homage of an English lordling, whose flatteries were the vilest calumny!"

And as she spoke, standing in the centre of the floor, her form upraised to its queenly stature, one fair white arm outstretched in sudden gesture, while the other, hidden in the folds of the snow-white sleeve, hung, with the small, delicate hand, drooping by her side, a queen in majesty of look, action, and gesture, Blanche Walford was disclosed in the light, a beautiful picture of womanly indignation and womanly scorn.

And over her face of beauty, shaded by raven locks of glossy hair, and over her form of queenly grace, robed in vestments of white, floating gracefully around the maidenly outlines of her shape, was flung the mellow light of the lamp beams; and her eye, full, black and shadowy, shone like a star from the shadow of the long, trembling fringes of the eyelashes, over-arched by the dark eyebrows; and her full cheek flushed and glowed with its rich vermillion bloom, bursting from the clear white of the maiden's countenance; while, heaving upward amid the folds of the snow-white robe, her bosom rose and fell with that beautiful pulsation which now avoids and now wooes the light; and from the calm, open forehead to the small and chiseled foot, each look, every gesture, each motion of the soft and rounded limbs, the extended arm, the trembling fingers, the breast heaving upward, and the proud arch of the queenly neck, all were alive and animate with thought, all were roused into action by sudden, and enthusiastic feeling.

The beams of the lamp, standing upon the centre-table, fell around the apartment, revealing the quaint carvings of the wainscotted walls, with here and there a picture framed in oak, and hung with folds of Highland plaid, while, over the hearth, broad and spacious, yet uncheered by fire, shone a broadsword side by side with a glittering rifle, inwreathed with the antlers of the wild deer; and opening to the south, were three large windows, reaching from ceiling to floor, the sashes thrown open, and the balcony without sweet with the perfume of autumnal flowers, the pleasant valley of the Brandywine beyond, and the distant hills, all silvering in the light of the rising moon, were disclosed to the view, while the silence of the air, scarce broken by the distant note of the night-bird or the murmur of the rushing stream, gave an air of thought and solemnity to the scene.

The parlor was carpeted with elegance; the furniture, the massive sideboard glittering with the signs of festival hospitality; the high-backed chairs, the circular mirror over the mantel, and the perpendicular glasses between the lofty windows, all were ancient in shape and fashion, yet there was an air of ease and comfort about the place that never found residence in the loftiest temple or the proudest palace, and it seemed well fitted for the home of rustic pleasures and woodland joys, combined with the luxuries of artificial life.

Sitting beside the centre-table, in a capacious armed-chair, was a man of some fifty years, tall and majestic in stature, broad in chest, and somewhat portly in figure, with a fine commanding face, marked by a bold forehead, surmounted by masses of dark hair slightly sprinkled with grey—large, expressive, grey eyes, an acquiline nose, high cheek bones, with broad, expansive cheeks, while the determined mouth and the full, square chin, gave some indications of the character and will of the old soldier, who, attired in the uniform of the old Provincial service—the blue coat faced with silver lace, the breeches of buckskin, and the square-toed shoes, brilliant with buckles of silver—now sat in the full light of the lamp, with his eyes intently fixed upon the form of the fair girl, who stood glowing and blushing before him.

" Blanche, you are a true Frazier!" exclaimed the soldier, as, rising from his seat, he took the maiden by the hand and led her toward the central window. " By the sword of Lovat, when I look upon your fair face, and mark the rich bloom deepening over your cheek, the clear light flashing from your full, dark eye, the lip wreathing with such pretty scorn, and the brow clouded by so pretty a frown, methinks I see one of the high-born damsels of our clan—the damsels of the olden time of blood and war—standing before me !"

" Uncle—nay, my more than uncle—my father !" the girl exclaimed, raising her proud form to its full height, while her beaming face was all affection. " My father, say rather, I am worthy of—thee !"

And as she stood in the full glow of the rising moon, her robes of white glistening in silvery light, and her form shown in all its beauty of proportion, its delicacy of outline, the uncle turned for a moment and gazed upon her fair face with all a father's love—all a father's pride.

The face was beautiful! oh, how beautiful!—Such a face as visits the poet in his dreams—the artist in his reverie—a face where thought, and tenderness, and love and innocence, speak in the glance, in the blush, in the slightest look, or the faintest smile—a face fair and lovely as the face of an angel form enshrouded by a gold-hued cloud, and looking forth smilingly on the gentle sleep of childhood—a face all dream, and vision, and grandeur, and beauty commingled—each outline waving with the line of grace—each look beaming with soul—every expression full of the magic of the mysterious fascination, which the loveliness of woman holds over the heart of man with a spell that may not be described, cannot be broken.

The uncle gazed upon that fair face again and again. The features, even and regular, were shaded by glossy locks of jet-black hair, swept aside from the open forehead and gathered within the circlet of a slight band of gold, brilliant with a single jewel, they fell waving along the cheek and over the snow-white neck. The nose was small and Grecian, the eyebrows dark and arching, the eyes full, black, and dreamy, the fringes long and quivering, the cheeks rounded and swelling, the lips small, and trembling with expression—while the hue of the maiden's countenance, clear and snowy-white, deepened into ruby on her lips, and bloomed into a delicate carmine on the smooth and velvet cheeks.

" Blanche, you spoke the name of—*father ?*" said Colonel Frazier, drawing the maiden nearer to the balcony, while, pressing her hand within his own, he looked upon her, with his keen grey eyes, with a look that was meant to read her very soul. " You spoke the name of—*father*, my niece ?"

A shadow came over the countenance of the fair girl, and her lip quivered, while her hand trembled in the grasp of her uncle.

" *Father !* said you the word, my uncle ?" she exclaimed, casting her full, dark eyes on his soldier-like countenance—" the word has ever been a strange sound to me. Other father than you, my uncle, had I never. Your daughter—my pretty cousin, Rose, was, it is true, denied a mother's tenderness, but then she had you—you, uncle, her—*father !* Father ! mother ! Ah, me !—the meaning of the words is all unknown to me !"

A tear emerged from each fringed eyelid, and stole down the swelling cheeks of the maiden.

" Uncle, tell me—tell me !" she suddenly exclaimed, as she grasped his hand convulsively, " the mystery—the gloom—the shadow—which has hung over my existence, aye, from very birth. What means it all ? My parents—who were they !" Her breath came thick and fast, and her bosom throbbed as though the heart were bursting. " And, uncle," she exclaimed, fixing her dark eyes upon his countenance, with a low and thrilling whisper, " my mother !—*my mother !*——"

The voice of the maiden failed—and, with throbbing bosom and gasping utterance, she started forward, gazing in the face of Colonel Frazier as though she would read his very heart of hearts.

" Blanche, the time has come !" exclaimed her uncle, leading her forward on to the southern balcony, where the moon-beams were playing amid the tendrils of the wild vines entwining around each gnarled and knotted column. " The time has come Blanche—the hour is calm and solemn—the Grange is silent. Your cousin, Rose, the mischievous minx, is not here to interrupt us with her girlish pranks ; you know she is on a visit to her uncle, Philip Walford down at Rock Farm, seven miles away. The hour is still and silent, and here, in the full glow of the moon-beams, will Norman Frazier tell to Blanche Walford the story of his life, and of her own !"

Blanche looked into the face of the soldier, with a look that was all interest and attention.

' Blanche !" exclaimed the Colonel in a voice that was strangely altered from his usual jovial and good-humored tones, " gaze upon yonder southern plain—the plain of the Brandiwine — how lovely ! The grassy meadow sleeps in the moon-light. Away and away it spreads, green and grassy, here and there a lofty tree, and yonder the uprising hills crowded and covered with woodlands, all gleaming and silvering in the moon-beams ! How like an undulating wave they rise---the hills of the Brandiwine ! How like a calm and rippleless lake they sleep---the meadows of the Brandiwine ! Blanche, what think you of the view ?"

" Lovely—most lovely !" whispered the maiden, leaning on the shoulder of her uncle, as they paced along toward the western balcony. " Lovely— most lovely !"

" Look, Blanche—look to the west !" continued Colonel Frazier in that same changed tone. " Through these tall elms and beechen trees, behold the meadows of the Brandiwine reaching toward the north. On this side slopes the hill of Wildwood-Grange. Winding at its base is the quiet stream, gleaming between the trees, and shimmering along through the foliage. Look across the meadow ; yonder is the inn of Chadd's Ford—a little further northward, a light gleams from the window of the old school-master's house, and, beyond, arise the undulating hills, sweeping suddenly, yet with a swelling ascent, upward from the grassy meadow ! Cattle are feeding upon the plain—the hills bloom with cultivation, and the scene is one of rustic, nay, of pastoral beauty. Is it not Blanche ?"

" It is—it is !" murmured the maiden, as she gazed wonderingly upon her uncle's face, warming with sudden enthusiasm—" lovely as a dream !"

" On a scene somewhat like this," resumed her uncle, traversing the bal cony, " on a scene somewhat like this—a quiet valley, embosomed among the highlands of Scotland—on a calm, summer night, in the year of our Lord 1745, the moon was shining as soft and silvery as she shines to-night —a quiet and lonely valley ! The hills, it is true, were more stern and abrupt in ascent, the steeps were clad less luxuriantly with green tree and verdant bush, but the meadows below were as green, and the sky above as clear as the sky and meadow you now behold. From the very centre of the meadows arose the dark grey walls of an ancient mansion, the home of a race descended from a long line of honored ancestors—and the moonbeams flaunted and played with the dark grey walls as now they shimmer over the quiet roofs of the Brandiwine. The scene was quiet and love ly, by moonlight. Morning came." He paused for breath, and Blanche heard his teeth grating against each other. " Morning came, Blanche," he whispered between his clenched teeth, " and a pile of smoking ruins arose, blackening to the sky like a thing of terrible omen and doom. A mother, a kind, a beloved mother, lay across her own threshold, slain and dishonored ! A father kissed the path leading to his home---his blood dyed and crimsoned his native hearth. Two brothers were strewn along the quiet garden walks---their limbs hewn and hacked, and their faces carved with

the sword-cut and the dagger-thrust ! The third brother, a youth of twenty
was stealing along the dark grey hills, while the dusky light of morning
broke over the scene. At his heels were the blood-hounds thirsting for
their prey—but on and on he sped, while closer and closer to his breast he
pressed the child—the fair and lovely child--scarce nine years old—the
girl—his *sister*—on he sped, holding her in his arms and clasping her to
his breast."

"And why was all this?" cried Blanche, as her eye flashed and her bosom heaved. "Why all this bloodshed—this wrong—this outrage?"

"I will tell you, Blanche," cried Frazier, turning his flashing countenance
to the moonbeams. "The footstep of the Englisher had been stamped on
the valley—and where was the footstep of Englishmen ever stamped without the mark of blood? The banner of the Englisher had floated in the air
—where did it ever float without the scent of blood? And they—the Englishers—oh ! * * * they—murdered my father, butchered my brothers,
and—aye, did they—they, hirelings of Hanover, outraged the mother of my
birth !"

Blanche spoke no word, but the dark eye flashed, and the lips were compressed.

"And why, Blanche, why?" resumed the soldier, "Because my father,
John Frazier, and his three sons, had joined the banner of old Simon Lovat.
They had joined the fortunes of England's rightful king, styled by his foes,
the Pretender—they had fought with him in his last battle, and for this did
Hanoverian rage march over the fair land of my childhood—"

Aroused to a pitch of terrible excitement, the soldier muttered between
his teeth a fearful oath, that may not be again repeated. He muttered that
fearful oath between his teeth, and then resumed his story.

CHAPTER FIFTH.

THE DOOM OF A FATED HOUSE.

"I FLED, Blanche, with my sister I fled to this fair land. Some gold and
jewels of our family, which I seized in the moment of my flight, afforded
me the means to purchase this land, and rear Wild Wood Grange. But
stay a single moment. On my way to this new world, I passed, disguised
as a beggar, through the English land—with my sister by my side, I fled.
I reached London—it was a fair bright day—and brave men were to die on
Tyburn. A whispered name reached my ear as I hurried through the
crowd—it was the name of Lovat!—old Simon Frazier, Lord of Lovat' I

rushed through the crowd. The brave old man stood on the scaffold, with the sunlight falling on a brow frosted with the snows of eighty winters! He looked upon the axe and smiled!—he looked upon the crowd and laughed: —he looked to the blue heaven, and, with his last breath, sent up a prayer for the Last of the Stuart Line. He was about to kneel, and place his head upon the block—I caught his eye! 'Ha!' shouted the old lord—' by thy broad cheek bones and by thy eagle nose, I'd take thee for a bonny Frazier!' ' I am—I shouted over the heads of the bystanders—I am a Frazier, heart and soul!' 'Then take this,' cried old Simon of Lovat, as the executioner was about to do his office, 'then take this, and use it as a Frazier should!' He flung me his good broadsword, and, as I hid the weapon 'neath my beggar rags, the head of Simon Frazier rolled in the sawdust of the scaffold! I escaped, and——"

" The broadsword hangs over yon hearth side!" exclaimed Blanche : " It waved in Braddock's war——"

" It will wave again ere long!" muttered the old soldier grimly. " But to my story, Blanche. I built myself a home, here in this quiet valley. Years past, and my sister grew up a fair and lovely girl—a thing of truth, a creature of innocence—all warmth, all affection! Two suitors sought her hand—they were brothers. They dwelt on a place called Rock Farm, about seven miles south-west of this Grange, and their name was Walford!"

" *Rock Farm, Walford!*" murmured Blanche, in an absent tone.

" They sought her hand," the uncle resumed, drawing Blanche towards the moonlight. The younger Brother, named Philip Walford—he was a widower, and his wife had scarce been dead a year when he sought my sister's hand—"

" He still lives!" murmured Blanche

" I never liked him!" exclaimed the uncle—" Cold, cautious, scheming, a trickster by nature, a cheat by birth, I never liked him—Philip Walford! John!—ah, me!—by the sword of Lovat, I well remember him! Noble in form, noble in feature, generous in heart, frank in soul, I ever liked the man! He won my sister's love—he married her—aye, on the very day I brought home to Wild Wood Grange, my wife—Mary Walford—the fair sister of John."

Blanche leaned forward, she clasped the hand of her uncle, and her eyes shone with intense interest.

" But harkye, Blanche, continued Frazier, lowering his voice to a whisper, ' one word concerning the family of Walford. Ask the meanest peasant who plods along yon valley, who are the Walfords, and he replies with a silence that says more than volumes. Ask the gossip at the fireside,—speak of the Walfords—ask who they were and what they were, and she will fill your ears with tales of horror and legends of terror! The Walford's are a CURSED, a DOOMED family. There is a ban upon them, a malediction on all they touch. Dark tales of murder, done at the mansion of Rock Farm, by the hoary father of John and Philip—tales of parricide, of fracticide—stories of murdered travellers, and butchered guests, are current along the valleys—every peasant repeats them, every schoolboy has them at his tongue's end. So it has been for more than a century, and generation after generation of the Walfords have been born but to imbue their hands in each other's blood—to quarrel for the undivided possession of the five hundred broad acres of Rock Farm—to quarrel, to cheat, to scheme, and to—die! Nay, Blanche, start not thus, nor let your cheek grow thus suddenly pale. John Walford—my friend—was as unlike his family as day is to night, and his sister Mary—my wife—she seemed a fair flower, blooming amid the ashes of a desolated hearthstone. John, I say, took my sister home to Rock Farm——"

"That dark and gloomy mansion!" murmured Blanche—"A fit scene for legends of horror!"

"A fair and lovely child blessed their union," resumed the uncle. "Scarce had it seen the light when, John Walford suddenly disappeared, no one knew whither. His wife returned to Wild Wood Grange—her cheek was pale, but her eye was tearless. In three months she died, Blanche—she died of a broken heart! From the day that John disappeared, to this hour —'tis now eighteen long years—never have I heard a single word concerning his existence or his death. All has been mystery—"

"But the child! uncle, the child?" Blanche murmured, leaning for support on the arm of the soldier, while her form trembled like an aspen leaf, and her very soul shone forth in her eyes—"The child, my uncle, the child?"

"It grew up in the presence of its uncle, a blessing and a charm," exclaimed Frazier—"The light of his home—dear to him as his own beloved Rose.—It was you, Blanche, you!"

She fell weeping on his shoulder; thick and fast fell the burning tears; her voice was broken by sobs, and her bosom arose throbbing to her very face.

"I have found thee—my mother, I have found thee!" The murmured words broke from her lips, and again and yet again she wept.

"Blanche, one word more and I have done," the uncle continued, in tones hurried by emotion; "the mystery of the story—the dark, the terrible mystery—ask me not, Blanche, ask me not. Let me speak volumes of agony to you in a single word. John Walford loved his wife to madness. He loved her till you were born; but a day elapsed—*he thought her false* —he believed she loved another—he fled from her sight, as from a polluted thing——"

"The cause, my uncle, the cause!" said Blanche, proudly raising her queenly form.

"I know not, I know not!" exclaimed Frazier, in a voice husky with feeling, "but a suspicion sometimes creeps upon me, Blanche," and his eyes lighted up with a wild flash, "and I feel my hand grasping for my sword. Would to God I knew my suspicions true or false! Were it true then, as God gave me being, Norman Frazier would avenge his sister's wrong, and Philip Walford—ha! ha! ha! the catiff!—never more should he betray noble man or generous woman!"

, "Philip Walford!" cried Blanche. "My uncle, what mean you?"

"Plainly this, my neice," exclaimed Frazier. "Philip Walford was the rejected suitor—Philip Walford lived in his ·brother's mansion at Rock Farm, as a—hireling! John Walford was the sole proprietor of the lands. By the will of old Aldrich Walford, the estate was devised to the eldest son, and in case of his death, to his eldest son ; or was a daughter born instead of a son, then the estate would fall to the younger brother, this Philip Walford! It was a glorious prize for Philip—the hired man—this estate of Rock Farm! But how should he be rid of this elder brother? There were a thousand ways. ' Might it not be done,' quoth Philip, ' by creating distrust between husband and wife? This John, my brother, is a generous fool— once satisfied of his wife's dishonor, he will not touch me his brother, but lay hands on himself, or rid me of his presence in some way sudden and sure! Then I shall be Philip Walford, *Esquire*, instead of Philip the younger brother—the serving man !' Do you see this devil's woof, Blanche? Do you see the thread of his villiany ?"

The maiden gasped for breath, and her eyes flashed until they seemed turned to things of living flame.

" The fiend in human shape !" she murmured, and her fair white hand was raised in the air as though she grasped a phantom.

" These were the suspicions I gleaned from the dying exclamations of my sister," resumed Frazier. " The day before her death, I rode over to Rock Farm, as though life and death were in my speed. I sought Master Philip Walford. I charged him with treachery—with falsehood—I branded him liar! I would have stricken him to the earth, but he seemed too mean a thing for the blow of an honest hand! How replied he? With tears, with solemn oaths of his innocence! The craven! After all, the idea haunting my mind was but suspicion. Had I but one single fact upon which to rest the justice of my purpose, Philip Walford would not have lived an hour !"

" And why, uncle, suffer you my cousin—your daughter, Rose, to visit the mansion of this man?"

" I'll tell thee, Blanche, replied Frazier; " if there's a thing on earth he favors with affection, 'tis Rose, and I wish to conciliate the man for your sake. I would have him believe I think him innocent, until I have certain proofs of his guilt. But, I wish so no longer! The memory of eighteen years ago is strong within me to-night. Rose shall come home to-morrow, and never darken his doors again!"

" And his sons, my uncle," said Blanche, " David and Walter—I have seen them but rarely—do they share the doom of this fated family ?"

5

" David, the taller brother, is sullen, unprincipled, and selfish !" exclaimed Colonel Frazier; " I like him not. You know, Blanche, they are twins ?—the children of Philip's first and only wife, who died a year before John married my sister. Walter, the other brother, more slender and less robust in figure, is kind and generous in disposition, but weak in principle, irresolute, and governed by impulse. They are foes by birth. Why ? The estate of Rock Farm, that fated estate, is the prize for which they will contend ! One alone can inherit the lands—one must yield to the other ! But, Blanche, you are wearied—you need repose—to your chamber, my neice, and if the fearful story which I have told you should scare sleep from your eyelids, then think that stern duty alone could have nerved me for the task !"

" Good night, my uncle !" murmured Blanche—" God bless you, my uncle !" she said in a low, soft tone, and then disappeared within the balcony window.

Colonel Frazier looked hurriedly upon the smiling landscape, lighted by the beams of the moon, and then, turning to the window, he also disappeared into the parlor.

In an instant he again stood upon the porch, but a good stout broadsword was raised in his right hand, and his eye flashed as he spoke aloud, in a bold and determined tone.

" The valley is lovely, but the scent of blood is upon the air !" he said. " Already the war hound snuffs his prey—already are the meadows of the Brandywine trodden by the spoiler ! Sword of old Simon of Lovat, you warred in the wars of Scotland—you shone on the field of Braddock—you will glimmer in battle-smoke again ere many days ! George Washington—I fought by his side when Braddock fell. I know the man, I will fight by his side again. In Scotland I fought for the Stuart—he was my rightful king ! In this fair land of the new world, every true man is a king. I will fight for my own arm, for the right of a freeman ! I will fight for Washington, and the sword of old Simon of Lovat will again cleave the battle-smoke ?"

And he stood upon the balcony, between two vine-garlanded columns of cedar, with the full glow of the moon falling upon his noble brow. His lofty form, and the extended arm, lifting the broadsword, all glowed in the moonlight, while at his back, unseen and unperceived, stood a fair and maidenly form, her arms upraised, her hands extended, and her beautiful face warming with the same generous enthusiasm that flashed over the features of the soldier.

" Ere this, the fair girls, Blanche and Rose, demanded my protection, and I could not away to the battle-field. *Now*, by my own hearthstone will I fight, and fight for them—for Blanche, for Rose !"

" And they will hold up your hands in the hour of battle !" murmured a low, soft, woman's voice ; " and in the hour of peril will they nerve you for the fight !"

1483882

CHAPTER SIXTH.

THE LIGHT OF AN OLD-TIME FIRESIDE—THE SCHOOLMASTER AND HIS STORY OR BRADDOCK'S WAR—THE HUNTER SPY—THE DEATH IN THE WILD WOOD—THE PACQUET AND THE WARNING.

' HE must, in truth, be a wondrous man, this George Washington !" said Gilbert Gates, as with his sly and insinuating smile he surveyed the group clustering around the table in the centre of the schoolmaster's room—" in truth, a wondrous man !"

" A wondrous man, friend Gates ?" cried the schoolmaster, as the light fell over his aged form seated in the capacious arm-chair with his face to the group, while his back was turned toward the fireless hearth. " What mean you, friend Gates ? Methinks there's a small piece of a sneer in your remark."

" Shortz Washington is a goot man, by Saint Christuffel !" exclaimed Gotlieb Hoff, glancing fiercely at the mild, saint-like countenance of Gilbert, and then at the pretty face of Mary Mayland, seated opposite her father. " By G—t, Gilbert Gates, if thee says he haint, thee's no man thee self !"

" Washington berry good gen'l'man !" observed the stout Negro, Ben, as, seated a little aside from the group, he folded his muscular arms on the cotton garment that clothed his Herculean form, " berry good man. Better not say he haint, Massa Gates. Ben Sampson ob Chadd's Ford, 'ab got bad temper—no like to hear broad brim abuse cocked hat. Ben Sampson's fader prince in he own country—George Wash'ton prince in his country. Berry good man, berry."

" Nay, friends, I meant no harm, in truth I did not," observed Gilbert, lowering his head meekly on his breast and looking sidelong at the blooming cheeks and fair blue eyes of Polly Mayland. " But that story of friend Washington's being made the mark of the Injins at Braddock's fight, without being wounded once ! That is true, is it, friend Mayland ? Daughter Polly, what does thee think ?"

" I have no thought about the matter," replied the maiden, without raising her eyes from her sewing, while an expression of ill-concealed scorn played on her pouting lip. " My father says it was so. Gilbert Gates surely cannot suppose that I will discredit my father's story because *he* may chance to doubt it."

" Nay, maiden, thee is rather tart," observed Gilbert, while a smile of peculiar meaning flashed over his sallow features. " In truth, said I but a

single word, and here ye are all saying bitter speeches to me. In truth, ye
are wrong. I meant no harm."

"Harm or not, what I tell you is a fact!" exclaimed the schoolmaster,
lifting his pipe to his mouth with his solitary left hand—the sleeve of the
right arm hung drooping by his side, "Now, I'll tell you all the truth o
the matter. Gotlieb, don't sit there makin' mouths as tho' you smelt
somethin' unpleasant—draw your cheer a bit nearer the table. Polly go on
with your sowin', and pick your ears, for this will be about the six thou
sandth time I've told the story. Sampson, man, move your black, shiny
face nearer the light—and Gilbert, do try and look a little less sick chicken-
like, jest while I tell the story, do. Its a story of blood and war, and may
hurt your feelin's. Stay a moment—I'll light my pipe fust."

And as the one arm'd schoolmaster raised the candle to the bowl of his
pipe, the beams fell warmingly over his aged yet still muscular figure, the
calm face, with the aquiline nose, the clear blue eyes, and the open brow,
with light, thin masses of snow-white hair falling over its front; while his
attire, the tarnished military coat of blue, faced with silver, the vest, with
enormous pockets and wide lappels, the linsey-woolsey breeches, the blue
worsted stockings, and the square-toed shoes, buckled with silver, all glowed
in the light, and reminded the lookers-on of the palmy days of Sargent
Mayland, as Hirpley Hawson would say, ' who'd been out in Braddock's
war, and fit the wild-cats and Injins like a hoss.'

"It smokes like a livin' creetur'," observed the schoolmaster meditatively
"Jest see how it rolls up to the ceilin'—puff, puff, puff! That's jest the
way I've seen the battle-smoke rolling over the dead."

"That's just the way thee'll see the smoke of thee house in flames within
three hours!" muttered Gilbert Gates in a murmured whisper. "I think
thee enjoys thee pipe very much, friend Mayland," he continued aloud.
"In truth, a pipe is a good thing."

"Now I feel quite comfortable," exclaimed Mayland, settling himself in
his chair. "In fact, if it were possible for an angel to look in for a minit
jest upon this scene, and my pretty darter there, he'd say I know'd what
comfort was, and so I do."

The picture was very quiet and peaceful in character. Side by side with
the scene that ensued but three hours afterward, it would have seemed like
a heaven in view of hell.

Polly Mayland—full, pretty, and womanly in figure, with a slender waist
and swelling bust, a rounded face, with swelling cheeks, a clear blue eye,
and dark, rich, brown hair neatly parted over the forehead and swept behind the ears within the pressure of a single comb—Polly Mayland was
clad in a neat boddice of well-fitting home-spun, terminated by a short-gown
of tasteful calico, beneath which appeared the folds of a brown linsey petticoat; while, seated opposite her father, her eyes were downcast on her
work, her delicate little hands, somewhat roughed by rustic toil, were busily

employed at the task, ever and anon interrupted by a covert glance at the ruddy face of Gotlieb Hoff, or a smile of scorn at the meek and insinuating Gilbert Gates, seated at the further end of the table.

A little in the back ground, sat the Negro, Sampson, his muscular arms, all bone, all sinew, folded across a chest of Herculean dimensions. His head—with the face of African features, the protruding eyes, the flat nose, somewhat aquiline in contour, the lips thick and large, yet determined or expressive, and the prominent chin—was slightly turned aside, while the jet black skin glistened in the light, and his eyes were fixed in silent cogitation on the whitened floor, which he regarded with a fixed moody stare that seemed to indicate that his meditations were any where but with the present scene.

Gotlieb Hoff, seated at one end of the table, had but one look and one object, and that was the face and figure of Gilbert Gates, who, with arms meekly folded on his breast, was smiling to himself as if something very good indeed had just stricken him, while his eyes wandered in sidelong glances from the face of the father to the daughter, and then, with a sort of squinting glimpse at the features of Dutch Gotlieb, the eyes of the worthy Gilbert were again fixed sadly on his knees with a look that seemed like a patient resignation to the divine will, and it only wanted a nasal twang through the nose to make the unoffending Gates a complete picture of a first-rate reformer, a capital builder of new doctrines, and a rare discoverer of fresh religions.

" Well, folks, you shall have my story," said the school-master, puffing his pipe, " and its a story of Braddock's war. Ye see, it was on a fine, clear day in June, more than a score of years since, that we started out from Fort Cumberland—we started out two thousand strong, with General Braddock, stiff and firm as a poker, at our head, and among his aids was a young Virginia Colonel, named Washington—aye, George Washington—a fine, tall, commanding officer, who rode his horse like a king and looked like an emperor-born from hat to heel.

" And then, at the head of our company—a band of Provincial rifles— was a brave young fellow from this same valley of the Brandiwine— Colonel Frazier his commission named him, although he commanded but a single company of riflemen.

" And out of Fort Cumberland, with the clear heavens above and the green woods around us, out we trooped on that fair day in June, while the sun shone on the scarlet dresses of the reg'lars and glistened on the green and blue coats o' the Provincials, and every heart felt brave, and every step was firm. Oh, we were goin' to conquer the French and Injins, we were, and General Braddock was to do it all with his parade ground manœuvres, his pipe-clay discip-lin, and his reg'lar lines o' march and what not, and we poor devils of Provincials, were'nt worth a straw in his eye, and yet the French were to be shot, the Injins were to be driven off, and all by a few

words of command—ordering live men and sound to march up to senseless
trees, present arms in reg'lar columns, and punish the bark, because, d'ye
see, an innocent Injin might happen to be firing away at us from behind the
trunk.   Well, well, we'll see how it ended.

"The eighth o' July came, and a broilin' hot day it was!   We were
marchin' in a pretty considerable style, way out among the grand old woods
—trees here and trees there, and trees everywhere—with a little glimpse of
the blue sky now and then through the intervals between the trunks.   We
were marchin' within ten miles of Fort Du Quesne, when all the officers
Colonel Washington among them, all gathered round Braddock, and besought him, for his soul's sake, to beware of an ambush—to send out scouts
and spies to track any red-skins that might be lurkin' in the woods, but it
was all of no use.

"General Braddock, to be sure, knew how to do the business himself.   He
was a general, us provincials were told.   He'd been brought up on t'other
side o' the water.   He'd a red coat on his back, and a gold epaulette on his
shoulder, and if he didn't know how to catch Injins, and lambaste 'em to
some purpose, he'd like to know who did!"

"It was early in the mornin', and we were advancing gaily thro' th'
woods, and the jest and the lively word, the thought of distant home and far-
away friends ran along the line, when, right in front of our march, we beheld standing under the shadow of a tremendous tall tree, a long, lean fellow
of a hunter, with a slouching hat covering his lean features, a rough coat o'
skins covering his back, and a rifle on his shoulder—(you needn't start,
Gilbert Gates, it's a fact I'm telling you.)   We saw this strange looking
hunter talkin' with the Commander and his staff, and presently information
ran along the line, that this individual had engaged to lead the troops, by
the safest and nearest cut, to Fort du Quesne, some ten miles off.

"And on we went.   And about high noon, the troops emerged, in gallant
order, from the immediate shelter of the woods, on to a level space of green
sward, starting from the clear waters of the Monggahaley, with the opposite
bank rising into a steep ascent, dark with interwoven trees and brushwood,
while on either side of our line of march was a deep and impenetrable wall
of lofty trees with a rich undergrowth springing up around the trunks.   On
we went, and red coat and green frock were all emerging from the wood,
and the van-guard were fording the river, when the General turned and
asked for the hunter, who had so kindly volunteered his services.   He had
disappeared—no one knew whither.   And then came a scene that would
have made your blood run cold, my daughter, Polly—a scene that would
have made you, Gotlieb Hoff, grasp your rifle with a firmer hold—and as
for you, Gilbert Gates, I question if it wouldn't a-made you show a well
made pair o' heels blessed quick !

"Sudden as lightning, there flashed from every bush, from every tree
around us, the fire of a concealed foe ; and about us, like a hail storm of

iron, fell the musket bullets ; and through the clouds of smoke, that so suddenly darkened daylight, I could see one red coat officer after another
falling to the ground, while around me, my comrades fell, wounded and dying, at every shot.

"It was a ter'ble time! Bang, bang, bang—pop, pop, pop—every second.
Clouds of smoke above—flashes o' flame around—men recoiling on their
comrades—all mist, all gloom, all confusion. And in the thickest of it all,
with his manly form towering above the smoke o' battle, and his manly
arm raised on high, beckoning courage and hope to the dismayed Englishers,
was George Washington—his chest a mark for every Injin bullet—his form
a target for every French musquet ball! In the thickest of the fight he
rode ; and, by his side, waving his good broadsword as he led us on to the
enemy, was our brave Captain Frazier,—but all was in vain! General
Braddock merely desired his men to advance in reg'lar order, and fire at
the bushes in parade-ground style—whether they were killed or not made
not a ha'penny's difference, so the thing was done in style, and the Injins
were showed what a wonderful thing it was to walk up to the chalk like and
be shot at according to some military rule o' three.

"Never shall I forget that day. How the ground was soaked with blood.
How the dead—their corpses all mingled, and their faces all hacked and
carved—strewed the ground and littered the green grass, while a hundred
little rivulets of blood poured along the sod and drippled into the waters o'
the Monggahaley.

"In one word. We were lambasted *com*-plete-ly. We fled for our lives,
—with the corpse of General Braddock we fled. But in flight or retreat,
George Washington was ever the same bold and determined soldier. And
Norman Frazier—God bless him for his kindness to the old soldier—'tis
his land I live on—'tis his house that covers my head—Norman Frazier
was never otherwise than a true-hearted man and a generous soldier. (Puff,
puff, puff—this tobacco is reg'lar fine.) Well, folks, you'd like to hear a
little about that hunter that led us into this trap, would you?"

"If thee pleshes to tell us, frient Mayland—y-a-h, by Saint Christuffel!"
exclaimed Gotlieb in his patch-work dialect. "Tat feller was a big enough
scoundrel to sell his grandmother's bones for horn buttons!"

"Berry great scoundrel that hunter," muttered Sampson. "Sampson's
fader prince in he own country. Some dam man-hunter led him in jist sich
a scrape—brought him here—made slave of him. Dat's reason why Sampson's here at Chadd's Ford. Poor nigga—berry poor—hab nuffin' to eat
weren't for Massa Mayland—hab nuffin' to wear weren't for Missa Polly."

And as some memory of the olden time came over the mind of the black
man, he ground his ivory teeth together and clenched his hands of ebony
upon his knees.

"Friend Gates, something seems to trouble you," said Polly Mayland
looking up from her work and turning with a mischievous smile to the demure

Gilbert. " Why, you are as restless as a cat in walnut shells—you look pale, and start and stare as tho' the company weren't agreeable. Pray, Mr. Gates, does anything pain you ?"

" P'raps he's sittin' on a chesnut bur," suggested Gotlieb, with a look of particular affection. " Frient Gates, ish thee verry pat indeed ?"

" Nothing ails me—nothing," said the Quaker, slowly, while his ashen countenance and rolling eyes belied his words. " Friends, 'tis merely a sudden pain—it is, in truth. Friend Mayland," he continued with a smile wreathing his white lips, " will it please thee to go on with the story of—of—this—hunter !"

" Sartinly," resumed the schoolmaster. " It was on the morning of the third day of our retreat, that I was a little in advance of our riflemen, when suddenly I burst thro' a clump of brushwood, and beheld a man sleeping on a log, his rifle by his side, his face very pale with fatigue, and his dress of skins all tattered and torn as tho' he'd been on a reg'lar tramp—but there was a purse of guineas resting in the grasp of the long, thin fingers of his right hand——"

" It was—it was—the—hunter !" said Gilbert Gates in a slow tone of voice, and as reluctantly as though each word were gold. " It was the—hunter, friend Mayland ?"

" Yes, by the lord ! I pinned him sleepin'. In an instant our riflemen surrounded him—the eye of Colonel Frazier was on him—and we gave him a short prayer and a long journey——"

" You seized him sleeping, friend Mayland ?" said Gilbert Gates, in a low quiet tone. " I am not a man of war, in truth am I not, but—but, methinks I would hate to kill a mouse in its sleep. But I am a foolish man, in truth am I."

" Seized him sleepin' ?" echoed Gotlieb—" by Saint Christuffel ! Tink of Braddock's field, mit te corpses strewn ober te groundt, and de Injins behind te pushes ! Shleep or awake, by Saint Christuffel, he was a purty feller—tam him !"

" Berry bad man," murmured Sampson. " Berry like he playing possum all time."

" But, father," exclaimed Polly, as her blue eyes were dimmed with tears, " You harmed not the hunter? You struck him not in his sleep ?"

" Devil a bit, girl," returned Mayland. " We gave him a fair trial. Certain papers found on his body proved him a French spy. He begged for his life ; but our men thought of Braddock's field as they loaded their rifles. Colonel Frazier gave the word——"

"*Colonel Frazier gave the word*," murmured Gilbert Gates, as a red flush for a moment blazed over his features. " Well, friend Mayland, thee story is very interesting."

" And as the sun went down we fired," continued Mayland.

" *We* fired," murmured Gilbert Gates.

" He fell, and died with the request on his lips, that we would lay his body across the log where we found him. It seems the scoundrel had a son out in the woods somewhere—on some errand to the white settlements. He expected his return an hour after sundown. So we laid him on the log —pinned a paper on his jacket, announcing that he had died as a spy, taken in the act, and that he was put to death by the Green Rangers, commanded by Colonel Frazier. I signed my name to the paper as Orderly Sargent——"

" And so he died, alone in the woods," exclaimed Mary Mayland with tears in her eyes. "Spy or not, t'was a hard death—alone in the woods— 'twas a hard death!"

" *It was a hard death !*" muttered Gilbert Gates between his teeth, while his grey eye blazed with something of human feeling. " *And I must fulfil my oath—ha, ha!*" He ghastily smiled as he said the words. " But, friend Mayland, 'twas not of this I came to speak with thee this autumn night. I have something to say to thee, and I may as well say it out before all the folks. Friend Mayland, thee knows me. I have a tolerably good farm up the creek, above Brenton's Ford. In truth have I. Thee daughter Polly is a fine girl—I will take her——"

" Will you, though ?" exclaimed the fair maiden, as her cheeks swelled with laughter, and mirth danced and gleamed from the corners of her bonny blue eyes. "Gotlieb what say you—shall *he* take *her ?*"

Gotlieb puffed and blowed, and made several very large fists, and half arose from his seat and then sat down again, and looked at Gilbert Gates as though he would very much like to do something desperate with him without the least possible delay.

" N-a-h !—by Saint Christuffel !" he roared in a voice of thunder. " Friend Gates," he continued in a calmer yet more urgent tone, "jist take off your shad-pelly coat for apout ten minutes, and giv' me a lambastin', or I'll give you a tozen of 'em. Do dis good turn for me, ant I promise to flux you mit a hearty good will."

" Nay, friend Gotlieb, I am a man of peace," said Gilbert Gates, turning away from the yeoman with a quiet sneer. " Friend Mayland, what says thee? Shall the maiden be wife of mine ?"

" Fudge of your'n, you mean Gilbert Gates," said Mayland, without turning his attention from his pipe. " You see the girl haint willin', Gilbert, don't you? Well, you might jest as well try to cut a hot poker with an icicle as to drive a stubborn girl into matrimony ag'inst her will."

" Then thee won't give me the maiden for a wife ?"

" You may set that down as settled, friend Gates. (Bless me, but this is fine tobacco.")

" Friend Mayland, I've got a good piece to go up the valley ere mid night. I would speak a word with thee at the door ere parting, in truth would I."

"In truth shall you," replied the school-master, slowly rising and moving toward the door. Now, friend Gates, what may it be your pleasure to say ?"

Gilbert Gates stood holding the open door, as he leaned forward and whispered in the school-master's ear, while the lower part of his face alone was touched by the light beams, the brow gathered in a wild frown, the grey eyes flashing with strange light, and the cheeks warmed by emotion, were all darkened by the shadow of his broad-rimmed hat.

"Friend Mayland," he hissed between his teeth in a serpent-like whisper, "'tis a week since a pacquet of important papers were stolen from the cabinet of Sir William Howe by a spy. These were most important papers—they detailed the plan of this campaign—they contained intelligence most important to Washington, most destructive to Howe, if perused by the rebel leader. This pacquet, mark thee, man, has been traced to this house. A single word more. 'You seized him in his sleep'—his voice sank to a whisper almost inaudible. 'You seized him in his sleep—he died alone in the wild wood.' Man, know you that the hunter-spy had a son ?"

"He said so, with his dying words," returned the school-master, wondering at the strange expression that came rushing over the Quaker's features. —"That son—what of him ?"

"*He stands before thee !*" said the Quaker, and the school-master in an instant found himself gazing at the closed door, while the sound of a hurried footstep was heard retreating without.

CHAPTER SEVENTH.

THE STRANGERS IN THE QUAKER TEMPLE—GATHERED BY THE LIGHT OF THE LANTERN AT THE MIDNIGHT HOUR.

THE light of a dark lantern, glimmering round the white walls of the silent temple,* with faint and flickering beams, now tinting the plain and rough-fashioned benches with sudden light, now shooting a gleam into some dark corner, and lighting up the recesses of a deep-silled window, or disclosing the panels of barred and bolted doors, shone warm and glaringly upon the faces and forms of two figures, one that of a young the other that of an old man, who seated on a rough bench, at the foot of the simple gallery which served for a pulpit, conversed in low tones together,

------

* It will be remembered that the Birmingham Meeting-House, is situated some **two miles** eastward of the Brandywine, and some three or four miles north-east of Chadd's Ford.

with gestures that implied the interest and importance of their topic of discourse.

Between them, on the bench of unpainted oak, was placed the dark lantern, disclosing the figure of the old man, leaning towards his companion with an extended arm, while the listener, with head slightly drooped aside, yet turned to the full glow of the light, and with arms folded on his breast, seemed to drink in each word of the speaker.

The lamp beams flashing upward, streamed over the face and lighted up each feature of the old man—the fine, bold, Roman countenance, with the lofty forehead, seamed by wrinkles, and relieved by long locks of dark black hair, sprinkled with grey—the prominent chin and the high cheek bones, clothed by a grey beard, sweeping aside over the full, determined mouth, and flowing in rugged masses down over the throat, down to the wild deerskin that clothed the chest of the stalwart man—while his arching brow, marked by bushy eyebrows of the same grey-white as his hair, overarched large expressive eyes, that might have been clear and blue in the days of youth, but were now flashing and grey with the thought of age. And on the countenance of the old man, for aged he was, but not with years, but with the weight of some terrible sorrow, there was written much of wrong endured, much of painful thought, and much of the power of intellect and the might of mind.

The face of his companion, as it glowed in the light, was marked by the striking beauty of early manhood, combined with a strange, and ever and again, a wild expression which riveted the attention of the spectator to the outlines of the youthful countenance, and gave utterance to the thought that the beholder looked upon the face of one young and handsome, it was true, but set apart from his kind by some dread fate, by some fearful duty, some early vow, whispered by dying lips to the ears of childhood, making life a terrible destiny, and existence itself, its joys and sorrows, the mere time for the fulfilment of some supernatural prophecy.

In hue, the face was dark and embrowned, in feature it was marked and characteristic — the brow wide and massive, with clustering locks of deep brown hair, falling to the shoulders—the nose delicate and aquiline in contour, with thin quivering nostrils—the mouth chiselled, with small lips full of manly expression, while the large, round, prominent chin, and the high cheek bones, indicated the distant aboriginal ancestry of the young man. The black mustache clothing the lip, and mingling with the slight beard that marked the outline of the chin, spoke of foreign adventure and travel; but apart from every other feature, the clear, dark, hazel eye, fixed the attention of the gazer, with its strange brilliancy, and shone out from beneath the arching brows like a star of thought, a star of mind, a light of wild and dreamy feeling. The attire of the twain was strangely and curiously contrasted.

A long and loosely fitting coat, a shirt of wild deer's hide, clothed the tall and stalwart form of the old man; his arms were covered with furs and his legs were defended by rough and rugged hose, fashioned of dark grey fur, and bound at the side by interlacing cords; his feet were clad in simple moccasins, while at his side lay the glittering rifle side by side with the cap of otter skin, wide and shapeless, and plumed with a bucktail.

A closely gathered coat of dark green velvet, marked by a single row of gold buttons in front, disclosed the muscular chest and agile form of the young man. A sword was suspended by a belt of dark leather encircling his waist. His legs were clad in buckskin, and he wore half boots of the same material, with wide slouching tops, and spurs glittering on each heel. Thrown back from the coat of green velvet, was a surcoat of blue cloth, faced with buff, and reaching to the knee, and over the right shoulder, drooping to the floor, hung the loose folds of a furred military cloak, while carelessly flung along the bench, lay the slouching hat, with diminished crown, topped by a plume of midnight blackness, and enwreathed with a green sprig, freshly gathered from the branches of some forest oak.

" Ask me not, young stranger, ask me not how I procured the pacquet," spoke the old man, in a bold yet hushed and whispered voice. " Hug it closely to thy heart. Part not with it, save with thy life. Away with it to Washington—to him it may be worth a nation's ransom ? For six long days have I borne that pacquet about my person. For six long days have my footsteps been tracked by the blood-hounds, and now, to thee, an utter stranger, do I consign the precious charge ! Swear, by the God above us, in the awful silence of this temple, while shadows flit around you, and all is still as the grave, swear to stay nor spur nor steed, until you have given this into the hands of Washington himself!"

" I swear !" said the young man, in a low, deep-toned voice, as he placed the sealed pacquet in his breast. " I swear by the God above me, and by the cause I serve !" And as he spoke, rising from his seat, the young soldier gathered his cloak about him, and was about to turn his steps towards the window opening on the Quaker grave yard.

" Stay—a single moment, young stranger," said the old man, motioning him to the rugged bench. " Our meeting has been a strange one ! Some would call it accident, some would call it chance. I call it fate ! Have you no wish to unravel the mystery ?"

" My friend, you know me not !" said the young soldier, drawing nearer to the old man. " My life, from very childhood, has been the creature of mystery and shadow. Is it time now to begin to wonder at another link in that chain of wild circumstance which has entwined its mysteries around every moment of my existence ?"

" And I have not been mistaken in you, then !" said the old man, leaning forward, and throwing the glare of the lamp full in the face of the young soldier, while he seemed to drink in each line of his magnificent face. " It is stamped upon you—the signet of an awful destiny !" he exclaimed, in a voice of wild enthusiasm. " Such a destiny as has made my life a *doom,* my existence a *curse!*". But it may yet be turned aside with you—the hand of fate may yet be stayed in its beckonings of doom. Oh, young sir! —tell me—has fancy, in your dreams, long time past, never pictured the simple walls of this Quaker temple?"

"It has! it has!" cried the young soldier, in a voice that shared the enthusiasm of the old man. "Long time past, in days of childhood—when a mother's corse lay stark and dead before me—when the OATH she exacted with her dying lips, yet rung in my ears!—then, then! I saw this simple temple in a dream—its bare walls, its rustic benches—in a dream I beheld the tombless graveyard without, and a voice whispered me, *here* shall the prophecy of a betrayed mother claim its terrible fulfilment!"

"And to-day, urged by a spirit of restless adventure as you call it, you rode from the American camp, now fixed away towards the west—you saw my lantern glimmering through the crevice of yon window—you sprang through the aperture—you confronted me—a word made us acquainted, and a sudden confidence sprang up between us. Speak I aright?"

"You do." returned the young soldier. "The moment I looked upon you, sitting here alone in the solitude of this temple, this rustic meeting-house, my heart told me that your life had been governed by a destiny dark as mine own! And now, Sir Stranger, your story. Can I ask its narration?"

"It may not, cannot be told!" exclaimed the old man, in a voice trembling with emotion. "At least not now, not *now*. Young stranger, I look upon you, and know that my future destiny is linked with yours. We shall meet again—I know it—I feel it. You ask my story? Who may tell it? I go—no one knows whither! I pass along the valley of olden time—no one calls me by name! I look upon *her*, and *she* knows me not! I come no one knows from whither! As a shadow and a dream among mine old familiar friends I pass—"

He clasped his hands in silent agony, and the big, large tears of man's despair, stood in his eyes.

"Yet stay, unknown friend of mine, a single moment stay," he said, in a bold and commanding voice. "Draw near to me, while I speak to your ears a wild prophecy connected with this simple Quaker meeting-house! Look around. Does it not look like a home for glooms and shadows? The glories of architecture enrich not these walls, and the vaulted arch and the fretted roof give no shade, no terror, no mystery to the place! Yet look around. Is there not something solemn and dread in the hour!"

"I must confess that there is a wild mystery about this rustic temple, which I never found in the recesses of Westminster Abbey, or Notre Dame," the young soldier returned. "The light! how it breaks in fitful gleams along the dark corners of the place! The walls—white, solemn, and sepulchre-like—how ghastly they glimmer in the lamp beams! And the hour! It is silent as though we were encompassed by the marble of a death-vault!"

" Here, my friend, long, long years ago, when I was a little child, on a fair summer afternoon, I sat upon this very bench, while the Sabbath sun light came streaming through the rustic windows, gleaming upon calm faces and peaceful forms!   Here I sat—how well do I remember the scene! An aged and venerable man stood up in yonder pulpit, and in soft and gentle tones spake to his brethren of the great beauties of the Christian faith, of its peace and its good will.   Suddenly a change broke over the preacher's countenance—the lineaments of his face lighted up with a strange expression—his eye flashed, his lip quivered, and while a thrill of terror ran round the place, thus broke the words of prophecy from his lips."

The countenance of the young soldier was all interest, and the fitful gleams of the lamp, falling around the lonely place, gave life to the mystery of the old man's words.

" ' Brethren !' he cried, ' this is a quiet and a holy place.   The Sabbath's sunbeams shine peacefully through the windows on your calm and happy faces !   But, lo ! the day shall come when the sunbeams shall shine through these windows as brightly as they shine now, but shine on heaps of dying and heaps of dead—piled up all gory and ghastly within these solemn walls ! The time cometh, and the quiet of this place is broken by the groan of mortal agony—the wail of the parting soul—the death shriek and the death yell !   The time will come when yon graveyard shall be cumbered with ghastly heaps of dead—broken limbs and torn carcases all heaped together in the graveyard of Peace.   And the bullet shall whistle through yon window-panes, and the sword shall gleam within these walls !'   His voice was the voice of a prophet as he spoke.   His manner was wrapt, his tone inspired ; and raising his form to its full height, he thundered forth the words, ' Lo ! the Lord God hath spoken it !' "

" And the prophecy will claim its fulfilment !" said the young soldier solemnly, " within three little days will it claim its fulfilment !"

" And I have passed through the valley like a spirit, waking its children up to a sense of British ravage and British wrong !" said the old man, grasping his rifle.   " To-morrow night the yeomanry of these valleys assemble in a lonely glen, some four miles south-west of Chadd's Ford.   At the same time a band of traitors, tories, and refugees assemble at a well known cabin at the cross-roads, in the woods, some three miles west of the Ford.   Is it your purpose to make one gallant effort to crush the enterprize in the bud ?"

" You judge me aright !" said the young soldier laying his hand upon his sword.   " With my gallant troopers of Wild Santee, will I adventure into the enemy's very den, make one daring blow to disperse this gathering of traitors, and rely in a good cause and a stout arm for success !"

And as he spoke the soldier moved toward the window, and, laying a hand upon the wide sill, sprang through the aperture.

' The friends of our cause may wish to join you in the attack—the sur prise.'' said the old man, unconscious of the soldier's sudden absence "What shall be your mutual watchword? Whom shall I tell them will lead on the attack?"

"The Captain of the Rangers of Santee!" shouted the young soldier, as the head of his golden-hued steed was thrust through the opened window, while the gallant barb was beating his hoofs against the graveyard earth without. "Tell them the Captain of the Rangers of Santee, will lead on the attack,—and as for the watchword, take the name that old tradition and the warm-hearted courtesy of his soldiers have given him—let the watchword be 'RANDULPH THE PRINCE!'"

CHAPTER EIGHTH.

THE VISION OF WAR.

In a small apartment, circular in shape, and lighted by a lamp depending from the arched ceiling, while the silence of the midnight hour gathered around her, sat Blanche Walford, half reclining on a couch of velvet, with her swelling cheek resting upon one fair white hand, and her form in all its maidenly beauty, was dimly disclosed in the light.

It was an oratory of prayer. An alter of snow white marble, an image of the Saviour, an opened volume, on whose pages were traced the words of religion, these all were there, in that silent temple with its solitary worshipper, the holiest place in Wild-wood Grange, while all was still and silent as death along the valley of the Brandywine, had the fair maiden retired for an hour of solemn thought. And as the memory of her uncle's story of fear and doom—the remembrance of her mother, her own long-sought and newly-discovered mother, she who had smiled upon her face when the light of life first played upon its young features, she who had pressed her to her heart ere its last chord snapped and shivered—as the memory of this mother came over her mind, mingling with the thought of the father—he who had gone forth from the home of his love, banned and cursed with the bane and curse of a blighted heart—as the mingled memory, the remembrance and the thought, came rushing over the mind of the beautiful girl, her full, dark eye gathered a strange brilliancy, and her bosom rose throbbing in the light.

Blanche ascended the winding stairway. In a moment she stood upon the roof of the Grange, and open to her gaze, sleeping in the mingled star-beams and the moonlight, lay the magnficent valley of the Brandywine, lovely as a poet's dream.

Resting her full, rounded arms on the balustrade, with her fair, white hands clasped over her bosom, while her robes of white fell sweeping to the floor of the roof, with a glistening eye and parted lip, Blanche Walford gazed upon the scene of pastoral loveliness.

Far away in the west, sinking behind the distant woodlands, the moon flung long columns of silvery light along the mass of forest, rising behind forest, a vast lake of foliage, undulating with the impulse of the night breeze, while winding around the base of the hill, from whose summit arose the Grange, the waves of the Brandywine—now shadowed by overarching elm, chesnut, or beechen tree, now open to the view—glistened and shimmered in the light, as flowing onward with the pleasant music of rushing water, mingling with the waving sound of the tree branches sweeping in its ripples, the stream so quiet, so pastoral in its beauty, wound along on its southward course, marking its pathway by a line of liquid silver.

Again and again did the beautiful girl gaze upon the view. And then her eyes were upturned to the sky, the vast and star girt sky, which arose in all its midnight magnificence—the dome of this scene of nature's more quiet glories—and there in all their unutterable beauty, shone the stars, the innumerable hosts of light, looking forth from their own blue heaven upon the lovely and lonely valley ef the Brandywine.

"The moon is sinking in the west!" murmured Blanche. "Slowly and in solemn grandeur she sinks! The woods gleam in the last beam of her light—it streams across the valley—it lights up the humble roof of the school-master—it trembles along the foliage of the hill beyond! And, *now* —all is dark ; and now, with a brightness more sudden and intense, the stars shine forth along the autumnal heavens!"

No land under the blue heavens is more invested with the poetry of tradition, now dark, now beautiful, now terrible, and now sublime, than is our own magnificent land of the new world. America no antiquities—no legends—no traditions? Not a hill-side in the land, but has witnessed some terrible scene of midnight slaughter—not a lonely dell but has been soddened by American blood, poured forth by hireling swords—not a tree, ancient and time honored, but has looked forth upon the scenes of battle—not a speck of dust blown along the wayside by the summer wind, but has once throbbed with life within the heart of some humble patriot, or yeoman soldier.

And along this fair land, blooms there never a valley so rich in legend, so rife with incidents of supernatural lore as the valley of the Brandywine. Among the most familiar of these legends, not regarded as things of fiction or dreams of fancy by the old denizens of the valley, but as settled histor-ical facts, is the Legend of the Prophecy of Battle, uttered in Birmingham meeting-house, the Story of Lord Percy's Dream, and the tradition of the vision seen by Blanche Walford when gazing upon the heavens some three nights previous to the battle-day.

And as the moon sunk down on that autumn night, while around gathered the shadows of the midnight-hour, Blanche Walford looked to the north, and started with an exclamation of wild surprise mingled with a stange fear, while her full, dark eyes were bright with sudden gleams of awe, and her bosom throbbed, and her breath came fast and hurried, in hushed and murmuring gasps, as leaning over the balustrade she gazed upon the northern sky with all its signs of omen and prophecy.

" It arises!" she murmured in the tone of an inspired sybil, " it arises! Sullen and grand, black it arises,—that dark, black cloud! It sweeps upward from the northern horizon—right upward it sweeps! It hovers above the quiet plains of Brandywine—in mid-air it hovers! Beyond its blackness I behold the stars! It hovers over the valley of the Brandywine! Look, look! One dark wing shoots along towards the quiet Quaker temple —the other wing of the terrible cloud hangs over the valley plain! And over the green woods, and over the peaceful farms, the midnight body of this fell cloud blackens and darkens like a spirit bird sent out to warn the sons of men of coming evil! How black and darker it grows!—its edges untinted by starlight—its centre unvisited by beam or streak of light! It rests not upon the horizon—it dwells not away in the distance, but right over the plain, in mid-air, dark, black and terrible,—how terrible! A thing of midnight, hangs the dark and lurid cloud, with the clear sky all around it—the clear heavens above—the sleeping valley below! Methinks it is a thing of life—not dull, not inanimate, but alive with spirit-hosts!"

The cold, damp chill stood upon her brow—her fair frame trembled from head to foot, and a feeling of terrible and intolerable AWE gathered around her heart and chilled her blood and iced her veins.

" A sudden gleam lights the cloud!"the maiden shrieked forth in a tone wild and terrible as the voice of one throttled by the vision of a nightmare. " Look, look! Bands of armed men—a strange host—are marching up the wings of the cloud —they are clad in scarlet—their arms glimmer, and their banners wave! On and on, trooping and gathering they cluster—and above them floats a massive banner, gory red, and blazoned with a cross of blood! They troop along the misty ridges of the cloud! Ha! Another host— plain and simple men, clad in blue, clad in homely attire, in coarse garments—they come trooping from the opposite wing of the cloud! And in their midst is one magnificent form—the form with the calm face and the clear eye! See! see!—they mingle in contest—the smoke of battle rolls over the cloud, Now, God help the banner of Azure, for the flag of Blood waves high over the cloud and the storm! Now all is mist, shadow and gloom! That shriek!—that terrible, that piercing shriek—that groan of

7

mortal agony!—comes it from yonder cloud? Oh, Heaven! the sight will drive me mad!"

She turned, from the phantasmal terrors she turned, and gazed upon the valley. A bright, ruddy flame shot upward near the dwelling of the school-master, on the opposite side of the vale. It shot upward, vivid and blinding girt with folds of blackening smoke, and darting into the clear heavens, while far along the meadow, far over the hillside and the distant woods, streamed the blood-red light, coloring rock and tree and stream with its fiery glare.

And figures were hurrying to and fro in that light, and the green sward was crowded by bands of men, their long shadows flung far over the meadow, and shouts broke upon the silent air; but high over the shout, and the yell, and the hurrah, shrieked one wild and piercing sound. It was the shriek of a mortal voice, it came sweeping along the night-breeze, it thrilled the heart of the maiden with fear, it smote her very brain with terror.

"Bands of men are hurrying to and fro in the flame," she whispered, gazing upon the scene which had arisen before her like the work of enchant-ment, "they are clad in scarlet! That sound that breaks along the air— it is the sound of a human voice!—the shriek of a strong man in mortal agony, dying a death of terror and massacre!"

CHAPTER NINTH.

THE TRAGEDY OF THE HAYSTACK OPENS WITH A CALM SCENE OF QUIET LIFE.

" GOODNESS me, but this pipe o' mine is like a livin' cretur'! Jest see how the smoke rolls and rolls and rolls away to the ceilin', jest as sassy like as if it knew every thing that was goin' on, and didn't care a fa'thin for no-body! Howsomever it is I don't know, but whenever I smoke a pipe near this spook hour, all the doings of my life seem to come up in gineral muster before me, not in single file or double file either, but four abreast, all in a crowd! Queer!—very queer world, this! One pipe o' 'bacco more, and then I'll to my bed o' rest——"

And, sitting in his capacious arm chair, the very picture of quiet ease and self-complacency—his coat thrown aside, his voluminous vest loosened, and his hose ungartered, with his legs resting on the small table, on which burned the flickering candle—the old soldier, Jacob Mayland, looked around the limited walls of his bedroom with a pleasant chuckle, which said much for the internal good humor of the old man with himself and everybody else, and then refilling his pipe, he watched the smoke as it wreathed around the apartment, floating above the neat coverlid of the bed, or clouding the glasses of the diminutive and deep silled windows.

"It's very queer!" he soliloquized. "All my life seems to come trooping up afore me! I see my wife, Polly's mother, with jest the same smilin' face as when I fust went a courtin' her! Dead and gone, now, fifteen long years! And then I see the old soldiers o' Braddock's time—the scenes o' the march, the fight, the retreat,—jest as plain as day. They're all gone, now! Old Jacob's all that's left, and he'll be seventy come next Christmas. Aye, aye, smoke away old pipe, you'll go out arter while—so will old Jacob. You kin be lit up ag'in old pipe—who'll light up old Jacob? Somehow, queer thoughts o' the next world are stirrin' in me jest now. What'll they do with me in th' next world? They won't have no use for soldiers there, and as for school-masters, why they haint got no little children there to be learned their 'a-b ab's,' and their 'b-a ba's'—"

Jacob looked very much puzzled at this point of his self argument, and then, knocking the ashes from his pipe, he resumed:

"Howsomever, my religion's a very plain one.—I think the good Lord that sent me into this world will take me out of it in his own pertik'ler way, and provide for me in th' next world, that's my religion—it's jest as good as clear weather, too. Providen' a feller don't cut up many capers in this world, and don't figure out too many shines, he's jest as good for the next world as tho' his face was two feet long and his voice always a twangin through his nose like the wind through a spavined bellows. Well, well, Lord forgive me my sins—(I feel quite solemn like to-night)—and help Polly arter I'm sleepin' in the Quaker graveyard—"

The door slowly opened, and in an instant Polly Mayland stood before her father, with her face pale as death, her lips parted, and her blue eyes wavering in their glance, while her rich brown hair fell wildly over her shoulders, but half veiling the full outline of her youthful bosom, gleaming into light from the scanty confines of her night dress, and with a loosened kerchief thrown lightly around her neck, with her arms, swelling and rounded in proportion, bare to the shoulder, extended in a gesture of sudden alarm, the maiden remained standing in front of the schoolmaster breathless and motionless.

"Speak, gal, can't you?" cried old Jacob, starting on his feet with surprise. "What in the name o' goodness is the matter?"

"Hist! father, for the sake of Heaven!" exclaimed Mary in a trembling yet energetic voice. "Fly, for God's sake, my, father, fly!"

"What's the matter Polly?" cried old Mayland. "What on 'airth d'ye mean?"

"Father!" gasped the trembling girl, "but a moment ago I was roused from my sleep by the sound of deep toned voices, whispering beneath my window. A thought, a terrible thought flashed over my mind on the instant!

I looked from the window! Our house is surrounded by men with their faces blackened—some were clad in red coats—all are armed with sword and gun. They are seeking an entrance into the house without alarming the valley. Not a word more, father, but fly—oh! for Heaven's sake, fly!"

" Not 'till I know more about this matter!" coolly returned the old man, ' What in the name o' natur' do the red coats want with me?"

" Can you ask, father?" whispered the maiden in a trembling tone. " A week since, you gave the protection of your house to a friendless stranger—a man clad in skins of wild beasts—he left a pacquet in your charge, a pacquet to which he affixed great value——"

" And that pacquet I gave back to him some twenty hours ago, afore daybreak," returned Mayland. " No, no, gal, the sold'ers can't want no-thin, wi' me——"

" Father! oh, father!" cried the maiden in a voice that was all pathos, all alarm, " these men are fitted, by drinking, for any act of outrage, any deed of horror! They whisper your name as Mayland the ' Spy!' They may kidnap you away in the darkness—they may steal you away from your home—and when they have you in the British camp, your act of hospitality will be made a sure, a certain witness against you——"

" Hallo, there! my name's Hessian Dick, be gaw!" growled a sup-pressed voice directly under the schoolmaster's window. " Is there nobody at home?"

" Pry the door!" whispered another voice—" D——n the rebel. Pry the door open with your bay'nets."

" Look to the pacquet!" mumbled the first voice, " damme, there's a good round sum on *that*. My name's Hessian Dick, be gaw!"

" Father, father, hear you that?" shrieked Mary Mayland leading the old man towards a closet in the wall, opposite the bed. " Not a moment more —but fly! A few seconds will place you in safety—the valley people will be roused—these ruffians driven back to their dens! Fly, my father, fly!"

" Whither, girl, whither?" exclaimed the one armed schoolmaster. " They are battering away at the front door! Shall I walk out among 'em and ask 'em not to stick their bay'nets in my breast?" The old man ground his teeth as he muttered—" Would I only had my good right arm back ag'in for about five minutes!"

" This way, father, this way!" cried the girl as seizing the light she flung the closet door wide open, " up with this board, father—quick!—quick! Do you see this ladder? It served us for a stairway before the staircase was built yonder in the centre of the house. It descends into the large closet of the schoolroom The floor is loose—a single movement of your foot will open you a way into the cellar——"

" And what 'ill I do in the cellar, Polly?" said the schoolmaster with confused glance. "Shall I go down there to be hunted like a weazel! By the Lord, no!"

"The door gives!" cried the voice without, as a confused murmur broke upon the air. "In a flash, be gaw, the old rebel is our man!"

"Father—quick, quick!" screamed Polly. "Descend the ladder. The lower closet is placed not directly over the cellar, but over the passage—you remember it?—the passage under the earth, walled in by rocks, and winding some twenty or thirty yards up the hill? It was used by the first settlers, in the times o' the Injins."

"I remember!" said the old man descending the ladder, while the light flashed upon his wrinkled face and grey hairs appearing above the closet floor. "This passage opens on the hill-side, about half way 'twixt the haystack and the little barn—it leads into that little mound o' earth near the haystack, which used to cover a spring o' cold water, but the water is now dried up, and the mound sarves us for a place to put our 'tatoes and tu'nips in winter."

"Yes, yes, my father!" cried Polly as a gleam of joy flashed from her pretty blue eye. "Descend into this passage—an old oaken door divides it from the cellar—remain there until you hear the soldiers in the house, then creep out o' the mound and make for the woods!"

"Another poke at the door boys!" cried the ruffian leader without, "and we'll have the old fox, be gaw! And as for his filly—ha, ha, ha! be gaw!"

"I don't think I'll go," said old Mayland in a determined voice, as arising from the ladder, he was about to step out upon the floor of the room. "What's to become o' you, gal?"

"Never heed me, father," cried the maiden placing the candle in his hands and motioning him to descend the ladder, "you have but one arm! your daughter has two. Your rifle hangs over the hearth—it was loaded by Gotlieb Hoff this very day, and——. Away, away, my father! Hark! the door is yielding to their attacks?"

The old man took the candle in his hand, and began to descend the ladder, and his fair daughter, leaning forward, gazed down the aperture with a look of intense interest, while the light, flashing upward, cast a ruddy glow over her face, now pale with alarm, now flushed with hope, and her maidenly form—the long slender waist, and the bosom, fair as snow, and swell'ng with agitation—was shown in the full glare of the retreating beams, as standing in the closet door, with parted lips and extended arms, the maiden watched the footsteps of her father.

"Ah! now the whole affair flashes on me!" cried the old man, slowly descending the ladder. "The threat of Gilbert Gates!—I see its meaning now!"

"Away! away, father!" cried the maiden, trembling with suspense "And as for that Gilbert Gates——"

" He is at .hee side !" said a mild and softened voice, as a cat-like foot
step trode along the floor. " Nay, maiden, start not, nor look thus alarmed,
I am at thee side for good. Thee father shot my father, but I can return
good for evil. Does not the Book say it is our duty? In truth can I——"

And holding a flaming pine knot in his hand, with the light flashing upon
the outline of his slender figure—the long, thin arms, the spider-like legs,
and the narrow chest—Gilbert Gates came stealing along to the side of the
maiden, while a faint smile wreathed his pinched lips, and his grey eyes
shot a strange and inexpressible gleam from beneath the shadow of the bushy
eyebrows.

" Back !" cried Polly Mayland, as a flush of anger brightened over her
features, " back, reptile !" she cried, with erect figure and extended arm.
" Come but a step nearer, and sure as God will nerve the arm of a true
maiden, so sure will I brain ye with this oaken brand !"

She seized a fragment of the closet floor, a tough piece of oak, knotted at
one end, and flinging her fair form in front of the closet, she confronted
Gilbert Gates with an erect port and a flashing eye.

The man started back, and quailed before the glance of the maiden.

" Quick ! my father, quick !" cried Mary, suddenly gazing down the lad-
der-way—" Ah ! ha !—Joy ! joy !" she shouted. " He gains the first floor
—he is descending into the cellar—a moment and he is saved !"

" Maiden, thee misunderstands me !" said Gilbert, approaching the school-
master's daughter, with an insinuating smile. " Thee must know, that
happening to pass this way, I beheld the soldiers around thee father's house.
My heart was touched with pity. I wished to save him—in truth I did !
' For,' said I, ' they will surely murder him if they catch him !' so I crept
into the back window down stairs—they were too much in liquor to see me
—I placed another bar and chain across the door ; it will take 'em jist five
minutes more for them to break in. And now, maiden, here I am, ready
and willing to save thy parent—oh, in truth am I !"

" Hurrah, there, be gaw !" muttered a voice without. " D—n the door,
it's made of cast iron? Another blow, boys, and a good one—now !"

" Oh, Gilbert Gates ! I know you !" cried the maiden, with a look of
ineffable scorn. " There is treachery in your look, man ! There is revenge
in your eye ! My father is your first victim—I am to be your last ! Back !
—not a step nearer ! Were you not coward as well as villain you would
seize me, as I stand—but ye fear this oaken brand !"

A gleam of human feeling lighted up the hard features of Gilbert.
" Maiden, maiden !" he cried, in a broken voice, " did thee know my direful
duty—had thee heard my OATH—thee would not taunt me thus ! One word
from thee may turn my fate—for—for—I do love thee, maiden !" A gleam
of fire lighted up his eyes as he noted her glance of scorn, and a malignant
smile crossed his features. " Thee will be mine, maiden ? In truth must
thee—or—or—thee father will die the death ! And"—he continued, with a

smile of peculiar meaning—"there is a certain Captain Howard who has looked upon thy pretty form, and a certain Sergeant Hamsdorff who will get an hundred guineas for thee—sweet maiden—an hundred guineas when that pretty form is delivered into the care of that Captain Howard!"

" I pity you, I pity you, Gilbert!" said Mary Mayland. " A heart like your's must be more terrible to its owner than all the tortures of the lost. He reaches the cellar!" continued she, in a murmured whisper—" His light flickers!—Oh, Heaven! I remember!—the door between the cellar and the passage is unbarred!"

A sound like thunder came booming from the room below, and a mingled shout and a hurrah startled the silence of the school-master's home.

" It gives way—this curst door—be gaw!" shouted a hoarse, boisterous voice. " My name's Hessian Dick, be gaw! Up stairs, boys, up stairs. Trap the old fox in his nest!"

The sound of trampling feet was heard in the room below, mingling with the clash of swords and the rumbling of musquet stocks, flung hurriedly to the floor.

" In truth, maiden, the men of war are in thee father's house!" quietly said the Quaker, moving to the door. " I will go to them, and persuade them not to give thee trouble. Meanwhile, thee had better remain here. In truth, there is some danger to thee father."

And with a malignant smile on his thin lips, this strange man disappeared, closing the door behind him, and Mary Mayland heard the lock grating as he closed it, while in the room below all was confusion and uproar.

" Now help me, oh my God!" said Mary, as her eyes swam in tears, and her form trembled from head to foot. "Hark! They are on the stairs! They think themselves sure of their prey. I will foil them yet!"

With a light bound she sprang down the ladder, drawing the closet door shut with one hand, while the other grasped the ladder rounds, and the bed-room of the one-armed schoolmaster was left to silence and darkness.

No sooner had Gilbert Gates emerged from the room, and stood upon the head of the stairway, than a mingled sound of threats and curses assailed his ear, and in a moment the shuffling of booted feet was heard upon the steps, and presently the light of the pine knot flashed upon the corpulent form of a portly trooper, clad in scarlet, with a face flushed by wine, covered with mustachios and grisly whiskers, and marked by large, rolling, vacant eyes, who came rushing up the staircase with a flashing sword in one hand and a torch in the other, while behind him appeared the faces of some half dozen dragoons, mingling with a half a score of ruffianly visages, blackened and craped for the purpose of disguise, and each man bore a sword or a rifle, and each voice swelled the tumult with drunken shouts and muttered curses.

" Eh! Broadbrim, here before us, hey?" shouted the leader of the band, as with a drunken movement he pitched up the stairway. " The old fox—

where is he? Caught, be gaw, eh? Damme, answer me man—my name's
Hessian Dick, be gaw!—where's the fox—old Jacob? Where's the robin
—pretty Polly, eh?"

"Friend, is it right to be a disturbin' a peaceful man's house at this hour
of the night? said Gilbert Gates, waving his pine knot with a pleasant smile.
"Surely did the folks of the valley hear ye they might think ye meant old
friend Mayland a deal of harm, in truth——"

"To the devil with your speech," shouted a stout, broad shouldered
ruffian, with a hat of felt drooping over his craped face, and a broad white
belt encircling his muscular chest. "We want the bundle of papers and the
rebel hound! Where are they smooth speech?"

"Aye, that's it," cried Hamsdorff. "We want the schoolmaster. We
want his pretty daughter. We want——"

"Oh, friends, if that's all ye want," returned Gilbert Gates eyeing the
group of ruffians, "friend Mayland and his daughter are looking after their
household affairs in the cellar, in truth they are."

With a mingled shout and yell, the troopers and the tory bravos swept
down the stairway, and Gilbert Gates turned again to the bedroom of the
schoolmaster. It was silent and untenanted by human being. He approached
the closet—he flung the door open—he gazed down through the aperture of
the ladder—a light faint and dim was shining in the passage of rocks below.
A smile wreathed the lips of Gilbert, and an expression of malignity that
was like the sneer of a devil's face came over his visage, as holding the pine
torch in one hand he gazed into the passage below.

"The old man has a single chance of life!" he said. "Just as I planned
it all! He takes to the cellar—he will emerge by the haystack—and, ha,
ha, ha! he will die the death! And she might have saved him. Brute
fools that they are, hark how they shout!—my dupes my tools. And she
loves her father, ha, ha! I never loved human thing—save—save,"—he
hissed the words between his teeth,—" save one, 'he died alone in the wood,'
ha, ha! I—I—am his son, his AVENGER!"

CHAPTER TENTH.

THE TRAGEDY OF THE HAYSTACK IS CARRIED ON RIGHT BRAVELY.

MERRILY around the old cellar walls flashed and flaunted the light of
glowing torches, tinting the grey stone with sudden light, and turning to
glowing red the massive rafters above and the hard clay beneath, while run
ning hither and thither with unsteady steps, the scarlet hued troopers, with

Hamsdorff at their head, sought their victims with loud oaths and terrible imprecations, and at their backs, by no means hindmost in the chase, came the craped and disguised bravos, with their stout captain of the white belt and the felt hat, leading them on and pointing their pathway with his sword, with the loud hurrah, the inhuman threat, and the half fiendish, half brutal yell.

"Ha, ha! What does this mean?" shouted Hessian Dick, rolling his corpulet form along the earthen floor. "A door—a door of oak, be g^w? Something behind that, my boys! Hunt 'em up, lads, hunt 'em up!"

'Force the door—force the door, Ravenso' the Hollow!" cried the white belted leader of the band of tory bravos, giving his men one of the score of choice names by which they were distinguished—"quick! Up with that log of hickory yonder—take hold of it, four of you, my boys! Now send it stavin' through the panels of oak!—now!"

And as he spoke, four of the bravos flung down their swords, their rifles, and their torches, and while the red coated dragoons wheeled to one side, and sable coated tories swept back to the opposite side, the blazing torchlight flashed around the scene and discovered the four stalwart ruffians starting backward from the massive door, each with his right leg advanced, and each with his right arm nerved, while the log of hickory swayed slowly to and fro in their vicelike grasp.

And, meanwhile, waiting at the opposite side of the door, where a dim light struggled round the rocks and crevices of the narrow passage, with its floor of stone, and its roof of rocks, there waited a fair and trembling maiden, her bosom bared and her brown hair all dishevelled and unbound, falling in glossy richness over her globes of snow.

"Father!" cried Mary, "onward, onward—to the mound, to the mound! The door has no bar, no bolt," she whispered in a lower tone—"but my right arm will serve for bolt and bar."

"One moment more, Polly, and I will break from the mound," the voice of the old man came faintly along the rocks of the subterranean passage. "There is a large rock laid right across the mouth. Ah! me, I fear I cannot lift it! This way, Polly—we will escape together!"

"In a moment, father, in a moment!" cried Mary, but she made no signs of moving. "Now let them force the door!" she exclaimed with a smile. —Through staple and through bar fastening was thrust her fair white arm —another moment and the hickory log would come thundering through the panels—another moment and the maiden's arm, snapped and shattered to the very shoulder, would fall in fragments to the earth, and over her prostrate body, crushed and mangled, would the pathway of the spoiler be made.

"Let your aim be certain!" shouted the bravo leader. "Strike in the centre of the middle plank! Now, my boys! right through the panel —strike!"

The log swayed slowly backward in the grasp of the four stout and muscular men—it came rushing onward, propelled with all the nerve and sinew of their giant arms! A heavy body, dark and sable, fell sudden as a flash from the small cellar window, right above the oaken door—it fell directly upon the centre of the log, arresting its progress and beating it from the grasp of the tories in the very moment of its contact with the oaken door.

Ere the troopers had time to breathe a word or raise a sword, right up from the cellar floor, before the door of oak, there uprose the muscular figure of an ebony skinned man, with a broad, black chest shining and glistening in the light and unbared to the waist, arms of almost superhuman nerve and sinew, thrown aloft, with the hands tightly clenched, and in the very faces of the ruffians, stared a wild, black visage, with large glaring eyes rolling madly from side to side, a wide mouth distorted by a hideous grin and disclosing two rows of ivory teeth jarring and grating against each other, while with heaving chest, and nerve and sinew trembling and quivering with passion, this strange apparition confronted the astonished troopers, and stood towering between the log and the oaken door.

" Look heah—look heah !" shouted the black man, shaking his arms aloft, while his face was convulsed by an expression like that of a maddened bull, " I'm dang'rous ! Ye gwain to go tru dat ar door ? S'pose ye am ! Ye must walk over dis niggah's dead body fust. I am a debbil, I tell you ! Stan' off ! Fader prince in he own country !—Sampson debbil heah ! Stan' off—s-t-a-n' off." He grated his ivory teeth together, and then brandishing his weaponless arms, he stood in the full glare of the lamp beams an animated statue of superhuman rage and supernatural strength.

" Be gaw, my name's Hessian Dick !" shouted the drunken trooper. " shoot him down ! Shoot the darkey down—damme, down with him !"

" Down with him," re-echoed the tory leader.

" Look heah !" shouted the negro, trembling from head to foot with rage, " You may tear dis niggah from lim' to liber, but you no pass dis door ! Hab been watchin' you dis ten minit. Dam scoundrels, all ob you ! My moder war sick—hab no friend in de world—war dyin'—Massa Mayland give her wittel—Missa Mayland gib her med'cin' ! S'pose I let you pass dis door ? Hah-a-whah !"—he screamed a wild, half fiendish shout. " I see you to de berry biggest debbil fust ! Stan' off !—s-t-a-n' off !"

" D——n the nigger !" shouted the white belted ruffian, darting forward and raising his clubbed rifle as he sprang. " No shootin' here, boys, it will alarm the valley folks ! I'll cut this lump of charcoal down.'

He sprang forward—he raised his clubbed rifle to the rafters—it descended with a whizzing sound—and the tories shouted as they already fancied the crushed skull and bleeding form of the prostrate negro. Sampson sprang aside from the blow with a nimble movement, retreated a step toward the door, and then lowering his head between his shoulders, pitched forward like a mad bull directly into the stomach of his antagonist, who reeled under the attack, and fell backward among the ruffians of his band.

Another moment and the whole body of dragoons and troopers had raised their swords and rifles around the negro. and with muttered curses and imprecations, proceeded to rid themselves of their sable antagonist in the shortest and most effectual way.

Sampson fought like an enraged tiger, bravely breasting his foes aside, parrying the sword thrust with his muscular arm, darting his woolly head into the stomach of one ruffian, and tripping up the heels of another; but it all was in vain. He was trodden upon the earth by the combined strength of the band. A fearful sword-gash severed the flesh of his right arm, and panting and bleeding upon the hard clay of the cellar floor, the negro, with his large rolling eyes, beheld the ruffians sweeping past him on their way to the door.

" Death and the devil!" shouted the white belted leader. " We lose time! Quick, my boys! Hurrah, Ravens! Lift the log, and send it through that infernal door!"

" Be gaw, I'd swear it was made of rebel oak!" shouted Hamsdorff, with a drunken attempt at wit. " Y-e-s, be gaw!"

The log was again raised—the aim taken—when, to the utter surprise of the whole band, the door creaked on its hinges, swung suddenly and slowly back, and the light of a dozen torches flashed along the narrow passage, along each pointed rock, in the hollow of each crevice, and over the stony floor and rocky roof of the cavern.

" Saved! my father, saved!" shrieked a female voice. " Bloodhounds, ye are foiled!"

And in the very path of the troopers, directly over the door-sill, there fell a maidenly form, with unbared bosom, and eyes closed in the faintness of a sudden swoon, while the cheek was pale as marble and the quivering lip livid as death.

" Be gaw! that looks quite nice," said Hamsdorff with a drunken leer. " One kiss, my dear girl, for the Captain's sake."

" D——n the hussy!" shouted the leader of the tory band. " Let us onward, Hamsdorff, this rebel hound lurks somewhere in this passage! Scatter, my boys, scatter!"

" Here, fellows, be gaw!" hiccuped the Sergeant, " lay hold of the pretty lass, and bear her up stairs. You know she's wanted somewhere, eh? My name's Hessian Dick, be gaw! Damme, let's catch the rebel!"

And while the ruffian band, with blazing torches, and swords and rifles upraised, swept on through the rocky passage in search of the fugitive, two of their number—tall, stout and athletic—remained standing beside the fainting maiden, with flushed countenances and eyes bloodshot, and noses purpled with wine.

" I say, Bill!" said the whiskered trooper, " she's a fine jade—and the

Captain 'ill give a round hundred, will he? Dev'lish clever. Let's take
her up stairs, and bear her off afore she wakes."

"Yes, Tom," the other replied, stooping down to raise the maiden. " I
tell you, though, my boy, but this Dave Walford, who leads them craped
chaps, is a roaring bird! Now, Bill, I can tell the reason why sich fellers
as you and me take to these fightin', plunderin' ways—'cause there was
nothin' for us but jails and starvation, the Newgate cell or the workhouse,
at home. But why these neighbors o' one another, as I mought say, should
go about burnin' one another's houses down—d——d if I can make it out.
Howsomever, there's a good deal of wine and brandy to be got for a cool
hundred guineas! So, here goes!—oh!—a-h—I'm done, for--d——n!"

The stunning report of a rifle thundered along the cellar—the stooping
trooper fell backward to the earth at the very moment his hands were about
to touch the fainting maiden. A quick, rushing footstep was heard. The
other trooper turned suddenly around, and as he turned, he received on his
skull the blow of a clubbed rifle, which sent him reeling to the earth. While,
standing above the unconscious form of the noble-hearted Polly Mayland,
was a stout manly form, with a face, light-hued and fair-skined relieved by
curling locks of golden hair, and flushed by excitement, looming boldly in
the torch-light, and a bluff, good-humored voice whispered the words—
" Mein gott!—nice work! Y-a-h—by Saint Christuffel!"

CHAPTER ELEVENTH.

THE TRAGEDY OF THE HAYSTACK ENDS IN DEATH AND FLAME.

He stood beside the haystack, with the faint glimpses of starlight falling
upon the green sward around him—he stood beside the haystack, while the
shout, and the yell, and the hurrah came echoing from the cellar windows,
with his slender frame upraised to its full height, with his chest heaving and
straining as though a tempest were pent up within his bosom, with the nerves
of his face creeping like living things, and his flashing grey eyes darting
with life from beneath the trembling lids, with his whitened lip quivering, and
his long, talon-like fingers clutching vacantly at the air—he stood in the
centre of the green sward, in the shadow of the haystack—a terrible picture
of human passion, hate, revenge and vengeance intermingling, roused to a
pitch of superhuman and fiendish malignity.

Around him lay the quiet valley of the Brandywine—the sloping hill-side,
the house of the schoolmaster, with its dark walls and gable roof, the haystack, and the small barn, all were shown faintly in the starlight—while the

level meadow, the rushing stream, and .he woods beyond, were all wrapt in impenetrable shadow.

He cast his eyes hurriedly around him, and glanced upward to the sky, and then his gaze traversed the masses of shadow that encircled the spot on which he stood alone and companionless, with the feeling of his revenge stirring each vein, blazing along with the life-current of his heart, flashing in his eye and trembling on his lip.

" Ha, ha !" he muttered in a voice changed and altered from his accus-tomed soft and insinuating tone. " By the Power that made me, and by the fiend that rules my fate—*this hour is mine !* Ha, ha !—how merrily the torchlight gleams from the cellar window ! They are on his track—the dupes, the tools of my vengeance ! Mine—mine ! father and daughter, both mine ! For him a death of horror !"—he shrieked the words forth—" for her, a—life of shame ! Ha, ha !" Some sudden remembrance of former years seemed suddenly to take him by storm. " It was sundown—and he lay dead in the wild wood !" he shouted, flinging his arms in the air. "Dead —butchered—murdered ! The only friend I ever had ; and I—I—never knew the name of ' love,' but I'd have given my life to serve my father ! Dead he lay—the setting sunlight falling over his ashen face. Ha, ha !— and his murderers must pin the proofs of their butchery to his blood stained attire ! But, the *oath*, the *oath !*—it shall be fulfilled ! First I will strike at this barnyard fowl—this Mayland and the pretty chicken, his daughter— and then, and then"—he wheeled suddenly round and shook his clenched hand toward Wild-wood Grange, rising above the gloom of the valley— " and then the hawk will speed his wing for the eagle's nest ! Ha, ha— how merrily the shouts break from the cellar and the earth hidden passage !"

As he spoke a long column of light was flung along the green sward, along the spot where he stood, as it seemed, from the very earth, and a huge rock was rolled aside from the mouth of the small and arching mound, while the shouts and yells of the ruffian band broke upon the air.

A figure sprang from the shelter of the mound—the figure of a weak and aged man, with his attire covered with earth and half torn from his person, while the small light which he carried in his solitary hand flashed over his wrinkled features, his blue eye wavering and trembling in its glance, and his long grey hairs tossing to and fro with the impulse of the night breeze.

He tottered slowly forward—he looked wildly around him—his steps trembled, and his gate was unsteady.

" God help me, but it is hard !" he exclaimed in a trembling voice ; " hard for an old soldier like me, to be hunted from my home like a mad dog ! Would I had my right arm back again ! Let me see—I must take to the woods !"

" Nay, friend Mayland, nay," said a mild and conciliating voice. " Thee has never trusted in me, yet, *now* will I save thee life! Not to the woods, for the bloodhounds are too near, in truth are they—but, to the haystack. Friend Mayland, to the haystack!"

"Gilbert Gates!" cried the old man starting back, "I trust you not! Traitor is written in your face!"

"Hark! hark!" cried Gilbert, "hear you the oaths, the shouts of your pursuers? Will thee trust to them? Does thee think, had I wished to wrong thee, it would not have been easy for me to have placed a file of them scarlet men in front of this mound? I beg thee to save thy life. I did feel some anger against thee for the refusal and the scorn of thy daughter, but 'tis all over, in truth is it. To the haystack!—to the haystack!"

A mingled expression of doubt, confidence, dismay and determination, came over the old man's countenance.

"To the haystack be it, then!" he exclaimed, hurriedly moving across the sward. Bless me, what does this mean? A hole hollowed out in the centre of the haystack!"

"I'll tell thee when thou'rt saved!" cried Gilbert Gates with his peculiar smile. "I heard of the plot of these men of blood—I heard it in time to save thee! In, friend Mayland, in! I will conceal thee hiding-place with this loose hay! They will never suspect!"

The old man hurriedly crept into the cavity which had been made half way through the stack—he crept along on his hands and knees, murmuring to himself as he disappeared into his hiding-place.

"It will soon be over, one way or t'other—God help Polly!" He murmured the words, and Gilbert Gates, seizing a small piece of square board from the sward, placed it perpendicularly across the opening of the stack, and then, adding other pieces of board, together with loose sticks and brushwood, in a moment he had smoothed it all over with masses of hay, and the haystack was round, uniform and compact in appearance, while in its centre, cramped and confined, scarce able to breathe, and trembling with the nervousness of age, was hidden Jacob Mayland, the old school-master.

"Fairer tombs have I seen, but none so warm!" said Gilbert Gates with a low chuckle, and a smile. "In truth, the pursuers come!"

And as he spoke, bursting from the mound came the corpulent Hamsdorff, forcing his unwieldly bulk with great difficulty through the narrow opening; and as he leaped out upon the sward, a torch in one hand and a broadsword in the other, the shouts and curses of his band broke upon the air, and the faces of the ruffians appeared over his shoulders as he advanced.

"Ha! Gilbert Gates!" he shouted, "which way went the 'spy?'"

"To the woods!" cried Gilbert. "I persuaded him to stay, but he would not, in truth."

"D——n your smooth speech!" shouted the leader of the craped band, advancing, while the light of a dozen torches fell over the figures of his sable band emerging from the mound, " I don't know what to make of you. If you've betrayed us, by G—d, I'd——"

" Be gaw, but this is d——d nice !" shouted Hamsdorff. " Here we are for at least twenty minutes, huntin' after a d——d old schoolmaster and a bundle o' papers, and what have we got for our pains ? Damme—damme —my name's Hessian Dick. It's a word and a blow with me——"

" Now, friend Hamsdorff, do not get in a passion," said Gilbert Gates, slowly approaching the Sergeant, " or, if thee does, do not commit any rash act"—he placed his face near the early countenance of Hessian Dick, and if ever a human face shone with a hidden devil, that face then shone in the light—" or, if thee does commit any rash act, do not, I beseech thee, *do not fire the poor man's haystack !*"

" Ha, ha, be gaw ! I understand you !" cried the Sergeant, Hamsdorff. " Don't fire the man's haystack ? Won't I, though, be gaw ? Hand me a torch, I say—a torch, damme, a torch !"

Torch in hand, he stumbled toward the haystack—he flung his right arm forth, and the blaze of the torch flashed among the hay.

" Fire the haystack, my boys !" shouted the leader of the tory band. " Fire the haystack, every man o' you. Burn the d——d rebel out o' house and home !"

And some twelve of the band ran forward, and encircled the haystack with a belt of flame ! Another moment !—a sudden puff of the night wind moving from the forest !—the haystack was all a flame. The fire whizzed, and cracked, and hissed, winding around the stack, shooting up to the star-lit sky, flashing abroad over the meadow, lighting up Wild-Wood Grange, crimsoning the leaves of the forest trees ; higher and higher, fiercer and redder wound the flame, while half in anger, half in drunken joy, the troopers and the tories, mingling hand in hand, danced round the burning pile.

" Hurrah for King George, be gaw !" shouted Hamsdorff, springing from his feet. " So perish all rebels !"

" So perish all rebels !" cried the leader of the tory band.

" So perish all rebels !" echoed the troopers.

And higher and higher rose the flame.

It flashed up to the mid-night heavens, paling the stars with its burning red. It flashed far and wide. It flashed over the green of the meadows. Up the hillside, and along the woods, was cast the ruddy light, and as in the blaze of noonday, lay the level sward, the grey stone house of the schoolmaster, the dark frame barn, with its fences and outhouses—while around the burning pile, merrier and gayer, danced the soldiers, flinging their gleaming swords in the blood red light, and sending the name of the good King George to the skies.

And a little in the back ground, some few yards from the burning stack, with his arms folded on his breast, and his head drooped slightly aside, stood Gilbert Gates—and there was a smile upon his face and a mer, y gleam in his eye.

Small and compact in form, the haystack whizzed and whirled away in clouds of jet black and dark grey smoke, strewn with sparks and fragments of hay, and but a few moments were required to level it with the sod.

"Fire the house! be gaw!" shouted Hamsdorff.

"Fire the barn!" shrieked the white belted leader.

"Fire the house!—fire the barn!" echoed the ruffians.

They turned to fire the house—they turned to fire the barn—but a low, moaning sound broke on the air—it caused the troopers, brutal as they were, to start with horror. The leaders of the tories wheeled suddenly round, bending his head to catch the slightest whisper, while the cheek of Hamsdorff grew pale as his sword belt.

That low, moaning sound swelled to a shriek—a wild, terrible, piercing shriek. It came from the bosom of the burning haystack—it swelled louder and more terrible—it whistled along the breeze like the yell of an unseen spirit! Another shriek, and another! Three shrieks, more dread, more terrible, never broke on mortal ear. And in a moment all was still as death, and something moved and struggled amid the last remains of the burning hay.

And higher and higher rose the flame.

"Be gaw!—I—I wished to catch the rebel, and if he was a spy, to hang him; but as for burning him alive! Be gaw—no!"

"D——!" muttered the leader of the white belt, "here's a pretty night's work spoiled! However, he was but a rebel after all! Away, boys, the valley people are rising!"

"Ha, ha, ha!" chuckled Gilbert Gates. "He died alone in the woods—and I, his son, am his AVENGER!"

And with these words he passed behind the barn, and was lost to sight.

And from the accursed pile of death fled the soldiers, spurring their horses to their utmost speed—with the fear and horror of coward guilt they fled—while round, far over the plain, far over the valley, came the men of Brandywine, roused from their sleep by the burning haystack—from the valley and the hill top they came, as the last embers of the fire were yet glowing upon the green sward.

And two figures emerged from the door of the school-master's house, the form of a stout muscular man, and the trembling form of a slender maiden.

"Gotlieb, it seems like a dream!" said the maiden. "The flight of my father, the chase in the cellar, the swoon! Thank God my father has escaped! But what means this sudden stillness around the house? What means yon flickering fire? They have burned my father's haystack!"

"Mein Gott! how prave dat was! By St. Christuffel!" returned Gotlieb, moving towards the embers of the haystack, "Polly, it's very likely your fader's took to te woods—p'raps dey are after him, I must go rouse te valley people, and start chase after te taint scoundrels!''

They reached the burning embers on the hill side, and stood for a moment gazing around the scene. A mass of burned hay, and a pile of ashes, mingled with the wrecks of some splintered boards, was all that remained to tell of the location of the haystack.

"What is that dark thing in the fire?" said Polly Mayland. "See, Gotlieb—draw the light nearer—it moves, it stirs! Quick, Gotleib, with the light!''

They drew nearer to the fire—Gotlieb flung the torchlight over the scene —and they both gazed downward among the embers for an instant.

One wild and piercing shriek burst from the lips of Mary Mayland—one look of horror—and she fell senseless at the feet of Gotlieb Hoff, while her extended hand rested among the embers of the flame.

" Mein gott!—mein gott!'' cried Gotlieb Hoff, gazing upon the glowing embers with the blackened mass in their midst.

The torchlight flashed upon a blackened mass of flesh and bones, scarred and burned to ashes, with cinders of clothing fluttering over the heap, while a whitened skull, with the face half turned to the earth, and the skin peeled from the brow—a whitened skull, soddened with blood, gleamed in the light, and grizzly arm bones, with long fingers, ragged with dangling flesh, were thrown out on either side, and the legs were drawn up under the blackened body, as it lay, a ghastly wreck of humanity, rendered yet more ghastly by the glow of the torchlight.

And while Gotlieb stood beside the shapeless carcass, dumb and motionless with horror, the inhabitants of the valley came gathering around, man after man looking with the curse and the imprecation upon the ruin of the spoiler, and silently taking his stand among the crowd who circled around the scene.

Where but a moment ago but one torch had gleamed, a dozen torches now shone on an hundred faces, on an hundred stout and manly forms, all gazing with the whispered word and the muttered speech upon the blackened mass, while above, the heavens grew darker, and around all earth seemed to grow more sad, and silent, and still.

" Make way for me, dar!'' cried a voice, and a muscular negro, with his arms all cut and gashed, and with blood upon his face and breast, strode through the crowd. " De debble himself, be 'shamed to do such a ting as dis! He kind to Sampson—he feed his old moder when she dyin'! And dey burned him alive!'' A low muttered word, and a wild howl burst from his lips, and he stooped down and kissed the blackened corse.

" It is a sight too terrible for a man to see!'' said a stout and muscular man, advancing. " He was my wife's cousin. Polly, the innocent girl, is his daughter! I tell ye, friends, this night's work has to be paid for in good red blood!''

9

A murmur, long and deep, arose from the multitude.

"Iron Tom, of Dilworth Corner, goes not to work again, makes no fire in his forge, or lays a hand to his anvil, until the last Britisher is driven from the soil!"

"Does the shoe pinch you now?" cried the sharp quick voice of Hirpley Hawson, advancing. "Will you look to the flint of your rifle now—hey hey? here's a sight to make a man sit down and weep like a suckin child!"

"And tell me, one of you, tell me," cried the commanding voice of Colonel Frazier, as he moved forward, and gazed at the corse, "Where did ever Britisher hesitate to slay the innocent or murder the weak? * * *" he muttered the oath between his teeth, "By the sword of Lovat, but the blood of this murdered man cries out for vengeance!"

"And the call shall be answered!" said a strange voice, and a tall and commanding figure advanced to the light, which shone upon an aged face, seamed with wrinkles, while the gazers noted that the stranger was clad from head to foot in a robe of skins, "and the call shall be answered! Look ye men of Brandywine—look upon this shapeless corse! Behold the justice of the Briton—behold the mercy of King George!"

"It is the mysterious stranger of the valley!" was whispered from one voice to another—"He who has been seen along the Brandywine, for a week or more—no one knows whither he goes or whence he comes!"

And tall and spiritlike, with his arm outstreched, his head erect, and his form of strength and dignity shown out in the full glow of the torch beams, the stranger stood, wnile around him clustered the multitude, at his feet lay the blackened corse, and the fainting maiden, and in the distance, unenlivened by starbeam or moonlight, lay the hills of Brandywine, wrapt in gloom and shadow.

"Men of Bradywine!" cried the stranger, "to-morrow night, as the sun sinks in the west, every freeman, whose true hand does not belie his stout heart, every man who looks upon this galling outrage, this grinding wrong of the ruthless invader, will meet the friends of freedom in a dense woods, some three miles north of Rock Farm, some four miles from Chadd's Ford! You have all heard of a curious rock which gives a name to this woods—a rock of massive granite, stamped with the impress of a human foot, side by side with a cloven hoof—"

"The Rock of the Devil's Footprint it is called!" cried the manly voice of the blacksmith.

"The same!" returned the stranger. "Here the friends of freedom gather from the north, from the south—from the east from, the west they gather! Do I look upon a man in this throng who will fail to be there!"

One answer ran around the crowd—a loud vell of vengeance, mingled with a hurrah.

The stranger flung a cloak of the wild deer's hide from his shoulders, he flung it along the grass, and then stooping slowly down, gathered the blackened carcass with its confines.

"I bear this terrible witness to the place of rendezvous!" he exclaimed, gazing round the crowd. "There shall the freemen of this fair land behold the justice of the Briton, the mercy of King George!" He raised his arm as he glided away from the crowd. "Remember! to-morrow night at sun down, at the Rock of the Devil's Footprint—there will the men of Brandywine gather—for Washington and Right!"

"To-morrow night, at sundown!" echoed the crowd. "At the Rock of the Devil's Footprint!" The echoes swelled in a loud hurrah. "For Washington and the Right!" shouted the freemen of the crowd—"For Washington and the Right!" The hills above, the hills of Brandywine returned the shout, and again and yet again, hill and wood, and stream, gave back the yell of vengeance and the wild hurrah. "At hour of sundown, at the Rock of the Devil's Footprint, will we gather! We will gather armed to the teeth —FOR VENGEANCE, FOR WASHINGTON AND THE RIGHT!"

END OF BOOK FIRST.

BOOK THE SECOND.

THE ROSE OF BRANDYWINE.

CHAPTER THE FIRST.

THE TWIN-BROTHERS OF ROCK FARM.

"Brother o' mine—look ye here! The blow has passed between us brother!" As he spoke, tne dark haired boy, leaned from his prancing steed, and while his slender form trembled with agitation, he shook his clenched hand in the swarthy face of his brother, who likewise reined his steed, in front of the porch of the old brick mansion—"The blow has passed between us brother! Aye, tne blow,—stout handed and strong armed, coward that ye are, you have stricken—and stricken me! And now while the mark of your blow, yet freshens over my cheek, do I pronounce a—curse upon you! A curse upon your life—a curse upon your hopes—a blight upon your death—"

"Walter—Walter—" cried the maiden advancing to the edge of the porch —"Walter oh, speak not these words!" she exclaimed while her hands were upraised, and her dark eyes blazed with feeling—"Oh, for the sake of heaven part not thus in anger—you are brothers—" her voice was choked by sobs, and with her full and maidenly form trembling with agitation, the girl covered her face with the fair and delicate hands, while the tears fell down the velvet cheeks, over the throbbing bosom, like drops of sunlit rain.

"Yes—yes—my boys—take the girl's advice—" said the old man as his gaunt and sinewy form, moved toward the edge of the rustic porch, while his nawklike eye, glanced at the figures of his sons, each mounted on a black steed, prancing and rearing along the green sod—"Do not part in anger my children. Consider your father, Walter—consider your father David. Rose do beg them not to part in anger—What will the neighbours say—"

"Oh, let the game-chicken crow, till the blood chokes his pipe!" exclaimed the stout, broad shouldered brother, as a grim smile passed over his swarthy face, with the low broad forehead, topped by stiff bristled hair, the prominent nose with wide nostrils, the large, heavy eyes, the wide mouth and the full square chin, dark with ragged whiskers sweeping behind each ear and along the throat—"Oh, let the game-chicken crow, till the blood chokes his pipe! Ha—ha—ha! Am I a dunghill fowl? Dave Walford fear him—does he? Maybe he does. Perhaps the blow pains ye brother—"

" *A curse*—" hissed Walter Walford between his teeth, while his small delicate features quivered, and his dark eyes flashed with passion—" A curse upon your life—a blight upon your hopes—a doom upon your death! Nay —smile, not so sweetly my brother—your horse is ready for the march and so is mine! The rifle hangs at your saddle-bow—the knife hangs at your side! Here is my rifle and here my knife! Brother we shall meet again —we shall meet in the hour of battle—we shall meet in the hour of death! A curse upon that hour, happen when it will! The curse of rifle and the curse of knife, and the curse of the hate I bear you! Brother—smile—oh! smile—Do you mark that hand so small and delicate—quite a woman's hand my brother!" he shook his clenched hand in the air, while the blue veins, writhed and struggled under the delicate skin—" But strike me again brother, and the delicate hand, and this small knife, shall work out for ye, the sudden reward of a brother's hate—"

" Walter—oh, Walter—you know not what you say—" exclaimed the fair girl standing on the porch, as her dark eyes, were fixed in a mild beseeching expression, upon the face of the young man—" For the sake of Heaven Walter, do not—oh, do not provoke this quarrel further—"

" What will the neighbors say?" cried the old man, raising his long talon-like fingers in a hurried gesture—" What will every body say of me, when my sons part thus in quarrel and in anger. Oh, David, oh, Walter is this the reward of your father's care, is this—"

" A father's care! Ha—ha—ha!" laughed Walter Walford, while a bitter sneer played over his thin lip—" A father's care? Who taught us to cheat, to lie, to scheme, to rob—aye to sell one's very soul, for gold? Who taught us the pleasant old story, of brother and brother, fighting each with his fellow, for the old brick mansion, and for these five hundred broad acres of Rock-Farm? Ha—ha—ha—a father's care! who drove to her grave, the mother that gave us birth—good, my father, was there not a storm abroad in that accursed hour?—Who? Ask yourself old man, whom I am bound to call —father! Ask your own heart—who was it that—"

" Walter, my son—" said the old man, while his sharp, irregular features, lit up with a sudden smile—" Have a care, my son. Your father pardons **words** of passion—but—but—my son—there is an old story of the Walfords,

—it has been said that the child who spit in his father's face, ever met a sudden death. Has it not David?"

"Dont ask me, old man—" replied the ruffian with a brutal sneer, as his stout black steed gave a bound, backward from the porch—"I've 'nough quar'ls of my own to take care of—I have by——. But d——n my —— if the boy dont speak true for once in his life! Ha—ha—ha! Father ye sow'd your field with spikes—ye must not complain if ye reap a good harvest o' crowbars—"

"And you—my pretty Rose—" cried Walter with a look that mingled love and hate—"You with your dark eyes—your pouting lips—your fair round neck and your maidenly bosom? Why stand you sobbing there? Your soft glance fanned the embers of this quarrel into a flame. Why weep and whimper at your own work? Look at me Rose—" he continued with that sneer which so strangely mingled feeling, warm and intense, with the bitterness which springs from that same feeling, when crushed and blighted —"Look at me Rosy—my pretty Rosy—I am your cousin Walter! I have looked upon you—I have loved you! Come death or come devil, come battle or come cloud, Rose Frazier you must be mine—"

"Yours? must be yours?" exclaimed the maiden with a proud elevation of her form of maidenly beauty—"Walter Walford, neither to you, nor to your brother, have I ever given, word, token or sign, to intimate, that the child of Norman Frazier, would in any case be the bride of a man, so doomed and cursed, by the doom and the curse of his own evil passions, as are ye both—brother and brother—both alike! Must indeed!"

"Look ye my boy—" shouted the ruffian David—"There's two words to that bargain, Rose Frazier must be yours? Ha—ha—ha! must she? Why boy do ye know that Dave Walford's ahead of you? The g-al is a fine g-al—Wild-wood Grange is a fine farm, and Dave Walford loves both —the g-al and the farm! These are times of battle Walter—the strongest hand bears the purse away! Ha—ha—Walter—will you discuss the p'int with a good rifle and knife?"

"To the death," shouted Walter Walford, while his face gleamed with passion—"Hark-ye, brother! I spoke of a battle-field for the settlement of this quarrel! By the * * * that made me, this field will do as well! Look ye, brother o' mine—the sun is setting in the west—over the wood-lands around us—over the level plain encircling this mansion—over the old brick mansion, streams the gaudy light of the dying day! Let it be the last day for one, or both of us, my brother! The sky is clear above us, brother—the woods are green and silent around us! The neighbors and farmer's-men, are away from the mansion—all is silent and still! Now, my brother, in the sight of our father, and this pretty maiden, let the quarrel be ended!"

"Oh, God, preserve me from these madmen!" shrieked Rose Frazier, raising her hands, while her cheek grew pale, and her form trembled from

nead to foot with affright—" Uncle Walford, for the sake of your own soul
do not see this murder done, in your very sight!"

The old man muttered something to himself in a low tone of voice, and
his cheek grew white as death, and his thin lips trembled with a short,
quick nervous movement. " When I gave *him* the bitter cup"—he mur
mured with the tone of one who speaks by an irresistible impulse—" I never
thought it would be given back to me again!" His voice grew wild with
sudden fear, and he shrieked—"My sons, for the sake of—of—" the words
trembled on his lips—" for the sake of God, do not drive this foolish quarrel further!"

" Walter my boy"—cried David with a sneer—" Your rifle is unloaded—
so is mine! The first man that loads his rifle, fires! Hey—brother ?"

" Be it so!" shouted Walter, as his dark eyes gathered a wild light—
" The man that first loads his rifle, first fires!"

And each man, leaning from his steed, proceeded to load his rifle.

The scene, was one of the many, dark and terrible pictures, which marked
the era of revolutionary terror, and the bloodshed-time of civil war.

Their stout black steeds, were placed haunch to haunch, along the green
sward in front of the porch, with the distance of a few yards intervening
between each horse. The broad-shouldered form of David, clad in a hunter's
frock, with breeches of buckskin, and boots of dark leather, with a skull-
fitting hat, marked by a wide rim, drooping over his sunburnt brow, was
slightly inclined to one side of his steed, while the ram-rod rose and fell in
his right hand. The slender-shaped youth opposite, was attired in a worn-coat
of course dark cloth, with breeches and boots of the same hue, a hat of felt
upon his head, with the rim drawn up from his forehead, and falling back
over his dark locks down to his neck. An expression of passion, mingled
with contending feelings flashed over his features, while, similar in action
to his brother, the fingers of his right hand, grasped the ram-rod, and forced
it ringing into the tube of the rifle. The porch of the mansion, with its shelv-
ing roof, and rough-oaken pillars—the trembling figure of the gaunt old
man, in his farmer's dress, with his hawk-eye and eagle-nose—the shrink
ing form of Rose Frazier, her hands half upraised, her lips parted with
terror, and her full dark eye flashing from beneath the fringe of the long
dark lasnes, while her look was eloquent of woman's fear and woman's
feeling :

This formed the foreground of the picture ; and above arose the dark
red walls of the mansion of Rock-Farm, the shutters and doors all closed
and fastened, the roof dark, moss grown and gabled, with the western sky
glowing with the light of the setting sun, revealing the heavy outlines of
roof-peak and chimney, while on either side of the edifice spread cultivated
fields, now shooting away as far as the eye could reach, level and flat as
meadow land, and now broken by spurs of the forest wild, thrown boldly
forth, until they reached within an hundred yards of the brick farm house,

casting their long shadows over field and plain, with an image of grandeur and of gloom.

"Uncle Walford, their rifles are loaded!" shrieked Rose—"oh, for the sake of Heaven, stay their hands, a terrible murder will be done, and every man in the land, will point to you, uncle, as the instigator of the deed!"

"What the girl says is true"—cried Philip Walford, as he trembled from head to foot. "David"—he shrieked—"I implore ye, I beg ye, do not fire! Walter Walford, a word with *you! Fire,* and so sure as the devil has now possession of you, so sure, will I, your father, shoot the brother-murderer down, as I would shoot a mad-dog!"

"Walter Walford"—cried David, as a ruffianly smile shot over his features—"my piece is loaded—a moment—"

"So is mine!" exclaimed Walter, wheeling his black steed around, with his face to his foe. "*Now,* strike me, coward! Fire!"

Their steeds face to face, their rifles poised in the air, each pointed at a brother's heart, in a single instant the sod would be stained with their blood, in a single instant, would old Philip Walford behold the forms of his dying sons, weltering in their gore, in front of the very porch on which he stood. It was a moment of intense horror.

"Fire!" arose the word from each lip, and each rifle was cocked and raised, and each brother took the certain and secure aim at a brother's heart.

"Hold!" shrieked a female voice, and then there was a hurried spring from the porch on to the sod, and a wild shriek rang upon the air. "Hold murderers, hold!"

She sprang along the sod, in an instant, one fair foot, small and delicate, rested on the left stirrup of Walter Walford, in another instant, she had thrown her lovely form along the neck of his steed, she had beaten the rifle aside from its aim, and with a throbbing bosom, and an eye all blazing with feeling, with parted lips and an extended arm, she turned her face toward the other brother, his piece still raised, his aim still taken.

"Fire—coward that ye are—fire if ye dare!" she shouted in a voice altogether changed from her soft and maidenly tones—"You may murder your brother—you may lay his lifeless corse along the sod—but you must reach his body thro' mine! Fire—coward! Man—I love you not, nor can I love you ever! I love not your brother—I can never be his bride! But I will not see ye slaughter each other, before my eyes, while my name is Frazier, while the heart of a true maiden beats within this bosom!"

"That's very purty, g-al, by —— !" laughed David Walford--"But just turn your head aside the least bit—yo're in the way. There now— I just want a glimpse of his top-knot! Its a pity for him—but he provoked this quarrel! Walter Walford I give you warning—"

The rifle was raised, the aim certain, Walter Walford endeavored to tear the hand of the maiden from the tube of his piece, the old man stood upon the porch trembling with an excitement, that might well be called madness, when the rushing sound of horses' hoofs was heard, bursting from the woods on the north, and in a single instant, a stout stranger, mounted on a sleek brown steed, rode up between the brothers, holding the bridle-rein of a small, black poney, prancing by his horse's side, with sweeping tail and mane, in one hand; while the other grasped a glittering rifle slung over his right shoulder.

"By St. Christuffel! Napor Walfordt, but tis is a purty bissness!' cried he stranger, turning his face from one to the other with an expression of ludicrous surprise. "Mein Gott! Rifles loaded and pinted at each other's prests? Y-a-h! By St. Christuffel! Miss Frazier in the scrape too—what would the Curnel say? You'd like to ask me, where I came from, Miss Frazier? You see your fader sent me, arter you tis mornin'—but te tamdt Pritishers chased me about te woods all day—they wanted to catch your poney, little Peter here! And here I am, Miss Frazier, and it's sundown! We must pe at home, seven long miles, before an hour! Yah by St. Christuffel! And dese goot gentlemen can den murter one another, as much as they likes—"

"Thank God, Gotlieb, you are come at last!" cried Rose, bounding from the neck of Walter's steed, along the sod—"Let us away from this fated house ere another moment!" she cried, springing into the saddle of the graceful poney, as he stood pawing the earth, and flinging his long dark mane to the breeze—"Never stay, Gotlieb, for my riding dress or my riding hat, but for home, for home! In this trim, with a mere kerchief thrown around my head, will I ride!"

"Yes, but tere's your colored maidt, Phillis, to be keered for too"—cried Gotlieb—"By St. Christuffel, but she'll have to wait till morning! And Miss Frazier—d'ye see, we can't ride home by te Philadelphy and Wilmington road, but we must take te pye-road, for it, right thro' the woods—te highway is scoured by parties of soldiers of both sides, and de biggest tevil is up in the country—"

"As you wish—as you wish!" cried Rose, arranging herself in the saddle—"any road at all, but let us away from this accursed spot!"

"Out of the way, Sour-Crout!" shouted David Walford, who had looked upon this sudden apparition with unfeigned astonishment—"Out of the way—We've a little business to settle here, in which you've no consarn—"

"Now my arm is free!" exclaimed Walter—"Fire, brother o' mine—fire!"

The old man, recovered from the first terrors of the scene, and springing from the porch, he hurried along the sod, and whispered a word in the ear of the stouter son.

"Fool that you are!" he murmered—"Why fight any longer with the hare-brained cub? Do you not see that she goes home, by the wood-road leading past the Rock of the Devil's-foot-Print? D'ye want the maiden? What so easy as to await her coming a this rock? You understand?

Away there, and gain this Rock by another road—a blackened face, and a dozen good fellows will accomplish all!"

"Gad, father, but you've hit it!" cried the ruffian—"then here goes for Marcus Hook!" he shouted aloud, suddenly turning his horse's head to the eastward—"Good even to you, brother, say I!" And the sound of his horse's hoofs, beating along the eastern road in full gallop, broke upon the evening air.

"Rose, tarry but a moment—" said Philip Walford, approaching the maiden, "You know when the unfortunate quarrel first broke out, I was about starting for your neighborhood. I've engaged to supply a friend up your way with provisions, and my team stands ready to start in yonder barn-yard! A single moment, and I will accompany you on your journey. But why are you so carefully armed, friend Gotlieb?"

"'Tis rifle is for te enemies of Shortz Washington!" returned the brave Pennsylvanian—"Last night de schoolmaster at Chadd's Ford was purnt alive, by te red coats—tis rifle is for de first damdt ropper dat comes mitin its aim! Y-a-h by St Christuffel!"

"You're a brave man Gotlieb—" said the old man, with a peculiar smile as he turned away towards the barn-yard—"a very brave man—" he shouted smilingly over his shoulder as he looked back—"but brave men are apt to meet sudden deaths—hot-bloods never die in their beds!"

"By St Christuffel!" muttered Gotlieb Hoff—"If cold bloods die in their beds, den you'll have a purty big chance, to die in a tozen feather peds piled on top o' one another!"

"To Marcus Hook!" murmured Walter Walford eyeing the retreating form of his brother—"That lie does not deceive me! He shall not escape me thus! Rose—Rose—" he cried flinging himself from his steed and approaching the side of the maiden, with a trembling gait and a faltering voice—"I blame ye not—" he continued, with all a brother's kindness, as he placed her delicate foot in the stirrup—"I blame ye not! Ye cannot love me—why should ye love one doomed and fated as I am? But oh, Rose—" and his voice trembled with emotion, and the tears stood in his manly eyes—"Could ye love me, there is not a fate, that I would pause to defy for your sake, not a deed but I would dare to do, for the sake of your fair face, and your bright eyes! Rose your love to me—is Heaven—your indifference is—hell!" And as he spoke his eyes were all passion, his voice all feeling—"But ye cannot love me!"

"I cannot—cannot help it Walter—" replied the maiden with a look of anguish, "God knows I cannot!"

"Fare thee well Rose—" cried Walter springing upon his steed—"Fare thee well Rose, and when you hear of Walter Walford, dying the unwept death in the ranks of battle, then believe, that his last thought was of—thee—that your name trembled on his whitening lips, and your form hovered over his eyes glazing in death! Fare the well Rose!"

With a bound and a spring his horse darted forward, along the farm-road leading eastward, and Rose beheld the form of Walter Walford, speeding away with the swiftness of an arrow, in the very path traversed by his brother.

As tho' the same spirit, the spirit of a demon, agitated the form of the noble steed, he swept onward, and in a moment Walter beheld the muscular figure of his brother, turning a bend of the farm-road, overshadowed by an ancient oak, with enormous trunk and wide leafy branches casting their darkness and gloom over the road side.

Onward, and onward he swept, and in a moment gained that brother's side.

" Whither go you my brother?" shouted David with a reckless sneer as he looked over his shoulder—" To the British or to the rebel army? The old man fights for the side that pays best—so do I !"

" We shall meet in the hour of battle—we shall meet in the hour of death !" cried Walter Walford raising his hand on high while the head of his steed was turned towards the gloom of the wood—" With knife and rifle shall we meet—" he shouted as his horse sped beneath the shadow of the trees—" The curse of our race, be upon that hour, chance it, when it will !"

CHAPTER SECOND.

THE GREEN GLADE IN THE FOREST.

The beams of the setting sun, fell warmly and with a golden light over the short wild grass, of a solitary forest glade, which crowned the brow of a wood-hidden hill, with dense masses of forest trees, encircling its verdure to the north, to the east and to the south, while far away to the west, the retreating branches, opened a pleasant view of a landscape, gorgeous with pastoral beauty, and the evening sky, with its clear azure, varied by massive clouds, piled in rugged grandeur over the dim woods of the distant horizon.

The glade was silent and still, and the woods around, glowing in the light of the dying day, were turned, each trunk, each branch and every leaf to living gold, while over the green sward streamed and floated the soft voluptuous light, giving the spot a strange dreamy appearance, which made it seem like the wild haunt of wood spirits, or the pleasant home of fairy beings, who danced in the sunlight, or trembled with each rustling of the deep green leaves, scarce changed by the breath of autumn.

It was sundown, and the disc of the broad and beautiful sun, had scarce touched the horizon of gathering clouds, when the sound of galloping hoofs broke upon the air, and presently the branches of the forest trees, to the south, were hurriedly thrust aside, and two horsemen, young, gallant and bold, came riding over the turf while the sunbeams flaunted over the trappings of their cavalier attire, and the swords of the riders clanked against each booted leg.

As they came pacing onward toward the full glow of the sunbeams, it might be seen that the first of the cavaliers, who rode the steed of dappled grey, and a noble steed it was, with its arching neck, the broad chest and the sweeping mane, was tall and slender in figure, with a youthful countenance, marked by a nose bold and prominent, and slightly aquiline, a determined mouth, a deep blue eye, and a clear open forehead, undimmed by a wrinkle, and strangly relieved by tangled masses of sand-colored hair, swept aside from the forehead, and carelessly disposed beneath the confines of the half-military chapeau, which the traveller wore, topped by a solitary plume, of snow-white brilliancy.

Attired in a military body-coat of fine blue cloth, faced with buff and thrown open over the chest, disclosing the silver-laced vest, the delicate white cravat and ruffle beneath, the traveller wore the gaudy epaulette of a general officer on his right shoulder, a star of gorgeous lustre on the left breast, while a belt of snow-white buckskin encircling his waist, supported the long straight sword depending from his side with scabbard of gold, hilt of steel, and an eagle-beak curiously fashioned out of the top of the handle of richly wrought ivory.

The cheek of the stranger was ruddy with the warm glow of nineteen summers, yet there was an air of thought shadowing his bold features, and it would have made the eye of an old warrior glisten to note his manly port, the ease and gracefulness with which he sate his steed, pacing along with the grace and majesty of a king.

The cavalier by his side, riding the steed, with the long sweeping mane and tail, white as the unsunned snow, with that singular mingling of white of yellow, and of deep rich brown in the hue of his glossy skin, best designated by the common term—cream-colored—was tall, straight and slender in form, with a prominent chest, shoulders of manly breadth, a sloping waist, mingling gracefulness and strength in its outline, while his marked countenance, in hue a rich olive, with the clear brilliant hazel eye, the slight aquiline nose, and the small determined mouth, wore an expression of wild dreamy thought, and unutterable resolve, which the beholder, might never forget. The open forehead, broad and massive, shaded by sweeping locks of dark chesnut hair, was indented by a single wrinkle, that compressed the dark eyebrows in a settled expression, which spoke volumes of the one idea, ever haunting the traveller's mind, and never absent from his thought or dream.

The sungleams fell warmly over his tight body coat of rich green velvet, fastened to the very throat with a single row of small gold buttons, and gathered around the waist by a belt of dark leather, supporting the long straight sword, while a surcoat of light blue cloth, faced with buff, thrown back from the shoulders, disclosed to every advantage the manly proportion of the stranger's form, and gave a pleasant relief to the breeches of light buckskin, terminating in short slouching boots of dark leather, bright with the knightly spur of gold.

On his head, he wore a slouching hat of dark felt, looped upward over the forehead, with a tall black plume, entwined with an oaken sprig sweeping to one side. The wide rim fell drooping over the neck and shoulders of the cavalier.

Pacing slowly onward, in a moment, the wayfarers, reined in their steeds, on the very brow of the hill, where the glade sunk suddenly down amid the rising tops of the forest trees, clothing the hill-side beneath.

" *Mon dieu!* The land is magnificent!" cried the cavalier riding the dappled grey steed—" Magnificent—magnificent!" he cried with a marked Frenchaccent, as drawing his sword from the sheath, with all the enthusiasm of his character he waved it in the air—" A land for freemen—a home for the gallant and daring of every clime! Massive forests, cultivated fields, cottages peeping out from luxuriant orchards, a stream of silver winding far in the distance, and the soft, autumnal sky over all! Magnificent— magnificent!"

" The home of the gallant and daring!" cried the dark-hued cavalier exultingly—" The land for freemen!" He flung his unsheathed sword in the air—" And here, my Lord Marquis, in the far ancient time, did the wild Indian wander, here did he hold undisputed dominion over forest and plain aye, here, did my father fight their foes, here they battled, and braved the pains of fire, and the doom of death—lords of the land, and kings among their tribes! Where are they *now?*"

"Driven to mountain fortress, and far away wilderness!" cried the Frenchman participating in the wild enthusiasm that blazed over the face of his companion—" Mon Dieu! Where I the child of such an ancestry, the sight of this lovely land, and yon fair plain, would fire my blood and nerve my arm! Ha—ha! 'Tis a land to fight for—by the best blood of *La Belle France*, a land to die for!"

" And here in the dim future time, the fight for freedom won, the invader driven back, shall dwell a free and happy people! And over yonder plain shall arise the sound of festival jubilee, and mingling with the chaunt of choral hymn and shouted with the name of Washington, shall swell your name—gallant stranger—the name of *La Fayette!*"

The Frenchman replied not, but his sword waved proudly in the air, and his deep blue eyes, glanced upon the far distance, as tho' he pictured magnificent phantoms of ambition, shaping their glories out cf the thin air and sweeping in grandeur along the azure sky.

"My gallant Randulph," he exclaimed, turning to his companion, "Often have you promised to tell to me, the strange story of your life ; we have now an half-an-hour at our command. Here on the brow of this hill, while the sun sinks in the distance, let the story be told. You claim descent from a line of the aboriginal chiefs—from a line of wild-wood kings ?"

"You shall hear the story of my life, my Lord Marquis"—replied the dark-hued cavalier—"In the fastnesses of Carolina, far away among the hills of the wild Santee, the sun looks down, upon a magnificent plantation, a garden in the wilderness, rich with cultivated farms, grassy hillsides, and verdant pasturages, while over all from the summt of a high hill, the mansion of Wyamoke, built of dark grey stone, towers grand and lofty, tho fitting home for the proud owner of the broad lands, and massive woods of this fair domain. Tradition states, that long, long years ago, an emigrant from a foreign clime, a banned and outlawed man, fled to the wilderness with the remains of his lordly wealth, and there conciliating the wild children of the forest, bought himself fair lands, and reared a princely home, amid the solitude of the forest——"

"His name"—asked the Marquis—"His name was ——"

"Randulph. No one knew from whence he came, no one knew aught of his origin. He gained the good will and fealty of the Indians, who haunted the woods of Wyamoke. The last of a magnificent tribe, the relics of a mighty clan, they owned the rule of an aged chief, and would have fought, to the death, for the weal of his only child—a daughter, who like others of her tribe, was marked by a brilliant clearness of complexion, and a beautiful regularity of feature, which attested the far-off oriental origin of the lonely clan of Wyamoke ——"

"Methinks I see your story now—" cried the Frenchman—"The unknown emigrant wedded the Indian maiden ?"

"It is a long story Marquis—" continued the cavalier—"But let me comprise the memories and histories of long years in a few brief words. Randulph, the German emigrant, married the Indian maiden ; their union was blessed by a daughter, fairer and lovelier than her own lovely mother. This daughter grew up to womanhood—the mother died—and the last relics of the tribe of Wyamoke, departed for the distant wilds of the land beyond the Alleghanies, never emerging from the solitude of the unknown wilderness save to pay a visit of friendship, to the fair child of their beautiful queen. Adele Randulph grew toward womanhood, lovely and beautiful as a dream, under the sensitive care of her exiled parent, who, buried from the world, yet surrounded by all the luxuries of European civilization, delighted to realize all the dreams of romance, in the nurture and education of his child. One autumn night, the father and daughter sat beside the hearth of their nome—a rifle-shot broke upon the quiet air—the father fell dead at the feet of the daughter—the house was filled by a band of hostile Indians combined with outlawed hunters and backwoodsmen——Adele Randulph beheld the tomahawk gleaming above her head—she heard the yells and shouts of the ruffians—when, sudden as a lightning flash, a stranger sprang through the window—a stranger clad in the undress uniform of a general officer in the British army. He beat the savages back—with his own unaided arm, he beat them back, and that very night, while the silence of her desolate home gathered around her, Adele Randulph, over the lifeless corse of her father, plighted the troth of a woman's love, to the gallant stranger. In one short month, they were married by the rites of the Catholic faith——

"And this stranger—who and what was he?" asked the marquis.

"His life is enwrapt in mystery. That he was young, gallant and bold, Adele Randulph well knew, but whence he came, or whither he went, his rank in his native country, or his object in journeying thro' the wilderness beyond a wild spirit of youthful adventure—all, all, is mystery and shadow."

"Gave he no history of himself? How ran his story?"

"He was named Captain Waldemar, and he held office under the Royal Government of the Carolinas. More than this, Adele Randulph never knew. Thus ran his story. He was attended by a single companion—a sort of a half-friend and half-servant—one Anthony Denys. Scarce had six months passsed over the union of the stranger and the descendant of a long line of native kings, when Captain Waldemar suddenly disappeared— no one knew whither. His wife never looked upon his face again—his child never once beheld the countenance of his—father ——"

"Randulph, your story is one of mystery. It interests—it enchains my attention. Your manner warms, my friend—your voice trembles. This child—this child ——"

"Grew up to youth on the domains of Wyamoke. He grew up with the pale wan face of a broken-hearted woman, ever gazing fondly and tearfully upon his boyish countenance—he grew toward youth, ignorant of the existence, or of the death, or the absence of his father. From his earliest years, the child remembered the sharp thin visage of Anthony Denys, who was prematurely old with care and scheming. This Anthony Denys seemed to hold a terrible and a mysterious power over the mind of the mother—he visited the estate once, twice and sometimes thrice a year. He claimed the respect due to a master from the tenantry, and with a sneer at his lean figure, and trickster-look, they were forced to grant him what he asked. The boy was now fifteen years of age ——"

"Mon Dieu!" cried the Marquis. "This Anthony Denys—what meant his mysterious power over the child of the Indian Queen? Heard the boy never a word of his father? What said the peasantry of Wyamoke?"

"The boy was now fifteen years of age"—cried Randulph, as his lip trembled, while his dark hazel-eye blazed with sudden feeling—"and the woodsmen and farmers of Wyamoke, gathered around him, with warm

courtesy and heartfelt respect.   Mysterious insinuations of the treachery of
a British Captain—of a wronged woman, tricked by a sham marriage—
coupled with vows of revenge against the traitor, reached the ears of the
boy.   His life became possessed of one thought—the thought of his father.
He grew old before his time.   His life became a doom—his existence a
curse!   And before him ever was the pale wan face of his mother, speaking volumes with that broken-hearted look—that uncomplaining and proud
expression, of a noble-minded woman, taming the soul with all its terrors
and its sorrows, down to the stern rule of secrecy and silence.

   " And now for the last scene of my story.   It was a night of storm and
terror—the boy was called to the bedside of his dying mother.   With an eye
glazing with coming death, yet flashing ever and anon, with supernatural
light she whispered the words, that sunk in my heart, never to be erased,
never to be forgotten.   She said, that soon after the disappearance of my
father, Anthony Denys, again appeared at the mansion of Wyamoke—he
whispered in the ear of the mother a dark tale of a father whose life was
endangered by crime—Anthony Denys had the proofs of that crime in his
possession.   The father had been forced to fly—Denys said not whither.
He had nominated this man guardian of his child—protector of his wife, and
this same Anthony Denys, produced a legal paper, signed by Captain Waldemar, which conveyed the estate of Wyamoke, the mansion and the woodlands into the possession of the stranger, ' for the sole use and benefit' so
ran the formal phrase of legal trickery—' of my wife Adele Randulph Wal-
degrave, and my child, in case a child is born.' "

   " Methinks I spy a villain in the same Denys!" murmured the Marquis
—" Your story is indeed a strange one, Randulph!"

   " And there, in that lonely room, while the storm was abroad without,
and the lightning flashed through the windows in the face of the dying, there,
in a voice broken with the death-rattle, and rent by the death-groan, and the
sob of the breaking heart, did this doomed woman—my mother, whisper to
my ears, the words of an oath, dark—wild and terrible!   I clasped the at-
tenuated hands of the dying—I drank the light of her lips blazing with coming death—I raised my hands to heaven, clasping the long thin fingers of
her trembling hands—I took the OATH—the last word lingered on my lips
—the thunder peal broke over my very head—and my hands clasped the
cold hands of a broken-hearted and betrayed mother."

   " The oath—how have you fulfilled it?" cried the Marquis leaning from
his steed, with intense interest.

   " Ask me not—ask me not!" cried Randulph—" I have sought him in
foreign lands—I have traversed England—I have journeyed from town to
town—my mission—*the sanctity of a mother's name.*   I have resigned the
estate of Wyamoke to the care of the minions of this Denys—I have measured
this wide continent in my search—and still my object is unaccomplished
Never have I found a clue to the existence of my father—never have I heard

a syllable, which might illumine the mystery that encircles his fate. And
as for the rest of my story Marquis—how I met you in London—how we
journeyed to this fair land together—how I again appeared at Wyamoke—how the hunters and woodsmen of Santee, arose around their favorite,
whom they familiarly name Randulph the Prince of Wyamoke—how we
hurried northward to join the army of Washington—all this is known to
you, General, and my story is done."

"Randulph—" cried La Fayette, leaning from his steed—"Has your
journey to this valley of the Brandywine, naught to do, with the fulfilment
of your oath?"

A shade of gloom came over the bronzed countenance of the young soldier,
and he flung his arm high in the air, while his flashing eye was fixed vacantly upon the distant horizon.

"*In a lonely grave-yard*", he murmured absently—"*beside a rustic
temple, unblessed by cross or altar, amid the din of battle, and the smoke
of war—there shall your mother's fame be avenged, there shall the prophecy of a wronged and betrayed woman, claim its terrible fulfilment!*' Her words—her solemn words—she spoke them in her hour
of death!"

"How his lip trembles—how his eye fires!" murmured La Fayette—"One
terrible idea—the idea of a wronged mother, and a treacherous father, preying upon his mind and absorbing his soul, has made his life a Doom!
And yet no sword is braver in battle, no heart stouter in the hour
of death!"

"Ah—ha, Marquis—" cried Randulph suddenly turning to La Fayette
—"Hear you that merry bugle note? 'Tis the trumpet-call of my merry
bugler Clerwoode Le Clere!"

"The Riders of Santee are holding a merry carousal in the woods!" replied La Fayette, "'Twill be a busy night with them—with us all! They
are drinking success to our 'knightly adventure' in a cask of good wine.
Let us ride forward Randulph and join the brave fellows!'

"Be it so!" replied Randulph Waldemar—"Their song swells higher
and louder, their emcampment is not far off! Away—away!" he gaily
exclaimed as he struck his spurs into the flanks of his cream-colored steed—
"It will be a night of sword-thrust and rifle-shot with us all—" he continued
eyeing the dense black cloud, that was sweeping up the heavens, over the
pathway of the setting sun—"And to many of us, it will be a night
of death!"

CHAPTER THIRD.

THE MERRY CAROUSAL OF THE BOLD RIDERS OF SANTEE.

" HURRAH for the merry bugler !" cried Long Ned Bean, raising the drink-ing horn of rye-whiskey to his lips—" Hurrah for Clerwoode Le Clere ! A song from the merry bugler—a song comrades—a song of war from Clerwoode Le Clere !"

" A song—a song !" echoed the stout broad-shouldered Sergeant Dan Davney, familiarly termed Devil-Dan—" A song from merry Clerwoode Le Clere !"

" A song—a song from Clerwoode Le Clere !" echoed the hundred troop-ers, extended along the sward—" Aye—aye—a song from Clerwoode Le Clere !"

" By the fame of our gallant captain !" exclaimed the youth, as perched upon a dismounted saddle, with a drinking horn in one hand, and a savory morsel of roasted beef in the other, he surveyed the throng—" By the fame of our gallant captain, but this is brave ! A hundred gallant fellows, gathered within the shelter of the green wood—gathered for a merry carou-sal—their swords by their sides, their rifles within reach ; their steeds—black as the raven's plume—reined in, within the shade of this oaken grove ready for mounting, and the blazing fire of our little camp shimmering 'hrough the trees ! It will be a crowded night with us all comrades—let this half-hour, ere sundown be a merry one ! Now for my song—"

And inclining his slight and slender form, to one side of the saddle, on which he sat, the merry bugler Clerwoode Le Clere, blew a joyous peal on his bugle, and then with the warm glow of the setting sun, falling over his back and shoulders with his handsome face all humor and merriment, he pro-ceeded to take a glance at the party, assembled for carousal within the forest glade.

An hundred stout oaken trees, swept round the green sward, in an oval form, and flung their branches overhead, each gnarled branch entwining with its fellow, while the rich verdant mass of foliage was alive with sun-beams, or glaring red with the light of the fire, blazing through the leaves, a little apart from the scene of festival mirth.

The beams of the setting sun, all warm and golden, came glancing through the thickly woven leaves, and shone gaily on the stout forms of an hundred bold troopers, all extended along the sward, in attitudes of careless ease, their slouching hats, marked by the oaken sprig entwined with the dark plume, thrown aside, and their attire, the coat of light green velvet, the breeches of buckskin, and the long black trooper's-boots, all standing out boldly in the light, while their stern and rugged faces, the visages of bold hunters and stern backwoodsmen, seamed by scars, and marked by many a sign of wild encounter with the forest-savage, or terrible fray, in the wilderness, were all shown in boldest light or darkest shadow, as grouped around that forest glade, the gallant riders of Santee, rent the air with the loud hurrah, the drinking song, or the merry catch of some patriot-strain, echoed and re-echoed far along the woods.

The figures of the troopers, were such as would have made the heart of an admirer of manly proportion, and muscular power, warm and throb to look upon. The sunlight falling lazily along the glade, disclosed the bold and prominent chest of each trooper, the arms all bone and sinew, the unbared throat, with its outline of rugged strength, the lower limbs, like the arms, all muscular power and sinewy vigor, while the rising calf, the sloping ancle, and the high instep of the spurred boot, completed the manly bearing of the bold Riders of Santee.

As the air echoed with the chorus of the manly laugh, or the sudden shout, the clatter of drinking vessels, or the rattling of sword against sword, thrown together in the convivial toast, or soldierly pledge, the scene formed a strange and various picture.

The glow of the sunbeams, falling along the forest-hidden glades mingled with the glare of the camp fire, built at a short distance aside from the grove, and the mingled light fell in fitful flashes along the sward, now crimsoning each bold face and gaunt-form with glaring light, now shimmering on rifle-barrel and sword scabbard, and again casting one broad bright gleam athwart the roof of over-arching foliage, the beams lit up the scene with sudden brilliancy, and then all was dark, shadowy and indistinct, while the bold outlines of the dark steeds of the troopers, fastened here and there among the trees of the forest, were shown in vague and gloomy shadow, or in strong and crimson light.

Slender and graceful in form, the youth, who sat perched upon the dismounted saddle at the eastern end of the grove, was attired in a tight body coat of green velvet, faced with gold, and encircled by a slight belt, supporting an ivory hilted dagger, breeches of fine yellow buckskin, while his small and daintily fashioned boots, gay with the golden spur and tassel, disclosed his fine leg, and delicate foot to every advantage. His face, dark and bronzed in hue, and relieved by clustering masses of glossy brown hair, sweeping down to his very shoulders, was marked by a forehead broad and massive, dark eyebrows, strongly defined, and over-arching eyes of hazel, now flashing with gaiety and humor, now brilliant with sentiment and feeling, a nose bold and prominent, large mouth with lips somewhat full, and a rounded chin, harmonizing with the other features, while the general expression of his countenance, indicated the enthusiast, warm and passionate in temperament, swayed by sudden impulse, fond of the daring and hazardous in courage, and generous with the quick pulsation of youthful blood.

"Fill your glasses boys!" cried Clerwoode Le Clere, with a merry glance of his hazel eye. "Pass round the flask, comrades—fill each glass and drinking horn! A toast for you Devil-Dan—a toast for you Lieutenant Bean! Heaven bless the Britisher for whom this Maderia was smuggled out of Philadelphia across the country, toward the red-coat camp——May all future consignments of fifty-year old Maderia meet with no better fate! Drink the memory of the forlorn red-coat in solemn silence, gentlemen!"

"In solemn silence, gentlemen!" echoed Long Ned Bean, turning his hard features, marked by a stiff wiry beard, toward the light. "In solemn silence, gentlemen! May the Britisher, for whom this Maderia was intended, drink nothing sweeter than jimson-weed-brandy, until his next cask o' fifty years old arrives!"

A loud boisterous laugh arose from the band, beakers were clanked together, and healths pledged, and none drank more energetically or shouted more lustily, than a stout broad shouldered yeoman, who seated at one end of the group with a coarse slouching hat of felt drooped over his face, and his muscular legs crossed one over the other, fixed his eyes meditatively on the ground, plying his beaker with one hand, while the other grasped the hunting knife, with the savoury steak hissing and steaming on its point.

"A health, comrades—a health to the jolly farmer, who aided us, in the attack on the British skirmishers to-day at noon!" cried Devil-Dan Dabney, as his broad face shone with convivial feeling. "Here's to the jolly old farmer of Chester County, boys!"

"Health to the jolly old farmer of Chester!" shouted the hundred voices of the band, with one bold shout, and every beaker was drained, and every glass emptied.

"We licked 'em, sartin—" murmured the stout farmer, without raising his head. "Licked 'em, hoss, foot and dra-goons! Made a reg'lar spill of 'em—they ran like hoss-thieves, sartin-ly we beat 'em. Howsomever, if that young sprig of hickory up yander haint no objections, I'd like to heer that 'are song—I would."

"The song—Clerwoode—the song!" shouted the troopers.

"Well, boys, here goes!" cried the Bugler, blowing a merry peal on his trumpet. "I'll give you a song, which I composed, as we rode to this forest glade, after our skirmish with the Britishers, to-day! It is a song in honor of our band—'The Men of the Oak! as they sometimes call us in camp. Leftenant Bean, unfurl our flag, there—the flag of the Mountain Oak and the Bald Eagle, and let the brave banner wave proudly overhead. while we shout The Hurrah of the men of the oak!"

And then in a clear, bold voice, that swelled away thro' the woods with all its intonations of manly melody, the gallant youth gave forth the words of one of the thousand songs, which, pointed and rugged, in design and execution, still served to while away many a weary interval, during the troublous days and dark nights of the Revolution.

THE HURRAH OF THE MEN OF THE OAK.

"They come from the hills the bold men of the Oak—
　They gather with knapsack, with rifle and knife,
　All gallantly mounted they speed to the strife,
The sword waves on high and there's death in its stroke—
　　　　Each rifle-ball carries a life!
　　　　Hurrah for the men of the Oak."

" Now, boys, now !" shouted Clerwoode Le Clere—"now boys—with an earthquake shout——

　　　　Oh, hurrah for the men of the Oak!
　　　　Oh, hurrah for the men of the Oak !"

Merry and bold, like a thunder peal, that chorus shout arose, far along the woods, and with a quick, piercing note on the bugle horn, the trumpeter gave forth the next verse of his song.

"In their coats of green, all gallant and bold
　With rifle on shoulder, with sword at the side,
　To the red field of battle all gaily they ride,
A stout band of steel—— a-hundred men told—
　　　All riding in glory and pride
　　　Hurrah for the gallant and bold!
　　　Oh, hurrah for the gallant and bold !"

" Oh, hurrah for the gallant and bold !" echoed the troopers, and again, and again the woods returned the echo—" for the gallant—the gallant—the gailant and—bold !"

"They sweep from the hills, in huntsman's array
　From the forest thy rush—from the wild-wood they pour,
　Lo! Around them swells up the battle's dread roar,
And the rifle-flash lightens the battle-mellay
　　　O'er a path sodden'd in gore
　　　By one bold charge they carry the day!
　　　By a bold gallant charge they carry the
　　　day !"

" Riders of Santee, charge your glasses to the brim !" shouted Clerwoode as he seized the banner-staff, and flinging on high the banner of the Bald Eagle and the Mountain Oak. " Riders of Santee, charge your glasses, and drain every man his drinking horn, as I give the chorus now—

"They rush to the charge with hearts that ne'er wince,
Around them their rifle shots scatter like hail,
Like the black mountain cloud on the wings o' th' gale
Sweeps on their brave Leader—bold Randulph the Prince!
Like the cloud on the gale
Rides Randulph the Prince!
Hurrah for bold Randulph the Prince!"

"Oh, hurrah for bold Randulph the Prince!" chimed in Lieutenant Long Ned Bean, as he flung his glittering sword in the air, and tossed the contents of the beaker down his throat.

"Oh, hurrah, hurrah for bold Randulph the Prince!" echoed the stout farmer, at one end of the group.

"Hurrah—hurrah for bold Randulph the Prince!" re-echoed the troopers emptying their glasses, and flinging their swords in the air—"oh, hurrah"— they continued, as the sound of horse's hoofs broke upon the air, mingling with the song—"oh hurrah, hurrah——"

"Hurrah for bold Randulph the Prince!" cried a strange voice, marked by a French accent, and a tall and handsome soldier, attired in blue and buff, stood in the centre of the group, waving his sword on high, and glancing around him with a flashing eye and a swelling chest. "Hurrah— hurrah, for Bold Randulph the Prince!"

"Our leader and his brave companion!" shouted Clerwoode Le Clerc "Riders of Santee, to your feet! Welcome to Randulph the Prince!"

One loud wild shout arose from the band, as the noble form of their leader emerged from the foliage, a loud, wild and piercing shout, mingled with the clash of an hundred swords, and the shrill neigh of an hundred steeds.

"Riders of Santee!" shouted Captain Waldemar—"A shout—a shout of welcome! Welcome to the brave foreigner—the chivalrous Frenchman— welcome to La Fayette!"

A murmur of surprise ran along the band, and even the stout yeoman of Chester raised his head for a moment in surprise, but in an instant, another thunder shout startled the wide forest. "Hurrah for the gallant French-man— Hurrah for La Fayette!"

"Mon Dieu! Captain Waldemar!" cried the Cavalier, with an enthusiastic voice and a flashing eye—"Yours is a gallant band! By the Great Conde, the sun never shone on men more fitted for deeds of daring, for deeds of death, than the gallant Riders of Santee!"

And flinging his manly form along the green sward, the young soldier glanced around him with a gleam of delight, as the sunbeams streamed over the hard visages of the Riders, each face warming with merriment and glee, while the beakers arose clanking in the air, and from side to side ran the song, the jest, and the quick return of soldierly wit meeting soldierly wit.

"Lieutenant, what information have you gathered concerning the movements of the British?" asked Captain Waldemar, seating himself beside the

French soldier. " I w many do they number ? What will be their next movement—where will their next position be taken ?"

" Captain, they're movin' towards Kennet's Square"—returned Long Ned Bean. " Kennet's Square, about seven miles from Chadd's Ford, which is in the neighborhood of three miles from this wood. They number 12,000 Britishers and 5000 Hessians. They are as proud as fighting cocks with their gaffs on, and intend to make a meal of one Mister George Washington and his men, without the usual trimmin's. Captain, I see, you would ask, how we come by all his provender—this Maderey wine—yonder smokin' hams, chunks of beef and other fixin's ? I'll tell you how. 'Bout noon, our band took position in a clump of trees, on the Philadelfy road, some miles east o' Chadd's Ford, Sun was shinin, very bright—observed a couple o' baggage waggons comin' down the hill—a driver, tall and square-shouldered lump of a fellow, walkin' a-head. Waggons were big as elephant-cradles. Reglar built Conestoga affairs. They were passin' us, and we saw yander stout-built farmer—the feller down below thar with the slouchin' hat over his face, a-walkin' near the team, a-squintin' at it in a sartin' way, and makin' himself ginerally queer, about it. ' Hallo, you sir, —he says to the driver—' whar you bound and what're got on board ?' ' Ya-ah'—replies the driver in Swabian Dutch. ' Who are you, and what side d'ye b'long to ?' again spoke slouchin'-hat. ' Yah'—growled the driver, in reg'lar Swope-dialect. ' Britisher or Blue-coat ?' asked the old farmer, in his pinted way. ' Y-a-h !' grunted the swope. ' Y-a-h—y-a-h—y-a-h !' ' It's my opinion, you've been told to say Y-a-h to everything and everybody, and that's suspicious as a blue-coat lined with red. Now, jist stop, will you ?' he remarked, seizing the driver, and at the same instant, pop—pop—pop, went half-a-dozen bullets from the bosom o' the foremost wagon —still slouchin' hat held on, and in a minute we took the whole party prisners. They proved to be a band o' Hessians, smuggling wine and Bologna sassages out o' Philadelfy, for the use of General Snitz-and-knep or Kniphaussen, or some sich a name And now, Capt'in, thar's the old farmer— he accompanied us this far on our way—and thinks of jinin' the blue-coat cause."

" The farmer is tall, stout and muscular"—exclaimed Randulph. " A magnificent soldier he would make ? But Sergeant Dabney—have you no story to tell of this day's adventure ?"

" W-a-l, Capt'in, mine's a story o' grease"—replied the Sergeant, as an expression of the most profound solemnity came over his broad visage. " You see, Capt'in, 'bout three o'clock, this arternoon, some light troopers of our party, with Clerwoode Le Clere—that mischievous boy up yander, and meself among 'em, were scoutin' near Chadd's Ford, when we observed three objects a-footin' down the Philadelfy road, toward the Ford. As near as we coulo see, they looked like three animated red-petticoats, topped by three short gowns, with three, round, fat, full-moon faces, shinin' in the

sun, while as many pairs of wooden shoes, were paddlin' away toward the
Ford. 'Three Dutch frows!' cried Clerwoode Le Clere, givin' a slight
touch of his bugle. 'Three Dutch frows—they may be spies in disguise'
—he went on, with a curious glance in his brown eye. 'Let's arrest 'em,
Sergeant!' And, no sooner said, than done, he orders the ladies to hold
up, and hold up they did, but with a considerable fuss, I can tell you.
"Who are you, what are you up to, whar you goin'?' ses I, rather rough
in my way. 'We're goin' over te Fordt—' cries the thickest and broadest
of the three. 'Me and Betz andt Peg.' 'And what mought ye be arter?'
ses I. 'Peg's got a childt sick mit de meazles—Betz's oldt man's got te
fever-an-agur, and I'm goin' to a berryin'.' 'Sergeant, there's somethin''
wrong about that party'—whispered Clerwoode Le Clere to me, and then
he mumbled somethin' else, which I shant tell ye. 'Howsomever, Sargent'
—he ses, 'it would be imperlite to sarch 'em—leave the matter to me—I'll
fix 'em afore they're many minutes older.' And with that, he rides up to
the three frows, with a perlite bow— 'Ladies, you must be tired'—he observed. 'Here's the Green-Tree Inn—'spose you walk in and take a rest.'
The ladies whispered and mumbled and grumbled, and even swore somewhat profanely in Dutch, but it was of no use. Into the bar-room of the
Green-Tree Inn they walked, waddlin' as they walked, like crazy sugar
hogsheads. W-a-l, as it happened, the queer-devil, one Hirpley Hawson,
who keeps the tavern, had kindled a-rousin' fire on the h'arth, and the place
was hot as a bake-oven. 'Walk up to the fire, ladies'—ses Clerwoode.
'Walk up and warm yourselves—there'll be a beefsteak ready for ye directly.
Here, Hirpley, hand the ladies a mug o' beer'—and with that, he gently
shoves 'em nearer and nearer the fire, smilin' perlitely all the time, and
lookin' as pleased as a young widower jist married to the fifth wife. Betz
looked at Peg, and Peg squinted at Sal, and all three of 'em made mouths
at one another, while Hirpley Hawson kept pilin' on the wood, higher and
higher, until the air was hot enough for a dozen sally-manders. 'Te tuyfel
Betz—I'm roastin'!' cried Peg, with a meltin' look. 'Mein Gott, Peg, I'm
fryin''—returned Betz. 'Dis *ish* a stew!' cried Sal, with a spiteful look at
the Bugler. 'I wonder weter te tuyfles men to eat us!' Higher and higher
did Hirpley Hawson pile on the wood, and Clerwoode Le Clere begin to
make observations round the dresses of the ladies, eyein' 'em curiously, and
winkin' at me, as he took a squint at the petticoats—red enough to be the
death of a dozen turkey gobblers. And the three frows? Oh, if you coula
have seen 'em—fryin' and stewin' and roastin' before the fire—large drops
o' sweat streamin' down their cheeks, while they panted and blowed like
bellowses, and the room grew hotter and hotter. At last one of the three
giv out. 'Mein Gott, Betz'—she screams—'I'm meltin' away! In a minit,
dere 'ill be no more of me, nor a handful o' chips!' 'Grasshus, what a
fine steak that is!' cried Hirpley Hawson, as he stooped down on the h'arth
'Gentlemen, jist look, see how the grease is runnin'! Did ever ye see sich

12

a steak !' And sure enough, the h'arth was all aflood with fat, right unde·
the wooden shoes of the three frows, and the air smelt as tho' somethin
live was roastin'. 'Another stick o' wood, Hirpley'—shouted Clerwoode
Le Clere. "The ladies is sufferin' with cold—another log, if you please !'
'Grasshus me !' screams Hirpley Hawson—' was there ever sich a steak !
Lord, jist look at the fat—how it streams down into the fire and over the
h'arth—and what's remarkable—' he went on in his own way—' and what's
remarkable, the grease o' this steak is all butter—now, I've seed a good
many green things in my time, but I never did see a beefsteak rain butter
afore.' ' Gott in himmel !' cried the stoutest of the three frows—' Betz,
dey've found us out ! And dere's all our tre dozen pounds o' grass butter
gone to the dogs !' And as she said this, Clerwoode Le Clere burst into a
loud laugh, and the three ladies, each produced, from the inside hem of their
petticoats, a dozen pounds o' butter a-piece, which they were smuggling
along to the British lines. It would a-made you laugh, to see each o' th'
frows a-stoopin' down, and unwrapping pound o' butter arter pound o' butter, all nicely did up in flannel, and sowed inside o' the petticoat ! And
then, when Clerwoode Le Clere asked one of the ladies, whether she was'nt
ashamed of doing an act so much against conscience and patriotism (he
meant, sellin' butter to the British,) to see the fat frow raise up her round,
chunky face, and ask him, so innocent-like— ' Weter konshentz andt patri-
otishm wasn't new names for te silver half-tollar ?' By the cocked-hat of
Gineral Washington, but 'twas too good !''

A loud laugh ran around the grove, and none seemed to enjoy the matter
more heartily than the French chevalier, while the stout farmer of Chester
at the further end of the group, shook with renewed fits of quiet and convulsive laughter.

"One song more, Clerwoode—" exclaimed Randulph—" One song more,
and then we must away toward Chadd's Ford."

"It shall be a song of one of the bravest of the brave !" shouted Clerwoode Le Clere springing on his feet—" The first in the charge the last in
the retreat—Mad Antony Wayne !"

A long loud hurrah awoke the silence of the woods, and every head was
uncovered, and every sword unsheathed, as the name of the bold Hero broke
upon the air.

"Now for my song !" cried Le Clere—" Ta-rila-larila !" pealed the bugle
note and then the words of his wild, irregular song, came bursting along
the air.

THE CHARGE OF MAD ANTONY WAYNE.

From the mountain-top gleaming, he came like a sprite,
Now riding in darkness, now dashing in light,
The Britishers revel and riot, along the green plain,
O'er their lair like a meteor bursts Antony Wayne—
                    Hurrah for Mad Antony **Wayne**.

Lo! swords wave on high and shouts swell on the air,
The swords of the foemen, the shouts of despair;
The British turn fighting—they charge but in vain!
O'er the fighting and fallen sweeps, Antony Wayne!
Hurrah for Mad Antony **Wayne**!

Have you seen the red-lightning hurled blazing from heaven?
Have you seen the stout-oak by the red-lightning riven?
Like the flame-riven splinters, the foemen lie scattered and slain,
O'er dying and dead, glares the thunderbolt Antony Wayne!
Hurrah for Mad Antony **Wayne**!

"Hurrah, hurrah, oh, hurrah for Mad Antony Wayne!" swelled the bold chorus from the trooper-band, and swords waved on high, and the banner of the mountain eagle and the oak, floated in the air, as the echoes, again and again, sent back the redoubled shout.

"Look—Captain Waldemar—!" cried the Marquis springing to his feet —"The hat has fallen from the head of the stout farmer of Chester! The open brow—the rich brown eye—the bold visage and the muscular form! Can you mistake them! 'Tis the hero himself—'tis—'

"It is Mad Antony Wayne!" cried Randulph the Prince with a gleam of delight "Troopers of Santee, a welcome to the General—a welcome to the brave General Wayne!"

And as the earthquake shout arose booming upon the forest air, the stout yeoman of Chester advanced and stood in the centre of the group. The last beams of the setting sun, shone strongly upon his muscular form, the prominent chest, the broad shoulders and the sinewy limbs; an l over his noble visage, the bold forehead, the clear sparkling brown eye, and the determined mouth, flashed a sudden and wild expression of chivalrous enthusiasm, as gazing around him, Mad Antony Wayne, beheld an hundred tried swords, gleaming in the air, while bursting on the air, like the boom of cannon, swelled the shout echoed again and yet again— 'Hurrah, hurrah for Mad Antony Wayne!'

"Antony Wayne begs to serve as a volunteer, for one night, in the gallant band of Randulph the Prince!" said the stout soldier advancing—"This good broadsword has flashed in the ranks of battle—it will gleam this night in the ranks of the banner of the bold eagle and the mountain oak!"

"Mount, my Riders, mount!" shouted Randulph the Prince as a loud and deafening hurrah arose upon the air—"Away—away—the sun sinks in the west, and we must make for the 'Lonely cabin of the wood' by way of Chadd's Ford!"

In a few moments, the sungleam shone upon the bald forms of the hundred stout troopers, each mounted on his jet-black steed, with the gallant La Fayette on his dappled grey, side by side with Wayne on his glossy brown charger riding at their head, while the magnificent cream-colored steed of

Randulph the Prince, flung his arching crest on high, and gave his long white mane to the gathering breeze, as his brave rider unsheathed his sword and pointed the course of the night march.

"Clerwoode a word with you—" said Randulph calling the youth to his side—"Your father fell in battle, fighting for his rights. Your widowed mother consigned you to my care—she bade me place you where the fire was hottest and the fight thickest. I have an adventure for you. Three miles to the southwest, hidden in the woods, there is a rock called the Rock of the Devil's Foot-Print. The friends of Washington and the right, gather there at sundown. Away there—ride for your life; the watchword is 'Randulph the prince;' tell their leader that I will meet them at the large oak, standing alone on the road-side some two miles west of Chadd's Ford, an hour hence; the band will then unite in the attempt to surprize the British refugees, who gather at the wood-cabin a mile beyond. God speed you Clerwoode. The adventure is one of danger—flying bands of tories beset the woods, and you may have to fight for your life. Away—Clerwoode—and remember your father's death!"

The young soldier leaned slowly from his steed, and bending his head to the saddle of his leader, he pressed the hand of Randulph the Prince to his lips, while his dark brown eyes flashed with the wild enthusiasm of his nature.

"I will remember the death of my father!" he shouted—"To the hilt of my sword and to the last pistol-bullet, to the last throb of my heart, to the last impulse of life, in this right arm, will I remember his death!"

And as the bold Riders of Santee, swept slowly onward, two abreast, along the forest glade, disappearing in the shadow of the woods toward the north with the sunbeams shining on the upraised swords, the flaunting plumes and the waving banner, the brown-haired boy struck the spurs into the flanks of his steed, and sped toward the southern woods, looking over his shoulder at the arching heavens as he sped.

"The cloud is gathering dark and black along the path of the setting sun!" he shouted flinging his arm in the air—"Let it gather! The cloud and the storm for me! Ha—ha!" he laughed and the words of his gay carol arose merrily upon the air.

THE TROOPER'S LIFE AND DEATH.

Oh, what's so merry as the trooper's life
The march---the alarum, the rescue----the fight—
His air is the storm, his pleasure the strife,
And the flash he loves, is the cannon's wild light----
Huzza----huzza for the troopers life!

And then when he dies, his last, long breath
Flies to the hymn of the rifle's rattle
'Mid his own green hills he meets his death,
And he dies as he lived, in the battle!
Ha—ha! Ha—ha! for the troopers death!

CHAPTER FOURTH.

THE ROCK OF THE DEVIL'S FOOT PRINT.

THE beams of the dark lantern, streaming along the green mossy turf, and glancing over the trembling leaves of the embowering foliage, discovered the spare, lean figure of a man prematurely old, half seated half crouched at the foot of a massive beechen tree, one hand extended grasping the lantern, while the other rested upon the glittering rifle at his side, as gazing wistfully around the recesses of the forest, his sharp, withered face, lighted by a small, keen, grey eye and marked by a low forehead, surmounted by thin locks of grizzled hair, a prominent nose, thin parched lips and a retreating chin, stood out boldly in the light, relieved by the background of the wide beechen trunk, and the shadow of th woods beyond.

"It is a dark night!" he whispered the words to his own ear—"The darkness has come suddenly down—and the moon is hidden by a vast, a gloomy pile of clouds. How still the air seems—how heavily it weighs upon my breath, like lead! I've seen many nights o' terror in my time— but this night will surpass them all! The night of *his* despair—" he chuckled as he said the words—"Ha—ha—he was my brother! He believed in truth—in a trusting heart, in principle—and what not. Behold his reward! The life of a wanderer—the death of a nameless vagabond! I— ha, ha, I believe in truth, in a trusting heart, in principle, and even in a God, that looks after the doings of the poor mites crawling and battening in this stale cheese—the earth, ha, ha, but the truth—heart—and God, all mean one thing in my way of thinking and that thing is—*Gold!* And I will manage my cards right! Philip Walford may be a curmudgeon and a niggard, but he shall be the richest curmudgeon and niggard in all the provinces! From the *South*, the news is cheering—Rock-Farm is mine—so is Wild-Wood Grange in the distance! *He*—the silly colonel—thought I had a sort of fatherly affection for his daughter Rose! So I have—after a sort. David must marry the lass, and then—and then—" he spoke slowly and distinctly, fixing his eyes in vacancy, and stretching forth his thin talon-like fingers as he spoke—"And then, there's a troublesome game o' blood and war to be played, but amid the cloud and the storm, the good fortune of Philip Walford rides onward, and the end is—"

"*Death!*" spoke a hollow voice, at the very shoulder of the scheming man.

He turned his face suddenly round, a sudden tremor seemed to seize his lean figure from head to foot, and with eyes starting from their sockets with alarm and terror, he beheld, a dark face, looking from the foliage at his back, and peering over his very shoulder, while two flashing eyes, gazed steadily into his own quivering orbs.

" Death, father, death—" said the same, sneering voice—"Isn't that the end of it all? You scheme, you plot, you plan—you gather the rich hoard of gold. You die. Who'll weep for you? I'll spend the gold—and the worms will be eatin' away at your carcase! Pleasant? eh? father."

And the stout muscular form of David Walford, with his blackened face surmounted by the slouching hat of felt, the rifle on his shoulder and the knife at his side, stood in front of the old man, while a fit of sneering laughter, shook his prominent chest, and convulsed the muscles of his brutal countenance.

" David—how you frightened me!" said Philip Walford, regarding his son, with a glance of surprize—" Boy, it is not well, to trifle with your—father! You are intoxicated—"

" Drunk, old man, drunk!" returned the ruffian rolling his eyes from side to side—" Drunk as a fiddler at a country-dance! Whoop! But where's the g-a-l old man? Where's the beauty? Where's old Frazier's farm, walkin' about in the woods in the shape of a purty g-a-l?"

" Listen boy, this is a busy night with me, and the sun is down—"
" ——— my ———" shouted the ruffian with a characteristic oath—" Dye think I'm an idler? I've got to run away with a g-a-l and marry her at that—there's an adventure waitin' for me up at Chadd's Ford—and several more things to do afore daybreak. I hope it will storm—hope it 'ill storm like * * * *!"

" David, I journeyed with Miss Frazier, and her two attendants, Gotlieb Hoff and the wench Phillis, as far as the cross roads, a mile and a half below this wood. I there discovered that I was pursued by a party of rebel skirmishers—I struck in the woods to the right—I delivered my load of flour and other provisions, to an agent of General Howe, and then gained this spot by a circuitous route. The Rock-of-the-Devil's-Foot-Print lies some fifty yards from this place—Rose Frazier will pass that way within ten minutes—it is just sundown, yet the woods are as dark as midnight! David your time is short—"

" I know it!" returned the ruffian—" I've got two things to do within ten minutes. Don't think old man, that I didn't know all you told me about the matter, afore you said a word. I've hung round the path of the beauty for an hour—almost a quarter of a mile behind her, a small party of rebel militia are footing along the wood-path—I intend to lay an ambush both for the g-a-l and the rebel dogs!"

Placing two fingers on his wide mouth, in a peculiar manner, the tory leader gave a long, shrill whistle, which echoed along the forest like the shriek of a night bird.

In an instant, six blackened faces, were thrust from the verdure of the

embowering foliage, and in another instant the light flashed upon the outlines of six tall muscular forms, attired in coarse dark coats, with slouching
hats drooping over each forhead, and each right arm grasping a rifle, with
the polished barrel glittering like burnished silver.

"Ready boys! Ready Ravens o' the Hollow? Will you follow me?'
shouted Dave Walford eyeing the band.

"To the death!" returned the ruffians with one voice.

"Lead the way father—lead the way toward the Rock—the Devil's
Rock!"

"David I do not wish to be seen in this matter!" whispered the father, as
the light shone upon his thin features, agitated by a mingled expression of
distrust and fear—"Can he wish to murder me!" he muttered to himself in
a voice that spoke the terrors of the coward and the sinner. "The prize
is a bold one and the hour is lonely!"

"You go with us father!" exclaimed David gazing sternly in the face of
his parent—"Aye to the pine coffin and the gibbet if need be!"

And without another word, the old man, for old he was, tho' he scarce
numbered fifty years, raised the dark lantern, and led the way along the
woods. Dark shadows of gloom and terror were around the party, the thick
growth of foliage overhead, shut sky and cloud from their view, and the light-
beams, fell with a ruddy glare over the stout forms and blackened faces of
the band for a moment, and then glimmered over the green turf, along which
they trod, and then all was black and vague again, and the sound of their
trampling feet, and the rustling of the bushes, alone marked the course of
their march.

"Here we are boys!" cried Dave Walford, as the wood-path suddenly
ended in a rock of granite, level at the top, and overshadowed by interlacing
boughs and interwoven branches, mingled with light shrubbery and brushwood. "Here we take our stand—right on this rock—through this tangled brushwood we pint our rifles—before us lays the wild glade of the Rock
—the Devil's Rock!"

He thrust the branches aside, and gazed forth upon the scene. It was
strange and wild—wild as the dream of the night-mare ridden, a fit scene
for a deed of treachery and bloodshed.

From an opening in the gathering clouds, half way up the heavens, shone
the moon, discolored and red, like a strange, spectral light, with dark piles
of storm clouds all around her path, and in the dim light of her beams, lay
a level piece of earth, covered with short wild grass, some fifty yards in
extent, with the lofty forest trees towering on every side, and wide masses
of granite-rock, flinging their shapeless forms in the air as they swept circling
around one side of the glade, each rough peak, each rugged point and
abrupt form of rock, silvering in the moonlight, while on the sward below,
stretched fitful shadows like belts of sable thrown over the turf, and in the
centre, brightening in the full glow of the moonlight, a solid rock, circular

in shape, rose like a platform from the glade around, with a human foot, stamped in its surface, side by side with the impress of a cloven hoof.

The night-breeze came sighing and shrieking along the forest, the tree tops waved gently to and fro, above were the blackened heavens, with their world of clouds, through which glimmed fitfully, the blood-red moon. The lurid lightning flash, now and then glared over the scene of gloom, while the rushing of a brawling streamlet, dashing onward, on the farther side of the rugged rocks, arose whispering on the air, its gentle music, strangely contrasting with the murmur of awe, which seemed to pervade all nature, on the eve of the approaching storm.

"A purty scene for our affair—aint it, boys?" exclaimed Dave Walford, gazing upon the blackened faces of his band. "Here Robinson—d'ye see that oak tree yander?"

"Dev'lish strange if I didn't"—muttered the tory. "It's right on a line with this rock, and its branches over-hang the wood path."

"Get you up into the tree, Robinson"—returned the ruffian. "I will conceal myself behind the trunk. Father, you will take care of the entrance to the wood-path, aided by these four good fellows of my band."

"David—you—will—not—harm the girl?" tremblingly murmured the old Walford. "Remember, David, that I—"

"Oh, d——n, old man, don't give yourself any trouble about the matter" —exclaimed the ruffian, as a meaning smile crossed his features. "Half-a-mile from this glade, in the thickest part of the wild woods, lies a lonely hut. There will I carry the maiden—and marry rhymes with carry, father! Old Frazier's daughter must be mine, afore she's an hour older!"

And old Walford beheld his son, taking his way across the glade of the Rock of the Devil's Foot Print, and in a moment, one of the tory band had ascended the oaken tree; another remained concealed, side by side, with David Walford, behind the massive trunk of this giant tree; and four stout hardy ruffians, with rifles levelled, and the fatal aim securely taken, stood upright on the granite rock, behind the shelter of the environing shrubbery.

A quick tremor of nervous fear passed over the form of the old Refugee, then the muscles of his face trembled and his lip whitened, but in a moment he had commanded his fears, and the cowardice of the physical man, was mastered by the stubborn will of the resolute schemer.

"It is a bold throw!" he murmured. "Wild-Wood Grange is a rich farm. It is a bold throw—it must be a sure one!" And the man smiled grimly, as he clutched his rifle with a firmer grasp, while over his face, his sharp and withered features, there passed an expression of solemn and settled determination.

Meanwhile, along a winding forest path, lighted by the glare of torch-beams, a fair maiden, urged her dark steed hastily along, while by her side, rode her sable female attendant, and at her bridle-rein, leading the way, was the manly form of Gotlieb Hoff, mounted on a stout brown horse, which

ever and anon he gave the spur, as the lurid lightning flashed along their
path, or the distant thunder growled a moaning alarum of the coming storm.

The light of the torch-beams glared over the stout form and handsome
features of the yeoman, with their expression of determined courage and
reckless daring; and the sable face of the Negro Phillis, with her large mouth,
with thick pouting lips, the protruding eye, marked by enormous whites, the
low forehead, gay with the ornamental folds of a parti-colored kerchief
shone and glistened in the light, as turning hurriedly from side to side, the
sable damsel glanced, with some fear and alarm, at the wild flashes of
lightning streaming over the path, in an instant, succeeded by shadows of
intolerable darkness and gloom.

" How dark the forest grows !" whispered Rose glancing at the masses
of shadow around her. " The air is heavy and the storm is gathering above !
Hark, how it thunders !"

And leaning to one side of her jet black steed, in an attitude of attention
and alarm, with one fair hand grasping the bridle-rein, while the other extended with a gesture of womanly fear, held in its tapering fingers, her
small and jaunty riding cap. Rose Frazier listened to the distant moaning
of the storm, and her bosom heaved upward with a sudden, convulsive throb
as the silence of the hour, and the loneliness of the woods, sent a strange fear
thrilling over her heart.

Gotlieb raised the torch on high, in front of their path, and the ruddy
glare of the torch-light fell glimmering over the face and form of the maiden.
And standing out from the back-ground of gloom and shadow, like the creation of a midsummer dream, was the face of the fair and lovely girl, with
the cheek warmed with the rosy hue of youthful beauty, budding into
womanhood, the straight Grecian nose, the small mouth with lips of ruby, the
ower one slightly projecting with a haughty pout, dark eyes fringed by long
dark lashes, and over-arched by delicate eyebrows of the same deep black
as the lashes ; a white forehead, neither very high nor very low, with a
striking relief afforded by the hair, which, dark and glossy, was parted, with
tasteful simplicity, in the centre of the head, and descending along each velvet cheek, fell in a cluster of graceful tresses, behind each finely chisselled
ear, bright, with a simple ring of gold

The countenance of the maiden was that of a lovely girl ; the beauty of
Blanche Walford was all dream, all ideal ; the face of Mary Mayland was a
pretty one, but Rose Frazier differing in her style of beauty from both, was
an embodiment of all the lovliness, which forms the character of the woman,
the all trusting, all confiding woman, whose being is love, whose soul is
affection, whose memory is the first dream of love, whose future is the happiness of the beloved.

" My uncle I fear has directed us, to the wrong path—" exclaimed Rose,
glancing anxiously around—" The midnight shadow of the woods deepens
The air grows heavier, the storm gathers darker and blacker—"

" Y-a-h by St. Christuffel !" muttered Gotlieb—" 'Tis one of te tuyfels nights! Te shadows jump apout like spooks, and te lightnin' plays among the trees like a drunken *Beltz-knickel! Mein gott, Phillis thee is as pale as a freshly white-washed pale fence! Te tuyfel gal—dont pe frightened—"

" Bress my goodness !" chattered the negro damsel—" All alone in de wood—arter sundown—lost our own selfs way—purty how d'ye do! Lor massey! Me frighten indeed !"

" St. Christuffel ! Hark at the tongue ov her !" observed Gotlieb—" Hey? What do I see ? A man walkin' a-head of us—"

" Berry likely ! It may be a sperrit o' some kind or-tother," chattered Phillis—" Spose massa Sour-crout an' spec inquire—"

" It is a traveller !" said Rose, glancing at the figure walking along in the gloom, some few yards ahead—" He is dressed like a plain farmer's man. Call to him Gotlieb and inquire the way,"

" I say neighbor—neighbor I say—" halloed Gotlieb at the top of his voice as the three horses sprang suddenly forward—" Neighbor I say !"

The traveller walking in front of the party, made no reply, nor turned nis head, but broke forth into a clear melodious imitation of the popular air of Yankee Doodle, while his hands were deposited in the unfathomable depth of his breeches pockets.

" Tam te fellow—cant he hear !" exclaimed Gotlieb springing forward— " I say neighbor, who are you, and which is the way to Chadd's Ford ?"

The light of the blazing torch flashed upon the form of a tall, spare man, clad in a threadbare coat, with a tail ludicrously diminutive, leather breeches patched and mended, and boots, that might have awoke the echoes of the ark, in their early days, while his head was defended by a small hat, of white felt, with a very narrow rim, drawn closely down over his forehead, to the very eyes, with the hair, all tangled and matted, forming a very good imitation of the various points of the compass.

" Oh-a-h—fine evening, barring a little bit of a storm that's gatherin'—" cried the stranger wheeling suddenly round, and gazing at the party with a lack lustre stare—" You see na-bor didn't hear you sooner. I'm rather deef, so much the better, cant hear the thunder—never mind my wife when she raises a rumpus—"

" What a fright !" murmured Phillis — " ugly as de berry debbil he own self!"

" Which way you going friendt ?" cried Gotlieb—" Can you tell me the way, out of this woods, to Chadd's Ford ?"

" Now you don't s-a-y !" exclaimed the stranger, walking along by the side of Gotlieb's horse with enormous strides—" I'm jist goin' there myself, got some business with a clever chap up that way—one Curnel Frazier."

* A familiar spirit of the " merry Christmas time."

"By St. Christuffel!" exclaimed Gotlieb, eyeing the vacant countenance of the stranger—"why I'm his hired man, and tis lady is his
daughter."

"Now that aint a fact—is it? What? Quite a purty girl." The
stranger gazed into the lovely face of Rose, with a wondering stare—"Jist
like my darter Sally down at Newark. Gineral Washington's army are
marchin' about there. And so that's his daughter!"

"There is something in this man, that strikes me with fear!" the thought
flashed over the mind of the maiden Rose—"His eyes seem dull and
vacant, and yet ever and anon there is a strange, wild gleam in its
glance!"

And in after times, it was told, how cheerfully the rustic stranger conversed with the man Gotlieb and the maid Phillis, in a long, drawling tone
of voice, as they wended along the forest path, how copious stories of
homely anecdote, and familiar discourse fell from his lips, and yet it is
said his presence impressed the mind of the maiden with a strange fear, as
gazing around the shadowed recesses of the forest, she marked the glare of
the torch light falling full and strongly upon his lean spare form, while his
face apparantly dull and expressionless, now and then lighted up with a
glance, that seemed born of an evil spirit.

"What part of te woodt are we in now?" inquired Gotlieb.

' Another bend o' the road, and we pass the Rock o' the Devil's Foot
Print!" exclaimed the stranger—"Strange stories are told of this spot
When I think of 'em it makes my blood creep—it makes my hair stand on
end. Do you know n-a-bor—" and wheeling suddenly round, he gazed
steadily in the face of the sturdy Pennsylvanian—"That when the Evil
Spirit fell from Heaven, he lighted upon that rock? He stamped the granit'
with the print of his feet—he did, and they do say these woods, is haunted
by ghosts and devils. Not many years agone a traveller was murdered at
the foot of yon tree—his spirit shrieks about the woods toward nightfall.
A little farther on, a mother was found butchered with her babe at her
breast. Hark at that moonin' o' th' wind? Can you fancy you hear the
mother cry for help?"

"Mein Gott! But you are one pleasant companion!" ejaculated Gotlieb
—"Its a wonder dey couldt spare you from home—your company's so
very agree'ble!"

"Bress my goodness!" whispered Phillis, all her superstitious fears
aroused by the allusions of the stranger—"I'd lay de berry best calico gown
I've got, but he's a witch!"

No words passed from the lips of the maiden Rose, but her dark eye
wandered with a trembling glance around the glade of the forest. The torch
light was thrown over the faces and forms of the travellers, with a red glaring lustre, the trunks of the giant trees were crimsoned by its glow, and the
leaves, quivered and trembled in its light. The lightning came flashing over

the path, it came flashing in pale, lurid light, and cast a blue sulphurous glow along the woods, now giving to sudden view, the distant corners and nooks of the forest, now darting into the very faces of the wayfarers, now bursting into mid-air and illumining the clouds above, while all below was dark and shadowy.

And then muttering and moaning growled the distant thunder, far along the horizon, like a thing of supernatural life, and then like the rushing of a vast chariot, it was heard rolling overhead, while the vivid fancy of the maiden might well imagine, the shrill yells of the æry coursers as an invisible hand guided their dread course along the path of clouds, mingled with harsh, crashing and grating sound that broke upon the air, like the noise of the chariot wheels sweeping over their way of terror.

" Here we are—yonder's the wild glade of the Devil's Foot print !" the stranger exclaimed pointing ahead—" Jist look at that tremendous oak, flinging its branches right over our path. They say that tree's three hundred years old. D'ye believe it ? Some folks pretend to declare, that they have seen the devil himself, walking about in this neighborhood, in the guise of a plain countryman like me !"

" Mein Gott !" ejaculated Gotleib, and in an instant, his eye wandered to the feet of the traveller—" I tont see, te club foot !"

" The place fills me with a strange terror !" murmured Rose, as her eyes glistened and her lips parted—" The light falls strangely and wildly around the forest glade, and the shadows of the rocks, flit hither and thither like spectre-forms ! It is a terrible hour !"

The party were now passing under the shadow of the giant oak tree. A massive branch flung its foliage directly overhead, barely allowing room for the passage of the travellers beneath, while before them wrapt in gloom, or illumined by the lightning flash, lay the wild glade of the Devil's Foot Print, with its rugged rocks and towering trees, the shrubbery and brushwood on one side, the strange piles of granite on the other, and the platform rock, invested with the mysterious interest of superstition, rising white and spectre-like from the centre of the level sward.

" Look above n-a-bor did ever you see such an oaken branch ?" cried the stranger—" Isn't the foliage thick and gloomy ? A fit roosting place for the devil !"

" Te tuyfel !" exclaimed Gotlieb with a feeling of superstitious terror expressed on his countenance—" What know you of the tuyfel ?"

" He stands before you !" said the stranger, and at the same instant Gotleib was driven to the earth, by a heavy body that fell from the oaken limb of the giant tree, like a weight of lead, and ere he had time to raise an arm in his defence, three dark figures with blackened faces, were bending over him, a gag was thrust into his mouth his arms pinioned, and three bared knives glittering in the light, were held extended across his throat.

It was the work of an instant, performed with the celerity of a lightning flash. Rose gazed around, with a flashing eye and throbbing bosom. The horse lately ridden by the negro maid Phillis was without a rider, Gotlieb lay bound and pinioned at his horse's feet; and moving along the sward with hurried steps, were dark spectre-like figures, while standing at her very horse's head, with the glaring torch raised aloft, its dark smoke rolling overhead, in fitful gusts, was the stranger, his tall, thin form raised to its full height, the ragged cap, thrown from his brow, each lineament of his countenance changed and transformed by a wild expression that blazed like fire in his keen grey eye, severed his thin lips apart, and sent the nerves of his face, writhing and creeping beneath his skin, like things of the serpent brood.

"Man or devil, what mean you?" shrieked Rose, starting forward from her saddle, and gazing wildly at the strange figure before her—"What means this strange assault?"

"He died alone in the wild-wood!" shouted the stranger in a changed and hollow voice, and then a shriek of wild laughter broke upon the air— "Ha—ha—I—I am his avenger!"

A dark figure advanced from the shadow, a slouching hat drooped over his brow and a broad knife gleaming in his hand. Rose gazed upon his blackened face with a new terror, throbbing at her heart, and in an instant, a coarse, hard hand was thrust rudely over her maidenly bosom, she was dragged from her black steed with a ruffianly grasp, and borne hurriedly over the sward, while her dishevelled hair, fell wavingly over her neck and shoulders.

"Robinson—" shouted the ruffian—" Turn them horses loose in the woods —drag the Dutch scoundrel and the negro wench down into the hollow —another gag down their throats and a knife—if need be." The dark faced ruffian, sprang upon the rock, opening the entrance to the wild wood path—" Old man—" he cried in a muttered whisper—" the rebel skirmishers approach. You must remain by this rock and 'bide the brunt. Nay, my pretty beauty—none o' this strugglin'! No shrieking--no uproar! Damme I'm not in the mood for trifling! Away to the woods my lass! Mine you are now—mine you will be ever!"

CHAPTER FIFTH.

THE FATHER LOOKS UPON THE FACE OF HIS SON.

"I HEAR the sound of horses hoofs!" said Philip Walford, looking forth from the shelter of the overhanging shrubbery, "The rebels are on our track; they follow us up, like bloodhounds trained to the chase! You carried away the Dutchman and the wench into the hollow—did ye?" he continued gazing in the blackened faces of the six ruffians, who stood beside him on the rock; "It is well—for in five minutes, or less time, each man of us will have to fight for his life. So far all is well—" he murmured looking at the priming of his rifle—"And David has the maiden—I will have Wild-wood Grange!"

He dashed the brushwood aside, and again looked forth upon the glade. The sound of approaching hoofs, grew louder every moment, and ever and again it was mingled with the clank of arms, yet unheeding the sounds of gathering tumult, the clank of arms, or the roll of the thunder above, the stranger, remained standing in the centre of the glade, with the warm glow of the torch which he held in his extended hand, falling over his erect figure, while his eyes glared wildly and his lip quivered, as he murmured incoherently to himself.

"Ha—ha" he laughed—"It comes—the hour of my revenge! The work of my life—the thing for which I was born! The storm in the heavens gathers wild and terrible—Ha! Ha! The storm on the earth shall rival the darkness of * * * *! And over all mid storm and cloud, rides on the spirit of my revenge! 'He died alone in the Wild-wood!'"

And with that peculiar sneering laugh, he disappeared within the shadow of the surrounding woods.

"Look to th' primin' o' your rifles, boys!" whispered old Walford, "In a moment the rebels will reach the oaken tree; when they pass between the oaken tree and this rock, each one of you mark his man, and as I give the word—fire! How dark the air grows—the lightning no longer flashes along the glade—the moaning of the storm is hushed! In five minutes boys, we will either be masters of this band or—ha, ha, the devil will have us all!"

And as he spoke, while a muttered curse, ran around his band, the sound of horse's hoofs was heard directly beyond the oaken tree, mingled with the words of whispered conversation, the clank of swords and the pattering of bridle reins. The darkness was intense, and seemed almost tangible with its density. In a moment the forms of some half dozen horsemen, were dis cerned, guiding their steeds around the bend of the road, the form of each man and the figure of each horse, appearing shapeless and indistinct amid the darkness of the atmosphere, while their conversation, low and murmured broke vaguely on the ears of the tory band.

"It is the spot—the spot of our gathering!" muttered a stout, manly voice—"The night is gloomy as death!"

"In a few short moments, the light of an hundred torches, grasped by the bold hands of freemen, will light up the scene!" whispered a voice, stern and solemn in its tones.

"Like de berry debbil's dinin' room"—muttered another voice—"Sampson's face white as chalk, alongside sich a-night as this!"

"They know nothing of the affair of the girl!" muttered old Walford. "Now, boys—let your aim be secure—spare not a man of them! There —take aim by the lightning flash. *Fire!*"

A sudden flash of lightning threw a spectral light along the glade. It shone over the form of a tall, bold man, with a wrinkled visage, white hair waving in the breeze and a white beard drooping to his breast, while his strange garments, fashioned out of the skins of wild beasts, looked wild and ghastly in the blue light of the lurid flame. The form of a stout, muscular man, riding by his side, was also revealed in the light, and it flashed over the dark skin and ebon features of a giant negro, in the very act of examining the barrel of a glittering rifle, while around him were shown the faces and figures of the remainder of the band.

"Take aim by the lightning-flash! Fire!"

The flash gleamed along the glade—the stunning report of six rifles broke upon the air—all was darkness and shadow again—and the startling groan of a strong man in mortal agony, came swelling on the air, mingled with the sound of a heavy body falling to the earth.

"May the fiend take the night!" muttered old Walford. "Boys, your aim was false! Club your rifles—for your time is short!"

A yell of execration broke from the patriot band, two riderless steeds dashed wildly along the glade, and then there was a strange dread pause of a single moment. Another moment, and four bold steeds sprang forward, and four gleaming swords glittered thro' the darkened air.

"To the Rock—to the Rock!" shouted the Figure in the robe of furs— "and remember—the death of the haystack!"

"To the sword hilt, and to the last rifle ball!" echoed the band, with one deep-toned shout.

They rushed forward to the hidden rock; it arose to the breast of each prancing steed; they struck with their swords among the brushwood, but all was darkness' gloom and shadow. Again, they reined their steeds upward against the opposing rock, again were their swords raised and swept thro' the over-hanging brushwood, when a lightning-flash illumined the fearful scene with its red glare, and six stout and stalwart figures, stood disclosed on the rock, their faces craped, their clubbed rifles raised in the air, each arm nerved, and each hand clenched for the death-blow, while on the very edge of the rock, his thin figure trembling with agitation, and his face darkened by a slouching hat, stood Philip Walford, a singular picture of the Power of the Will, struggling with strong nervous fear, and physical cowardice. "Let each blow be sure!" murmured the old Walford, with his teeth set together. "To the skull and to the eyebrows, strike! No quarter!"

"Strike home—we have them!" arose the loud shout of the stalwart mechanic of the patriot band. "Strike for Washington and Right!"

And the half-human growl of a negro voice broke strangely upon the air.

The clubbed rifles descended, in darkness and in gloom they descended —they were met in mid-career by the upraised swords of the freemen, and then there was the sound of bodies falling to the earth, and horses darting madly aside, while a half fiendish yell broke from the giant-negro, as the groans of two dying men arose upon the storm-darkened air.

"Tories and traitors, ye will have our blood!" shouted one of the patriot band, whose face was veiled by a drooping plume, as he urged his horse toward the wood-hidden rock. "Ye will have our blood, but it shall be paid for, drop for drop, life for life!"

He struck the rowels into his horse's flanks; the steed sprang forward, with one wild effort, and while all around was darkness and confusion, he succeded in planting his fore feet upon the rock, where stood the tory band, nerving their arms for another blow of death.

The horseman leaned over the neck of his steed; he planted one foot upon the rock, and, in an instant, old Philip Walford felt the fingers of a strong man at his throat, clenched in a gripe, terrible as the grasp of death, and in his face, there flashed two bright eyes, vivid as coals of the living flame.

"His grasp is at my throat"—murmured old Walford. "He will throttle me! 'Tis like the grasp of death—like the grasp of a devil! My veins swell, and mine eyes are starting from their sockets!"

A low moaning call for aid died on his lips—tighter and closer wound the grasp of the plumed Horseman—he was dragging him from the rock—he was throttling him—his breath came thick and fast, in short convulsive gasps, and the senses of the old man swam, for a moment, in horrible confusion.

He stretched his hand wildly forth; it rested upon the hilt of the knife, inserted in the Plumed Horseman's belt, in a moment, the knife arose, gleaming like a light in the darkened air, and then it came hissing down with one wild sweep of the Tory's right arm, nerved by desperation and strengthened by superhuman hate.

One wild, terrible yell broke along the woods; it was the shriek of the Plumed Horseman; the knife had entered his throat behind the left ear. Ho fell prostrate along the rock, while his steed sprang away with a sudden bound.

As he fell, the storm burst over the woods, heralded by one terrible and blazing flash of lightning, which threw its lurid glare along the forest trees, and over the rocks and massive trunks of the wild glade.

Philip Walford stood erect upon the rock, his eye blazing and his hands upraised, dripping with blood, while around him was the terrible glare of lightning, and the scowl of angry men whose swords were whetted for his life.

Philip Walford gazed downward, he gazed upon his victim. The prostrate form of a young man was thrown across the rock, his arms outspread, his face turned to the thunder-riven heavens, while the knife stood out from the gash along his throat, and the blood spurted in a torrent from the wound.

Philip Walford gazed upon the face of the dying man. A low murmuring sound broke from his lips.

"I would have saved her!" he murmured, and then his eyes rolled ghastlily, and his chest throbbed with the throes of coming death.

Old Walford slowly lowered his head. A sudden and supernatural spell seemed to have taken possession of him, and the group of combatants withheld their blows for a moment, in anticipation of some scene of superhuman horror. Philip Walford knelt down on the rock. All was darkness for the lightning flash had passed away. He passed his hand over the face of the dying man—the levin flame again blazed along the heavens, and the grizzled hair of old Walford, swept along the visage of the patriot, contorted by the spasm of approaching death.

One long, one fixed gaze, and then from the very heart of Philip Walford, there shrieked, a wild and terrible howl, and a single exclamation burst from his lips—

"My son!" the yell of terror swelled along the woods, and the murderer raised his quivering eyes from the face of the dead. He raised his quivering eyes, and their glance was met, by the vision of a tall and majestic form, clad in white skins of the beasts of the forest, looming awfully in the light of the lightning flash, while the glare of two eyes, strange and spectral in their gaze, was fixed upon him, with a look that froze his very blood.

Around were the figures of the patriotic band, looking dim and spirit like in the light of the lightning flash : the form of the stout blacksmith, his steed half turned aside, the giant outlines of the negro's figure, with his black face glistening like the visage of a demon, while on the edge of the rock, grouped around the murderer and the murdered, stood the Tory-bravoes, starting aside with the impulse of a strange and sudden fear, and in the centre of the terrible picture knelt old Walford, his upraised face, fixed in an unearthly gaze upon that tall and majestic form, towering in the light, like a being of

14

the other world, an awful Intelligence sent back from the tomb, for the punishment of unnatural crime, the avenger of superhuman wrongs.

" They are around me !" shrieked Philip Walford raising his blood stained
hand on high—" The thunder yells above—the lightning flashes around—
each thunderbolt bears a spirit on its wings—each lightning flash reveals a
thing of Death !   Her face is gazing on mine—he stands before me—dread
and terrible he stands !   The grave gives back its dead—they have thronged
hither to witness this deed—ha, ha, ha !" How strange and hollow yelled
the laugh along the woods—" The son murdered at the father's feet—the
knife sticking in his throat !   And that father the murderer, and that father's
hand, the hand that dealt the blow !"

He said never a word more, but springing on his feet, shook his clenched
hand at the storm darkened heavens, with a wild gesture of defiance, invok-
ing the vengeance of the Awful Unknown, and then while the thunder rattled
above, and the rain came sweeping down, while the forest trees, swayed to and
fro, groaning under the terror of the hurricane, while all above was thunder
and flame, and all around was storm and death, the Son-murderer, sprang
backward from the rock and fled wildly along the wood, shrieking and yelling with horrible laughter as he fled.

CHAPTER SIXTH.

THE RUFFIAN HAND WOULD GATHER THE ROSE.

THE flickering light of a pine-torch, was cast around the apartment, disclosing the low ceiling, with the rafters, crumbled by decay, the narrow
walls, of rough boards, leaning inwards, with the storm beating thro' each
nook and crevice, while the straw that half concealed the earthen floor was
wet with damp and rain, and the scanty fire burning in the rugged hearth,
cast a melancholy glare around the lonely place, and flung strange and
flitting shadows, along the walls and ceiling.

Seated aside from the fire, on a rough block of oak, coarsely strewn with
damp straw, with the light of the pine torch, affixed to the wall at her back,
streaming over her head and shoulders, the maiden gazed wildly around the
apartment, with her hands clasped over her bosom of virgin beauty, as it
rose with its globes of snow, heaving in the flickering light, while her full
dark eyes shot quick and trembling glances, from beneath the shadow of
the quivering lashes, and with lips dropped apart, a cheek now flushed with
all the bloom of the damask rose, now pale with all the whiteness of the

uly, the fair girl, turned her head, to listen, as the shriek of the storm without fell upon her ear, and startled the silence of the lonely cabin.

"Now God save me !" the words fell tremblingly from her lips—"Hark —How the storm yells and shrieks along the woods ! The trees groan and totter—the wind sighs like a spirit, and the branches of the forest oak beat mournfully against the roof of this lonely cabin ! The ruffian will return— he will return with his band of merciless robbers ! I am at the mercy of a fiend in human form—they are ready for any deed of violence, any deed of death ! Oh, would to Heaven, it may be *death !*"

And as a fearful thought, flashed over the heart of the lovely girl, more lovely in her sorrow and loneliness, than in her joy and happiness, she gathered her dress, wet with rain, and torn by the branches of trees, close over her maidenly bosom, while a weight seemed pressing against her heart, and then came a wild suspicion, and that fearful thought again, mingling with a quiet picture of her peaceful home, now far away, the face of her father, and the dreamy countenance of her cousin Blanche.

She flung herself on her knees, her hands were upraised, and the torch fell upon her beaming face, all glowing with voiceless prayer, while her eyes shone with a clear liquid light, as her inmost soul, arose to Heaven, seeking that protection which man denied.

"May God help me !" murmured the maiden—"Or the terror of this night will drive me mad !"

The door suddenly opened, a footstep brushed along the straw, and a coarse rough hand was laid upon the maiden's shoulder.

"W-a-l—Rosy ! How d'ye feel g-a-l—" laughed a bold harsh voice— 'How are ye by this time, I'd like to know. Any better g-a-l ?"

Rose turned hurriedly round, and her eye rested upon the stout, burly form of David Walford, his face agitated with inward laughter, a brutal leer in his large rolling eyes, a sneer on his sensual lips, while his brow was darkened by a frown.

"David—oh David—" shrieked Rose, bounding on her feet—"Save me—save me !"

"That's what I will g-a-l—" chuckled the tory captain—"Save you ? To be sure I will. D'ye spose I'd a run off with you if I did not mean to save ye ? Come Rosey we're goin' to be married, we are. Ha, ha, g-a-l, how ye blush !"

Rose sprung aside from the bravo as if an adder had stung her, and in a flash, the whole plot of the ruffian, darted over her mind.

"David Walford are you crazed ?" she said in a low even tone of voice with a glance, that the Tory leader in vain endeavored to look upon without a quailing eye—"Know you that for the deeds of this night, you will have to render a terrible account ?"

"W-a-l—g-a-l, I'm obleeged t'ye for the hint—" said David Walford, drawing close to Rose—"And so to secure myself ag'inst all accidents I've concluded we'd better be married. I tell you g-a-l I've looked upon you often when you'd no idea of such a thing, and I love you. D——n my —— if I dont. Curnel Frazier would hash me up small, if he cau'ht me in this bisiness, but I kind o' 'spose he wouldn't be very hard upon yer lawful husband. Sounds well g-a-l? Hey?"

He gave a long shrill whistle, and in an instant a long slim figure, robed in a sweeping cloak of black, came gliding thro' the narrow door of the hut, with a scull-shaped hat, marked by a voluminous brim, concealing his face and features from the view.

"Now g-a-l here's the parson—" shouted Walford, as he leered sideways at the maiden—"Here's the jolly parson—he'll marry us in a trice—"

"Does thee take this man to be thee wedded husband?" a keen and biting voice whispered from beneath the shelter of the slouching hat—"In truth marriage is a divine institution. It is sacred maiden, tho' the place may be gloomy and the hour lonely. Thee takes this man, David Walford, to be thee weeded husband—does thee Rose Frazier?"

A proud smile curved the haughty lips of the maiden, and then her cheek was flushed, and her bosom rose throbbing to her dimpled chin.

"David Walford you are too mean a thing for my scorn—" she proudly said—"And ye think to frighten me with this childish mummery! Ha —ha—ha—"

"David Walford does thee take this maiden to be thy wedded wife?" asked the voice from the figure in black.

"Yes I do—" growled the ruffian—"I'll be d——d if I dont—"

"Then are ye man and wife. David Walford take thee bride by the hand—"

And as the figure in black glided from the lonely hut, silently as he had entered, the ruffian sprang toward the maiden, his large rolling eyes blazing with passion, and his brutal face, convulsed by a sensual expression, that gave it a greater resemblance to the visage of a hyena, than the countenance of a human being.

"Back ruffian!" shrieked Rose Frazier as her lovely form, arose swelling to its full stature, while her eye blazed like a thing of flame—"Come not a step nearer on the peril of your immortal soul!"

"Ha—ha—ha—" laughed Dave Walford—"And who shall save ye now? And where is there help for you now? Yes, proud beauty—scorned despised; and contemned as I have been by you, still must you be *my* bride Ha—ha—ha—yer lip is lovely maiden—yer cheek blushes like yer name sake gal, and yer my bride! Mine you are now—all airth cant save you! All * * * * cant tear you from me—

"God will protect me!"

And as the words fell from the maidens lips, the torch beams came streaming over her figure erected to its full stature, the full rounded arm upraised to heaven, the head erect, the eye flashing and the face crimsoned by a glow of emotion, that sent the warm blood flowing from her heart, while her beautiful bosom, rose swelling in the light, all alive with agitation, and trembling with excess of feeling.

The ruffian was struck with awe. There she was all alone with no protection but her own lovely arm, with no voice to plead the cause of innocence, but her own maidenly tones, with the light of her beauty, floating around her like a veil, alone and companionless she stood, and the ruffian dared not assail her form of loveliness, he dared not raise a hand to contaminate her with his touch.

It was but for a moment. He recovered his manner of reckless daring in an instant, and rushing forward, the fair and delicate hand of the maiden was clasped within his own, and his muscular arm was wound around her slender waist.

There was one wild pause of agitation and horror. The hot breath of the ruffian swept over the cheek of Rose Frazier, his arm was around her waist, his large rolling eyes, were glowering upon her with a glance that shone with the gleam of sensual passion. She felt her heart beating against her side as tho' it would burst from its confines, she felt her breath come thick and gaspingly from her throat, she felt her brain whirling, and her thoughts mingling together in a strange confusion, and then, with one wild impulse, scarce knowing what she did, Rose Frazier flung forth her arm, her hand sought the belt of the Tory-Leader, and then rose upward in the light, but the delicate fingers clasped a hunting knife, and the keen blade glittered like a meteor in the torch-beams.

It was her last resort, her last hope.

The knife descended, urged with the strength of a pure maiden's despair, it descended, but the blow was turned aside by the upraised arm of the ruffian. The arm was severed in a fearful gash at the wrist, and the blood spouted, and the sinews dangled from the wound.

"May d——n seize the hussy! She has maimed my left arm! Now, fair lady, you'll give me that knife if you please. No strugglin'. I tell you, you are mine; mine by ——!"

"Oh, save me now, my God!" The shriek arose from the maiden's lips, but closer wound the grasp of the ruffian. "Save me, oh, save me now my God!"

A wild shriek arose outside of the hut, a shriek that came thrilling over the heart of Rose, like the yell of a lost spirit. The door was flung open. A tall thin figure came rushing over the floor, with eyes madly glaring from their sockets, while slight locks of grizzled hair fell aside from a withered face, from which all color of life had fled, and as this strange figure rushed forward, two outstretched arms, with long bony fingers, grasped wildly at the vacant air.

"It is a spirit!" murmured Rose. "A spirit of the dead!"

" The light, the light—oh, give me light !" yelled the Apparition, cower
ing down beside the scanty fire, with his knees touching his chin, while his
outspread fingers were thrust toward the flame.   " You see, they chase me
in the dark—they shriek at me in the wind !   They flash in my face with
the lightnin'—they tramp over my head with the big, red thunder-bolt !
Near the light—nearer, nearer yet !   Let the flame whiz and whirl around
me !   It scares them—it scares them off !   *Her* face is so pale ; the eyes,
the large, black eyes are fixed upon me—his face is so ghastly—the brow
lowers at me !   Ha—ha—ha !   It drips in the flame—his blood—my own
son's blood !   Each drop becomes a face—each drop a ghastly face.   Ha !
Ha ! Ha !   The light —the light, oh, drag me from it—oh, veil mine eyes,
ha, ha, ha !"

And, struck with sudden awe, David Walford stood gazing downward
upon the prostrate wreck of his father, with a strange expression of terror
on his brutal countenance, as he gazed.   He had released his hold of the
maiden, and Rose Frazier stood alone, pale and trembling, while her thoughts
swam in wild confusion, as she gazed upon the strange scene passing within
the lonely hut.

" What in the name of the fiend's the matter with you !   Hey ?   Old
man ?" David Walford sank on one knee as he spoke.   " Who's been a-
huntin' you ?   Whar you struck ?"

" In the throat I struck him—in the throat !" muttered old Walford, and
he cowered along the damp hearth, with the crouching movement of a whipt
hound.

And David Walford, with his face to the fire, and his back to the maiden,
stooped down in the attempt to raise the form of his crazed father.

" Lady !" the soft whispered word reached the ear of Rose, and suddenly
turning round, she beheld the handsome form of a young soldier, attired in
a coat of green velvet, with a dagger and a glittering bugle at his side,
standing before her, while a slouching hat, with the dark plume falling back
from his brow, discovered a wild daring face, relieved by sweeping locks
of dark brown hair, marked by dark eyebrows, rich dark eyes, full cheeks
flushed by a spirit of adventure, and a prominent chin, well rounded and
determined in its outline.

" Lady—one word, and then away !   I tracked the villain to this den—
I waited an opportunity to foil his purpose.   This is the time, lady, for escape.   My horse stands ready at the door.   Let us away lady—away
thro' the woods !   In life or in death shall the arm of Clerwoode Le Clerc
be your defence and shield !"

Scarce knowing what she did, Rose suffered herself to be led toward the
door by the gallant young soldier.   In a moment, she was mounted on the
back of a stout war horse, in another instant had the young soldier flung
himself by her side, and then thro' the darkness and storm of the wild
forest, broke the sound of horse's hoofs in full gallop.

"D——n what noise is that?" shouted Dave Walford raising his head—
'The sound of horse's hoofs!"

"The prey has escaped!" said a mild soft voice, and the Figure in Black appeared in the doorway—"Thee is very dutiful to be 'tending there upon thee good father, when the shouts of the rebel pursuers is heard to the south—the sound of retreating hoofs to th' north! Thee prey has escaped!"

The Tory leader sprung to his feet, and a terrible oath broke from his lips, as he perceived that the maiden had fled.

"My horse Gilbert—my horse!" he shouted—"Your neck's as much in danger as mine! Old Frazier's not the man to forgive a thing o' this sort, We must catch that g-a-l come death or devil. Hark! They take the bye-road leading towards th' Wilmington and Phildelfy highway? They've got five good miles to go, afore they reach Chadd's Ford! Hark, Gilbert from the south? The ribbles are arter us—now for't!"

And as the sound of their horses hoofs, beating northward in full gallop, broke upon the air, mingling with the shouts of the patriotic band pursuing from the southern woods, old Walford crept nearer and nearer to the flame, fixing his eye upon its light, with a cold vacant glare, that would have froze the blood of a gazer to look upon.

"The storm's abroad without—and there's hell within!" he laughed—"Ho, ho, ho! Such a foolish fancy! That *he* had risen from the grave—that *she* with her ghastly face was, was——ah!" He shrieked a yell of horror, as half starting from his crouching position, he flung forth his long fingers toward the fire, while his eyes, all red and bloodshot lit up with a fire, that was not of earth—"There they are—now, now! All around me they gather, and—and—the knife sticks out from his throat!"

CHAPTER SEVENTH.

THE GATHERING OF THE MEN OF BRANDYWINE, BY THE ROCK OF THE DEVIL'S FOOT PRINT.

AROUND the lonely glade flashed the glare of an hundred torches, casting a crimson glow over the front of the encircling rocks, each peak, each projection, each rugged point, turned to burning red, while high above the lofty trees, waving in the storm, flung their thickly grown foliage, each quivering leaf and trembling branch, into the ruddy light, and over all, darkened and rolled the storm clouds, now sending forth the thunder peal, now brilliant and grand with the forked lightning, and then rocks, trees and sky, were al. one mass of sheeted flame.

Around the glade, shoulder to shoulder, and side by side, were grouped the men of the Brandywine, the farmers of Chester, a long line of stalwart forms, and sunburnt faces, each sturdy right hand grasping a glittering rifle, while the left hand, pointed to heaven, held aloft the blazing pine torch, with its columns of dark smoke winding away amid the shadows of the trees.

Beside the rock, in the centre of the glade, was the muscular form of the stout Blacksmith, his manly face, with its expression of dogged courage, glowing in the light of the torch which he raised on high, while at his side, silent and motionless, the colossal form of the negro Sampson, with its muscular chest, each rugged sinew and thewe, bared to the waist, was disclosed in the full glare of the torch-beams, one stalwart arm, resting upon the handle of a glittering scythe, while the other was laid upon the head of a magnificent dog, which crouching by its master's side, stout in form and white as snow, with short ears, a keen blazing eye, wide mouth, marked by teeth of ivory whiteness, seemed prepared for the chase of man or beast, as keenly snuffing the air, the noble animal scented the smell of human blood.

The scene was grand and terrible. The light of the hundred torches flitting from the rocks, to the trees above, falling along the green of the glade in sudden flashes, or casting a fixed glare over the stout forms of the yeomen, clad in their rustic attire, with each man his hunting knife, his belt of leather and his powder horn; the rock in the centre, with the bundle of sable resting upon its summit, the contrasted group circling around its base, the tall blacksmith, the giant negro, and the snow white hound, the strange silence that reigned along the glade; each lip stern and determined in ex. pression, each voice hushed, and every footstep firm, all formed a scene of strange and peculiar interest, while the sounds that broke the silence of the atmosphere, the *sough* of the wind thro' the trees, the rolling of the thunder, and the crash of falling timber, added awe and terror to the scene.

The torches flickered suddenly to and fro, where two tall rocks arising against each other, opened a passage to the stream beyond, and as the yeomen beneath the shadow of these peaks of granite, stepped aside for a moment, a tall and majestic figure advanced toward the light, and the torch beams shone over the high forehead and determined visage of Colonel Frazier, while a subdued murmur of greeting ran around the throng.

He advanced to the Rock of the Devil's Foot Print, with a calm and measured step, and then ascending the Rock, his proud form towered to its full height as he glanced with a swelling chest and a glistening eye upon the scene around him.

" Men of Brandywine we have met for Vengeance !" The words broke from his lips in a calm, determined tone.

"For Vengeance, for Washington and Right!" echoed the hundred voices of the gallant yeoman band.

"For Vengeance for Washington and Right!" returned Colonel Frazier "Dwelling in the quietude of our own lonely valley we thought the storm of war might pass over our heads—" he continued in a tone of bold and manly eloquence—"We thought the storm of war might pass over our heads. We shared not in the strife. We invoked not the vengeance of the Invader. But his footstep has been stamped upon our soil, and the print of blood soddens the ground. His banner—the banner of the red-cross has waved in the air of our peaceful plain, and the smell of human blood is on the breeze. At the dead hour of night, an old man—an unoffending old man—one-armed and defenceless was dragged forth from his peaceful home —the flames arose blackening to the heavens, and the crumbling remains of the aged soldier, strewed the earth, the sod of his homeside, while the fire hissed and crackled around the peeled skull and the scarred bones. He was burned alive. We have met to revenge his death—we have met to carry fire and sword and death into the camp of his murderers, we have met to rear the gibbet for his assassins, the gallows for his butchers!"

A mingled shout and a yell ran around the group, and each man grasped his rifle with a firmer hold, and then each lip was compressed, and each brow curved in a frown.

"Men of Brandywine—" said Colonel Frazier in a bold and commanding tone—"Whom do ye accuse of the murder of the one-armed school master Jacob Mayland?"

The stout Blacksmith, Iron Tom o' Dilworth corner advanced in front of the Rock, and raising his hand on high, glanced around upon the long line of determined faces as he boldly spoke.

"I accuse one Richard Hamsdorff, a sergeant in the British army, one Gilbert Gates, a spy in the employ of the British, living near Brenton's Ford, and one David Walford, captain of a band of Tory Partizans,—I accuse these men of the wilful murder of Jacob Mayland, the one-armed school-master of Chadd's Ford! And for the truth of my charge I call every living man in this wild wood to witness!"

"Do ye witness the truth of this accusation, thus solemnly made, while the storm rolls above—while the earth is still around? Raise each man his rifle, and point each man his knife in the air, that will support the truth of this charge to the very death!"

"We do witness the accusation! Hamsdorff, Gates and Walford are the murderers!"

And each rifle was raised, and each knife was pointed in the air, while Sampson swung his scythe on high, and patted his dog on the head.

"What shall be the punishment of the murderers?"

"Death!"

"The old man died without a moment's warning. He was hurned from

15

the silence of his chamber to the scene of death—he was hunted like a dog thro' the passage of the cellar—in another moment he was burned alive within the haystack.   How shall the murderers die ?"

The Blacksmith raised his voice on high, and shook his glittering knife in the air.

" They shall die on the spot where the hand of the avenger shall first overtake them.   Without prayer, without warning, without mercy shall they die.   Cut down in their sins and crime, when the iron is hottest—when the fire of life burns brightest !   And if there's a death more terrible than that which old Jacob Mayland died, then let them die that death !"

" Dey shall shall die by this scythe !" Sampson muttered—" Marcy for de wild bar, marcy for de tiger and de painter—none for the Britisher ! Sampson fader prince in he own country—prince nebber forget kindness, nebber forgive wrong !   Nebber !"

And then while the storm clouds rolled darker above, Colonel Frazier raised his broadsword on high, and as the memory of British tyranny and British wrong, came flashing over the soldier's mind, the sinews of his good right arm, seemed to creep and writhe beneath the skin, as grasping the sword-hilt with a vice like grasp, he shook the glittering blade in the air:

" Men of Brandywine !" he shouted—" circle round this Rock, and take the solemn oath !"

And ere the brave yeomen were aware, a tall and majestic figure clad in a robe of skins, with a noble face and a commanding brow, stood at the shoulder of Colonel Frazier, glancing with his keen flashing eyes around the group.

" Men of Brandywine behold the mercy of the Briton—the justice of King George !"

And stooping slowly down, he flung aside the covering from the blackened mass, resting on the top of the rock.

A yell of horror, ran around the throng, as the torchlight, flashed upon a mangled mass of scarred flesh, with the peeled skull and whitened bones, glaring ghastily in the ruddy light.

There was one wild yell of horror, one wild rush forward, every man moving with the same impulse, and around the Rock of the Devil's Foot Print, with rifles brandished on high, and knives glittering in the air, circled the hundred yeomen, eagerly pressing onward, and gazing with flashing eyes and knit brows upon the mangled carcase of the schoolmaster, while over all, towered the lofty frame of Colonel Frazier, side by side with the magnificent form of the unknown stranger, in his wild forest robes.

Each eye was fixed upon the corse, every gaze was centered on the blackened heap, when the negro Sampson started suddenly forward, and leaning over the ghastly skull, stretched forth his right arm with its outline of iron muscle and sinew.   In a moment, his hunting knife had passed like a flash over the ebon skin, and the warm blood spurting from the wound, fell, drop by drop, on the skull of Jacob Mayland, the one-armed schoolmaster. The eyes of the negro flashed, and his dark countenance worked as with the throes of a death spasm.

"Sampson mingle he blood wid de blood ob de dead. Sampson hab but one life—dat for de one-arm schoolmaster. Sampson hab but one death—dat for de one-arm schoolmaster! Revenge for his murder—all Sampson ib, for all Sampson die for! Revenge!"

The example was irresistible. It was no time for cold calculation, no moment for cautious prudence. A terrible murder had been done, the blood of the yeomen had been roused, and by every word and sign, they panted to confirm themselves in their purpose of revenge.

"What, will ye suffer the negro to be a-head of you in the good work?" shouted the stout blacksmith, glancing around on the excited throng. "Let us bind ourselves to the deed, by mingling our blood with the blood of the dead! Revenge for the death of Jacob Mayland! Revenge to the last ball of the rifle—revenge to the last stroke of the knife!"

He flung his right arm over the blackened mass—his knife flashed in the light—the warm blood fell, drop by drop, on the skull of the murdered man

And, wildly pressing forward, each man bared his right arm of iron muscle, and in a moment, the mingling blood-drops fell in a shower o'er the corse of the dead, and Colonel Frazier stooped, and the Stranger leaned forward, and their arms were bared, and their blood mingled with the blood of the patriot band, pattering down upon the skull of the one-armed schoolmaster.

And the dog sprang forward and lapped the blood, and howled, and man and beast were bound together in the work of vengeance.

At this moment, the storm clouds rolled away overhead, in vast and heaving masses, and the calm stars looked forth upon the place, and then, the bright and beautiful moon shone over the forest glade, over the bared arms and the raised knives, over each determined countenance and manly form, — the scene was grand and terrible.

"In life or in death——Revenge for the murder of Jacob Mayland! Death to his murderers!"

Like the sound of bursting thunder, arose the fierce shout on the air of night, and the torches flashed on high, and the rifles were upraised, and again, and yet again, arose that thunder-shout ——

"Revenge for the murder of Jacob Mayland! Death to his murderers! Vengeance, Washington, and the Right!"

A hurried step ran along the glade, and the form of a stout man, with his dress all torn, and his face all wild and haggard, came rushing toward the light, and Colonel Frazier recognized the face of Gotlieb Hoff.

He sprang to the side of the soldier, and a few quick whispered words passed between the twain.

" Men of Brandywine—" shouted Colonel Frazier raising his head, while a warm glow flashed over his face—" One word and then to horse! My daughter has been spirited away by a band of tory-bravoes. The same band that attacked a portion of our company, in this wild glade half an hour since."

" How say you, Blacksmith, was your pursuit of the ruffians unavailing," He continued suddenly turning round to Iron-Tom o' Dilworth Corner— " Had you no suspicion of this outrage ?"

" I confess the Refugees, had the 'vantage o' us—" spoke Iron-Tom— " In the fust place in their ambush—in the next place in their retreat. All we could do was to return to this glade, and send the wounded off to Wild-Wood Grange as you directed. Had I a suspicion of this outrage? By the G * * that made me, Iron-Tom o' Dilworth Corner would not be standing here now, had he dreamed of sich a thing in the least pertikler. All we found o' the refugees was old Walford, half-dead and altogether crazy in a hut, a half mile from this place. But to horse boys—no time's to be lost! And let us teach the tory-robbers a lesson they'll never forget! Who knows but that Hamsdorff, young Walford and smooth Gilbert Gates are consarned in this very business ! To horse, to horse !"

" To horse, to horse !" shouted Colonel Frazier—" Scatter in every path, spread along every highway, scour the woods, and sweep the valley of the Brandywine! To horse volunteers of Brandywine to horse !"

CHAPTER EIGHTH.

BLANCHE WALFORD AND GEORGE OF MONTHERMER.

" The night is dark and the storm rolls terribly above! Look from the window Mary—see, how dark and heavy sweep the gloomy clouds !"

" And the tall trees around the mansion, Miss Walford, rise strange and shadowy in the darkness. Hark ! That terrible thunder peal! Said you Colonel Frazier would not be home till midnight ?"

" He may not be home until to-morrow morn. How silent and still every thing seems about the mansion—the lamplight falls gloomily around my chamber—and the storm beats on the window-panes. We are alone Mary —and strange fears flash across my brain—"

' Strange fears ! Ah me, no fear however dark or terrible can be strange after—God of mercy help me—after the scene of last night !"

" *His* death will be avenged! Most terribly and fearfully will it be avenged—but see! Come close to the window Mary—Is that the form of a man, flitting along under the shadow of the trees, in the grounds without the mansion?"

" The storm-clouds are breaking away above us, and a beam of moonlight falls along the plain of Brandywine! It falls over the desolate hearthsider and over the green sward, blackened by the embers of the haystack—"

" There Mary, I see that figure again! It flits along under the shadow of the trees—"

" Miss Walford, I thought I saw something gleam from among the shelter of the brushwood. Look! I see it again—the gleam of arms—"

" And men are hurrying around the lonely mansion! Hark—the tread of armed men—no hand is near Mary to protect us now from British ravage —the valley people have all hurried away to the scene of the patriotic gathering—"

" Hist! Miss Walford—I hear the sound of voices!"

And while Blanche drew nearer to the side of the orphan girl, and flinging her full rounded arm around her maidenly neck, pressed closer and yet closer to her bosom, the hushed sound of low muttered voices was heard without, and the subdued tread of hurrying feet, mingling with an occasional clank, like the jingling of a bridle-rein, or the rattling of a sword.

Nearer drew the maidens one to the other, the lovely Polly with her full and swelling form, her locks of brown, and her eyes of blue, twining her arms round the queenly form of Blanche, with her hair of lustrous blackness, her eyes full, dark and dreamy in their glance, while the loosened folds, of her robes of white, displayed the bewitching outline of her shape, gleaming thro' the dim light of the lonely chamber, with a fascinating combination of soft tints of light and delicate masses of shadow.

" Hark! Miss Walford there is the sound of feet on the balcony without —the rose branches rustle and quiver, and—"

" I fear some terrible evil, even now a hovering over my head. I fear— oh God I fear—"

" Fear nothing for I am at your side!" The tones of a calm and deep toned voice, broke on the hushed and silent air.

Blanche turned hurriedly round. She turned with a strange trembling feeling at her heart, with gasping breath and a cheek now flushed with all the blush and bloom of womanhood, now pale as snow-white alabaster.

Standing before her, was the commanding figure of a young and handsome man, with a form of manly beauty, upraised to its full height, the right hand extended toward her, while the left, rested upon the sword-hilt of gold; with full, black eyes, flashing and glowing from beneath dark brows, fixed in a strange and settled expression, with a compressed lip and a face, rigid and death-like with an immoveability of feature, that betokened strong internal feeling, and struggling passion, the stranger stood silent and motionless gazing upon the beautiful countenance, and the queenly form of Blanche Walford.

She returned his gaze with a glance mingling a thousand feelings in one. Their eyes met, still silent and motionless he stood, regarding her with the same settled glance, which seemed as tho' meant to read her heart of hearts.

And while face to face, they gazed upon each other, a manly form, clad in a dress of scarlet, with a handsome face, and a gallant air, glided from the balcony along the room, and in an instant, a muscular arm was wound around the waist of Mary Mayland, while the hand of a soldier was placed over her mouth with its pouting lips and bewitching outline.

" Now, d-o-n-t ye be n-o-isy"—drawled a soft, indolent voice. " Now, d-on't you struggle, my pretty lass. 'Pon honor, it's all in such bad taste."

And as he spoke, despite the maiden's struggles, he bore her from the room along to the balcony, without the action being noticed by Blanche, or the Stranger, as gazing upon each other, with a glance which seemed like a spell, they were dead to all other sights, and breathless with a strange emotion.

" What mean you?" said Blanche, low and tremblingly, and then her eye flashed and the warm blood came flushing over her cheek. " What means your presence in the chamber of an unprotected maiden, at this un-wonted hour?"

The Stranger advanced. He essayed to speak. Wild thoughts blazed from his eye, and a whole world of burning eloquence seemed about to fall from his lips. He advanced. He paused and hesitated, and then flung himself wildly at the maiden's feet.

" Blanche"—he shrieked—" Blanche, I love you !"

And her hand was clasped within his own, and his dark eyes, upturned, were gazing in her own.

" With a love that danger cannot appal, that difficulty cannot daunt, that death cannot dismay ! With a love that overleaps all human forms, that sacrifices rank, and makes a mock of power and grandeur, love I you, Blanche—mine own Blanche !"

And the maiden trembled, and gazed upon him with a feeling of unutter-able agony. and then came the trembling words —

" God help me—I love you not !"

" George Percy, of Monthermer, is at your feet. He takes your hand, he looks upon your face of beauty. He whispers to your ear the words he never before spoke to woman's ear. He casts aside rank as a bauble, he resigns the power and grandeur of lordly birth as a thing of no value. He woos Blanche Walford—he asks her to give him this fair hand—and with the fair hand to bestow the love of that stainless heart !"

"I cannot—cannot love you!"

"He loves you, maiden, with a love that his heart never knew, until he gazed upon your beauty. You are his Fate—his Destiny! Oh be not also his—Doom—the beautiful instrument of a terrible Judgment! You hold over his soul in power which has passed beyond his will, or his control. It urges him on to any deed—it fills him with a desperate resolve. Yes—yes —Blanche Walford—you must be mine! By the awful Power of a Will, resolved to any deed, and strong for the accomplishment of any purpose, I tell you, maiden, you must be mine!"

"Never!"

"Blanche, you know not what you say. Maiden, you are the Fate of George Percy of Monthermer. It arises before me now—now, while in this lonely chamber, kneeling at your feet, I plead my love. I see it all, clear and vivid as on the night of the ocean storm ——"

He leaned forward, and while over his face there gathered a strange, dread expression, his voice sank to a low, muttered whisper, as tho' he communed with a spirit.

"God help me!" whispered Blanche—"his voice fills me with terror! His eyes glare wildly, and his face is not like the face of human thing!"

"I see it all! It arises before me—the dream—the ocean-dream! The vision that has swayed my fate with its terrible Prophecy! A calm and lovely valley, blushes in the beams of the afternoon sun. Pleasant hills arise around, undulating they rise—woods, green and luxuriant, crown the hill-tops, and over all, arches the autumnal heavens. A plain fabric, rugged and rustic in form, arises on the hillside, and in its front there spreads a lonely grave yard. And the clouds of battle roll over the valley, and the musquet shot, and the cannon glare, turn the clouds to blood. The fight sweeps into the lonely grave yard—it deepens—it thickens! A form leads on the British charge—that form is mine! A corse falls, crimsoned and ghastly, along the tombless graves! The corse is mine—and then, all is gloom and mist and shadow ——"

"The vision is terrible as mine own!" murmured Blanche.

"And thro' the mist and the gloom and the shadow, glides on, one fair and dreamy form. She smiles on the corse—it springs to life, and the valley again is calm, and the sky again is cloudless. That form is thine, Blanche Walford—you alone may turn back my fate! You alone may arrest my doom! Oh, Blanche, love me!"

"My Lord, all this is idle and vain—I cannot, cannot love you!'

Lord Percy turned his head aside for a moment, and his lips writhed and his woven brows, gave a dark and terrible gloom to his brow.

"Maiden—" he cried leaning forward, and pressing her hand with a convulsive grasp—"For your sake will I renounce the British name. Aye start not, nor gaze on me with such wild surprize—for your sake will I unsheath this sword under the banner of Washington! My name a byeword in the land of my birth—a traitor—a rebel—my land confiscated, and the axe and the gibbet, glimmering and blackening, over the hearth of my childhood—all this, all this Blanche Walford will I dare for your sake!"

"Oh would to God I could love him!" murmured Blanche—"If ever man loved woman, he loves me. And I cannot, cannot—God knows I can not love him!"

Oh, how beautiful she looked, as standing there in all her queenly loveli ness, her form inclined gently aside, her glance of deep emotion, was fixed upon the kneeling figure of the handsome Lord, who grasped her hand, in that lone chamber, while their eyes met, and mingled their strange and contrasted glances.

"Lady will you love?"—said Percy as his manner of wild agitation subsided into a deep and settled gaze and tone—"Lady will you love me?"

"Release my hand my Lord—away from this chamber!" And as she spoke the form of the proud girl, rose swelling to its full height, and her tone was dignified with energy and command. "My Lord, this interview—un-forseen and untimely—has been protracted too far, already. This very moment my Lord, I command you to quit my chamber—"

He arose slowly to his feet, and a bitter smile passed over his lips.

"And did ye think to frighten me with words of maidenly command?" He sneered as he said the words. "Release your hand? I will but to clasp it with a firmer grasp—'Quit your chamber? I will Ladye—but you go with me!"

"My Lord you forget yourself!" Blanche exclaimed with a proud smile —"An American maiden is never unprotected from insult!"

"Away and away, ere the morrow's dawn, shall we flee!" And as in a tone of wild enthusiasm he spoke, his arm encircled the waist of the maiden—"Away and away to the wild-wood, where the eternal solitudes of the forest, are untrodden by the footsteps of civilized man! Rank will I for-sake, death will I dare for you Blanche! Away to the wilderness with me shall you fly—in the wild-wood the gold of George Percy will rear us a home, and there shall you be mine, and mine alone! Nay maiden—my purpose is firm—struggle not, nor endeavor to free your waist from my arm! My steed stands ready without—and ready without, wait twenty good soldiers, whose swords, whose lives are mine!"

In vain was the struggle of Blanche, in vain her efforts to release her form from the grasp of the desperate man. With one stride he sprang toward the window of the chamber, and Blanche felt his arm wind closer around her waist, while his dark eyes were fixed upon her with a gaze all flame, all passion.

"Love rules you not—" cried Lord Percy with a sneer—" My Will shall rule you, and my Will points to the far away paths of the wild forest—"

" I hear the sound of horse's hoofs—" murmured Blanche—" The clatter of hoofs and the clank of swords ! I may yet be saved !"

" There is no time to be lost—" cried Percy with an oath—" No power can save you now proud girl—no foe may stand in my path—"

" Death stands in your path !" The tones of a deep toned and determined voice broke upon the air, and at the same instant George Percy of Monthermer was hurled aside from the maiden, by a strong and sudden blow, and Blanche Walford beheld, standing in the full glow of the lamplight, a tall and imposing form, clad in a uniform of green velvet, with a slouching hat and plume drooping over his bold forehead, while his dark hazel eye, was fixed in a steady glance on the face and form of the English Lord.

Blanche Walford glanced upon the stranger, and a strange feeling came gathering round her heart, and flashed like lightning over her brain. She looked upon the stranger, and beheld the form of her Dream.

Percy rushed forward, and was met, midway, by the Stranger, also rushing forward toward the light. There was no time for words of parley, or muttered imprecations. Both swords rose glittering in the light, both arms were nerved for the blow and Blanche Walford stood contemplating the scene with every emotion of surprise and terror.

" Your life or mine !" shouted Percy, as his sword swung around his head—in mid-air it swung—when, sudden as a lightning flash, his good right arm dropt senseless by his side, his lips parted, and his eyes glared from beneath the woven brows, with a wild expression of terror and astonishment, as tho' the gazer, while looking on the face of the stranger, recalled some strange and terrible dream.

Blanche gazed upon the Stranger. His eyes were flashing with the same wild expression that agitated Percy's countenance, his brow of manly dignity was darkened by the same wild frown, his lips were also dropt apart, and with a nerveless arm, his sword swung loosely to the floor.

" Man or devil—what are you"—shouted George of Monthermer, extending his arms with a wild gesture. " I look upon you"—he continued, in a muttered tone—" and the form of my father stands before me !"

" Huzzah for bold Randulph the Prince !" the clear shout of an hundred voices, burst like thunder on the silent air, without the mansion.

" The rebels are upon us, be G-a-wd !" yelled a single hoarse and rugged voice. " To your swords, my boys—be G-a-wd !"

" They must always meddle with something nice"—drawled a soft indolent voice. " Such bad taste !"

" Strike troopers—strike for Randulph the Prince—strike for gallant La Fayette—strike for Mad Anthony Wayne !"

And while the noise of the sudden tumult, the clanking of swords, the sound of pistol shot, and the pattering of horses' hoofs, swelled fiercer and louder on the air without, Blanche Walford beheld the tall and commanding form of the Stranger—that form which she had beheld in her Dream—sweeping onward to the side of the English Lord, and then, bursting the mutual spell that bound their arms, their swords joined in conflict, and foot to foot, and eye to eye, they fought, each man for his life.

" The likeness between them is strange and terrible !" murmured Blanche. " The Stranger is like the Lord, and, on the brow of each soldier, there rests the same dread expression of some supernatural doom !"

The contest was short and decisive. Lord Percy parried the blows of his antagonist, and exerted all his skill in returning thrust for thrust, but closer and closer to his side, pressed Randulph Waldemar, and nearer to his breast, gleamed the sword of the Partizan Chief, whose flashing eyes and compressed lips, betokened the interest he felt in the struggle. Again the sword waved on high—it descended, and shivered to the hilt, the weapon of Lord Percy, fell in fragments to the floor.

Randulph sprang forward, with a flashing eye and an outstretched arm, he sprang forward, and a wild desire to take the life of the man who stood before him, had fired his soul.

" Die, lordling—slave of the tyrant, die !" he shouted, and the keen blade circled his head, preparatory to the last fatal lunge.

" George Percy of Monthermer fears not death !"   And as he spoke he smiled and folded his arms across his breast.

" Man—I cannot kill ye !" shouted Randulph Waldemar—"I look upon your face, and the vision of a Dream is before me ! Away and save your life ! Away—the shouts of my soldiers arise without—away by the eastern balcony ! Speak not—breathe not a word—but away !"

" And when again we meet—" said Lord Percy in a low and thrilling whisper—" The time will be the hour of Death !"

" Strike for bold Randulph the Prince !" arose the thunder shout without the mansion—"

" Over them boys—upon them—over them !" rang the deep-toned war-cry of Mad Antony Wayne.

" Mon Dieu !   A blow for Washington !" mingled the hurrah of La Fayette, and then there was one wild storm of clashing swords mingling with the sound of retreating hoofs, the quick and piercing pistol shot, the cry of mortal agony, and the yell of defiance.

And as Lord Percy, strode slowly toward the western balcony, the chamber was filled with armed men circling at the back of Randulph the Prince, who stood holding Blanche Walford in his manly arms, while his face fired with a feeling of unutterable passion, as gazing downward upon her face of dreamy beauty, the eyes closed in a death-like swoon, and the ruby lips slightly parted, the thought flashed over his soul that for that lovely form, death would be willingly faced, that for that dreamy countenance, not a peril in heaven and earth, but might be dared, not a doom, however terrible and dark that might not be defied.

"Well, boys we've driven them off!" cried the bold cheerful tones of General Wayne—"I take it, they'll not try this game again in a hurry!"

"We've driven them off General—" said a well known voice, as the form of Colonel Frazier advanced to the light—"But the assassin Hamsdorff has escaped—my child has been stolen away by British ruffians, and the peaceful silence of my home violated! Away—men of Brandywine—to horse, and let my child, be restored to her home ere the light of another morn!"

As he spoke a shout of execration broke from the soldiers, as they beheld the majestic form of George of Monthermer, standing near the window of the western balcony. He regarded the group with a smile of quiet contempt and bitterness.

"Upon the ravisher!" shouted the soldiers with one impulse—"Upon the coward and the robber!"

And they sprang forward, and a score of broadswords glittered in the air. Percy betrayed no sign of emotion. He stood silent and motionless, a clear glance in his eye and a cool smile of contempt on his lip.

Randulph raised his gaze from the beautiful face of Blanche Walford. His eye flashed, and his brow gathered a frown, as he glanced upon the advancing forms of his men, with swords upraised and rifles levelled.

"Riders of Santee, my word is pledged to this man—" he said in a calm deliberate voice—"Advance not a step nearer, on the peril of my honor!"

It was a strange and impressive scene. The light falling full and strongly over the form of Randulph the Prince, with his arms wound around the slight yet budding figure of the beautiful maiden, each fold of her snow white dress, each outline of his attire of velvet, shown in beautiful relief; the form of Lord Percy, standing slightly apart, facing the group, also shown in the full glare of the lampbeams, the strange frown on his brow, and the bitter smile on his lip, while on the remote side of the apartment, gleaming vague and shadowy in the darkness, was the manly form of Colonel Frazier, the iron figure of Wayne, with the lines of his bold visage disclosed in the light; the slight form and youthful face of La Fayette, appearing amid the throng of daring soldiers, with jovial Gotleib Hoff, standing aside in the background, his muscular arms thrown around the waist of Pretty Polly Mayland, and over the whole scene, the mingled gleams of light, and masses of shadow threw an air of solemn and imposing mystery.

"Aye, aye, let one viper of the scarlet brood escape!" exclaimed Mad Antony Wayne with a smile—"Even at this moment, the troops of the

Continental host, are crowding over the plain of Chadd's Ford. There will be a battle anon—and then in the field of death, foot to foot and hand to hand, will the men of Brandywine, teach the British ravagers, the meed of foul outrage and atrocious wrong !"

"We will meet again Sir Captain—" cried Lord Percy as his face trembled with emotion, ere he proceeded to spring thro' the balcony window— "We will meet where the battle rages hottest, and the fight swells most terrible—"

"For me, or for you—" cried Randulph, as his face warmed with the same wild feeling that blazed over the visage of the Lord—" For me or for you there is a—Doom."

"And that doom" cried George of Monthermer, "is the doom of the unwept grave and the nameless Death !"

END OF BOOK THE SECOND.

EPISODE.

It was the night—the Eleventh of September.

The Earl stood beside the door of the second chamber, the light uplifted by old Bernard, flinging its ruddy glow over his pale face. For he was pale, and weak and trembling. His white hairs were glued to his brow, by cold, beaded drops moisture. In two brief months, he had grown ten years older. Age, agony, remorse; were written upon his wrinkled cheek and woven brow.

He stood beside the second door, his hand trembling on the lock. Not a word was spoken, by the old servant; all throughout the castle was terribly still. At last, an expression like the determination of despair, came over the face of the Earl. The lights in his hand, he unlocked the door, and entered the room.

"Wait without," he said in a hollow voice, as he closed the door, "and let no one enter, on the peril of your life!"

Bernard waited without, Thus on every return of this terrible anniversary, he had waited for twenty years. He listened for a long while, not a sound was heard; but at last a groan, so deep, so heart-wrung, so tremulous, came through the thick panels of the door.

The hours passed on, their awful silence only broken, by the indistinct sounds, proceeding from the second chamber. Deep groans, heart-broken sighs, half-muttered words; these pierced the old servant's ear and chilled his blood.

At last all was still. The hours of the night wore slowly on. Morning came. The Earl was still, enclosed within the walls of that fatal chamber. The sun shone warmly into the room, over the figure of old Bernard, and yet his master did not come. Noon was there, and yet no sound was heard. Bernard stooped down, listened; not even a sigh, not a breath disturbed the silence of the room.

At last he placed his hand upon the lock and shuddered. What was he about to do? To enter that room was death; the Earl had sworn it, a thousand times.

At last trembling from head to foot, he pushed open the door. All was dark within, darker than night or the grave. Bernard listened—no sound! He advanced into the darkness, feeling his way with his extended hands. The echo of his footsteps frightened him. Presently his hands reached an object, which

(125)

arose in the night of that fearful room. It was a coffin. The upper part of the lid was open; he felt the gold plate on the front; and then, with palsied hands, the cold face of the dead.

He started with a gurgling cry of horror. His foot touched a prostrate form. He raised it, bore it from the room, and beheld the insensible face of his master, glaring upon him with glassy eyes. He laid him on the bed and watched by his side until the setting of the sun. Then for the first time, the Earl moved his lips.

"Bernard," he said in a husky voice, "has she gone?"

"Who my lord?" gasped the affrighted servitor.

"Who?" thundered the Earl, springing up in the bed, "Who! Can you ask me, that! The Countess—married but four years—and then! Found dead in her bed one morning, with the mark about her throat, The mother of Percy, has she gone—tell me, has that tall woman, with the mark about her throat, retired from her *husband's* chamber?"

That word *husband*, was pronounced with a frightful contortion.

A light shone into the old servant's soul. All at once, the dark mysteries of years, dissolved like rolling clouds.

"She has gone!" he whispered, determined to humor the phrenzy of his lord.

"Bernard, she conversed with me all night. She told me words that burned my blood. Get holy men to pray, that I may die, before the fourteenth of November—for ah"—

He fell over in the bed, muttering with a groan these words:

"For now, even now, the clod is on his breast, the grave-worm about his brow!"

BOOK THE THIRD.

THE BATTLE MORN.

SEPTEMBER THE ELEVENTH, 1777.

CHAPTER THE FIRST.

THE GROUP OF BRAVE MEN CLUSTERED UNDER THE GIANT CHESNUT TREE.

IT broke calmly and it dawned in quiet beauty—the day of battle—with the sky all cloudless and serene, arching above lovely valley and grassy plain, while around the hill-tops of the Brandywine, curled and waved in spiral columns, the thin light wreaths of autumnal mist, winding away into the glow of the uprising sun, as the first glimmer of his beams tinted the azure of the zenith.

The first beams of morning light, faint and dim, were revealing the beauty of uprising woods, winding rivulet and lovely plain, with the rustic cottage peeping here and there, from amid the luxuriance, of embosoming verdure, while the vast figure of a giant chesnut tree, with a trunk like the proud column of some Druid fane, with branches, wide, massive and gnarled by age, covered with foliage, and thick with broad green leaves, rose towering in the air, from the summit of a grassy hill. Under its broad shadow were grouped a band of men, clad in military costume, each face the face of a hero, each form the form of a soldier, while the steeds of the band, the hand of every warrior resting upon the empty saddle, circled around the spot, their heads aloft, their manes waving to the breeze, as the eye flashed and the nostril quivered with the excitement of the coming battle.

The light of the breaking dawn, stole faint and dimly around the spot. The figures of the warrior band, rose tall and grandly in misty shadow, with each scarred and veteran face, turned toward the warrior who stood in their midst, one hand grasping a pacquet, while the other was laid upon the neck of his gallant war-steed.

He was tall and majestic in height with a form of iron muscle and sinew, marked by broad shoulders, a prominent chest, long arms, and long lower limbs, terminated by large yet well proportioned feet. He stood upon the sod, like a king among his battle worn peers. His military costume, displayed the majesty of his figure to every advantage. His brow calm and open, was shaded by the triangular chapeau; his coat was of blue, faced with buff, with the wide lappel of his vest, seen beneath the collar and fac- ing, thrown open on either side, and a long straight sword depended from his waist; while the military boots of dark leather rose above his knees, with the knightly spurs, glittering on each heel.

He advanced a step from his position, and his noble face lighted up with a gleam of a true warrior's joy, as glancing over the heads of the encirc- ling chieftains, his eye rested upon the level plain of Brandywine, a half mile distant, with the green meadow of Chadd's Ford, dotted by the white tents of the American host, while over all, scarce stirred into motion by the faint whisperings of the breezy air, waved and streamed the broad banner of the New World-freedom, the signal of hope to the men of that iron-time, the flag sacred to the rights of the human race, blazoned with the armorial bearings of the stars, and gorgeous with the heraldry of the skies.

" The time has come," the warrior exclaimed glancing around him as a smile of pride wreathed his compressed lips; " The time has come. The Doubt of the past ten days is over. At last we have brought the enemy to a field, where he must fight his way thro' our ranks or be driven back to the Chesapeake. This day may decide the fate of the American arms. Our force now repose along the Brandywine—the British yesterday took post, as our information serves to tell us, at Kennet's Square, seven miles beyond the Ford. And action, must certainly take place within two hours. Gentle- men, I desire your opinion, in the plan of battle—"

A murmur of interest extended through the group, and each warrior leaned forward with deep attention, as the General unfolding a map of the battle field, pointed to the various posts and distances.

" Here gentlemen is Chadd's Ford," Washington continued turning to the brave men around him, " The main body of our army, lies posted here, with General Wayne at their head. General you will fight to day, on the ground of your childhood, for the rights of man. General Sullivan, you are posted with the right wing of the army, two miles above Chadd's, in the heights between Chadd's and Brentons's Ford. The left wing, under your command General Armstrong, comprising the militia of the state, are posted at the Ford two miles below Chadd's—and General Greene, the reserve, with yourself at the head, have taken position at this spot, near Dilworth corner, some three miles, from Chadd's Ford. This is our position gentlemen. Now what think you of the intended movements of the British? Where will their first attack be made?"

General Wayne threw his arms carelessly across the pommel of his saddle, and glanced at the notches on his unsheathed sword, as he spoke.

" Your Excellency must remember, that I'm not much fitted for the planning of a fight. I usually like to have my work laid out for me—" he continued with a grim smile—" And then, when I know I've *so* much fighting to do, and so many minutes to do it in, I can go right about it, and so can my men—"

" Like the story they tell of you General—" whispered La Fayette in an aside tone while his face was all alive with quiet laughter—" With regard to the message you once sent to the Commander in Chief. ' The General wants me for Council does he? I'm no fellow for a Council. But I can do. Tell Washington to plan an attack on Tartarus, and I'll storm the gates!' *Mon Dieu, Generale!*"

" However, I think the chief point of attack will be Chadd's Ford—" Wayne resumed. " The enemy may make a feint of attacking elsewhere but they may threaten Jefferis' or Trimble's Ford, but my word for it, the battle will be fought in yonder valley—"

" I agree with General Wayne," said a bold, determined voice, as every eye was fixed upon the form of the speaker, the brave Sulivan, with his noble face and eagle eye—" The great point of attack will be Chadd's Ford."

And a murmer of assent arose from the sagacious Greene, the brave foreigners, De Kalb and Steuben, the gallant Stirling, and the chivalric La Fayette.

" As for me"—said a bold rugged voice, and the dark hued face of Count Pulaski shone with a smile, that wreathed the mustachio on his determined lip—" I also agree with our comrade, General Wayne. However, I am better fitted to execute than to plan. The charge suits me better than the Council."

" I am also of the opinion, that Chadd's Ford will be the principal point of attack," Washington continued, as the light of morning broke clearer and brighter around the scene. " But here is a pacquet of papers, placed in my hands by the brave Partizan Chief, Captain Waldemar of the Riders of Santee. It contains a plan of operations, traced by the hand of Sir William Howe. Here are descriptions of the tract of country around the Brandywine, together with a statement of the number of persons, disaffected to the American cause, the condition of the various fords, along the rivulet, as well as other important and interesting details. Gentlemen, from this pacquet, I glean the idea, that the attack at Chadd's Ford, may be, nothing more than a feint, while the main body of the enemy will cross the river seven miles above, either at Trimble's or Jefferis' ford, and by turning our right flank, accomplish the confusion and discomfiture of the Continental army. Here is the pacquet, gentlemen. Examine these papers, and tell me, whether there is any foundation for the idea."

A murmur of surprise ran around the group, as Washington broke the string of the pacquet—it was the same pacquet, for which the schoolmaster had been murdered—and, as the papers flew around the throng, each manly countenance assumed an expression of deep and absorbing interest, while a frown gathered on each scarred and wrinkled brow.

"These papers, your Excellency, it appears, were stolen from the hands of a Tory Refugee, one Gilbert Gates"—thus spoke the brave Sullivan—"by the ingenuity of a good Whig, and from this Whig, Captain Waldemar received the pacquet. A suspicion flashes over my mind, that the whole matter, may be a feint of Sir William Howe, to direct your attention from his real plans of battle. It may have been his design, to convey these pa-pers to your hands!"

"Aye—and suppose the main body of the Army is withdrawn from Chadd's Ford?" Wayne exclaimed, eyeing the pacquet of papers; " Or, suppose, that one division alone, is advanced to the northward. May not the enemy concentrate his entire force at Chadd's, and thus win a half fought battle? Ten chances to one, the pacquet is a strategy of the Britisher."

A murmur of assent arose from the throng, and Washington was about to speak, when a horseman, mounted on a golden hued steed, was seen spur-ring in hot haste from the direction of the American encampment, at Chadd's Ford, and the light of the morning's dawn revealed the outlines of a tall and commanding figure, with a slouching hat looped up on one side, drooping over his face, while the folds of a military cloak, depending from his saddle, swept the flank of his horse, and sank trailing to the very ground.

"It is the brave Partizan Chief!" shouted General Wayne. " The gal-lant Randulph Waldemar!"

And ere another word could be said, the horseman dashed into the very centre of the group, flung himself from his steed, and in an instant, Randulph Waldemar, his flace flushed with excitement; stood before General Washington, with his slouching hat extended gracefully in his right hand.

"I hasten to inform your excellency, " he exclaimed with a soldierly sa-lute—"That the main body of the enemy, at all events, the brigade of Hes-sians under General Kniphaussen are in full march for Chadd's Ford. They number five thousand strong. From all the intelligence my men can gather, it is not at all improbable, that Lord Cornwallis accompanies this division. In fifteen minutes their arms, will glimmer over the heights of Chadd's Ford."

"To horse gentlemen!" the bold word of command rang from the lips of Washington, as he sprang to the back of his gallant grey—" The first gleam of sunlight, falls gaily over the plains of Brandywine—let the last gleam of sunset be as glorious !"

And they sprang to their horses, the Chiefs of the American host, and bright swords dinted with notches, each notch, the remembrance of some glorious fray, rose glittering in the air, while the tall figures and commanding forms of the brave Leaders, were disclosed in the majesty of active manhood, as the first gleam of the rising sun, broke over the plain, like an arrow of slender gold, leaving a track of light in its path.

And in the light of the rising sun, was revealed an impressive picture, of the enthusiasm of the American chiefs, as they anticipated the coming battle. Mad Antony Wayne shook his sword aloft with joy ; the boy-general Gilbert Mortier De La Fayette, kissed the glittering blade of the warrior-drover's sword, with a true Frenchman's enthusiasm ; Count Pulaski smiled grimly, and his eye flashed and his whiskered lip quivered, as he seemed to scent the far-off battle, with the glory of a true war-horse, trained to deathly struggle and terrible mellay ; Lord Stirling glanced around with a proud look of command, the flashing eye of Maxwell was fixed upon the heights of Chadd's Ford, Steuben muttered a soldier's oath, De Kalb laid his hand upon his sword hilt, the face of glorious Nathaniel Greene was all sagacity and calculation, while in the centre of the throng side by side with the form of George Washington, was Randulph Waldemar mounted on his steed, with the arching neck thrown aloft, giving the mane long and waving to the breeze, while the figure of the Rider of Santee swelled to its full height, his nostrils dilated with excitement, and over his brow there broke, a flash of the warm enthusiasm of youth.

" Oh who would spend a life of inglorious ease, when the peril of war may minister such quick joy to the warm heart, such terrible excitement to the daring soul !"

" Away to your posts gentlemen !" shouted Washington as his calm face, lit up with all the excitement of his younger days—" The morning light falls brightly over the American flag—let its folds wave as proudly in the last beams of the setting sun !"

CHAPTER SECOND.

THE FIGHT AT THE FORD.

On the summit of a green knoll, rising suddenly from the plain of Bran-dywine, the gentlest of the range of eastward heights, with the golden light of morn, falling on the embankment at his feet, stood Mad Antony Wayne, his towering form raised to its full stature, standing boldly out in the glow of the sunbeams. With uncovered brow, and right hand resting upon the hilt of his stout long sword, he gazed with a flashing eye and compressed lip, upon the plain of Chadd's Ford, extending green and grassy below him, with the silvery waves of the Brandywine glistening and trembling with ra-diance, as gleaming from beneath the shadow of the overhanging trees it swept, on its way of beauty and of beams.

He stood upon the summit of the embankment, the American chieftain with the ponderous cannon resting at his feet, while his attire, the coat of blue with facing of buff, the breeches of buckskin and the long military boots, were disclosed in strong relief, and his long sword hung trailing to the earth, while over his head waved the broad folds of the banner of Freedom.

Resting his prominent chest on the uprising embankment, with his hand near the feet of Wayne, was the stout Blacksmith, Iron Tom o' Dilworth Corner, his muscular arms folded across his breast, with the rifle in their embrace, the sun shining gaily on his rustic attire, on the clumsy slouching hat, with the oak leaf inserted under the band, while his eye, keen and piercing in its glance, was fixed upon the silent woods beyond the Brandywine.

At his side, giving a terrible interest to the picture, stood the negro Samp-son. His form, with its brawn and muscle was raised to its full stature, his jet black skin was bared to the waist, his dark face, with the thick lips steadily compressed, the eyes fixed upon the woods beyond the Brandywine, received on the cheeks faint touches of sunlight, while his giant right arm twined around the handle of a glittering scythe, and his massive left hand rested upon the head of the noble white dog, panting and gasping at his side.

And a little further on, with his slight figure, carelessly laid along the em-bankment, the fingers of his long talon like hands, grasping a rifle, much taller than himself, was the growling host of the Green-Tree, Mr. Hirpley Hawson, with his uncouth features, distorted into any number of faces, as eyeing the opposite woods he waited the approach of the Hessian band. A large oak leaf decorated his hat, and his figure was enveloped in the folds of a grey coat, evidently made for a man of twice his size.

Wayne glanced around, and his cheek glowed and his dark eye flashed. There was the beautiful valley of the Brandywine, extending green and grassy below him, with small bands of American riflemen, hurrying over its verdure, with the outlines of Wild-Wood Grange, peeping from among the woods, on its further side, a short distance below the Ford, while over the rich mass of forest, the sunbeams fell in a shower of golden rays.

He looked to the north. The American army, each soldier resting on his arms, each war horse standing ready for the battle-leap, spread over hill and over height, their swords gleaming from among the woods, their rifles glistening in the light, amid all the windings of the valley hills, far away as Brenton's Ford. Each eye was fixed upon the opposite shore, and every hand was nerved for the struggle, as the peal of drum and trumpet broke upon the ear.

Wayne glanced upon the wide plain to the south. There were banners waving and bayonets glistening in the sunlit air, there were stout forms ready for the fray, and gallant warhorses waiting for the plunge into the ranks of death, and circling along the plain, and around the foot of the knoll, on which stood the American leader, were extended the band of the Continental host, resting on their arms, and silently listening for the signal-note of battle.

" By the good Lord above me, but it's a grand sight !" the stout Black-smith murmured, with a flashing eye. "To see so many, good men and true, come out to die, that their children, and children's children, may have plenty o' quiet and freedom. It's a grand sight—my wife and child are away at Dilworth Corner—and the blue sky arches so smilin' above us all, jist as in the olden times ; I've a sort o' a feelin' this day 'ill be my last job on airth. Well, God take me sperrit once for all, and the sperrits o' them I'm goin' to send afore me ! And now, I'm ready to die—"

" Die ? The d——l !" whined Hirpley Hawson, turning round with a quick peevish movement.

The white dog started forward and howled. Hirply had unconsciously uttered the name given him, by his sable master.

" Down, Debbil, down"—muttered Sampson. " Why can't yo' be quiet, Debbil ? Hab tasted Massa Mayland's blood ! Shall hab some dam Hessian blood, afore an hour. Hab your tooth in Hamsdorff's trote. Dat satisfy you ? Down, I say, Debbil, down."

The Negro laid his hand gently upon the head of the dog, and showed his white teeth in a grim smile.

" What d'ye mean, Darkness ?" cried Hirpley in the same peevish tone. " What d'ye mean by comin' out here to fight with that scythe and an ever-lastin big dog ? Hey ? D'ye think the Britishers is wheat-stubble, that you kin cut 'em down like a whiff o' smoke ? Hey Charcoal ? D'ye know,

Sampson, I sometimes take you for a sperrit, and yei dog for a real devil, pure grit, of the tallest material, jist from the lower market house! You die Tom Davis! Stuff! Pooh! Take you a week to die—you'll die by small divisions at a time, you'll go off in little squads. You will. Takes a feller like me to die. It does. Why I'll go off jist like *that!*"

And Hirply snapped his finger and thumb in the air, and was about to continue his discussive remarks on things in general, when the voice of Wayne hushed his chattering tongue into silence.

" I hear the peal of drum, and the notes of bugle!" exclaimed the gallant Leader in a low muttered voice. " It breaks louder and nearer, over the valley. The Hessians are coming, at last! Their arms are gleaming thro' the woods on yonder height—they are occupying the position above Chadd's Ford! By the God of Battles, this will be a glorious day—a glorious day for the fight!"

" They are comin' "—exclaimed the Blacksmith. " Look, Hirpley, how their arms glisten along yonder height, how their tall, black caps darken the woods! Wonder if Gineral Snitz-and-keep is among 'em!"

" Spring, every man to his cannon!" shouted Wayne, and some four or five whiskered soldiers, attired in the artillerist uniform of the Continental troops, sprang forward from among their comrades, each man holding a lighted match in his hand.

" Stand back!" cried Wayne, glancing below the height of the embankment, where he stood—" stand back, and give, each man of you, his torch to these brave men. I have seen them do good service. They shall have the honor of the first fire, in this day's fight."

And as the Iron Blacksmith, the loquacious Hirpley, and the stalwart negro, Sampson, took their places, beside three of the cannon, the lighted match in hand, and every eye centered upon the opposite heights, the scene became one of terrible and absorbing interest.

Along the brow of the western heighths of the Brandywine, came thronging in all the pride of military discipline, the Hessian bands of the enemy, file after file, rank after rank, emerging from the thickest recesses of the forest, their well burnished arms glaring in the sun, each bayonet silvering in the light, the tall black caps of the grenadiers, their heavy accoutrements, their stout forms and whiskered faces, all bursting into view, while the terrible tread of armed men, moving to battle, mingling with the tramp of war-steeds, echoed like distant thunder along the woods, and the roll of drum, and the peal of trumpet, broke gaily and merrily upon the morning air.

On the side of the Americans, all was intense interest and expectation. Every eye was fixed upon the Hessian bands, every war-horse was starting forward for the terrible charge, and along the whole line, was seen nothing but erect figures of brave men, their brows darkened by a frown, their lips compressed with determination, each hand grasping the sword hilt or the rifle stock, with the fierce grasp of freemen, fighting for their homes, and for their lives.

The valley of the Brandywine, the meadow of summer verdure, and the winding stream of silver, lay between the armies ; above, arched the calm and unclouded heavens, and up from the eastern horizon came the sun, glowing over wood and plain, over embattled legions, and over upraised bayonet and upraised sword, over waving banner and glittering plume, over all the gallant array, and gaudy tinsel of the splendid game of war, shone and flaunted the golden light.

It was a moment of intense and terrible expectation. An awful silence brooded on the air.

A solitary bird uprose from its perch, on a tall oak, and sailed slowly over the armies. The flapping of its wings was heard, distinctly along the American and Hessian lines. It was a raven. Extending its wings, with a wild scream, it hung poised in mid-air, over the bayonets of the opposing armies.

" Iron Tom, point your cannon toward the brow of the hill, overlooking the Ford," exclaimed General Wayne—" Sampson you take aim at the same point ; the Hessians are descending toward the Brandywine, Hirpley, you give it to them half-way down ; now, let your aim be sure—fire !"

" Here's to th' old Schoolmaster Jacob Mayland !" shouted Iron Tom, and his lighted match waved on high.

" Ten Hessians for one old soldier !" cried Hirpley Hawson, also waving the lighted match.

A low muttered sound, broke from the clenched teeth of the negro Sampson, he patted—" Debbil" on the head, and then flung the lighted match on the priming of the cannon.

" Take dat yo' debbils !"

The sound of the three cannon broke like thunder on the air, the fierce and vivid blaze flashed like summer lightning over the plain ; and around the towering form of General Wayne, circled and circled the thick wreaths of white battle smoke, winding away toward the heavens of cloudless azure, in columns of massive grandeur.

At this instant, the raven which had hung in mid-air darted suddenly down, and was lost in the clouds of smoke. Did the bird of evil omen, already scent the battle dead?

Another moment ! The blaze of cannon flashed from the opposite hills, the smoke enveloped the green woods in its lurid folds, and came rolling over the stream and plain of Brandywine, while the earth was dashed in scattering sand full in the face of the stout blacksmith, as standing at the feet of Wayne, he marked the effects of their fire, and the cannon balls swept like hail against the embankment of earth, rising up to his very breast.

Wayne sprang aside, and in a moment reined in his war horse, near the edge of the fortified knoll, the soldiers leaped forward, to reload the cannon, and oetween the intervals of the battle smoke, over the rivulet, the Hessians were seen rushing down in the attempt to ford the stream, while from the opposite side, poured the band of Maxwell's riflemen with the brave Porter-field at their head.   The rifle blaze flashed in the air, and streamed from amid the foliage of the overhanging trees, and thicker and darker rolled the lurid smoke, sweeping around the lonely mansion of Wild-Wood Grange, and winding upward to the heavens.

" Look Hirpley—look Sampson, d'ye see that are ?" shouted the Black-smith raising his rifle on high—" Do you see them hundred fellers, each with an oak sprig in his hat, each with a good rifle in his hand, a-creepin' along under the shade of the trees, a hundred yards north o' Chadd's Ford ! There's Curnel Frazier at their head, the sword of old Lovat wavin' on high, while he leads them onward thro' the battle smoke !"

" He's just got back from Jefferis' Ford, where he went huntin' arter his daughter stole away from him by that Devil-bird, Dave Walford. Wonder if he's found her ?   There they go—right into the centre of the muss ! D'ye see the Curnel's sword—d'ye see his arm sweepin' up and down like one of your own hammers Iron Tom ?   We must have a hand in that scrimmage—here goes !"

And the whimsical Inn-keeper, sprang over the embankment side by side with the stout Blacksmith, speeding toward the valley plain, with their rifles raised on high, while at their heels, sweeping onward with long bold strides, came the negro Sampson, the glittering scythe upraised on his shoulder, the dog bounding forward at his side.   The clouds of white smoke, curled round his sable form, in wreathing folds.   He seemed like the Demon of this fear-ful scene, laughing aloud with glee, as he viewed the work of carnage and blood.

" At 'em Debbil—at 'em !" shouted this singular being, in whose heart, a wild principle of Fidelity, was the ruling passion—" Massa Mayland kind to your massa—dey burn him alive !   Sampson hab but one life—dat for Massa Mayland—Debbil hab but one death, dat for Massa Mayland ! At 'em Debbil, at 'em trote !   Ha—ha !'

With a wild howl the dog sprang forward, and the white battle smoke, rolled around the ebon form of his giant-master.

And while the carnage thickened around the Ford, while Wayne looked from the knoll, at the gathering fight, and Washington glanced hurriedly over the scene, the thick and gloomy battle clouds, swept in rolling masses, around the mansion of Wild-Wood Grange, as it arose from the summit of the hill, directly above the scene of the riflemen's contest.

Gazing from an upper window of the mansion, with her form of grace and loveliness, clad in a loosened robe of white thrown slightly forward, was a fair and beautiful maiden, her dark eyes fixed upon the smoke and glare of the fight, her cheek flushed with excitement, and her lips dropped apart, while her breath came in quick convulsive gasps, and her throbbing bosom, rose like a billow, heaving into light.

Along her neck of alabaster, and over the bosom of snow, swept the dark masses of her uncinctured hair, glistening and glowing in the light, and affording a striking relief to the swelling outlines of the maiden's countenance, with all its dreamy beauty, aroused into strange and sudden expression, by the terrible excitement of the battle scene.

" Alone—alone—a weary day, a long and dreary night—" the maiden Blanche murmured—"no living soul in the mansion, but myself, and a wounded man—my uncle not returned—no word of my cousin Rose—how dread and heavily hangs the time ! And I could not desert him Walter Walford —wounded and helpless as he was, I could not desert him ! Tho' I bade Mary Mayland leave the mansion for a place of greater safety last night, and was left in the dread silence of this place alone ; alone, in the solitude of the sick chamber, yet I could not desert the child of my father's brother ! And now while around me swells and darkens the battle, I will not leave the wounded to die, for the want of the cup of water, which this hand might place to his lips !"

Her soliloquy was interrupted by the sound of a low, hollow voice. It came from the bed, placed at one side of the chamber, faintly illumined by the light of morn, now clouded by battle smoke. A wan and ghastly face, with large rolling eyes, cheeks hollowed and sunken by sudden disease, and thin lips, livid and blue with mortal pain, was thrust from beneath the folds of the coverlid, which fell suddenly aside, disclosing the throat and shoulder of the wounded man. There was a bandage around the throat, yet the ghastly wound, was but half concealed, for the hands of the delirious man, had partly torn it aside, in the fever and terror of a bewildered brain.

" Rose, oh, Rose," the words broke wildly, from the thin and livid lips of Walter Walford, " I would have saved you—ah, 'twas kind in you—that cup o' water—but ye see there is a curse upon our hands, and hearts ! The Walfords are all a doomed race. And the night was dark, and the old man —hush,—do ye know I sometimes think it was my father ? He struck home—right into my throat he struck. And—and—I will save ye—I will save ye Rose—"

He sprang from the couch, with one wild bound, he sprang into the centre of the floor, with the long white sheet, hanging loosly from his upraised form, and extending his arms, with a maniac gesture, he seemed warding off the attacks of some invisible foe, while his eyes glared from their sockets, and his pale face was distorted by an expression, that looked like the terror of a lost soul.

" The wood is dark—but I will save ye !" he shouted—" The thunder cloud darkens above, the lightning is around—but I will save ye ! Hark ! The sound of rifle shots—he is my own brother—yet, yet—" he hissed t

18

forth in a low whisper—" He must die! They bear her away—they strike me down—but I will save you Rose !"

He glanced madly round him, and then with a sudden spring, disappeared thro' the door of the chamber, laughing wildly as he fled.

Blanche Walford was left alone. She turned to the door, for now all reason for remaining in the mansion, was past, she turned to the door, but volumn of thick and blackening smoke, came rolling thro' the aperture, and swept into the apartment. It stifled her breath and choked her utterance, and she fled to the open window for air. A sudden suspicion came icing over the very blood of her heart.

" The mansion is in flames !" she exclaimed—" The lower story is occupied by soldiers—hark ! The tramp of men, and the sound of battle ! The smoke rolls blacker and thicker thro' the door way ; I hear the fire blazing ; — I hear the crackling of the flames ! There is no hope for me !"

" Ha, ha, ha—all is hope for thee my Blanche !" laughed a bitter and sneering voice—" What meddling hand, shall tear thee from me now ?"

And the form of George Percy, stood disclosed amid the smoke and gloom.

CHAPTER THIRD.

THE BRANDYWINE.

" The battle smoke is gathering thick above the Ford, but I cannot yet think, the enemy will pass at this point of the stream ;" and as Washington spoke, he glanced from the heighth of the knoll, where he had reined in his gallant grey war horse, he glanced over the valley of the Brandywine, and then surveying the anxious visages of the officers of his staff, he continued —" Kniphausen will make a feint of passing here, while the main body of the enemy force their way above—"

" General, I think you're right," exclaimed Mad Antony Wayne, spurring his brown steed, a step forward to the edge of the embankment, while his keen eye, drank in the vivid scene of the fight, in the valley below ; ' Still I think it would be just as well for us to rush over stream, and give 'em a warm Chester County reception ; Hessian gentlemen as they are, and clever fellows, to boot."

" By the spirit of the great Condé !" cried a voice at his elbow, and the form of La Fayette, came riding forward to the General's side—" The scene stirs a man's blood to look upon! The smoke hangs over the ford—from the dark curtain rush bodies of armed men—from its folds glares the flash of rifle, and the blaze of musquet shot! While on either side, pitched upon opposite hills, the two armies, like bloodhounds in the leash, are waiting to spring at each other's throats! A grand scene by the spirit of the Great Condé!"

"Look yonder General! Look at the golden-hued steed, speeding along the valley road! He speeds towards us—his rider waves his hand. 'Tis the gallant Captain Waldemar by my soul; he bears intelligence of the movements of the British host!"

And as Washington turned to gaze upon the new comer, he beheld speeding along the road, toward the rising knoll, the gallant form of Randulph Waldemar, mounted on his beautiful steed—whose hue was like sunset gold —the neck arched, the mane waving to the breeze, while his broad chest stood boldly out in the light, and his nostrils trembled with the excitement of the battle field.

In a moment Randulph the Prince, came riding up the knoll, and reined his steed by the side of Washington.

"I have left my Riders of Santee, with the division of Sullivan, near Brenton's Ford," exclaimed Captain Waldemar, "and hastened southward, with additional intelligence of the movements of the enemy. One of my Riders—Sergeant Dabney—not half an hour since, espied a large body of British, passing northward of this spot, some seven miles, on their way to the Forks of Brandywine. Various rumors are abroad, in the country, but all seem to agree on one point. It is thought, the movement at this Ford with the Hessians, is but a mere feint, but that the principal attack will be made some miles above."

A shade of anxious thought came over the brow of Washington. He whispered a word to Randulph Waldemar, and then turning to the countenance of the gallant La Fayette, a hurried sentence passed from his lips

"Will you follow me?" the sentence was audible to the group who circled round.

"To the death!" whispered Randulph Waldemar.

"To the death!" echoed General La Fayette.

And, in an instant, the commanding form of Washington, the manly figure of Randulph, and the youthful form of La Fayette, were all enveloped in long, grey fatigue coats, concealing the color of their uniforms, and reaching to the tops of their long military boots.

"Gentleman"—cried Washington, turning to the officers of his staff, clustered on the height of the embankment—"I will reconnoitre, the position of the enemy, in person. I desire you to remain here, clustered on the height of this knoll, above the battle-field. General La Fayette, and Captain Waldemar, we will away to yonder stream. Across the meadow, and up along the banks of the Brandywine, lies our path. Away!"

And ere a sound of exclamation arose from the group, the three were speeding away, down the knoll-side, and over the meadow, their eyes fixed upon the thick clouds of battle smoke rolling above the Ford, while, thro' each interval of smoke and flame, the bands of the Hessian army were seen, clustering, in all the pomp of arms, and of banners, along the windings of the opposite hills.

"The smoke arises thick and gloomy," exclaimed Washington, "and the fire of battle flashes over the valley. Yet, thro' smoke and gloom, lies our way! In a moment, gentlemen, we will be in the very path of death!"

And ere they plunged beneath the curtain of overhanging smoke, the eye of Randulph Waldemar glanced hastily over the field of battle, over the meadow, and over the uprising hill, where, gleaming thro' smoke and gloom, towered the mansion of Wild-Wood Grange. A strange, wild expression lit up the face of Captain Waldemar, his lip quivered and his eye flashed.

"A form appears at the window, her white robes waving in flame and battle-smoke!" he murmured. "It is *her* form"—he exclaimed, as the whole story of the appalling situation of Blanche Walford flashed over his mind. "I must save her, and by the honor of a true man, I will!"

Meanwhile rushing beneath the cloud and gloom of battle-smoke, rushing on toward the waters of the Brandywine, with the thick-leaved foliage arching above his head, the dark, rough trunks of giant trees spreading around, Colonel Frazier led on, the men of Brandywine, to the fight, the sword of 'Old Lovat' waving on high, while the tall form of the old warrior, his lofty brow, his chest of strength, and his arms of sinew, were shown in the fitful flashes of battle light, as clustering his men along the eastern shore of the stream, behind the trunks of trees, and beneath the cover of brushwood, he waited the approach of the Yager * bands of the Hessian army.

At the feet of Colonel Frazier, rolled the Brandywine, its clear waters rippling and bubbling with a song of rustic melody, as it swept onward with the clear sands of its bottom, rich, yellow and golden, beaming from beneath the sparkling waters. Along the opposite shore, the bushes were rustling and crashing with the march of armed men, and in a flash, each bush gave out its glittering rifle, and then a stout Yager, clad in green velvet, with ornaments of gold, sprang from the shelter of each tree. Two hundred rifle men, stood disclosed in the light, each eye flashing, and each whiskered lip wreathing with the courage of the trained bloodhound, lapping the first drop of foeman blood.

"They spring from the shelter of the brushwood," shouted Colonel Frazier. "They spring into the waters of the stream! Men of Brandywine, mark, each man of you his man; Let your aim be sure! Remember the watchword ——"

* Hessian Riflemen.

" Remember your daughter, torn from you by the hand of violence," the deep-toned voice, startled the ear of Norman Frazier. " Remember the desolated hearthside of your infancy. Remember the long and bloody Charter of British Fraud, and British Wrong, written in the life-blood of millions. Remember Jacob Mayland, and then—*Fire !*"

And as the word rung thro' the grove, the tall and muscular form of the grey-bearded Stranger, stood, side by side, with Colonel Frazier, his glitter-ing rifle poised at his shoulder, while his attire of whitened furs gleamed in the light, and his face, with its outlines of premature age, and its expression of wrong suffered, and despair endured, stood boldly forth, from the back-ground of massive trees. a d smoke clouded foliage.

" They plunge into the stream," shouted Colonel Frazier. " Mark, each one of you, his man ! *Fire !*" And then, like the crash of mingling thunderbolts, meeting over the head of the benighted traveller, the report of an hundred rifles broke along the wood, and then a plashing   d ruffled the waters of the Brandywine, and the waves, came rollir   o the green shore, crimsoned with blood.

" Upon them, draw your knives, and upon them !" shouted Colonel Fra-zier, springing into the stream, side by side with the stranger, the sword of Lovat waving on high, as he sprang. " Remember the butchered school master, and then, think of mercy, if ye can !"

There was one terrible moment of blood and horror ; the men of Brandy-wine springing from the shelter of the green foliage, each hand raised, with the hunter's knife glittering in the light, the Yagers, in their attire of green, recoiling in the middle of the stream, while the upturned faces of the dying, sent red currents of warm blood, spouting over the waters. While the Yagers recoiled, and the volunteers of Brandywine sprang into the rivulet, there appeared, on the eastern shore of the stream, a giant negro, holding a snow-white dog in his grasp, with the left hand, while the right swung aloft a glittering scythe.

" Ha-ha—Debbil !" the negro shrieked with a yell of wild delight. " Flame—smoke—rifle-flash—death-groan ! Berry good ! Debbil, see dat ar ? Hey ? Smell de blood ? Debbil grow fat on Hessian puddle 'fore a minit ! Look 'o de hill, Debbil ! Ha, ha,—see dem red-coats—see Hams-dorff ? Ha-ha—Debbil—at 'em trote, at 'em trote !"

He sprang into the water with a wild yell, and at his side leaped the snow-white dog, following his sable master to the death.

" I say there's a muss and no mistake !" shouted Hirpley Hawson bound-ing from the woods—" Look Iron Tom, and remember the hay-stack ? Whoop ? Hey ?"

" For Vengeance, for Washington and the right !" pealed the shout of the Blacksmith, as he sprang into the waters, marking his victim as he sprang.

In mid stream breast to breast, met the foemen, the whiskered Hessians, and the stalwart Pennsylvanians, hand to hand, foot to foot, with the water gurgling from the mouths of the dying, and splashing upward in the faces of the living, and the glittering knife of the hunters, clashed against the short sword of the Yagers, and the clubbed rifle was raised on high, while thicker and darker, swelled the tumult of the fray.

And amid the storm, and smoke, sweeping right onward with giant strides, came the negro Sampson, his glittering scythe describing a quick circle around his sable head, and then sweeping downward, with a force that no arm might resist, while a loud yell arose from the African, as Hessian after Hessian fell dead amid the waters, with the teeth of the terrible white dog, clenched in the gashed and severed throat.

" Another blow and we have them !" shouted Colonel Frazier, as in the very van of the fight, waved the broadsword of old Lovat—" Men of Bran-dywine to your mettle ! The watchword—Vengeance, Washington and the Right !"

And at each word, a Hessian, bit the sands of the rivulet's bed.

" Remember the haystack !" shouted Iron Tom o' Dilworth Corner, parry-ing the thrust of a Hessian sword, aimed at Hirpley Hawson's throat— " Death to the slaves of the British Tyrant !"

" That's jist what I say—" shouted Hirpley with an expressive grimace of his ugly face—" Dam 'em for their cussed impu'dence ! To try to cut a feller down in that ar' way ?"

" I say you dam Hessian, don't you grin at me in dat ar' way !" shouted Sampson waving his glittering scythe aloft—" De larf aint on your side, by a jug full ! Down dog—at 'em trote Debbil ! Dar's a dog for ye ! Hah-a-whah ! at 'em trote !"

" They give way !" shouted the stranger as his clubbed rifle was raised on high—" They yield ! Look Men of Brandywine, look how the bodies of your foes, cumber the waters ! The waves run crimson with blood—your own blood and the blood of your foes ! Another charge and we drive them back, step by step, to yonder shore !"

And with one wild rush over the dead bodies of comrade and foe, the Men of Brandywine swept thro' the stream, driving their astonished foes, before them at every step, while the mingled curse and the yell, broke wildly on the air ; the smoke clouded the face of day above, and the gleam of arms flashed over the troubled waters below.

" For Vengeance, for Washington and the Right!" shouted Colonel Fra-zier, as red with the blood of his foes, begrimed with smoke, and wet with the splashing of the water, he led on the encounter, driving the Hessians back to the opposite shore, in terrible route and disorder.

" Look yonder !" shouted the grey bearded stranger—" The cavalry of the enemy are charging upon us ! They sweep down the hill—the red coats In a moment they will be upon us !"

And as the Hessians gave way on either side, a band of the enemy's dragoons, some fifty strong, came dashing from the shelter of the underwood, their stout horses springing forward in the mad plunge of the battle charge, the neck of each steed arched, with mane and tail flung wavingly to the impulse of the breeze, and on gaudy red coat, towering cap of fur gay with plumes, on uned sword and helmet, glared the sudden rifle flash, as with one sweep the red coated dragoons, came plunging into the waves of the wood-hidden Brandywine.

" Over the rebels — " shouted the Leader — " over the rebels be-G-a-w-d !"

" The ruffian Hamsdorff leads them on !" shouted Iron Tom Davis—" Men of Brandywine remember your oath !"

A shout of execration burst from the yeoman-band as they beheld the corpulent form of the ruffian, his red, round carbuncled face, hedged with whiskers, and his large eyes, gleaming with an expression of brutal ferocity, as with shout and haloo, he led his men onward to the charge of the stream.

The yeomen of Brandywine stood the charge like men. Every form erect, every hand with the knife uplaised, every eye fixed upon the front of the advancing troopers, they stood the charge, and as the Britishers came rushing on, the patriots sprang suddenly forward, to the necks of the foemen's horses they sprang, their huntsmen-blades glittered aloft, wresting the flash of the ruffian sword, and every sword dealt a death, and every knife, sent a soul wandering to its last account.

The charge was terrible. Each tiny wavelet of that fair stream turned to blood, the faces of the dying, contorted with the spasm of violent death, thrust from beneath the waters, the last dreadful encounter of the wounded, with the living, ere they plunged below, the shout of the Britishers, the yell of vengeance, bursting from the patriot band, the hurrying of the foemen, to and fro, in rapid conflict, the confused gleam of mingling swords and knives, the smoke, the flash and the flame, all formed a scene of death and horror, that would have made, a demon laugh to look upon.

" Now Men of Brandywine, another blow for the murdered schoolmaster !" the shout arose from the lips of the mysterious stranger, as a knife waved on high in his grasp; " These bloodhounds recoil ; up to their horses necks each man of you, and we have them !"

And while the terrible fight was renewed, on toward the opposite shore, flinging red-coat and patriot aside, with an iron hand, strode Colonel Frazier, the sword of Lovat waving aloft in his grasp, while his eye was fixed upon the figures of a band of Tory-Partizans, who attired in sable garments, with large slouching hats, and raven plumes, came gathering from the shade of the woods, along the western bank of the stream.

" Ha—Ha—Ha—Ravens o' th' Hollow !" laughed a bold sneering voice

—"Here's fun for you but not much plunder! The last affair we were engaged in, was tolerably rich in the article of fun ; we carried *her* off for sartin. W-a-l as I live, yander's her daddy's farm, which Gilbert Gates, says
we'll all share when its confisticated ; that's the word I guess? And by
* * * * here's the old man himself—"

"David Walford, you have a sword," exclaimed the stern tones of a determined voice, as Colonel Frazier came rushing thro' the waters, "That
sword cannot save you now. Give me back my daughter ; without stain,
without dishonor, and there shall be no quarrel between us—"

A coarse smile, wrinkled the muscles of the ruffian's visage.

"Without stain, without dishonor?" the sneering words burst from his
lips, as he glanced around the faces of his fellow ruffians. "Ha, ha, ha
boys. Good—aint it?"

A flush, brightened over the manly countenance of the old soldier ; his
lip quivered for a moment, and then the clear flashing glance of a determined man, shot from his grey eye.

"You have spoken your last word!" shouted Norman Frazier, as with
one bold bound he sprang upon the grassy bank, and as he sprang the sword
of Lovat, rose whizzing round his head—"Now by —— you die !"

And quick as a lightning flash Dave Walford lay prostrate on the sward,
driven to the earth by a half-parried blow of the stout broadsword, while
his companions, thunderstricken by the sudden movement, started hurriedly
backward, and Norman Frazier stood with his sword at the throat of the
helpless ruffian.

A moment of quick and terrible action ! The old soldier with his sword
raised on high, the ruffian eyeing the descending blow with one wild glance,
the band of shrieking ruffians, and the terrible fight in the waters of the crimsoned rivulet.

"Coward and liar, this blow is for my daughter !" shouted Colonel Frazier, and the blow came hissing thro' the air, when a quick splashing sound
of the waters broke upon his ear, then a wild and hurried footstep, and like
a thought of terror, a strange spectral figure, stood between the soldier and
his victim, with a half clothed form towering in the light, with bared arms,
raised on high, while a face, deathlike and colorless, with large, rolling eyes,
glared in the visage of the prostrate ruffian.

"Walter !" shrieked the Tory-Leader with a look of horror, as he sprang
wildly on his feet, while Colonel Frazier started backward to the stream,
with involuntary surprise—"Walter ! Risen from the dead—I will not
fight ye man !"

"The knife is at my throat—the wood is dark—" shouted the maniac,
throwing his arms aloft, while his eyes, quick, vivid and blazing in their
glance, glared with the light of coming death—"But I will save ye Rose,
I will save ye yet ! Father—ha, ha—the stab was sure. Brother—" he
shrieked leaping forward, and seizing David Walford by the throat, with his

long, talon-like fingers—" Brother the hour has come. The curse of our race is upon the hour. It is the hour of death."

Each brother sprang to the other's throat, their bared hands, were inter-locked in the wild struggle of life for life, and the terrible yell of the maniac brother, broke wildly and fearfully above the clamor of battle.

" Retreat boys—the rebel dogs are too much for us—be-g-a-w-d !" shouted a voice from mid-stream, and the hurried sound of the trooper's steeds, sweeping thro' the water, burst upon the air—" To the hill, boys to the hill be-g-a-w-d !"

Colonel Frazier turned hurriedly, and glanced over the waters. The form of the burly Sergeant Hamsdorff, met his eye, as with sword up-raised and head turned over his shoulder, the ruffian, urged his men, toward the eastern shore of the stream, while at their horses flanks, hung the men of Brandywine, dealing death at every blow, or dying like brave men be-neath the foemen's sword.

Frazier confronted the advancing ruffian ; the sword of Lovat waved on high in his grasp; again and again, was the steed of Hamsdorff, driven back from the western bank of the stream.

" Traitor and rebel—" shouted Hamsdorff—" Stand from my path, or I'll pin ye to the sod, be-g-a-w-d !"

Colonel Frazier sprang forward, the pistol of the ruffian was pointed at his throat, he sprang forward, but his right foot slipped along the sod into the stream, and thrown suddenly down upon his left knee, he was at the mercy of the trained assassin.

The eye of the bravo was fixed upon the form of Norman Frazier, the aim was taken, the levelled pistol pointed at his heart.

" This for the traitor !" shouted Hamsdorff—he fired, but the ball whistled away among the trees, and relieved from certain death, the soldier sprang forward, upon the grassy bank. He glanced at Hamsdorff. A large, white dog was clinging to the Hessian's shoulder, the teeth, glistening and white, were fastened in his throat, while the red, round face of the ruffian was up-turned, to the heavens. He flung the pistol aside ; he endeavored to tear the dog from his throat, but in vain.

" At 'em trote—ha, ha—whah !" shouted a well known voice, and the giant form of Sampson, scythe aloft, and arms upraised, came rushing thro' the waters. " Dar's a Debbil for you ! At 'em trote—lap um Hessian blood ! Marcy for de wild bar—Marcy for de painter—none for de Hessian ! Lap am blood, Debbil—at 'em trote—fast, fast ! Ha !"

The teeth of the dog sank in the Hessian's throat ; a low muttered growl broke upon the air. The bravo made a desperate struggle, he flung his arms of sinew and muscle around the body of the snow-white dog, spotted with blood, but in vain. The teeth struck deeper, his face was flushed and burning red, and his large, rolling eyes were starting from their sockets.

"Take the dog—the dog off—" yelled Hamsdorff. "Take the brute off —take—"

"Remember the haystack!" the shout broke from the negro. "He shriek for marcy—you burn him 'live! 'Spose you hab a tousand lives! Sampson hab 'em ebbery one, and he dog hab de oders! At 'em trote, Debbil!"

The scene swam, for an instant, before the vision of Colonel Frazier—he looked again—the riderless steed of Hamsdorff was dashing up the hill-side—the face of the ruffian was thrust from the crimsoned waters, while his burly form, plunged to and fro in the desperate contest, with the snow-white dog.

"Off, Debbil—off!"

The dog sprang aside, the scythe rose glittering in the darkened air, and then, while the shout and yell arose thundering along the grove, it circled around the head of the giant negro, it swept downward!

"Captain—be-Gaw-d, tell Percy Lord—I tried to carry the jade off—but —Be-G-a-wd ——"

A shapeless corse floated on the waters, with a terrible gash severing the prominent chest from side to side, and thick masses of curdled blood crimsoned the waters round the negro, as he gazed on the face of the dead.

"Massa Mayland—look heah! Dat ar counts One for you! Hah-a-whah—Debbil!"

Norman Frazier looked not, upon the scene, with a second glance, but sprang forward, to join the patriots of Brandywine, who, in mid-stream, were driving back the troopers of the enemy, with terrible bloodshed and havoc. As he sprang forward, at his very back, concealed by the clouds of enveloping smoke, David Walford, sank kneeling on the sod, with the gaze of his brutal eye fixed upon a stiffened form at his feet, half-veiled by the white folds of a blood-spotted sheet, flowing round the bared limbs, while the ghastly face relieved by sweeping locks of jet-black hair, was upturned to the heavens above, the eyes fixed and glassy with death.

"And soh, Walter is gone!" the Ruffian murmured, while a scowl darkened over his face. "We fought in our mother's womb—we fought in the cradle—we fought when boys—we fought when we were men—and there *he* lies! We'll fight in the next world—we'll fight in * * * *!"

* And he struck the lifeless corse in his rage. A faded ribbon, encircling the chest of the dead man, was severed by the blow—a withered rose-bud fell quivering upon the sod.

"I: was *her* gift! Fool! He kept a woman's gift till death! Ha, ha, ha! Rock Farm is mine—*now!*"

Folding his arms, with his rifle locked within their embrace, David Walford fixed his eyes upon the earth, and, unheeding the glances of the ruffians

---

* Let those who pronounce this scene unnatural. look around the walks of every day life, and then pass judgment on a brother's hate.

of his partizan Band, strode gloomily up the hillside, and, in a moment, was lost in the shadow of the woods.

" There he stands —" he exclaimed, as emerging from the opposite side of the wood, the valley of the Brandywine was opened to his view. " Yander stands the old man—half-recovered from his fit of madness ! He thinks he killed his son, night afore last ; let him think so still ! And with him, stands Captain Howard, and Colonel Ferguson—all eyeing the movements of the rebel party, on t'other side of the Brandywine—Ha ! What do I see ! ' Them' three figures in grey coats ridin' along the stream, within rifle-shot of yonder party ! They're officers of rank ; I'd swear the middle one is Washington himself ! Quick Dave Walford, and your fortin's made !"

The Ruffian sprang suddenly forward, with his eye fixed upon the three figures, in grey uniforms, riding leisurely along the opposite bank of the stream, with wreaths of battle-smoke floating above their heads. " If I can reach yander knoll, where Captain Howard is standin', the rebel leader is mine !"

Ten vigorous steps he sprang forward, he reached the knoll, where stood old Walford, the complacent Howard, and the manly Colonel Ferguson, with his snow white hairs waving in the breeze. The Bravo levelled his rifle at the tallest of the three soldiers, who were dashing onward, on the opposite side of the Brandywine.

" What would you do ?" exclaimed Colonel Ferguson, eyeing the sturdy form of David Walford, which had thus suddenly been thrust before his vision. " You will not shoot yonder men, when their backs are turned toward you ?"

" No d-o-n-t fellow—" drawled Clarance Howard—"I don't like shootin' a man behind his back—It's in such d——d bad taste."

" Colonel Ferguson—" cried old Walford, as his hawk-eye glanced over the stream—" You know not what you say. The tallest of yonder three soldiers is—Washington !"

And here, tradition states, that the gallant old Colonel advanced a step forward, and impelled by some indefinable impulse, struck down the barrel of the Tory's rifle.

*" It may be the rebel leader—" he said—" or it may be nothing more than an aid-de-camp, but be it as it will, God never made that man, Washington, for such a death !"

And as the fatal aim, was stricken down, the three soldiers in overcoats of grey, swept onward along the stream, and were lost to view, in the encircling folds of battle smoke.

" The Hessians, muster along the hills in formidable numbers ;" exclaimed

---

* This incident is no fiction. This narrow escape, made by Washington on the morning of the fight of Brandywine, the singular impulse which actuated the British Colonel, are alike matters of common tradition and accredited history. Eternal honor to the brave Briton, who although the officer of King George, saved the life, of Washington.

Randulph Waldemar, turning his face, to the noble visage of Washington —" Think you General, the attack will be made at this Ford ?"

A shade of solemn anxiety came over the brow of the chieftain, as having completed their hazardous reconnoitre, they turned their steeds, across the plain of Brandywine, while the hand of the American General unconsciously wandered to the hilt of his sword.

" Would to heaven," he exclaimed in a low, yet impressive tone, with that wild glance of his eye, never noted, save in the crisis of some terrible game of battle—" Would to heaven, this sword alone might fight the matter out! The valley swarms with spies and tories, and I know not, whom to trust !"

" By the Spirit of the great Condé—" shouted La Fayette as they sped over the plain—" The pacquet may be right after all !"

A rolling cloud of battle smoke swept around the gallant band, and Randulph Waldemar, was separated for a moment from his companions.

His eye rested upon the hill of Wild-Wood Grange, distant some two hundred yards. The mansion was veiled in one enormous cloud of smoke —the smoke was swept aside for a moment, and a pillar of flame shot upward to the heavens.

" The mansion in flames! She is in danger—her robe flutters from the window! Now by the * * * above me, I will save her, or die in the ruins of yon burning pile !"

He patted the arching neck of his golden-hued steed, and the noble animal sprang forward, with its gallant rider, speeding for the hill, wrapt in clouds, and lighted by the flame of the burning mansion.

CHAPTER FOURTH.

THE HOUR AND THE MEN.

" HER form appears at the window ; now the flames sever on either side !" muttered Randulph as he swept onward, over the valley plain, the bullets whistling around his path at every step,—" The smoke gathers thicker around the window ; the flames shoot upward, far above the woods, away to the very zenith! I must haste, or all is lost !"

And striking the rowels into the flanks of his gold-hued steed, he darted onward, with a flashing eye, and a lip compressed with the terrible excitement of the moment, while over his soul in that dread instant, flashed all the memories of his life, like presentiments of coming death. The thought of his wronged and broken hearted mother, mingled with the thought of the mystery, that hung round his own path ; and then came a dim and shadowy, yet impressive belief, that the young and gallant English Lord, whom he had encountered two nights agone, had some mysterious connection with his destiny ; that some terrible duty, bound them together, in the work of a hidden fate.

And then came the thought of Blanche, whose love, had not grown up in his heart from the intimacy of early years, not been nurtured by habit, or fostered by acquaintance, but dawned over his soul in sudden brightness, as tho' a new star, had been created in the heaven of his being, and with its sudden glory cast all former thoughts into forgetfulness.

" My love was not the thing of a year, nor a day, nor an hour!" the thought flashed over the mind of Waldemar—" It arose into being with the first look, it dawned into light with the first glance ! One glance at her dreamy face—one glance at the eyes grand, and dark as night, and Love sprang into birth. The glory, and the soul and the passion of her intellect, mingled with my own being, as our glance met, and mingled for the first time. And now she is in danger, hemmed in by flame, overshadowed by death ! Shall death tear my new found love from my soul ? Perish in the flames she may—but on the same pile shall blacken the corse of Randulph Waldemar!"

He gained the base of the hill, his noble steed darted like an arrow upward, thro' the intervale of the age grown trees. And as he sped upward and onward, parties of American riflemen crossed his path, fleeing from the heat of the burning mansion, and his cheek was burned by red hot cinders, swept along the woods, by the morning breeze.

He gained the summit of the hlil; all before him was thick and blackening smoke ; all above him was red and forked flame. The leaves of the surrounding trees were all a flame, the smoke concealed the mansion, like a pall of death, enveloping some funeral vault, and no sound of human voice, not even the death groan, or the cry for quarter, broke the dread silence of the scene.

Randulph plunged his steed amid the folds of the overhanging smoke, and in a moment, he stood in front of the southern balcony, with the hall door, yet untouched by the flames, which hissed and circled around its pannels, and ran along the crumbling walls, like vast serpents, with forms of living fire.

He flung himself from his steed, he rushed to the hall door, and started with astonishment as he beheld, fastened to one of the pillars of the balcony, a magnificent war horse, of ebon blackness of skin, with broad chest and arching mane, and an eye of fire, that glared with horror, as the sinews of the noble animal swelled and writhed, with the terrible excitement of the scene.

" I will save her yet !" muttered Randulph, as rushing between the columns of the portico, he entered the hall of Wild-Wood Grange, filled with flame and darkened by smoke—" The smoke gathers around and the flame flashes above—but I will save her yet!"

He glanced forward thro' the smoke and gloom, and discerned the outline of the stairway, fronting his path, with the flames creeping round the bannisters, with their forked tongues blazing on high, while smoke, dark and dense, swept overhead thro' the passage above, in stifling masses, and the steps of the staircase, crackled and trembled, with the fire raging underneath.

His first step was on the stairway; his eye was fixed on the gloom above, when a footstep met his ear.

And ere he turned to gaze, onward thro' flame and smoke, swept a tall and magnificent form, clad in robes of snow-white furs, with the strange glare that gave its wild lustre to the hall, falling over a calm and majestic brow, impressed with the lines of suffering and thought.

" The mysterious stranger of the valley !" muttered Randulph, and as he spoke, the stranger glided upward along the crumbling stairway, like a ghost, and the smoke gathering thick and dense on either side, in a moment shut him from the view.

Randulph sprang forward, half stifled by the stifling smoke, he sprang forward, and the sound of voices met his ear.

" The smoke gathers thick ; the stairway rocks and trembles ; I will save her yet ! I hear the sound of voices in the room. Her voice—the voice of Blanche—and the other voice ? By Heaven 'tis the voice of the English Lord ! A moment more and she will be saved ! A single moment !"

He had reached the top of the stairway, and all around him was dark as midnight. The massive planks of the landing floor were heated with the intensity of the flames, raging underneath ; before him all was gloom ; behind all flame ; above all darkness. The sound of a voice again broke on his ear.

" Mine *now*—mine forever !" spoke the tones of that deep toned and determined voice—" Mine in life and mine in flame and death ! Ha—ha—" and the sneer came echoing thro' the gloom and smoke—" Ha, ha—proud girl, have I won you at last ?"

" Never !" resounded the voice of a woman, aroused to sudden indignation—" Lord Percy advance a step nearer, and I will leap from this window into the flames below !"

And as the sound of a quick, hurried struggle broke upon his ear, the smoke was suddenly wafted aside from the path of Waldemar, and he beheld a scene, that gave a brighter glow to his eye, a quicker throb to his heart.

Standing in the centre of a large room, seen thro' the open doorway, was the stranger, his tall form, rising grandly amid the clouds of rolling smoke, while on one side in a shrinking posture, her arms clasped across her bosom, stood Blanche Walford, beautiful as a dream and on the opposite, side, driven back by a sudden blow George Percy of Monthermer, was gazing with a half drawn sword and a flashing eye, upon the sudden apparition, that had separated the maiden from his grasp.

One glance at the clouds of smoke that darkened the walls, the ceiling and the windows of the apartment, one glance at the singular mingling of light and gloom that played around the strange picture, and Randulph Waldemar sprang to the side of the maiden. She raised her full dark eyes —their gaze met. She hailed him with a faint cry, and then a wild ringing shriek of joy burst from her lips.

" My own, my beautiful Blanche—" murmured Randulph as he gathered her form of beauty within his embrace ; " let us away from this scene of flame and death !"

She said not a word, but her eyes of midnight beauty were fixed upon his face, and her arms clung closer to his form.

He sprang toward the opened doorway, his foot was upon the threshold ; he started back with sudden horror. The smoke had rolled aside from the landing place, at the top of the stairway, the flames were bursting from the oaken floor ; all hope of escape was over.

Thicker and darker gathered the smoke, and fiercer crackled and hissed the flames, while the fire below roared like a furnace.

" Never, tremble Blanche ; never fear !" exclaimed Waldemar—" I will save ye yet !"

And as he spoke, the tall and handsome form of George Percy stood at his shoulder, his eyes flashing with rage, and his lips firmly set together.

" Unhand *her*—" he shouted—" or by the * * * who made me, we'll perish in the flames together ! You have a sword—*coward*—defend yourself !"

He sprang forward, with his sword raised on high. The blade glittered over the head of Randulph, and with one arm girdling the form of Blanche Walford, with one foot on the threshold and his face turned to his foe, Waldemar drew his sword and stood on his defence.

" She is mine—mine and none other than mine !" shouted Lord Percy, when his sword dropped suddenly to his side, his face changed to an ashen paleness, and he sank upon his knees, with his flashing eyes fixed upon the burning floor. A small pacquet with broad seal, marking the carefully folded paper, lay on the very verge of a widening crevice in the burning floor. The violent movement with which Percy had rushed forward, had loosened the ribbon that encircled his neck, and bound it to his heart, and the pacquet had fallen to the floor, as he was in the act of raising his sword.

It was terrible to see the mingled expression that came over Percy's countenance, as groping along the floor, he extended his hand to grasp the pacquet, with the fear, that it might be consumed in the flames, visible in all the changes of his face, in the fixed glance of his eye, and the nervous trembling of his lip.

"Quick! Captain Waldemar!" muttered a voice at his shoulder, and the lofty form of the Stranger, stood before him sword in hand—"Look—I have riven a panel from the wainscoting—it is thrown across the floor of the landing—you may reach the stairway, in safety! In * * *'s name—speed ye, speed!"

It needed no second word, no second look. With one firm arm gathered around the waist of the beautiful girl, while her head, with all its midnight tresses falling loosely around the beaming face, was pillowed on his manly breast, the chieftain, sprang forward, and tho' the plank quivered and trembled like a reed beneath him, he gained the top of the stairway. It was encircled by smoke, and illumined by the glare of the raging flames.

Another moment! He descends the stairway, his noble form towering thro' smoke and flame. The steps creak and tremble beneath him; the flames sweep against her dress of flowing white. He holds her aloft in his manly arm—she gasps for breath, her bosom trembles, and her dark eyes flash. A terrible crash resounds thro' the burning mansion; the stairway has fallen; the flames sweep upward, and his noble form is lost to view.

A solid step rings on the floor of the mansion hall, and thro' the smoke and flame, sweeps on the form of Randulph Waldemar.

"'Twas a terrible leap Blanche; and the crash was terrible, but I have saved ye!"

And with the word, he sprang from the bosom of the flame, he sprang along the scathed sward in front of the mansion door. His noble steed was standing beside a lofty tree, with the loosened bridle-rein falling along his arching neck, while around and above him, gathered and blackened the smoke of the burning mansion.

In a moment Randulph Waldemar was mounted on his gallant war horse, the bridle rein in his right hand, while his left arm gathered to his heart, the queenly form of Blanche, with her dark hair streaming in wild luxuriance over her neck and shoulders, while a sudden flush brightened over her cheek, and a gleam, like the light of a shooting star, intense, vivid and flame-like, glanced from her midnight eye.

"Fear you aught, my Blanche?" exclaimed Randulph with his dark hazel eyes fixed upon her kindling face—"my steed sweeps down the hill —he speeds away toward yon plain with its pall of battle! Fear you aught my Blanche?"

"Fear Randulph? I feel no fear!" replied Blanche with a wild glow of enthusiasm as she flung her arms, closer around her lover's neck, "The battle flame flashes around us; and the smoke gives forth its glare and meteor light, but I feel no fear!"

He pressed the maiden closer to his heart, and then his steed sprang down the hill, and soon was speeding along the valley plain, with all its glory and its terror, darkening and flashing around him.

His way of escape lay directly over the valley, with the American army clustering along the eastern heights, while the western steeps were darkened by the hordes of the Hessian band. In front of his path all was smoke and gloom, with skirmishing parties of either army, engaging hand to hand along the green sward, while the bullet whistled along the air, and the glare of the cannon, flashing from the heights of the Ford, gave a wild, lurid radiance to the scene.

"We will speed along the valley road between the two armies," whispered Randulph—"We will speed for Dilworth corner, where I will place you in safety until the fate of this battle day is known. Blanche cling closer to me now—we approach yon cloud of death and flame; closer Blanche; in a moment all danger will be passed, in a moment—"

A bullet came whistling along the air, from the Hessian army ; the snow-white robe that gathered round the maidenly bosom of Blanche, was stained with blood.

And as Randulph beheld the crimson stain, with a kindling eye, the sound of horses hoofs, beating in hurried pursuit, struck his ear, and turning he beheld the dark steed of Lord Percy, rushing onward in his very path, at the utmost stretch of his speed. His rider, George of Monthermer, leaned over the arching neck, with his drawn sword gleaming on high, with his glance, vivid and flashing, fixed upon the object of his pursuit, while his countenance was impressed with one wild determined expression, that spoke of his fixed purpose, and resolved soul.

"She is mine !" came the deep toned shout of the desperate man—" And on the field of battle, will I tear her form from your embrace !"

He came rushing on, in a moment his horse, would be side by side with the steed of Randulph.

"It must be !" muttered Randulph, as his eye beheld the crimson stain on the snow-white robe of the maiden, "Blanche our death bed may be this valley plain—from this green sward our souls may wing their way to the world beyond ! Fear you death, love of mine ?"

"Not with you !" murmured Blanche, and her eyes beamed brighter, and more beautiful was the glow of her young face, as she clung to her lover's heart.

"Coward, turn and defend yourself !" shouted a stern voice, and the steed of Lord Percy, came sweeping along by the side of the American Chieftain ; the sword of Monthermer was raised in the air, his flashing eye was fixed upon the face of Randulph, and his arm was nerved for the blow of death.

Randulph raised his sword to parry the descending blow, and as the steel glittered in the light, the eyes of the antagonists met, and at the same mo

20

ment, some wild and terrible thought blazed from each eye, and paled each cheek.

" *The* HOUR *has not yet come !*" murmured Percy, his sword swung to his side ; and at the same moment, his ebon steed reared suddenly on high with his forefeet thrust wildly forward, and then, with a quick and startling bound, he fell heavily back on his haunches, with the mortal wound of the cannon ball, severing the black skin of his glossy chest.

And over the horse and his doomed rider, thrown along the green sward of the field, rolled a cloud of gathering smoke ; it shut them in from the sight, like the death pall encircling the coffin and the corse.

" 'Tis a glorious scene, Blanche !" murmured Randulph, as his steed dashed onward ; " The armies clustering on the opposite heights, the gleam of bayonet and the pomp of banners ! Might I choose my death, 'twould be a death on a battle field like this !"

The voice of the lover suddenly faultered, as he gazed upon the stain of blood, that crimsoned the robes floating around the maiden's breast.

"She may be fatally wounded !" the thought flashed over his brain. " I will away from this field ; I will seek a place of safety !"

And while he gathered Blanche to his heart, with a firmer embrace, his steed swept along the valley, with the speed of wind. It was a strange sight, that gallant rider, dashing thro' the smoke of battle, the white robes of the maiden fluttering in the breeze, while the outlines of the golden-hued steed, the waving mane, the arching neck, the proud toss of the head, and the magnificent proportions of the limbs, were one moment seen, revealed in sudden and vivid light, and the next instant, veiled in as sudden tho' blackening shadow.

On and on he swept, speeding along the valley plain, with his steed urged to the utmost extent of his speed, and Chadd's Ford was soon left behind ; the house of the murdered schoolmaster was passed, and the pleasant shadow of a green dell, reposing between two high hills, brilliant with the sword and bayonet of the American host, was presently seen, thro' the wreaths of cannon smoke ; quiet and peaceful as in the olden time of halcyon rule.

Randulph struck for the lovely dell, he dashed thro' a party of American rifles, he sped along the woods, and then a track of green fields, and whitened buckwheat traversed, he was soon speeding along a winding road, leading eastward to Dilworth Corner, overhung by long lines of magnificent forest trees, here the giant trunked chesnut, with its broad green leaves, there the grey sycamore flinging its massive shadow over the brown earth of the road side, and a little farther on, a clump of the white oak, the ash, and the beachen trees, arising on some green knoll by the road side, mingling their rich and luxuriant verdure, faintly tinged by the breath of autumn.

Many a pleasant field was left behind, many a green hill ascended, many a lovely hollow passed, and then, ascending the steep of a lofty hill, Ran dulph beheld, within cannon shot, the brick walls of the deserted town of Dilworth Corner, the dark timbers of the blacksmith's shop, and the cottage with its uprising well pole, all occupying the rising ground in the vicinity of the four cross roads.

"Yonder, Blanche, you may remain, until the fate of this battle-day is known"—whispered Randulph, as he suffered his horse to pace the road side, with a less hurried movement. "The broad blaze of day streams over this luxuriant land; 'tis yet unclouded by battle smoke!"

"How still, how quiet, how dead, seems everything around us!" whispered Blanche, fixing her full dark eyes on the visage of her lover. "It seems as tho' all nature, was hushed in solemn awe of the approach of battle!"

"Blanche, your dress is crimsoned with blood!" exclaimed Randulph, "and yet, your cheek pales not, your eye still gleams with its wonted fire! Are you wounded, Blanche?"

So hurried had been their flight, that the maiden had not noted the stain of blood crimsoning her dress. She cast her glance hurriedly downward, and in a moment, her fair white hand was placed, within the folds of her dress, upon her bosom.

Randulph held his breath, and gazed upon the maiden with all the anxiety of his soul, pictured in his countenance. Blanche drew her hand from her snow-white bosom. The hand was stained with blood. She whispered a word to her lover.

The wound was slight, the bullet had but grazed her bosom, crimsoning her dress with a sudden tho' slight effusion of blood.

"You are not injured then, Blanche, God be thanked!" exclaimed Randulph, as his bronzed visage lit up with a sudden flush of joy. "But here we are, at the Cross Roads of Dilworth Corner. Look around, Blanche—not a sign of life meets your eye. No living being within sight; all is silent, hushed and dead!"

And as he reined his steed, in the open space, forming the centre of the Cross Roads, Blanche raised her head from his breast and gazed around.

All was silent as midnight. The full blaze of the morning sunbeams fell warmly, and with a golden light, over the massive brick walls of the deserted inn, the sloping roof of the cottage, and the circular wall erected around the well, but the tavern was untenanted by human being, the cottage was voiceless and silent, and no merry sound of clanging anvil, or ringing hammer, broke the silence of the blacksmith shop of Iron Tom o' Dilworth Corner.

All was still and silent as tho' a plague had swept the place.

The Inn of Dilworth Corner, was a structure of massive brick, with a porch extending along its western front, and a lordly buttonwood tree, ascending from the sward, and flinging its wide branches over the roof of the mansion. A wild vine hung, trailing, along the northern gable, its green leaves, contrasting with the dull red of the brick.

At a few rods distance, on the opposite side of the road, was the cottage of the stout blacksmith, a one storied structure, with a neat garden in front, a well on one side, and a mass of foliage on the other. Like the Inn it was silent as the grave. The morning was rapidly approaching, the noonday hour, but a voiceless silence hung upon the landscape. Not a shout, or the bray of a watch-dog, or even the gentle sound of lowing of cattle was heard.

The * inn and the cottage were deserted by their denizens ; war had disturbed this quiet nook of rural solitude, and with it, brought a dark presentiment of coming horror.

" Look to the south, Blanche ! Yonder are the white tents of Greene's division, dotting the hillside. How proudly the American banner waves in the morning light, over the lines of brave men, drawn up in order of battle."

Blanche gazed to the south, and her eyes brightened with a gleam of pleasure. Within the distance of a quarter-of-a-mile, arose a green hill, its summit crowned with woods, and the gentle slope of its breast, whitened with the tents of the American soldiers. The broad banner of the stars, waved proudly over the General's marquee, toying with the breeze and sunbeams, as gaily as though no stain of blood, was to redden its folds, ere the close of day.

Suddenly the echo of horse's hoofs was heard, toward the north. So deep was the silence, which lay upon the landscape, that this familiar sound, struck upon the ear, with a strange emphasis. It came from the bye-road, leading toward Birmingham meeting house.

In a few moments a dark bay horse, emerged from the shadow of the trees, in front of Iron Tom's cottage, and came, dashing at full speed, toward the Inn.

A wild cry of joy, burst from the lips of Blanche.

The rider of the strange steed, was a woman, and though her dress was torn and soiled with dust, Blanche recognized her cousin at a glance.

It was Rose Frazier !

Ere a moment, had flown, Blanche flung herself from the arms of Randulph, and Rose was at her side, they gazed in each other's face, with a look of deep joy, and then were buried in each other's arms.

While Randulph, gazed upon the forms of the fair girls, in mute surprise, a sudden rustling, was heard, among the shrubbery, in the rear of Iron Tom's cottage, and a noble steed cleared the thick hedge at a bound.

---

* The Inn of Dilworth Corner, (as I am informed by my esteemed friend, the Senator Myers, of Delaware County,) was tenanted, about the time of the battle, by Major Harper who proved himself, an able soldier, on the well contested field of Brandywine.

The dress of the rider, was covered with dust and spotted with drops of blood. His dark brown hair, hang lank and wet about his neck. His broken plume, drooped over his heated brow, and it was evident, that he had ridden, far and long, at peril of life and steed.

" Clerwoode !" exclaimed Randulph.

The new comer made no reply, but urging his horse to Randulph's side seized the extended hand of the chief, and wrung it with a vigorous grasp.

For a moment there was silence.

Randulph's manly countenance reddened with a warm glow of pleasure, his dark hazel eyes grew bright and then dim. A manly tear stole down his olive cheek. Clerwoode gazed in the captain's face with evident signs of emotion. His upper lip quivered, and he brushed his left hand, partly across his eyes.

" Clerwoode I am glad to see you !" said Randulph in a quiet but emphatic tone. " When we left the hills of the Santee, I swore that I would keep you, as the apple of my eye. How could I have entered the presence of your widowed mother, without you ; without her only son ?"

" Well—well—Captain," exclaimed Clerwoode, in a hasty tone, assumed to hide his emotion, " I swore I'd fool the Britishers, and by the Lord I've kept my word !"

Meanwhile standing in the centre of the road, Rose and Blanche, were buried in each other's arms. Their emotion was too deep for words or tears. Blanche had feared that her cousin was lost to her forever ; for the two past days, a fearful presentment of wrong and outrage had rested on her soul. Rose, had dared death, and untold dangers worse than death ; she too had feared she might never behold a face from home again.

And now they stood locked in each other's arms, Blanche's raven black hair, streamed over the shoulders of her cousin, while the face of Rose was buried in her bosom.

This scene, was broken by the voice of Randulph, after the lapse of a few minutes. In brief words, he spoke of the necessity of his return to the army, with the young soldier Clerwoode Le Clere.

" An hour may decide the fate of this day. This inn will be a safe retreat, Blanche, for you and your friend, until the close of the fight. The fight once over, I will return to you again. Till then Blanche farewell. Come Clerwoode, we must away !"

He spoke in a hasty tone, as though he feared, his manhood, might be shamed, by an expression of the emotion, which throbbed throughout his heart.

Blanche and Rose, stood side by side on the porch of the inn, while Randulph and Clerwoode, turned their horse's heads toward the valley of the Brandywine.

A look from each soldier to each maiden, a wave of the hand and they were gone. The echo of their horse's hoofs rose on the air; the sunlight fell over their retreating forms, and the maidens were alone, in the silence of the hour.

Rose gazed in the face of Blanche, with a look of deep meaning. Her dark eyes dilated, with an expression, whose import, Blanche, could not fathom. It was wild and fearful and full of some dark mystery.

"What mean you, Rose?" exclaimed Blanche, gazing wonderingly into the face of her couzin.

"Come," whispered Rose, moving along the porch, to the open door of the inn, "Come! I have a story to tell you, Blanche, so sad, so fearful, that my heart grows cold to think upon it! But God is just, and *He* will avenge the innocent, ere the day is over. Come Blanche, I will tell it to you, this story of a hideous wrong."

CHAPTER FOURTH.

HIS GRACE, GEORGE, DUKE WASHINGTON, VICEROY OF AMERICA.

A GENTLE knoll, lifting its grassy bosom, from the level of the meadow, its summit crowned with trees, and its sides decked with flowers. A gentle knoll, encircled by the greenery of wild vines, from whose leaves are thrust the hues of flowers, with the tall grass waving in the autumnal air.

A gentle knoll, uprising from the valley, like a brave warrior, sleeping after a hard fought fight, a robe of flowers, round him, and a lofty plume of trees upon his brow.

Yonder is the meadow of the Brandywine, one unbroken sheet of summer green, yonder, winding along in light, are the waters of the rivulet, with a sombre battlement of woods, arising on its western shore. To the north among the hills of Brenton's Ford, you behold the gleam of Sullivan's arms; to the south, you hear the clangor of Wayne's battle music. This knoll uprises between the two points of fight, a quiet spot, amid the terror of battle.

Even at this day, many a traveller turns aside from the beaten road, and fastening his horse, to the rustic fence, ascends the gentle knoll, and from its height, as from an altar, gazes over the valley of the Brandywine. Yes, with eager steps, he brushes among the wild vines which beset his path, he stoops to deck his bosom, with the wild flowers which grace the hillside, he ascends the knoll, and stands beneath the shadows of the trees, upon its brow.

Lordly trees, by Heaven! Five oaks, encircle the brow of that mound-like knoll. Five oaks, with beech and chesnut and maple trees between, leaving a circular space in the centre, whereon, grows a thick and tufted moss. These oaks have trunks like the columns of some temple, dark, rugged and massy. These oaks, have stout and wide reaching limbs, thick with broad green leaves. The chesnut and the maple, and the beech, have died and been reproduced, again and again, but these five old oaks, who shall count their age?

When these five old oaks were saplings, there were gallant red men in the land, stern warriors, whose religion, was honor and love and revenge. This knoll was an altar, yonder sky its roof. Hundreds of years have past, since then; the red men have been crushed beneath the blood-stained feet of Christian civilization, a nation has arisen from a family of provinces; a Republic has sprung into birth, from the gory sea of revolution.

Still the five old oaks, raise their proud forms on the brow of the knoll and reach forth their hundred arms to the sky.

God avert the day, when these oaks, shall arise in a Despot's kingdom! God avert the day, when Priests and Factionaries, shall have done, their work of treason, and transformed the America of Washington, into the America of Anarchy, Civil war and Despotism!

Oh, would to God, that every Priest or, Demagogue, or Factionary, who essays, to do his little work of cant and hypocrisy, might come to this valley of the Brandywine, might ascend this knoll, and kneel down in the place of holy memories.

Here, while kneeling on the moss, which is consecrated by religion, by history, by patriotism, in sight of this valley, whereon, the tide of battle flowed, on the renowned eleventh of September, here, while kneeling, under the shade of these five old oaks, the words of treason, would be forgotten in the syllables of prayer. Here under this green sod, would be buried, and forever buried, the watchwords of discordant factions and ambitious Priests; their cant about the Bible, which they read but to distort, about that Slavery, which they attack but to strengthen, about that Human Progress, which like the car of Hindoo superstition, is to crush, our holiest institutions and dearest memories, under its wheels.

For the summit of this gentle knoll, was consecrated by a scene of the deepest interest, on the memorable battle day of Brandywine.

It was eleven o' clock in the morning; that moment, when an awful pause, a fearful expectation, intervened between the fight of the morning, and the battle of the afternoon; it was eleven o' clock, when a solitary traveller whose way had lain, along the Brandywine road, approached this knoll of the five old oaks, and ascending its side, disappeared within the foliage of the trees.

The branches of the old oaks, mingling with the leaves of the chesnut, and maple and beech, enclosed him like a curtain. Flinging the rein on the neck of his grey horse, he dismounted. Trembling beams of sunlight, fell through the thick leaves, over his kingly form. A solemn silence, reigned within the shadow of the oaks. Thickly clustered green leaves, above, and softly tufted moss below; massive trunks all around; the scent of flowers on the air, which came rustling through the trees; and a glimpse of the blue sky, visible through an opening, in the foliage, the place, was well adapted for deep and absorbing thought.

The traveller, with his back against a giant oak, at one end of the glade, and his arms folded on his breast, gazed intently on vacancy, with his dilating eyes.

A mighty emotion, shook his powerful frame. Yes he, the man, who in battle, was calm, as an image of carved marble, now felt the throes of an agitation, which quivered through every fibre of his soul.

That face whose commanding features, were never shadowed by an emotion, when exposed to the gaze of men, now quivered in every muscle. That calm grey eye, so full of mild benignity, at all times, even when it gleamed over the ranks of battle, now dilated and blazed. That massive chest, heaved and writhed, beneath the folded arms. From head to foot, this mighty man, trembled with an emotion, whose intensity cannot be told in words.

WASHINGTON, was in the presence of his GOD.

Yes, yes, he had hastened from his army, to the quiet knoll, for a few brief moments, to hold converse with his Maker. Washington was in council with Jehovah.

A world of thought flashed over his brain. Hope, fear, joy, triumph and doubt, by times, assumed the sway, or mingling together, deepened the emotion, that shook the chest of the mighty man.

It is my solemn duty, to fling off the covering of frost work, with which posterity, has enshrouded Washington; to show the man, as he was, all feeling, and enthusiasm and all MAN.

Ever and again his thoughts found utterance in words, now quick and hasty, and again low, deep toned and prolonged.

"Would it might be so, would it might be so!" murmured Washington, as he paced up and down the sheltered glade. "Would that it were the will of God! That this day might be the last of the war! The last day of the long and bloody massacre! Yes, yes, were the position of the enemy, the invader, but once taken, could I but behold, his ranks drawn up in order of battle, I would advance to the charge, I, myself would head the army of freedom, and by one determined onset, decide the fate of the war!"

For a moment he stood like a statue of carved marble. Not a fibre of his commanding frame, but was firm as adamant, not a muscle of his set features, but was fixed as steel. His eye, alone, betrayed emotion, for glaring on vacancy, it shone like a flame.

" Could my life determine the war," he said in a deep and solemn tone, " this very day, would I pour out my blood, an offering to God, for the freedom of my land !"

There is a sublimity of tone and manner, which shames the poverty of words. That sublimity of the will, centred in one object, was in the manner and tone of Washington, as he spoke these words.

" Would that my death, could end the war, and give freedom to this land !"

And then, as if the multitude of overpowering thoughts and hopes and fears, crowded like phantoms, on his soul, he sank slowly upon his knees.

Clad in his warrior costume, with head uncovered, he raised his hands, and spoke with his God.

With his face upraised, his eyes lifted to heaven, his brow radiant with emotion, he plead with God, that he might lay down his life, for the freedom of his land.

It was a picture for history to cherish with pious reverence.

The grove of trees, the massive oaks sweeping round the scene, that man of iron strength and muscular frame kneeling in the centre of the sward ; his warrior costume, the coat of blue and buff, the sword trailing on the sod, the long military boots, and the epaulettes glittering on each shoulder ; these formed the details of the picture. Then that face, whose features, seemed to have been formed in a mould of deep serenity, now quivering with agitation, while the grey eyes, lifted to heaven, burned with a sublime resolution.

The voice of Washington, fell round the grove, with that softened and most impressive murmur, which links itself with the syllables of prayer. Meanwhile the grey war horse, stood with the rein thrown over his arching neck, quiet as some statue-steed, erected in the crowded city, a witness of a warrior's triumph.

" Merciful Father ! The contest has been dark and bloody. Armies have sunk to death, in this cause ; the bones of the dead have whitened every battle field. Massacre, and wrong, and outrage, have tracked their footsteps, over the land, in the blood of an innocent people. Now, O God, let the humblest of thy servants beseech Thee, that war may pass from this land ! Thy name has been with me, as a sword and a shield, in the darkest hours of this contest ! In the battle, in the triumph, and in the defeat, in camp and in field, I have called upon Thee, and heard thine answer in the death cry and the battle shout !

" Now, kneeling on this soil of my native land, thy humble Minister, whom thou hast commissioned to work out a nation's freedom, I send up my prayer to Thee, and with the memory of a thousand fights, passing before my soul, I beseech Thee, let the sword of the Destroying Angel, wave no more over the land !

"In the name of the Martyrs who have died, blessing Thee, on ten thousand battle fields, in the name of the patriots of every country and clime, who, having each fulfilled their mission on earth, now surround thy Throne, in the name of Jesus, our Saviour, I beseech thee, hear my prayer.

"Let me, O God, this day, lay down my life, an offering in the cause of freedom ! Let my blood be a sacrifice, acceptable in thy sight, in the cause of that liberty, which is true Religion ! Yes, yes, O, FATHER, with heart, and voice and soul, I beseech thee, take my life, and give freedom to this land, even before yon sun has set !"

He paused and looked up to heaven. With clasped hand and burning eyes, he paused, while his voice died in his throat.

Here was a scene for the Christian to contemplate, while his soul wandered back to the groves of Gethsemane.

There JESUS, with the blood-drops starting from cheek and brow, plead for the salvation of the world. Here, in this quiet grove of Brandywine, WASHINGTON plead, with God, for the salvation of his country, with an agony, second only in intensity, to the sorrow of Christ the Redeemer. With reverence be this spoken ; but let no dry formalist, or complacent Pharisee, carp at this record, which names Washington, in the same breath, with the Saviour, whose Minister he was.

Bowing his head, in voiceless prayer, for a few moments, he was silent as the grave. While thus occupied, the foliage at his back was thrust aside, and the face of a man appeared among the green leaves. Had you been there, you would have started with surprise, as you remarked, how like the face of Washington, was this strange countenance.

Suddenly Washington arose ; he turned ; he beheld the face, and, ere a word might pass his lips, the foliage was thrust aside, and the form of the stranger stepped from beneath the shadow of a giant oak.

They gazed upon each other in mute surprise, Washington and the stranger.

There stood Washington, clad in the military costume of his army, with the sword by his side, and the epaulettes glittering on each shoulder. There, too, confronting the Chieftain, stood the stranger, his form, bearing in its height, its breadth of shoulder and outline of chest, a marked resemblance to the powerful frame of Washington. He was clad in a long grey surtout, buttoned up in front, and reaching to the knees of his booted legs. He wore a plain farmer's broad-rimmed hat ; and his right hand grasped an oaken staff.

There was something mysterious in the manner of the stranger. Gazing steadily in Washington's face, he slowly uncovered his head, as though he stood in the presence of a king. It was strange, to see the likeness which his face bore to the countenance of Washington. His features were cast in the same massive mould ; his brow, bold and thoughtful, his nose prominen.t, his mouth determined, his chin resolute, Evei his hair was arranged like Washington's, after the fashion of the time. As he stood there, confronting the Man of his age, his face bore the same resemblance to Washington's, that an inferior copy does to a portrait by some world renowned master. His face lacked the soul of Washington's countenance, his eye the fire, his brow the expression of indomitable energy.

For a few moments, Washington and the stranger stood regarding each other, in silence. Each seemed to feel, that in the other, he beheld, the Incarnation of some great principle.

"Pardon me, Sir," exclaimed the stranger in a tone of gentlemanly courtesy, "I am a stranger in this part of the country, and have lost my way. I would thank you to direct—"

He paused suddenly, as though some secret feeling, had mastered these words, uttered in the quiet tones of a well-bred man. He paused, he advanced a step, and a solitary exclamation broke from his lips—

"You are Washington !"

"And you—" hesitated Washington.

"My name is Howe," exclaimed the stranger quickly. As he spoke his grey surtout flew open in front. With a start Washington beheld the crimson uniform of a British General, which with its gaudy trappings of gold, had been hidden beneath the overcoat.

There was a moment of deep silence, and deeper surprise.

"General Sir William Howe," continued the Stranger after this pause, "Commander in Chief of his Majesty's forces. This morning, ere daybreak, I rode from our camp at Kennet's square, and lost my way, among the bye-roads of the valley. Passing in the vicinity of this grove, a few moments since, I heard your voice, and having fastened my horse to yonder fence, came hither to enquire the way. I am now—"

"On American ground," exclaimed Washington, gazing upon the British Commander, with a meaning glance.

"Hah! American ground?" echoed Howe witn a slight start. "One word from you, and I am prisoner, in the heart of the *reb*—that is the continental army."

"The American forces are within pistol-shot, from this knoll, both on the north and south," calmly replied Washington. "Across yonder meadow, and up yonder heights," pointing to the west, "lies your way. To be plain, w.th you, General Howe, you are in my power, but I cannot take an ungenerous advantage of an enemy. Yonder lies your way; it needs but five minutes gallop, across the meadow, and over yonder hills, and you are in the heart of the British army—"

Howe advanced toward the tree, beneath whose shade, he had entered the glade, and then suddenly turning, confronted Washington again.

"Sir, let me beg the privilege of a moment's conversation with you " ne exclaimed in a quick tone. " And let me confess at once, that it was with the hope, that I might encounter you, that I rode forth this morning—"

" Encounter me ?" echoed Washington. " And with what motive did you desire an interview, with the commander of .he American forces ?"

" Sir, I beseech you hear me, for one moment. The King my master, has heard of your self-denial, your indomitable energy, your sincere, although mistaken patriotism. He has heard of all your personal qualities, which alone have dignified, this revolt, with the name of a war. Believe me, his admiration for your character, is sincere. And it is to you, that he appeals, and by your oath of allegiance, asks you to stay this rebellion, in its desolating career. Yes, Sir, the King my master, has commissioned me, to appeal to you in person. His majesty has more confidence in your honor, than in your Congress, or in any ambassadors or commissioners, whom either party, might appoint, to settle the difficulties of the colonies with the Mother Country."

" I know not the drift of this appeal," replied Washington with stern dignity ; " but you can tell your King, that a spirit has been raised throughout this wide land, which will not be laid to rest again, until these colonies, are recognized by his majesty and the world, as an Independent empire."

" Independent empire !" echoed Sir William Howe. " That is a vain delusion, Sir. Rebellion in all the history of man, never found any termination, but punishment from the Sovereign, whom it defied, or Anarchy from the miserable success, which it won. No, Sir ! Let it be yours to act the nobler part, and merit the gratitude of the King and the world—"

" In plain terms, brand my name with the epithet of Traitor ?"

" The King commissions me to inform you," continued Sir William Howe, without appearing to notice the indignant exclamation of Washington ; " That any efforts of yours, to restore peace to these colonies, will not be forgotten by him—"

He paused, as if to note the effect of his words. Washington stood calm and immoveable, with his gaze fixed upon the face of the British General.

" In fine," pursued Howe, " I am instructed to offer for your acceptance, a *title*, which no subject ever won, by his simple merits, in all the history of Great Britain—"

He paused again. As though deeply impressed by the words, Washington folded his arms, and suffered his head to droop on his breast. His eyes were fixed upon the ground.

" Let us imagine a case. By your means, the colonies return to their loyalty, and the royal government is firmly established. In that case Sir, I am instructed by the King my master, to offer to George Washington, Esquire, the Vice-royalty of his majesty's kingdom in America, with the title of Duke—"

He stood awaiting his answer, with his eye, fixed anxiously on Washing-

ton's face. Washington, remained in the position, which he had assumed,
at first, with his arms folded, his head drooped on his bosom, and his eyes
cast to the earth.

Duke !

Aye Duke Washington, second alone to the King himself, in rank and
power !

Say, was not this a glittering, boon to hold before the eyes of a simple
Virginia gentleman, one plain Master George Washington ?

"Have you no answer, to this offer, from his Majesty ?" exclaimed Howe
after a long and anxious pause.

Washington slowly raised his head.   His look was full of quiet
dignity.

"I have just been thinking of the ten thousand brave men, who have laid
down their lives, in this cause. I have endeavoured to recall the horrible details of each battle-field, where brave and virtuous men, sank down to death,
fighting for their native land.   I have tried to bring up before me, the memories of Bunker Hill, Lexington, Quebec, Long Island, White Plains and a
thousand nameless frays, where your arms, were crimsoned in the blood
of peaceful men."

"And you wish to terminate this disastrous war ?"

"And your King, wishes me to barter the blood of my countrymen and
the whitening bones of her battle fields, for the bauble of a coronet, the
empty jingle of a title !"

The manner of Washington was withering, as he gave utterance to the
sentiment.

"Go, and tell your King," he resumed extending his good right arm,
"That were George Washington, to betray the trust reposed in him, there
is not a soldier in the Continental army, who would hesitate to shoot the
traitor !"

Howe was silent.   His frame shook with emotion, and he turned his head
away, for a single moment.

"O, Sir, your King has a most elevated estimate of honor and faith and
manliness !   What though thousands are butchered for a shadow, what
though a nation of widows and orphans, heap their curses on this war, what
though the land grows rich with the graves of its massacred children.
Your King would pay for it all, with a ribbon and a bit of tinsel !"

Howe extended his hand, and with a sudden movement, and seized the
hand of Washington.

"I am a Briton," he said in hurried tones, "A British General, and the
subject of a British King, but I do—I do respect you as an honest
man !"

He said these words in a voice of deep emotion : when Washington looked
around again, the British General was gone.

Casting his gaze towards the meadows of the Brandywine, in a moment he beheld the form of a horseman, attired in grey, and riding a noble white horse, speeding rapidly toward the rivulet. As Washington looked, there was the sound of a musquet shot, followed by two others in quick succession, but the horseman passed on unharmed, he gained the waters of the Brandy-wine, he passed the stream and disappeared, beneath the shadow of the trees, on the opposite bank.

Washington was alone again. At his feet, distinctly relieved by the green of the moss, which formed the carpet of the glade, lay a large square pac-quet of white parchment, encumbered with a massive seal.

It was the royal seal of England. Washington raised the pacquet, slowly unrolled it, and with a calm smile, perused its contents.

These words were prominent, among the multitude of royal phrases and legal tautologies :

—GEORGE, DUKE WASHINGTON, *our well beloved* VICEROY OF AMERICA—

It bore the signature of the Idiot-King of England, and was, nothing more nor less, than letters patent from his Majesty, constituting the Ameri-can leader, for his high services, in restoring the revolted colonies to their allegiance, Duke Washington, Viceroy of America.

George Washington gazed upon this glittering manifestation of royal favor, with a smile, and then, with one quick movement of his muscular arms, tore the parchment into fragments, and trampled the royal seal of England under foot.

"To thee, O, God, do I resign the issues of this day! If the gift of my poor life, will bring freedom to this land, then, O, Father, I will most gladly lay it down, a sacrifice upon the battle field!"

With this voiceless prayer, Washington mounted his steed, and descended from the knoll of the five oaks.

And on this knoll the moss grows green as ever, the trees arise, with trunks like granite columns, and limbs as large as the trunks of common oaks ; there are green leaves still overhead, and soft turf still beneath. And here, as the autumnal day went down, have I lain, while the purple gloom of twilight gathered over the valley. The shadows of Washington and Howe, have risen before me, in the silence of that grove, as an old soldier, whose white hairs swept his shoulders, spoke, in trembling accents, this tradition of Washington, who was too proud to be a Duke with a princely revenue, too proud to be the Viceroy of a British King.*

* This incident was related to me by an old veteran, who pointed out the knoll, on whose summit it occurred. In an old English magazine. I find an allusion to a circumstance of this kind ; it is hinted that the King sought to purchase Washington, by the offer of a Duke-dom, about the time of the Battle of Brandywine.

Whether a vain tradition or a solemn fact, this incident is fraught with a sublime moral.

CHAPTER FIFTH.

THE DREAM.

It is but a Phantasm, a dream, and yet unlike the dreams of most romancers, it is a dream with a meaning, a phantasm with a moral.

All men are dreamers. The geologist dreams, when he gravely attempts to reason himself and others, into the belief of a Pre-Adamite world; the historian dreams, when from a few puerile fictions, he constructs a solemn and truthful chronicle; and a very dreamer is your portentious Divine, who would convert the world, by describing, in lively colors, the terrors of hell. All men are dreamers, from the niggard of a Dollar-worshipper, who builds up a fortune, to be squandered by his profligate heir, to the Ideal Perfectionist, whose supreme elixir for the evils of society, is, by turns, a very popular theory of government, where every man administers justice for himself, with Knife and Torch; or an Association, which herds men, women and children together, in a farm, like cattle in a barn-yard, or yet again, a Flesh-abhorring society, which, holding the butcher and his stall in superlative abhorrence, confines itself to saw-dust bread and raw turnips.

All men are dreamers, and some have blessed, and some pernicious dreams; some are beautiful as light, some ugly as a cankered heart; some are nightmare convulsions, full of revolution and horror, and some are like the golden visions, which come over the soul, in the sleep of the summer's dawn. Yet, all are dreams.

Why should not your Romancer have his dream, as well as your geologist, your historian, your divine, politician, or perfectionist?

Here, then, is our dream, which came over us, while the incident of the last chapter, was yet green in our memory. The reader is fairly warned, that this dream has no connection with the mere story of the book, but is an Episode, which intervenes between the more stirring incidents of the plot, like a quiet vision of memory, breaking in upon the the stirring prospects of the future.

It is morning, in a populous city. An immense crowd blocks up the avenues, around a massive building, whose lofty walls arise, from among green bowers of foliage. Trees, and walls, and roof-tops, are black with people. Here are grey-haired men, and blooming maidens, here are mature matrons, with babes in their arms, and here are the bronzed faces of early manhood, and the careless visages of youth. The wide city has given forth its populace, who come thronging around this palace, eager to behold a strange and wondrous scene.

The marble palace arises in the centre of a spacious park. Gates of iron, and massive railing, with points sharpened like spears, defend it from the pressure of the crowd. Here, within this park, you behold winding walks of brown gravel, contrasting with gentle slopes of green lawn ; here are statues and fountains, trees and flowers.

The palace is a massive structure of marble. Its outline arises from among the trees into the sky, like an image of vague immensity. From its windows, so lofty and impressive in their architecture, float cloths of gold, and banners inscribed with many a quaint yet meaning device. High, over all, over trees, and fountains, and marble walls, and dense masses of people from the dome of the palace, floats the broad banner of England, its colors of blood sweeping gaily into the clear blue sky.

Along one of the wide walks, leading to the palace, are files of soldiers, attired in crimson, a massive fur cap on each swarthy brow, a musquet to each shoulder, and the broad banner waving overhead. In two brilliant lines, one on either side of the walk, they extend along the park, from the iron gates, to the massive door of the palace.

In all that vast crowd, every eye is fixed upon the palace door, in mute expectation. Suddenly the deep silence, which marks the anxiety of the populace, is succeeded by the clangor of trumpets, the roll of drums and the thunder of cannon.

A wild murmur breaks on the air, and then a wilder hurrah. From the main door of the palace, a gorgeous pageant emerges into light ; a gorgeous pageant of courtiers, attired in silken robes, with a man of noble presence at their head.

He stands alone, on the marble steps of the palace, that man of commanding stature and kingly look. Royal robes of crimson droop from his shoulders ; a glittering coronet flashes from his, brow, the sword of state, gleams along his thigh, and stars and ribbands, heave into light, with every respiration of his muscular chest.

Who is this man of noble presence? Hark ! How that shout swells on the air ! Ten thousand voices shriek one name, ten thousand eyes are fixed upon one form. Mothers lift their babes on high, pointing their gaze to that man, whom to look upon is glory ; grey-haired veterans uncover their heads in honor of his name ; bearded men send that name in thunder to the skies.

How name you this city, the time, and the man ?

The city is Philadelphia, the year 1800, the man——Listen to that shout for his name.

" Hail to the Viceroy of the King ! Hurrah, hurrah for His Grace ! Hurrah for DUKE WASHINGTON !"

Yes, Duke Washington ! He comes forth from his palace, to receive the shouts of a pliant populace. He walks beneath the shadow of a British ban-

ner, he walks between long lines of British soldiers, he stands erect, a British
Duke, the Viceroy of a British King.

Our dream assumes another form.

The golden sunlight is streaming through the emblazoned windows of an
apartment in the palace of St. James. In that gorgeous anti-chamber, are
clustered a band of Lords and ladies, arrayed in all the lustre of stars and
coronets. The walls are hung with pictures, on whose faded canvass are
delineated the triumphs of the British empire. And, among the glittering
frames, along the tapestry which conceals the walls, are grouped the banners of many nations, won on the red field of battle, by British arms. Here
are trophies from all the world. The *oriflamme* of France, the rude flags
of far distant Barbarian kings, the gonfalon of Spain, the broad banner of
the United Provinces of Holland, these all are grouped among weapons of
battle, the tomahawk of the Indian, with the sword of the French knight,
the flame-like crease of the Malay, with the javelin of the Hindoo. Here
are innumerable proofs of the greatness, the glory and the fame of England.
Where are the proofs of her crimes? Leave that to God and the Last
Judgment!

Here, in this anti-chamber stored with flags and trophies from all the
world, are gathered the lords and ladies, the proud nobility of Britain.
Every tongue is hushed, in expectation of a scene, fraught with the deepest
interest.

The Viceroy of America, and his Britannic Majesty, will, in a few moments, meet face to face, in that ante-chamber of St. James.

Suddenly a massive door is flung open. The gentlemen in livery announce the King. At the same moment another door, on the opposite side
of the chamber, rolls back on its silver hinges. Those gentlemen in livery
announce the Viceroy.

The King and the Viceroy meet in the centre of the ante-chamber. Need
you ask, which is the Master, which the Servitor? That fine old gentleman, with the vacant face and the bulging eyes. that good humored old man,
with his portly form bedizened with a robe of crimson, his receding brow
glittering with a crown, his fat, gouty fingers grasping a sceptre, that is
King George the Third, of England.

Then that man, in whose presence lords and courtiers seem to stand in
silent awe, that man, with his towering form, arrayed in ducal robes, with
his calm and imperturbable visage, whose every lineament betokens command, surmounted by the vice-regal crown; how name you this kingly
stranger? His Grace, George, Duke Washington, Viceroy of America.

The humble Virginia planter has become a Duke, the rebel has been
transformed into the Viceroy of the King whom he defied, the Father of his
country, into the courtier of a tyrant.

He kneels he kisses the hand of Majesty; in low tones and set words,

22

he announces to the King his master, that rebellion is crushed, and loyalty triumphant, in the Provinces of America.

Then that corpulent old gentleman, with the vacant face and the bulging eyes, answers in short quick sentences, and testifies his delight, that his faithful servant of Mount Vernon, has returned to his duty, and crushed the rebels of America.

The Duke Washington rises to his feet, he stands erect, in the pride of his commanding look and kingly stature, he feels the vice-regal crown upon his brow, the vice-regal robes upon his limbs, and gazing on the pitiful old man, whose gouty fingers have bestowed these honors, he exclaims,

" For this, I betrayed my country !"

Such would have been the position of George Washington, had he betrayed the liberties of his country, for the smile of a king.

Again the dream changes. It is a dark and fearful change.

The scene is Tower Hill. In the centre of a dense mass of human beings, arises a blackened and hideous spectacle. In the centre of that vast theatre, whose stage is the hard earth, whose walls are houses, castles and steeples, tapestried with human faces, whose roof is the calm blue sky, there glooms a strange panorama of death, a scaffold, with the executioner, the victim and the axe.

All London gives forth its crowds, to-day. Lords and beggars, bankers and thieves, fine ladies of the court, and courtezans of the sidewalk, the starving populace of St. Giles, and the sybarite nobility of St. James, are here assembled, waiting patiently for the commencement and the end of the bloody drama.

Two figures stand on the scaffold, beside the block. Is not the block itself a pleasant sight ? So grim and grisly, with the saw dust strown all around it, and many a harsh notch dented in its oaken surface ? These notches are but the rugged handwriting of the executioner ; each notch testifies to one death. The block is the Doomsman's ledger. On that block have been laid the heads of England's proudest nobility, those gallant men who fought against the Usurper of Hanover for their rightful King : that heap of saw dust has drunk their blood.

That grim figure, standing on one side of the block, with his face veiled in crape, and the glittering axe in his hand, that is the Executioner. The other figure, standing erect, in all the pride of godlike majesty, with his calm face, motionless as marble, his dilating grey eyes, raised fixedly to heaven, that is the rebel and the traitor, George Washington.

He stands there, firm as he has stood amid the conflict of many a glorious field, waiting for his doom. You descend from the scaffold ; you ask the meaning of this spectacle ; you have your answer from ten thousand voices.

" That is the traitor, who rebelled against his King in America. He was defeated at Yorktown ; his army massacred ; and his fellow rebels forever crushed. He was brought to England in chains, tried in Westminster Hall, and, to-day the Felon dies !"

The Executioner approaches ; he disrobes his victim. Yes, those rough hands of the Deathsman, ungird Washington's sword, strip the warrior's coat from his shoulders, and he stands erect, with his bared neck ready for the stroke.

Another dark figure approaches ; this is not an Executioner, but a priest. He bids the rebel prepare for his doom. He urges the traitor to repent his foul sin, of revolt and treason. He entreats the Felon, to make full renunciation of his felony.

Not a word from Washington's lips. One brief prayer to his God, with uplifted eyes, one brief prayer for his country, now bleeding, in her bondage, and then, he kneels. The mob of lords and ladies, beggars and courtezans, this populace and nobility of England, hold their breath.

Washington, kneeling on his scaffold, is like a God reposing on his shrine. He lays his head upon the block. The sun shines upon his bared neck, and on the glittering axe. That axe sweeps in the air, it glimmers for a moment, and then sinks with a heavy sound. The head falls upon the saw dust of the scaffold.

" Behold !" croaks the Deathsman, seizing that head, and holding it up to the gaze of myriads, while the life-blood falls in a torrent upon the quivering body ; " Behold, the head of a traitor !"

Such would have been the fate of George Washington, had he fallen into the power of the British king.

Our dream, now, becomes wild and confused. It hurries us, with the celerity of thought, from the State House of Philadelphia, to the streets of London, Edinburgh, and Dublin. In each of these cities, an awe-stricken crowd is gathered around the ghastly fragment of a human body, hung on high, for public scorn ; a festering limb, or an arm, or a trunk, that bleeds in the hot sunshine. On the State House in Philadelphia, over the very door of the Hall of Independence, is nailed a human head ; green with corruption, clammy with decay ; horrible and sickening to look upon. It is the head of Washington. Yes, yes, he has died the death of the traitor, and his limbs are scattered abroad, as a terror to all rebels ; his head is nailed to the door-posts of Independence Hall.

Our dream is over. It has served to show you, how gorgeous a traitor to his country, Washington might have been, had not his soul been pure, as his arms were triumphant. It has also served to show you, how generous would have been the mercy, which George the Third would have extended to Washington, had he been unfortunate or unsuccessful.

Our DREAM is past, and in its place comes a beautiful and blessed REALITY In the hearts of millions, the name of Washington dwells, like a saint in its shrine. Throughout this wide land, whenever a mother would ask God's blessing on her boy, she links, with her prayer, the name of Washington. Whenever an old veteran, who stands on the borders of Time, with one foot crumbling in the sides of the grave, would teach the religion of patriotism, to a new generation, the name, that falls from his lips, only surpassed in sanctity by the name of God, is the word, Washington. We treasure that name in our prayers, we link it with our hopes, we join it with our memories, aye, we, the People of the United States, send that name, morning, noon and night, on the common week-day and the Sabbath of rest, as incense to the skies, a sweet smelling savor to the throne of Almighty God.

WASHINGTON! That name is the GENIUS of our land, the SOUL of our liberties, the Patron-Saint of our soil, whose shrine is in the hearts of fourteen million worshippers.

CHAPTER SIXTH.

ROSE AND BLANCHE.

ROSE and Blanche, sat by the window, with the cool breeze blowing freshly in their faces. There was a wild vine, with thick green leaves and yellow flowers, trailing along the window, and the light of morning, came faintly and softened, into the chamber. It was a fine old room, with a massive cupboard, painted a dull blue, occupying one corner, a bed with snow white counterpane, placed opposite, and high backed oaken chairs, grouped around the white washed walls. There was an air of honest comfort, and good humored ease, about the place.

The maidens had passed through the deserted hall, they had ascended the wide stairway of the Inn, they had traversed the spacious entry on the second floor, and entering this chamber, they had seated themselves, in two high backed chairs, beside the window looking to the north. There was another window, facing toward the west, with a snow white curtain, drooping to the floor.

And there in that deserted mansion, while all around was silent as midnight, sate the maidens, their faces and forms, presenting a beautiful and effective contrast.

The queenly form of Blanche, was inclined gently forward, its outlines revealed by the white robe, spotted with crimson along the bosom, while the more diminutive, yet full and well-proportioned figure of Rose, was seated opposite, its rounded symmetry disclosed to every advantage by the close-fitting folds of the green riding habit.

Leaning gently forward with one hand upraised, while her tongue gave utterance to a story of fearful interest, the lovely face of Rose grew tremblingly eloquent with emotion. Her eyes, distinguished by that softening hue, which melting a dead azure into expressive grey, gives such witching power, to the glance of woman, now enlarged and burned with deep emotion. Her dark brown hair, gathered behind each ear, in a mass of curls, gave a beautiful relief to that fair countenance, which now glowed with the hues of the damask rose, and now was pale as a shroud.

Her lips, dropped gently apart, disclosing the white teeth, were singularly expressive. Her upper lip was marked by a short curve, which at times, gave it an expression of laughing scorn, while the lower one, slightly projecting, with its hue, matching in dewy beauty, the heart of the torn rose-bud, was full of womanly voluptuousness.

The hair, the eyebrows and the eyes of Blanche, were black as midnight. Her dark hair, parted in the centre of the high forehead, was tastefully disposed, around a face of swelling outlines, with skin, as clear and transparent as a snowflake tinted by a sunbeam. Her eyes, were large, intensely dark, and full of enthusiasm. Her mouth like the rest of her features, was faultlessly formed, and on its curving lips was wreathed the same expression of calm beauty which spoke from the high brow and swelling cheek. Her form with its commanding stature, its full bust, drooping into the slender waist, and the widening proportions below the waist, presented an effective contrast to the figure of Rose, which shorter in stature, was yet moulded with more roundness of outline, more voluptuousness of shape. Blanche was the lily, slender and white, yet graceful; Rose was like the flower, whose name she bore, more rounded and swelling, more compact in outline, yet of a beauty, which came warming and blushing into its perfect bloom.

In one word, Blanche was the ideal of that enthusiastic temperament, which makes life itself, but one continuous dream; Rose, the incarnation of that more womanly organization, which is formed to love, to bear, and revere.

And there, as they sat in that lonely chamber, a story of fearful interest, fell from the trembling lips of Rose.

" The last gleam of sunset, streamed through the deep silled windows of the ancient chamber. I was alone. Crouching in one corner of that dreary room, my hands clasped, and my head drooped on my bosom, I listened, intently for the slightest sound. My brain was frenzied with the incidents of the last forty eight hours. Two days had come and

gone since I had been a prisoner, in this dreary room of Rock Farm.
Two days were gone, and I had endured the threats, the brutal in-
solence of this ruffian, who shrunk from no crime, not even from murder
nor —— God of heaven! From that which tongue grows palsied to
name!

"I sank down in one corner of the room, while the last beams of the sun
came streaming through the windows. You know, Blanche, it is a dark and
dreary place? The walls are concealed by dark walnut wainscotting, the
floor is painted black, and the spacious hearth, surmounted by heavy carvings wears the same dull and dreary hue. I sank down in one corner of
the chamber, my brain fevered by the incidents of the last two days. That
fearful night when the storm howled over the forest trees, and the lightning
flash alone, illumined the wild-wood path, while Clerwoode urged his horse
forward, amid all the terrors of the tempest; that terrible moment, when
Clerwoode fell bleeding on the earth, and the ruffian of Rock Farm again
claimed me for his victim— These thoughts, Blanche, were with me, as
sinking down on my knees, I listened for the faintest sound.

"All grew dark around me, all was silent throughout the mansion. Over-
powered by the fearful memories which darted through my brain, I fell into
a feverish slumber. I was dreaming of my home, of my father, of you,
Blanche of you, when I was suddenly awakened, by a faint sound.

"In the dimness of the twilight, I beheld standing in the centre of the
room, a tall figure, whose dark outlines were faintly relieved, by the light
from the window. It was David Walford.

"Come girl," said he, in his rough tones—"You've trifled with me long
enough! Look at the trouble I've had on your account. Weren't we married two nights ago? Didn't I strike that boy in uniform, from his horse,
when he tried to carry you off? Don't yo' remember, how like a corpse,
he looked, as he lay, without sense or motion on the hard ground, with the
lightnin' quiverin' over his face? And then that wound, that deep gash
over his forehead—ho, ho, girl, d'ye remember that?"

I listened to the ruffian's taunts in silence. Well I remembered the scene
in the wood, well I remembered the terrors which darkened over my soul,
when I was conveyed to Rock Farm, a prisoner in the hands of this reckless man; I remembered it all! But no word passed my lips. For two
days, I had listened to similar taunts; I had resolved to suffer, in silence.

"Come, girl, you've carried on this game long enough," exclaimed David
Walford, with a lowering scowl. "Do yo' know that I've a notion, to
bring matters to a pint, mighty quick. Yer my wife; we were married two
nights ago, an' if you like, we kin have the ceremony performed agin. But
out o' this house, you shant go, until you own me as yer lawful husband—"

"I will die first!"

"The scowl gathered darker on the brow of the ruffian. He gave utterance to a brutal laugh.

" D'ye know Polly Mayland, the old Schoolmaster's daughter? One Captain Howard was in love with her ; the girl was mighty proud, but he brought her to terms in a jiffy ——"

" What mean you ?" I exclaimed, gazing in the face of David Walford, while my heart grew heavy with a strange presentiment.

" ' This afternoon not more than an hour ago, Polly Mayland, was strayin' about near Wild-Wood Grange. This minit, Polly Mayland is safe in this house, and so is the Captain. You look thunder struck my girl ? Oh, I had not any thing to do with bringing her here, upon my word, I had not. My band—the Ravens o' th' Hollow—did not carry her off—oh no ! Ha, ha, d'ye hear that ?' "

" As he spoke, a wild and piercing shriek thrilled through the lonely chambers of the desolated farm house. I started to my feet, in horror. My God ! That shriek pierced my heart, like a death knell. As I stood listening in silent awe, it rang through the mansion, yet again and again. I felt my heart throb, and my veins swell to bursting. With one sudden bound, I darted from the ruffian's embrace, I sprang through the door of the chamber, and in a moment, I was speeding along that dark and gloomy corridor, which traverses the entire extent of the mansion. My footsteps were stayed before a massive door, from whose crevices flashed red gleams of light. There was a shriek, a deep groan, and then all was still. The next moment, the door flew open ; I beheld the form of an officer in British uniform, and then, Blanche, I beheld a woman's form, standing erect, in the centre of that large and gloomy chamber, with the beams of a lamp falling over her face. She stood like a thing of marble, so straight, so motionless, so silent, so like a spirit from the other world. That wan face, that look—oh, God, I shall never forget it ! Blanche, it is noonday, and the glad sun, and the free air, come freely through the window, but a midnight darkness covers my soul, when I think of that awful scene. Let me draw closer to you, Blanche, let me utter the full horror of this story, in a whisper, let me ——"

With an eye darting unnatural light, Rose half-raised her form from the oaken chair, and flinging her arms around the neck of Blanche, spoke the last words of the fearful wrong, in a husky whisper.

Blanche grew pale as death.

" And you escaped ?" she exclaimed.

" Last night, David Walford and his ruffian band, conveyed me from Rock Farm, some eight miles northward, into the limits of the British camp. Need I repeat the story of my escape ? This morning, Clerwoode Le Clere this gallant young soldier, appeared in the farm house, where I was imprisoned ; in a few moments, I was on my way to Dilworth Corner. Clerwoode had not been severely wounded, in the conflict, on the night of the storm. Laid insensible on the earth, by a blow from the cowardly ruffian, he did not recover his consciousness until the following morning. From

that time, until the moment of my escape, he hung round my path, like a
guardian angel, determined to rescue me, or die in the attempt."

"Have you seen Mary Mayland, since last night?"

"I beheld that wan face, I encountered that maniac look, but for a mo
ment, and then fell insensible on the floor. When I again unclosed my
eyes, Mary was gone!"

There was silence for a few moments. Blanche and Rose sat gazing in
each other's faces, while the hideous crime, which had been committed in
Rock Farm, the night before, rose, in all its horrors, before their souls. It fell
with a deadening, stunning weight upon the heart of Blanche, depriving her,
for the moment, of the powers of speech and sensation; while Rose contemplated the memory of that crime with affright. The face, the look of
Mary Mayland, were with her ever, like a phantom, hovering before the
eyes of the dying.

So deep was the horror, which each maiden felt, that all other incidents
of the past two days, sunk into nothingness.

The scenes at Wildwood Grange, the presence of Washington and his
brave generals, the manner of her father, Randulph, his confession of love,
and her trembling response, all were for the moment forgotten by Blanche.
Nor did Rose call up to remembrance, the face of Clerwoode, his hurried
words of passion, her own hurried answer, when, in the moment of her escape, she sunk on the bosom of her preserver. All thoughts of love were
forgotten in the horror of that nameless wrong.

"Did you not hear a groan?" exclaimed Blanche, with a look of alarm.

"It was but fancy," replied Rose, "it was ——"

The words died, half-uttered, on her tongue. A low, deep moaning
sound thrilled through the mansion. With an involuntary movement, Rose
hastened to the door, and, followed by Blanche, hurried along a gloomy
entry, in the direction from whence the sound was heard. In the obscurity
of the passage, the maidens listened with painful intensity. Again, that
low moaning sound, half sigh, half groan, came, subdued and deadened, to
their ears.

Rose softly opened the door of the room, in front of which they stood,
and the maidens beheld a sight of deep and fearful interest.

The beams of the morning sun were pouring through the broken sashes
of two small windows, into a contracted apartment, destitute of all furniture,
or ornament of any kind. There was the glaring ceiling, and the bare
walls of a cold dead white hue, there was the simple fireplace, with the embers of extinguished flame smoking on the hearth, and there was the heavy
mantel-piece, grotesque with cumberous carvings; but furniture, or ornament, of any class, there were none.

In the centre of the oaken floor, beside the prostrate form of a woman
knelt two figures, one at her head, and one by her side. The manly form
kneeling beside the prostrate woman, was attired in a half-military uniform,

a course grey coat, buttoned to the throat, and crossed by a broad belt, supporting a powder horn. The broad brow, the ruddy cheeks, and blue eyes of this muscular man, were relieved by thick curls of clustering golden hair.

Kneeling beside the head of the prostrate woman, was a giant negro, his dark skin bared to the waist, while his right arm was entwined around the handle of his blood-stained scythe. The other arm was laid upon the head of a magnificent dog, whose white fur was spotted with crimson stains.

The figure of the woman was silent and motionless as marble. She lay extended on the floor, the graceful and rounded proportions of her figure but scantily concealed by the short petticoat of coarse cloth, which formed her only dress. Reaching to her knees, and terminating at her bust, it laid open to the light the faultless proportions of her foot and ankle, the unstained whiteness of her motionless bosom. Her arms were extended stiffly by her side, while her eyes were closed, her lips parted, and her rich brown hair falling in disordered clusters over her shoulders.

Gotlieb Hoff and the negro Sampson, knelt beside the insensible form of the wretched and ruined Mary Mayland.

Rose and Blanche stood in the doorway, gazing, unperceived, upon the scene, while their hearts were frozen with an intolerable anguish.

" Dat groan was her last," whispered Gotlieb, in a husky voice. " Does thee hear, Sampson? Polly May—as I used to call her—is teadt, mein Gott, teadt! Does thee hear, negur?"

" Hah-hah! I does heer, don't I, Debbil?" exclaimed the giant, with a convulsive laugh. " Dis mornin', you see, Massa Hoff, we comes along de Fildelfy road; we finds dis gal, ravin'-mad, by de roadside. We ax her who had done her harm; she answer, " Cap'in Howard!" Den we brings her to dis tabern; and dar she am, dead as a rock. I heers—hah-hah! Don't I, Debbil?"

The dog looked up in his master's face, and uttered a deep moan. The tears rolled down Sampson's cheeks, over his ebon chest, which heaved with a spasmodic movement.

" Dam yo', Debbil, why don' you shed no tear? Dat ar gal feed you and you' Massa, several hundred time. Her foder feed you, yo' dam dog, and you hab no tear for his darter? Dat gal 'tend on Sampson, when him sick—why you no cry, Debbil?"

The giant raised his hands to his eyes, and then wept like a child.

" Yah—yah! Tis is badt, oh, tis is too badt! Mein Gott! Won't thee open thee eyes, never again? Many andt many a time, Polly May, have I set by thee, in thee fadder's house, andt now, Polly, tere thee lies, teadt — Mein Gott—teadt!"

A wild howl, like the yell of an enraged tiger, escaped from Sampson s heaving chest.

" Hurray, Debbil, sharpen yo' teeh, Debbil! You hab British blood.

23

Debbil, by bucket's-full ! You drink it, Debbil, you swim in it, Debbil, you feed on it, Debbil ! Yah-hah !"

The dog rose on his feet, and surveyed the insensible form of the girl, with a look almost human in its consciousness. Then crouching down beside the prostrate woman, with his fore feet resting on her arm, he uttered a prolonged and dismal howl.

It was a strange, yes, an awful scene. That muscular man, with his ruddy face quivering with emotion, that giant Negro, weeping like an infant, that noble white dog, howling beside the insensible girl, as though he knew that some mysterious horror tainted the very air.

" I tells you, what it is, dis must be paidt for, yah ! Te British must pay for dis ! As Gott gibs me breath, for every hair on yer headt, Polly May, a British tog shall bite te groundt !

As he spoke, the eyelids of the girl slowly unclosed. Half raising herself on one hand, she gazed around with a glance of unutterable terror, while her long brown hair fell trailing over her neck and bosom.

" Mercy !" she muttered, gathering her arms over her bosom, and shrinking as from a threatened blow. " Mercy, Captain Howard, mercy !"

No words can depict the pathos of her look and tone, as she uttered this appeal.

" Polly May, dere's no one here to harm thee. Look up, Polly—don't you know me ? I'm Gotlieb, Gotlieb Hoff !"

The girl slowly swept back her brown hair from her face, she pressed her hands against her brow, and gazed intently in Gotlieb's eyes. The effort was in vain ! She did not know him ; all she saw was the form of Captain Howard, all she felt was the danger of the threatened dishonor.

" Mercy !" she again shudderingly exclaimed.

All was silence, unbroken, save by the sobs of the giant negro, and the groans of Gotlieb Hoff. Blanche and Rose stood gazing upon the scene in mute horror.

" Kill, kill !" shrieked Mary Mayland, as with her blue eyes glaring on vacancy, she stretched forth her arms, in a gesture of trembling prayer " Kill, kill, but do not dishonor !"

She uttered these words, she sprang into a kneeling posture, and again her shrill accents rang through the chamber—" Kill, kill, but do not dishonor !"

There was a moment, when she looked sublime. There was a moment when sinking on her knees, with her hands upraised, her fingers quivering in the air, her face lifted heavenwards, her large blue eyes glaring on vacancy, while her brown hair fell, in rich clusters, over her white bosom, there was a moment when she looked sublime. An image of trembling supplication, maidenly beauty and horror !

That moment passed, while the word ' dishonor' yet quivered on her lips she fell back heavily to the floor. She fell back, dead.

A moment passed, a moment of speechless horror, and this strange scene was revealed by the light of the morning sun.

There was the corse of the ruined girl, laid along the floor, the limbs crampeo by death, the arms resting stiffly by her side, the white bosom, the fair countenance, and the blue eye, fixed by death, glowing ghastlily, in the light of the sun.

At the feet of the corse stood Rose and Blanche, their faces bathed in tears, their lips quivering and their eyes flashing, with a thousand emotions, mingling pity, and horror, and speechless woe.

Beside the body of the dead girl, his manly face expressing the vacant stolidity of despair, his hands listlessly clasped, and his lips wearing a mocking smile, knelt Gotlieb Hoff, the lover of the ruined maiden.

At the head of the corse knelt the negro, with his white dog by his side. The sunbeams poured over the massive outlines of his figure ; over his immense chest, with the ebony skin, bared to the waist, over the arms, all sinew and muscle. over the face, black as midnight, bathed in salt tears, and quivering with agony, and over the clenched right hand and the glittering scythe poured the glad beams of the morning sun.

A moment passed. Rose advanced and closed the eyelids of the dead girl ; Blanche composed her limbs.

Gotlieb took a hunting knife from his belt, and severing one glossy cun of her brown hair, thrust it within his bosom, close to his heart.

END OF BOOK THIRD.

BOOK THE FOURTH.

RANDULPH THE PRINCE.

CHAPTER FIRST.

THE THEATRE OF DEATH.

The afternoon sun is shining over a lovely landscape, diversified with hills, now clad with thick and shady forests, now spreading in green pasturages, now blooming in cultivated forms.

We ascend yonder high hill, rising far above the plain, yonder hill, in the north-east, crowned with a thick forest and sloping gently toward the south, with its grassy bosom melting away into a luxuriant valley. We ascend this hill, we sit beneath the shade of yonder oak, we look forth upon the smiling heaven above, upon the lovely land beneath.

Yonder, toward the south, arise a range of undulating hills, sweeping toward the east in plain and meadow, and gently ascending in the west, until they terminate in the heights of Brandywine.

Gaze upon yon hill to the south-east. It rises in a gradual ascent, and on its summit, thrown forward into the sun, by a deep background of woods, there stands a small one storied fabric, whose quiet and unpretending appearance may well contrast with the deeds soon to be done, within its peaceful walls. With steep and shingled roof, with walls of that dark grey stone, peculiar to the county of Chester, this unpretending structure, is connected with a wall of the same dark grey stone, which extending north and east, and built high as the breast of a man, encloses a square space of ground, all green and grassy, and varied by gently rising mounds.

(180)

This fabric of stone rests in the sunlight quiet as a tomb. Over its ancient walls, over its moss-covered roof, streams the red sunbeams. And that solitary hill standing in the centre of the graveyard—for that enclosed space, is the last resting place of the dead, although no gaudy tombstones, or marble monuments glimmer in the light—that solitary tree, quivers to the breeze, and basks in the afternoon sun.

That is, indeed the quiet Quaker graveyard; and yon simple looking fabric, one story high, rude in its architecture, and contracted in its form, is the peaceful Quaker temple; the Meeting House of Birmingham.

It will be a Meeting House, indeed, ere the setting of yon sun, a meeting house, where Death and Blood and Woe shall meet; where Carnage shall raise his fiery hymns of cries and groans; where Mercy shall enter, but to droop and die.

Now let us look forth, upon the land and sky. Let us look forth, from the top of this hill—It is called Osborne's hill—and survey the glorious landscape.

The sky is very clear above us; clear, serene and glassy. A light cloud drifting here, and there, only serves to render the mellow azure of the autumnal heavens, more lovely by contrast.

Look to the south. Over hill and plain and valley. Observe those thin light wreaths of smoke, arising from the green of the forest some two or three miles to the south-east: how gracefully those spiral columns, curl upward and melt away into the azure; upward and away they wind, and are lost in the heavens.

That snowy smoke is hovering over the plain of Chadd's-Ford, where Washington and Wayne, are now awaiting the approach of Kniphausen across the Brandywine.

Change your view, a mile or two eastward, and you behold the camp fires of the RESERVE, under the brave General Greene; and then, yonder, from the hills north of Chadd's-Ford, the music of Sullivan's Division, comes bursting over wood and plain.

We will look eastward of the Meeting House. A sight as lovely, as ever burst on mortal eye. There are plains, glowing with the rich hues of cultivation, plains intersected by fences and dotted with cottages; here a massive hill; there an ancient farm-house, and far beyond, peaceful mansions reposing in the shadow of twilight woods. Along these plains and fields, the affrighted people of the valley, are fleeing, as though some blood-hound tracked their footsteps.

They flee the valley of the Birmingham Meeting House as though Death was in the breeze; Desolation in the sunlight.

Ask you, why they flee? Look, from this high hill, look to the west, and to the north-west—What see you there?

A cloud of dust rises over the woods—it gathers volume—larger and

wider—darker and blacker—it darkens the western sky, it throws its dusky
shade, far over the verdure of the woodlands.

Look again—what see you now ?

There is the same cloud of dust, but nothing more, meets the vision.
Hear you nothing ?

Yes. There is a dull, deadened sound like the tramp of war steeds—
now it gathers volume like the distant moan of a storm in the ocean—now
it murmurs, like thunder rolling in the caverns of the earth beneath, and
now ! Hah ! By the soul of mad Antony Wayne, it stirs ones blood !
Now, there is a merry peal bursting all along the woods, drum, fife and
bugle all intermingling, now arises that ominous sound, the clank of the
sword against the boot of its wearer, and the rattle and the clang of arms ;
all suppressed, yet terrible.

Look again. See you nothing ?

Yes. To the north and to the west ! Rank after rank, file after file,
they burst from the woods—banners wave and bayonets gleam in the light
In one magnificent array of battle they burst from the woods—column after
column—legion after legion—and on burnished arms and waving plumes,
shines and flaunts the golden sun.

Look, far through the woods and over the fields ! You see nothing but
gleaming bayonet and gaudy red coat ; you behold nothing but bands of
marching men, or troops of mounted soldiers. The fields are crimson with
British uniform ; the red cross of St. George gleams through the forest trees
and flutters in the sun.

Again turn we to the South ! What see you there ? There is the gleam
of arms, but it is faint and distant, but that *sound !* Is it thunder, is it the
throbbing of an earthquake ? No ! The legions are moving. Washington has scented the prey—doubt is over. Glory to the God of Battles,
glory ! The Battle is now certain. There, there, hidden by woods and
hills, advances the banner of the New World, the Labarum of the rights of
man. There, there, the boy-general La Fayette gaily waves his maiden
sword—there white-uniformed Pulaski grimly smiles—there calm-visaged
Greene is calculating chances, and yonder, far away above the meadow of
Chadd's-Ford, Wayne—Mad Antony Wayne ! Hah, what does he now ?
He shouts for joy. His hand to his sword, his torch to the cannon that
surmounts his embankment, he shouts for joy, and like an old racer, trembling ere the word is given, he snuffs the battle, he prepares to spring forward
in the race of death.

And on they come, the American legions—over hill and thro' wood,
along lonely dell, band after band, file after file—and now they move in columns ! How the roar of the cataract deepens and swells ! The earth
trembles, and all nature gives signs of the coming contest.

And over all in mid-air, unknown, and unseen, sits the Fiend of Carnage, like a colossal vulture, with the head of a demon, there there, he sits, and spreads his dusky wings with joy. He will have a rare feast ere sundown, a dainty feast! The young, the gallant, the brave, are all to sodden yon graveyard, with their blood. Near the foot of this hill, under the shade of yon wild cherry tree, a spring of clear cold water, shines in the sun. Ere the set of yonder sun, that spring will be thick and red and foul, with the ore of a thousand hearts. Is it a vain fancy, to imagine the Incarnation of all this woe, chuckling over the scene of man's wrong to man? The biter and biting wrong of selfish tyranny, that sheds blood in rivers, for the shadow of a pretext, and slays millions under the sounding name of " the good king George !"

Yes, while the good natured Idiot, with vacant eye and hanging lip, babbles in the halls of Windsor, here to this peaceful valley, come his hirelings, thirsting for the blood of innocent men. Here come his assassins, ready to butcher men like dogs.

Yes, yes, while the crazy man, called George the Third, sits counting the buttons on his coat, or watching motes floating in the sun, or picking threads from the royal robe, here comes his red banner, over the hills of freedom, waving in the glad sun, as though not ashamed to face the light, with its dishonored folds.

Be that banner accursed in thy sight, O, God! Tear from its polluted folds, thy Holy Cross. For that cross is stained with the blood of millions. Yes, that cross, emblematic of the agony of the Blessed Redeemer, on that foul banner, has become the emblem of atrocities, too foul to name. The blood of the Irishman, the Scottish mountaineer, the peaceful Hindoo, aye, and the blood of the English brave drips from that red flag ! The Ghosts of the slain, rise up from battle-fields in millions, and cry day and night for vengeance, vengeance or that gory banner !

For the Englishman, we cherish no feeling but fraternal love. But for this Juggernaut called British Power, we cherish the deep hatred of the Mother for the snake, that crawls into the couch of her child, and stings it while it sleeps.

Vengeance, vengeance on that gory banner !

Such was the cry of nations, on the Battle-Day of Brandywine, but now, that cry has became a groan from the whole earth, heaving up to God, calling day and night for vengeance.

Napoleon ! Yes, upstart leveller, Imperial demagogue—these are the epithets of his enemies—Napoleon, thou Man of Destiny, we stand upon the rock of St. Helena, by thy side, with all the glories of thy meteor fame around us, we stand upon that rock, and hurl thy Prophecy at England's banner !—even as the blood of millions, drips from its folds.

" *When the cup is full, then God will make them drink the blood, they have shed!*"

It was this blood stained banner, that now advanced from the hills of Brandy'wine, to the valley of the Quaker temple.

And on and on, over hill and valley, on and on advances the Banner of the New World.

Glory to the God of Battles, how fair that banner looks in green woods, how beautiful it breaks on the eye, as toying with gentle breezes, it mingles its stripes with green leaves, and pours its starry rays among forest trees ! But now, advancing over hill and field, it comes swiftly on, and on ! It comes in grandeur ! Now it gives its stars to the sky, it flings its blood-red stripes, across the heavens, and comes gloriously on. The eagle, sailing in yon azure, see his banner from afar. It is his own, his beloved. He swoops down with one rushing motion of his pinions, he perches upon his banner, and there, scenting the battle, sits with unfolded wings ! Hail to the Labarum of freedom !

Sit THOU enthroned above that banner, GOD ! Guard it with thy lightnings, fan it with thy breezes, shield it with thy thunders. May it ever, as now, move on, in a cause, Holy as thy light. May the hand that would dare pluck one star from its glory, wither. May treason fall palsied, beneath the shadow of its folds. May it ever advance, as thy ark in the olden time, holy in the sight of angels !

But should it ever advance in the case of tyrrany and wrong, should its folds ever float over hordes of traitors or slaves, then O, God, crush thou that banner in the dust ! Tear from its dishonored folds thy stars. Rend it with thy lightnings ; let thy winds scatter its fragments, to eternal space and night. Then, take back to heaven, thy stars !

Yet, O God, may that dread moment, never cloud the earth in darkness. May that Banner, ever advance as now, a holy thing in the sight of angels, this Labarum of Freedom.

May that banner move on, and on, over this broad continent,—freedom's pillar of cloud by day, her pillar of fire by night—until from the ice-wilderness of the north to the waters of the southern sea, there shall live, but one name, one nation, one religion.

That name, AMERICAN ; that religion, THE BROTHERHOOD OF MAN ; that nation, THE CONTINENTAL EMPIRE OF THE PEOPLE.

Be THOU enthroned above that Banner, GOD !

CHAPTER SECOND.

BEFORE THE CURTAIN RISES!

AND now while the afternoon sun, is serenely shining over the valley, while Carnage whets his scythe, while the armies are mustering for the fight, let us take up the threads of Fate. Let us look forth, and see, who are they that come hither, to the quiet valley, from the north and south ?

The mysteries of our story, will all be solved in yonder Quaker graveyard.

Hither comes George Washington, in the name of God and freedom.

Hither comes William Howe, in the name of King George and Monarchy.

Hither from a far southern home, comes Randulph, the child of Adelé Waldemar, that last descendant of a royal line, hither comes Randulph the Prince, seeking to clear his mother's name.

Hither from the mansions of a ducal line, comes George Lord Percy of Monthermer, with his father's pacquet in his bosom, and a strange omen upon his brow.

Hither comes Philip Walford, having in his possession the secret by which Anthony Denys holds the broad lands of Randulph the Prince.

Hither comes the Forest-Stranger, seeking to know the mystery of his wife's dishonor.

Hither comes Blanche of Brandywine, whose fate is entwined with the fate of George Percy and Randulph Waldemar.

Hither comes Colonel Frazier, like the victim to his doom.

Hither comes Gilbert Gates, with his father's death to avenge.

Hither comes Captain Clarence Howard, the ravisher of Mary Mayland, and hither also come the avengers, Gotlieb Hoff and Black Sampson.

Hither to battle, comes the brave boy Clerwoode Le Clere, and hither also, the Rose of Brandywine.

Hither comes the bravo and assassin, David Walford.

Hither come the avengers of Jacob Mayland, the schoolmaster of Chadd's-Ford. With them, the iron-handed blacksmith—A dark cloud hovers over his forest home.

Hither also, from a far land comes a strange and unknown form, gliding like a spirit by the side of Lord Percy of Monthermer.

These are all the instruments of Fate. These all approach the Quaker graveyard. These all blindly and unknowing are led forward by their Destiny. Meanwhile the sun shines brightly over the green grass of the Quaker graveyard.

24

CHAPTER THIRD.

THE sun was shining through the thick forest leaves over gay uniforms, waving plumes and glittering swords. A gallant company of warriors were advancing along a bye-road, which winding through the forest and field, led up to the summit of Osborne's Hill. Here the fairest and noblest of England's chivalry rode onward, encircling the form of their chief, General Lord Cornwallis. The grove was alive with the clashing of swords; the blaze of the blood-red uniforms was reflected on the leaves of the forest trees.

First, following the windings of the bye-road where it led through woods almost impervious to the sun, came a man of noble presence, mounted on a gallant grey steed. His commanding form was clad in scarlet cloth, his manly chest was loaded with gold lace; an epaulette of gold glittered on each shoulder, and over his heart there shone a solitary star. His face was mild, dignified and commanding. His hair was powdered, and he wore a plain chapeau, heavy with lace of gold. He sat erect on his steed, with his head slightly bowed, while an expression of deep thought shadowed his manly visage. This was the Lord Cornwallis. And around him, mounted on stout war-horses, whose frames were rendered somewhat gaunt and lean, by a tedious voyage, rode the generals of the British army, their portly forms heavy with gold lace, their shoulders glittering with epaulettes of gold; and their dainty white hands concealed in gloves of buff. They were silent as they gazed upon the thoughtful face of their leader. He was contemplating the fearful chances of the coming battle.

After this company of titled men, with some twenty yards between, came the officers of Lord Cornwallis' staff, mounted on gallant war-steeds, and blazing with scarlet uniforms. They seemed to be careless, handsome, laughter-loving men, who had left the dissipations of London, for a pleasant hunting party in the New World.

In their midst, rode an officer, who was the object of every eye. His slender, yet manly form, clad in a uniform of green and gold, presented a strong contrast to the scarlet uniforms around him. He sat erect on his golden-hued steed, while his cap of dark fur, with its waving white plume, gave a bold and dashing look to his handsome face, with its dark eyes, and clustering locks of jet-black hair.

Near the side of this officer, rode a youth whose slim yet handsome figure, clad also in an uniform of dark green velvet, yet without the star on the breast, or the epaulette on the shoulder, was in deep contrast with the tall and manly forms around. His dark hair was gathered stiffly beneath

nis fur cap, and with a face of almost effeminate beauty, this youth rode silently along, while the song and jest passed from lip to lip. His dark complexion so clear and rich and deep in its brown ripeness, gave additional
beauty by contrast, to his dark red lips. His eyes were vividly bright, yet
as black as midnight. They startled you with their mild yet vivid blaze.

And thus in light-hearted mirth, rode Lord Percy and his brother officers,
through the forest, while Ensign Frank De Lorme, riding by the side of his
Colonel, gazed steadily forward with his jet-black eyes.

The history of this youth was singular. One night, previous to his departure from England, Lord Percy was met in the street by a young man,
poorly attired, who calling him by name, solicited to enter his regiment as a
recruit. At once struck by the manner of the stranger, Percy interested
himself in his behalf, and having learned that he was the only son of an old
officer, who after serving his country had died a beggar, he procured him a
commission as Ensign in his regiment. Since that time the youth had
manifested a quiet disposition to serve his benefactor. He said but little,
but there was a speaking eloquence in the deep gratitude which shone from
his large black eyes.

While one party are wending their way through the woods the terrible
tramp of ten thousand men shakes the earth for miles around. Every now
and then, as the breeze sweeps the forest branches aside, you can obtain a
glimpse of the gayly attired British soldiers, moving on to the battle field.
In front and in the rear, you hear the sound of marching legions.

And there in all the pride of crimson coats and gallant steeds, rides the
regiment, commanded by Lord Percy, who this day is detailed for duty,
near the commander-in-chief. There also speeds his gallant company of
picked troopers, attired like their leader, in uniform of green velvet. These
were the noblest forms and stoutest hearts, from the peasantry of the ducal es-
tates of Northumberland. With the carbine slung at each back, with the
sword by each side, with the fur cap on each brow, these stout Englishers
await the command of their Captain, Lord George Percy of Monthermer.

Strange coincidence! Was it a whim of that Fate, which frolics with
men, while it crushes them?

Here we have Lord Percy and Prince Randulph, riding to the same battle-field, mounted alike on golden-hued steeds; each attired in green velvet,
each leading on a company of picked men attired in the same green uniform.

Now while these gay young gentlemen are following in the wake of Lord
Cornwallis, let us laugh and talk and sing with them.

" Ha, ha, Clarence," cried a smooth-faced stripling in a drawling tone,
"So last night you won the soft beauty? You lured her to the farm house,
you told her how much you loved her, and then kissed her cherry
lips, and ——"

" Now De Vere that's in such bad t-a-s-t-e," drawled Captain Clarence
Howard as he gave his brown steed the spur. " Do'n't nev-er mention

these little things after they are past. Man is man, and woman is woman !"

" You are deeply philosophical!" said an officer with a striking aquiline nose, and blue eyes. He was named Colonel Clifford.

" W-e-ll if you must have something to talk about," drawled the hand some Clarence, " There's our friend Percy. He fell in love with a valley beauty. He tried to carry her off, once, twice ! Two efforts, as I'm a sin ner. Bad taste, that ! His last effort, this morning at Chadd's-Ford, where he had his splendid black horse shot under him ——"

He paused, as he noted the deep wild light in Lord Percy's eyes.

" You are quite amusing Clarence," said Lord Percy in a tone of affected gaiety. " Go on, I pri'thee ! Tell how George Percy played the fool, for the sake of a proud peasant girl ; go on I pri'thee, my good fellow ! Ha, ha ! It is too ridiculous ! To think how I have been led by this proud beauty !"

" Was you indeed in love with her ?" asked the effeminate De Vere.

" He had his horse—worth five hundred guineas—shot under him for a peasant girl ?" said Clifford, in a tone of mock astonishment.

The grove rung with the laughter of the gay young officers. Ensign Frank De Lorme, alone was silent.

" Look ye, my good fellows," cried Lord Percy, glancing round upon the handsome forms and laughing faces of his companions, " Enough of this ! Spare me your jests. I have made a fool of myself : does that satisfy you ? Let me tell you frankly, and at once, that I even offered to marry the peasant maid ——"

" To marry her !" exclaimed the whole party, in a breath. " Bad taste," quietly suggested Clarence. " Deuced bad !"

Their horses were now ascending a slight elevation in a quiet walk. Lord Cornwallis and his generals were for a moment lost to sight, behind a sudden angle of the road.

Lord Percy gazed into the countenance of his brother officers. His face wore an expression of strange meaning. There was a cold sneer on his chisselled lip, and yet a deep agony flashed from his dark eye. He spoke in a light and careless tone, however, as turning to Clarence, he said ——

" Clarence, my boy, keep this gold watch for my sake ——" Captain Howard received the jewelled watch with a look of blank amazement.

" Why, Percy ——" he began

" Captain De Vere, accept this ring. I hope whenever you look upon its diamond, you will remember that you once had a good-natured acquaint-ance, named George Percy ——"

" Good God, Percy !" ejaculated De Vere. " You surely ——"

" Colonel Clifford," calmly continued Lord Percy. " Here is a Turk.sh dagger, of exquisite workmanship. Take it. it is yours. Wear it for my sake. Nay, do not decline the gift. Major Charaloix, there is a full blooded Arab horse, with my company yonder. I call these gentlemen to witness, that I now give this steed to you. What, are you surprised? Colonel Delcombe, should the horse on which I ride survive this day, it belongs to you. Captain Wyvil, after the battle, this sword is yours. Here is a broach, Major Windham, which has been somewhat highly valued, by my ancestors; keep it. What, gentlemen are you surprised? Why this amazement? Is George Percy such a niggard, that his *legacies* create such dumb astonishment. Are you not satisfied with his bequests?"

No sound broke through the forests, save the sullen trampling of the horses' feet. The young officers looked into each other's faces in silence. With one instantaneous movement, they reined in their horses, and paused beneath the shade of a beechen tree.

"Frank," continued Percy, turning to the Ensign, with a slight tremor in his voice. "My personal effects, which you will find with my camp equipage after the battle, I now bequeath to you. What do I see? Tears, my boy? Phsaw! This is folly——"

He said it was folly, yet his voice trembled, as he noted the dark eyes of Ensign De Lorme, bathed in tears. There was something touching in the gratitude of the boy.

"Look ye my boy, will you do me a kindness? Then take this miniature, and when you return to England, seek out my father, the Earl of Monthermer. Ask to see the Lady Isidore of Monthermer. She is the niece of my father, and his ward. She is the heiress of broad lands, and queenly revenues. Seek out the Lady Isidore, give her this miniature, tell her that George Percy wore it in his dying hour, that he loved her to the last gasp——"

"That he wore it in his dying hour," echoed the Ensign, as if endeavoring to impress the words on his memory, "That he loved her to the last gasp——"

"Now mark ye Frank, and tell her this, for though I never loved her, but with a brother's love yet Isidore I believe—Pshaw! It will make her happy to tell her so. Give her this miniature—it is mine—and tell her that I died like a man in battle!"

It was interesting to note the regard in which that dark-eyed Frank De Lorme held his Captain and friend. His red lips turned white, as he placed the miniature within his breast. Then brushing his hand across his eyes, he was self-possessed again, and looked his benefactor steadily in the face, though his dark eyebrows were contracted in a slight frown.

"What my good fellows? Are you dumb?" cried Percy, gaily, as he looked around upon his brother officers. "Why do you halt? Whence this amazement? Why look in my face as though you all saw a ghost—"

"Good God Percy," ejaculated Clarence Howard. "What do you mean?"

The other officers awaited the answer in mute suspense, gazing into each other's faces, with looks of vague astonishment.

"What I mean?" exclaimed Percy with that cold sneering smile. "I mean that this day I will die in the battle-field. That is all."

"Nonsense!"

"This is madness!"

"Pshaw! Percy trifling on such a subject is in such bad taste!"

Notwithstanding these scattered exclamations, which coupled with oaths, went round the group, yet every man felt a heavy feeling at his heart, when gazing in Lord Percy's face with that black eye blazing with deadly light, so deeply contrasting with the sneering lip and careless tone.

"This day I will leave my bones upon the battle-field. But look you my good fellows, I will not die before I have gratified my love and my revenge! As for my revenge, that dark-faced rebel who tore the proud girl from my grasp this morning, shall feel my sword ere night, or by * * *'s sunlight I am a coward! Some mention has been made of the proud beauty. You have been pleased to laugh at my ill-starred *courtship*. Now mark you! By the word of a dying man I swear, this proud girl shall be mine! Yes, amid the roar of battle, the thunder of cannon, with death groans of the wounded in my ears, will I gather this girl to my heart, and taste the sweetness of her lip and bosom, though the very next instant I fall a corpse!"

There was a fiendish expression upon his face as raising himself in the stirrups, he slowly lifted his hand to heaven, and with corrugated brows and set lips, he took this solemn oath:

"I have sworn it by my soul's salvation! I swear it again, by the word of a dying man!"

His dark eyes started from their sockets until the white enamel was exposed to the light.

"Yes, yes, proud beauty," he said with his features quivering, "I have offered you wedlock; now you shall accept shame! I have loved you with a pure and spiritual love worthy of an angel. That love you scorned! Now you shall accept the love of a sensualist. Yes, yes, that love which looks upon a woman, as but a rare delicacy after a feast, or another bottle of wine at a drinking bout. Yes, for the freshness of your lip, for the voluptuous beauty of your bosom, will I love you! This day, you shall be mine!"

"How will you obtain possession of the girl?" faltered Clarence Howard.

"She is now at Dilworth Corner, not two miles beyond the battle-field. Let but the first cannon give note of the fight, and I will crash through the rebel route, and bear this girl away!"

There was a determination in the look and tone of that man, like the fierce energy of despair. That look and tone was thus translated by Lord

Percy's comrades—"I have so many hours to live: well! Ere I dash the cup of life from me, I will drain it to the last drop."

At this moment, a gaily uniformed officer rode up to our party, from be hind the angle of the forest road, and stated that Lord Cornwallis wished to speak to Lord Percy, for a single moment.

In an instant Percy gave spur to his steed and with the officer disap-peared, beyond the angle of the road.

The gentlemen of the staff looked in each other's faces.

"Is it a dream?"

"Can he be mad?"

"No—here is the ring he gave me!"

"Here my dagger!"

"Here's my gold watch, too. But curse me, if I like this. I cannot say it's in good taste!"

The Ensign De Lorme said nothing, but drawing his fur cap deeper on his brow gazed steadily upon the vacant air. His black eyes were thick with moisture; his white lips were fixedly compressed. It was plainly to be seen, that he loved his captain dearer than his life.

"Come, Captain Howard," exclaimed the smooth-faced De Vere, "Give us an account of your amour, with the — rebel wench ——"

This was said in a tone of affected gaiety, with an effort to bring back the conversation to its usual careless tone.

"That would'n't be in very good taste," drawled the handsome Captain. "However; here goes ——"

Then with every addition of his lively fancy, Captain Howard related the story of the ruined Mary Mayland. He was a handsome man, a splendid looking officer, in short that monster of treachery and meanness, intituled a man of the world. What was the ruin of one poor peasant girl, to such a glorious Briton as Captain Howard?

Pity for him, that even at that moment while he told the story to his laughing comrades, Black Sampson in the fields, not two miles distant was whetting his scythe, while Gotlieb Hoff sharpened his knife, and muttered to himself, "It was padt—tamdt padt—Mein Gott!"

"We must crush these rebels at a blow! We have stolen a march on them, we have taken them by surprise. We must, this day, put an end to rebellion. Yes, yes gentlemen, we must teach this half-starved, half-clothed band of rebels that treason is a dangerous word to speak, a deathly thing to practice. Stealing from the woods, we must crash upon them like a thun-derbolt, and crush them with a blow. The army of Mr. Washington, once crushed, then Philadelphia and the rebel Congress are ours. Then let us hope that justice will be done upon their leaders; then let us hope that a little well-timed severity, will bring this people to their senses. Hah!

My Lord Percy, I salute you. Excuse me gentlemen, for a single moment; I would speak with Colonel Percy——"

As the Lord Cornwallis spoke, he spurred his steed, and separating from the party of field officers, joined Percy, some few rods in advance, where they might converse at freedom.

They walked their horses slowly along the road, under the shade of the forest trees. They were now within a hundred yards of the summit of Osborne's hill, from whence a magnificent prospect of hill and valley for miles around, broke on the traveller's eye.

It will be remembered, that neither Lord Cornwallis or Lord Percy, had ever looked upon this lovely landscape. They were approaching the summit of the hill for the first time.

"George," said Cornwallis in a kind and familiar tone, " When you arrived in this country, you gave me a letter from your father, in which he besought me to watch over you with parental care. I have endeavored to do so. Yet for days past, George, I have noticed that you were silent and gloomy. I have seen your brow darkened by a strange sorrow; I have seen the light laugh die on your lip; I have seen the sweat stand on your forehead, while your features writhed as if with mortal agony. Tell me, George, why is this? Open your heart freely to me, my boy, and if I can aid you in any way, you may command me!"

The tone of Lord Cornwallis was kind and paternal. It touched Lord Percy to the heart. For a moment he bowed his head, low on the neck of his steed, and then raising his livid face, for it was pale and livid with terrible emotion, he spoke in a husky tone, broken by frequent pauses:

" There is a Presentiment of sudden death upon my soul. It has haunted my brain since first I trod the American shores. It has crept like a phantom beside me, in broad daylight; it has brooded with images of horror, over the calm hours devoted to sleep. It is ever with me, fearful, vague, and shadowy, that dark presentiment of sudden death!"

" He labors under some strange hallucination," muttered Cornwallis gazing with deep sympathy on the livid face of the young lord. " George," he said aloud, " Shake off this strange folly, make one strong effort of the will, and it is gone."

" One night my lord, when crossing the Atlantic, when the ship's timbers creaked and groaned, in the fierce contest with storm, while the lightning played over the deck, and the thunderbolt came crashing down the mainmast, then, Oh God, then I had a dream! I beheld a lovely valley, a rustic fabric, too rude for a lordly church and a quiet graveyard. There were no monuments, no gaudy tombstones in that place of graves. Around the rude temple and over the valley, swelled the tide of battle; for it was a battle, fierce and bloody. The graveyard was choked by combatants. Suddenly they parted, they opened in the centre; I beheld a form thrown prostrate on a green mound, with the warm blood pouring from the death-wound near his heart. That form was mine! Yes, yes, I saw the streaming blood, yes, I beheld the clammy brow, I beheld the eyes glaring upon the blue heavens, with the glassy stare of death!"

His voice rose to a half-shriek, as he poured forth the secret of that fearful dream. Lord Cornwallis turned his head aside, to conceal his emotion.

" Be calm," he said after a moment's pause. " Remember this is only a strange haliucination. Determine in your own mind, that you will not yield to it, and it will fly from you. Have you not read the story of the German student, who was afflicted with a hallucination somewhat similar. He fancied that he was to die on a certain night at twelve o'clock. This fancy robbed him of health and nerve. When the fatal night came, a friend put back the clock ; the hour passed, the student was saved. George, you can save yourself, by a simple exertion of the Will. Come—be a man—this bugbear will affright you no more !"

His words were not without their effect, on the mind of the half frenzied man.

" Oh, that it were so, oh that it were so !" he said bitterly. " Believe me, my lord, I do not fear death. But to die in this manner, to die away from my native land, to die after having been harrowed by the knowledge of my fate, for long days and nights before its occurrence, to contemplate every moment the scene of my death, to behold every moment that corse flung over the mound —— Oh God, —— to die, with my father's request unfulfilled ——"

His head dropped on his bosom. He shook from head to foot with agony. He dropped the bridle-rein and with his white hands clutched madly at his throat. His agony had swelled the veins in his throat, to suffocation. There was silence for a few brief moments. While Percy sate with his hands clasped, and his head bowed low, his gallant steed paced gently on. Cornwallis rode beside the young soldier, gazing silently in his face.

Presently their horses emerged from the shade of the forest trees, and stood on the brow of the battle hill.

At this moment, Lord Percy raised his face. At a glance he beheld the glorious landscape.

An expression of horrible agony distorted his face.

" My dream! My dream !" he shrieked rising in his stirrups and spreading forth his hands.

And then with straining eyes, he looked over the landscape.

A single small black cloud hovered in the blue heavens. It hovered in the blue sky, right over the Quaker temple. Hill and plain and valley, lay basking in the sun. Afar, were seen pleasant farm houses, embosomed in trees, delightful strips of green meadow, and then came the blue distance, where earth and sky melted into one.

25

But not on the distance, looked George Percy of Monthermer, not on the blue sky or glad fields, or luxuriant orchards.

His straining eye, was fixed upon the valley at his feet, upon the Quaker temple, and the quiet place of graves.

"My dream! My dream!" he whispered, as leaning to one side, he grasped Lord Cornwallis by the arm and pointed to the graveyard on the opposite hill.

Cornwallis muttered an oath between his teeth. "Accursed coincidence," he murmured. "This will kill him! Yes, yes, 'tis just as he pictured it, in the story of his dream!"

At this instant the sound of a pistol-shot echoed through the woods, from which they had but a moment emerged. It passed unheeded. Lord Cornwallis did not even turn his head; while Lord Percy still grasped his arm, and pointed to the graveyard.

And yet that pistol-shot echoing through the woods, had a strange connection with the fate of George of Monthermer.

There was a brief pause. Lord Percy released his grasp on the arm of the General; he sate proudly erect in his stirrups, all violent traces of emotion had vanished from his face. He still was deathly pale, but his eye and lip were firm.

"Enough of this," he said, in his usual tones. "What are your commands, my Lord?"

Even as he spoke, the broad slope of Osborne's hill was thronged with the columns of the British army. Tramp, tramp, tramp, the troops of horse scattered along the hill; the infantry came moving in solid masses, and the artillery with their glittering brass cannon, thundered by. It was a glorious sight. The broad bosom of the hill was one mass of scarlet and gold and steel. An hundred banners fluttered in the air, with the Red Cross standard waving over all. Still on they came, the twelve thousand of the British host, on and on, with an earthquake tramp, with bayonets glittering and banners waving, on they rolled, breaking from the woods and fields of the north-west, and displaying their formidable front, along the bosom of the hill, and through the adjacent fields.

As Lord Percy with his steed reined on the summit of the hill, gazed on this scene with all a warrior's rapture, the tramp of steeds was heard directly to his left, and a gallant company came thundering on.

A gallant company of British officers, arrayed in gaudy scarlet and glittering with stars and orders. In their centre rode a man, whose tall stature and commanding look, would have reminded an American spectator of George Washington. But not as we this morning beheld him, was this man attired. Not in the coarse overcoat of grey with the farmer's hat slouching over his brow. His broad chest stood out in the sunlight, in all its muscular outline, arrayed in dazzling crimson, with a single star, rising and falling with the pulsations of his heart. The epaulette on each shoulder, the laced hat shading his brow, Sir William Howe rode hurriedly on, with all the port and dignity of a man, who had seventeen thousand lives at his beck.

"Look—we have them!" he shouted, as he neared the side of his brother general. "Look—my Lord Cornwallis, we have them! See, yonder, far in the fields, how the rebels are rushing forward. Yet we have them! We have turned their flank, we have chosen our field of battle, and now, Washington and his army, are ours! Away every man to his post, as alloted in the council of last night—away! This day rebellion shall be crushed!"

As he spoke, from the shelter of the trees on the opposite hills, broke the first gleam of the Starry Banner. Far, far below through the fields were seen the hurrying bands of the Continental host. Already the Quaker graveyard was thronged by bands of American soldiers, and there, floating above the heads of a gallant company of horsemen, robed in forest green, waved the blue banner of the Eagle and the Oak.

"It is he!" exclaimed Lord Percy, as his dark eye hurrying through the confused bands of the graveyard, sought out a single form, rising proudly erect, on a golden steed. It was Randulph the Prince.

"This day rebellion shall be crushed!" exclaimed Sir William Howe, in a tone of fierce determination.

Then, with Lord Cornwallis by his side, he surveyed the glorious prospect, while from the shelter of the woods, on the brow of the hill, broke the gallant train of field officers, attached to his brother general, followed by the gentlemen of the staff, whom we left a moment since, riding gently along the forest road. And nearer, and yet nearer, through the trees on the opposite hills, gleamed the advancing Banner of the Stars.

CHAPTER FOURTH.

THE LADY ISIDORE.

WHEN first the valley, beneath the battle-hill, broke on Lord Percy's eyes, the sound of a pistol-shot echoed along the forest.

It now becomes us to show how this pistol-shot, affected the destiny of George of Monthermer.

We will return to the party of young officers, riding so gaily through the forest, while they listened to the story of Captain Howard.

"Ha, ha, ha, a capital adventure," laughed the effeminate De Vere "So you lured the pretty girl to the farm house. Her name was Polly, was n't it? And so you made love to Polly with a little ' gentle severity, as my friend, Lord Cornwallis would say. Ha, ha, ha, a capital adventure !"

" Ha, ha, ha, a capital adventure," echoed the lively band of Britons. Ensign Frank De Lorme was silent. He was too deeply interested in the fate of his friend Lord Percy, to give much heed to such trifling matters, as were involved in the ruin of a peasant girl.

" Bye-the-bye, Howard, what is this story we have heard of Percy, being in love with his pretty cousin, the Lady Isidore of Monthermer ?"

And Colonel Clifford, turned to the complacent Howard, and awaited his answer with an air of languid *non chalance.*

" He never was *in love*, with that lady, my boy," exclaimed Howard. "I know all about it. Percy has not seen Lady Isidore, for these four years at least."

" Not seen his betrothed for these four years ?" ejaculated Colonel Delcombe. " You speak mysteries, my conqueror of a peasant girl, named Polly !"

" I know all about it. Have pa-ti-ence," drawled Clarence. " Have pa-t-i-ence, and I'll tell you. The Lady Isidore is an orphan, and an heiress. She is the child of Lord Lyncliff, the younger brother of the present Earl of Monthermer. Her father died some seventeen years ago, when Percy was a little boy, and the Lady Isidore, an interesting baby, playing with rattles and pap spoons. Previous to his death, however, Lord Lyncliff, made a contract with his brother the Earl of Monthermer, which stipulated that the little boy Percy, and the little baby Isidore, should enter in hy-m-e-n-e-a-l bands, when said baby became a sweet young lady of nineteen. Good ! The Lady Isidore has been reared at Monthermer, under the care of her guardian, the present Earl. Percy has not visited his native halls, for some four years. Why ? His studies at Oxford, his dissipations in London, his rambles on the continent took up his time. Consequently, he has not seen the Lady Isidore, since she was a sprightly Miss of fourteen. However, he has received whole bundles of letters from his betrothed, and answered them, with similar bundles, crammed with sentiment, passion and the usual compliments, you know ?"

" This is a strange story," exclaimed Captain Wyvil, " Did not Percy see his father, previous to his departure from England ?"

" The old gentleman came up to London. They had quite a time ; father and son. Considerable weeping on the part of the Earl—moodiness and melancholy, on the part of his son. All in bad taste ! What's the use of crying or pouting, when life's so dev'lish short ?"

" This Lady Isidore is pretty ?" inquired Colonel Delcombe.

" I never saw her, because her guardian buried his interesting ward away from the life of London, in the hermitage of Monthermer. I pity his taste ; bad ! Rumor, however, says that the Lady Isidore is a lovely maid of eighteen, with eyes like stars and —— I never poet-ize, you know ?"

" Bye-the-bye Howard," exclaimed De Vere, " What became of your pretty maid named Polly ?"

" I left her last night, raving somewhat wildly to herself, at the farm house. These women have their little prejudices, you know ? It's astonishing, when one thinks of it, how like the princess is to the peasant girl when placed in a pe-cu-li-ar position. They all rave and start, and go into hysterics ——"

" Ha, ha, ha, I suppose you question their taste ?" exclaimed De Vere.

A loud laugh resounded through the grove.

" Ha, ha, ha ! Howard is such a droll !" ejaculated Captain Wyvil.

" Why do'n't you laugh, my boy ?" exclaimed Clarence, turning to the moody Ensign De Lorme. " It's suc'. a bore to have to say, good things, when there's a gloomy fellow in the company, who never laughs !"

The dark eyes of Ensign De Lorme lit up with fire, as he encountered the careless self-complacent gaze of Howard.

" Captain Howard," he said quickly, with that scornful intonation, which no man likes to hear.

" Sir ?" replied Howard, startled out of his usual *non chalance.*

" You are a coward !" said De Lorme, in a quiet, but deep and decided tone.

" What are you pleased to say ?" drawled Clarence turning his head slowly round.

" By your own showing, you lured an innocent girl from her home," exclaimed De Lorme, as his dark eyes flashed like flame-coals. " By your own showing, you brought this innocent girl to shame. You used *force,* to accomplish your wishes. You are a coward and a villain !"

This was said in the deep tones of indignant scorn. Had a thunderbolt fallen in the midst of our party, they could not have exhibited deeper astonishment. With one impulse, they reined in their horses, clustering round Captain Howard and his youthful antagonist. In mute silence they awaited the answer of Howard. A moment elapsed before he spoke. Turning his head over his shoulder, he surveyed the slender form of De Lorme, from head to foot. Then he lowered his head on his breast, and patted the sleek neck of his bay steed. Then turning his head over his shoulder again, he looked De Lorme in the face, and said with an air of mock-compassion ——

" My * * * ! My dear fellow, do'n't you know I'm a dead shot ?"

There was something so coolly contemptuous, and withal so self-complacent in the tone and look of the handsome Captain, that his comrades burst into an involuntary laugh.

" I take these gentlemen to witness, that I here, proclaim you a coward and a villain !" exclaimed De Lorme, with a fierce and biting emphasis.

" 'Sdeath boy," shouted Captain Howard. " Do you want to fight me ! Pshaw !" he added in a softened tone. " This is all in questionable taste.

Take back your words, my fellow. Your friendship with Lord Percy shall protect you. Take back your words, De Lorme. I confess, that a moment since, I felt inclined to sting your cheek, with my open palm, but that kind of thing is in bad taste. Come Frank—I like you—tell me, that you are sorry ——."

" O, you are a brave man !" said De Lorme, with his dark eyes flashing scorn. " A brave man in the presence of a friendless girl, but here in the presence of your equals —— Ah ! villain, coward !"

Howard reddened to the brows with rage.

" Come, stripling, come ! This matter can be shortly decided. Yonder is a smooth piece of grass—Delcombe will you act as my second ?"

" Pshaw ! This is folly !" broke in the voice of Colonel Clifford, " Let this matter go no further. Frank your language is harsh—unwarranted. Take back your words, and Howard do you let the matter drop ——."

" This thing must be settled according to the laws of honor," cried Captain Wyvil, who was one of those thin faced, gimblet-eyed men, who always delight in a duel or a dog-fight. " There is no going back ——"

" Clearly so," lisped De Vere, " Come Frank I will be your second.'

Frank silently dismounted, and tied his bridle rein to a tree limb. Howard and the others followed his example. In a moment the pistols were prepared, and all preliminaries arranged.

The scene of this strange combat, was a quiet piece of level sward, encircled by the gnarled trunks of age-worn trees. The sunbeams came fitfully through the intervals of the overshadowing foliage. All was silent as death around the spot, though from afar was heard the tread of legions.

There, on that green sward, breast to breast, with five paces between, stood Howard and De Lorme, the slender figure of the Ensign, presenting a marked contrast, to the muscular form of the Captain. They stood, each with a pistol in his hand, while their comrades surveyed the scene, from the intervals of the massive forest trees.

It was the awful moment before the signal word. De Lorme had grown deathly pale. His cheek was bloodless, and the cold sweat stood on his brow, while his lips, from their red and mellow hue, had changed to livid white. He gave one look at the trees, he inhaled one eager breath of God's free air, and then with lips compressed stood ready for the signal.

Howard, handsome, calm, self-complacent as he was, ere this fatal quarrel, surveyed his antagonist with a pitying smile.

" Come Frank, let this matter drop ——" he began.

The dark eyes of the Ensign darted an indignant answer. " I will avenge this ruined girl !" he said between his set teeth, and then, as a single ray of sunlight fell over his pale brow, he dropped his glove upon the sward. This was the sign, for the second of his antagonist.

" One—two—three—Fire !" shouted Delcombe.

With one movement they raised their arms ; their separate shots, sound-ed as one. The green foliage was concealed by blue wreaths of smoke. A light breeze wafted the smoke aside; the seconds and officers rushed from the shelter of the trees, and gazed around.

There stood Clarence Howard, with that eternal smile on his handsome face, and there, separated from his antagonist by five paces of level sward, stood Frank De Lorme, as fixed, as erect as marble, his dark eyes starting from their sockets, and his quivering lips parting in a ghastly grimace, while he flung his outstretched arms to heaven. Thus he stood for a moment, and then, with a half-uttered shriek, he fell. His graceful form lay extended on the sod, as stiff, as motionless as stone.

" By * * * you winged him !" cried Captain Wyvil.

" Yes—see—his green velvet coat is torn over his heart," exclaimed Clifford. " Poor fellow ! He is gone !"

As he stood over the inanimate form of Frank De Lorme, the tramp of a horse's hoofs was heard, and a tinselled aid-de-camp of Lord Cornwallis, rode into the circle of the sward.

" Gentlemen, your immediate presence is desired by Lord Cornwallis !" he said, with a military salute.

At that word each man, left the wounded soldier, and started to his steed.

" What must we leave the poor fellow ?" said Clarence Howard. " God knows I bore him no malice ——"

" Away, away !" cried De Vere, " The commands of the General, do not brook denial or delay ——"

And he put spurs to his steed, and followed by his comrades darted along the bye-road. Captain Howard was left alone, in the centre of the road, with the vision of that pale face and motionless form, full in his sight.

" Hah ! Death ! Hah—Blood ! Are you here ?" cried Howard, as two strange and hideous figures, advanced from the shadow of the trees. " Look ye ! Here is gold ! Look to yon wounded man—no plundering mark ye ! Seek out the Surgeon of our regiment, and bring him hither. I will look to you for that brave fellow's life, by Heaven !"

And flinging the yellow guineas on the turf, he gave his steed the spur, and dashed along the road after his comrades.

The two strange shapes grasped the gold with their eager hands, and approached the wounded soldier. As they stood above his senseless form, they looked like the hideous images of some nightmare dream. One, was the caricature of a man ; the other, the grotesque semblance of a woman. They were the vilest of the vile followers of the British camp. Their delight was to revel amid scenes of corruption and blood ; they grew rich on the plunder of the dead. They were known by no other names, than those given them by the rude soldiers of the camp ; slang titles which acquired a strange meaning, when their hideous shapes, were taken into consideration.

BLOOD—the man—was a short, stout thick-set figure, whose broad chest and bony arms, were arrayed in faded crimsom. His thin and knotted legs were concealed in tawny boots, reaching above the knees. His middle was encircled by a belt of rough leather, in which was stuck a pistol and a sheathless knife. His huge head was all one mass of matted hair, red as blood, which fell over his forehead in thick and tangled points. A short, thick snub nose, a wide mouth, with thin lips, a beardless and receding chin, skin hideously freckled into spots, by wind and sun, and two small grey eyes, peering with sleepless malice through the knotted locks of his overhanging hair; these complete the details of the disgusting picture. Such was Blood, the camp follower of the British army.

DEATH—the mockery of a woman—was a short and stunted figure, whose withered limbs were clad in a gown of flaunting calico, girdled around the middle with a cord, ornamented with a knife and pistol, and drooping around the thin and skinny arms, in wide and hanging sleeves, from which the bony hands protruded like claws. The head of this creature was hideous. Imagine a skull, clothed with discolored parchment, which leaves each harsh outline distinctly visible. Let this parchment be drawn tightly over the forehead, the cheek-bones, the mouth and chin; a hideous indentation marks the place of the nose; and from the eye-sockets, gleam two large white and clammy balls. Then around this living death's head, wind a flaming red 'kerchief, tied over the forehead in a gay knot, leaving the long ears distinctly visible. Such was the face of Death; this vulture follower of the British army. And to complete the loathsome picture, you must remember that that this wretch is stone blind. No sight blesses those clammy eyeballs.

The language of these creatures, was a strange compound of camp-follower slang, and idiotic mummery. Blood, the man, spoke in a cracked emasculated voice, like the tone of an Eastern eunuch. Death spoke in deep bass, which coming from those hollow jaws, thrilled a man's blood to hear. And these two hideous shapes, stood bending over the graceful form of Frank De Lorme, as he lay pale and motionless at their feet.

"Is the kitten dead Nan?" said Blood as turning away, he proceeded to conceal the gold, which he had received but a moment since. "One—two —three—only three sogers! Dang that Cap'in he maught a gi' me four. Is the kitten dead Nan?"

"I'll zee Deek," said the guttural voice of his hideous partner. And stooping down, Death applied her thin long ear to the lips of Frank De Lorme, listening with a grotesque grimace, for the faintest whisper of breath.

"Not a puff, I tell 'ee," exclaimed Death, as her companion stood with his head turned away. "This skin," she chuckled, passing her skinny hands over the gay uniform, "Will sell for twenty sogers, that it wull!"

And then, with a dexterity peculiar to these vile plunderers of the dead, she unbuttoned the velvet coat, and lifting the body of the Ensign, with a harsh movement, stripped it from his shoulders. His buff vest, slightly stained with blood over the heart, shared the same fate. As Death knelt grasping her plunder, in her skinny hands, Blood turned suddenly round, with a screech of surprise.

There on the grass, at his feet, lay the body of the Ensign, stripped to the shirt and boots, with his arms laid helplessly by his side. The shirt of snowy cambric with its diamond broach unfastened, lay open on the chest, and there, gleaming in the light, was the soft glimpse of a woman's form, with the rounded globes of the bosom, white as alabaster, resting motionless as death, while the blue veins traced their delicate lines on the transparent skin.

" Gi' us y'er hand Nan, gi' us y'er hand," screeched Blood, and seizing the bony fingers of Death, he passed them roughly over that snowy bosom, " It am a woman, by * * * * !"

" He, he he," chuckled Death, tearing the fur cap from the forehead of their prey, " Deek, I zay Deek, I feel her curls !"

And the dark hair, released from the disguise of the powdered wig, fell in thick and streaming masses down over the face, and along the white bosom of the unconscious girl.

Blood squatted on the grass, and with his huge hand examined the wound near the heart. He tore the shirt aside, and with a howl, beheld the miracle. There, right over the pulseless heart, lay the miniature of Lord Percy, with the pistol ball imbedded in its centre. The fair skin was only slightly bruized, beneath the jewelled case.

" The kitten aint dead, I tell 'ee Nan ; I feel she heart go bump—bump —bump——"

" Look 'ee I'll soon settle she," grunted Death, seizing the sharp knife from her belt. " This trumpery 'ill bring us twenty sogers ! And mind 'ee Deek, this is the first dead 'un we've 'ad to day !"

Crawling near the form of the unconscious girl, this monster brandished the knife over her white bosom.

" No—No-o-o !" screeched Blood, as his grey eyes gleamed through the points of his red hair, with a look of infernal malice. " No blood Nan ! Jist put one knee on she's mouth, and one on she's bosom, and I warrant 'ee she 'ill never zay word ag'in !"

And crushing down the wild grass in the action, Death placed one knee on the white bosom of the girl, and the other over her mouth. It was terrible to see the rolling of those sightless balls, the working of those discolored lips, as the foul creature began the work of murder.

" Quick ! Quick ! One push, and it's done !" screeched Blood, placing his hands on his knees, as he surveyed the scene, in a half-squatting posture.

At that moment, as the bony knee of the camp-follower pressed upon her mouth, the eyelids of the unconscious girl slowly unclosed, and her dark eyes rolled in their sockets with a vacant stare.

And there, in the power of these hideous wretches, lay the **Lady Isidore of** Monthermer.

CHAPTER FIFTH.

BLACK EAGLE.

Our story now returns to the Inn, at Dilworth Corner, two hours before
.ne incidents, related in the previous pages.

It was high noon.

Rose and Blanche, with their arms entwined around each other's necks
were gazing from the window of the Inn, which commanded a view of the
northern road.   The faces of these girls, so pure in their virgin loveliness
presented the most delightful contrast, as bending from the window, whose
dark frame, half-concealed by vines and flowers, surrounded their forms,
with a striking relief, they gazed in silence upon the landscape.

Before them lay the quiet cottages of Dilworth Corner, the rude roofs of
the blacksmith shop, the well-pole arising from the verdure of a bowery garden, and a delightful sweep of fields and trees, with the autumnal sun shining over all.

And in the interval between the blacksmith shop and cottages, was seen
the northern bye-road, its brown earth visible for the space of two furlongs,
when it was lost in a mass of trees.

Suddenly the deep silence of the landscape, was broken by the sound of
horses' hoofs, and bursting from these trees, there came a soldier and his
gallant steed.   Even at that distance, the white foam flecking the black skin
of the horse was visible, while his rider, attired in a uniform of forest green
waved his arms wildly overhead, and urged the speed of his noble beast,
with frequent shouts.

The horse came thundering on, with the rein thrown loosely on his neck,
with head thrown forward, and mane waving in the wind, on and on, he came,
with arrowy speed.   But a moment ago, he burst from the woods, and now
three-fourths of the way between the forest and the Inn, lay behind him.
And now, the maidens leaning from the window, saw that the quivering
nostrils of the horse, reddened the roadside dust, with drops of blood, while
his rider's face convulsed with a strange fear, streamed with sweat, as with
loud shouts he dug his spurs into the flanks of his steed.

And on, and on they came, the streaming horse and his rider.   And now
as he neared the Inn, he lifted his trooper's cap from his hot brow, and
dashed it into the dust of the road.   Then tearing his green coat from his
stout breast, he hurled it down, and then his pistols. his sword, his powder
horn, fell ringing on the roadside sward.   With his shirt thrown open on
his rugged breast, with hair flying back from his red brow, the affrighted
soldier flung his form on the neck of his steed, and dug the spurs into the
bleeding flanks, as his shout burst on the air—

"On! My brave fellow, on! Ten miles in twenty minutes that is 'n't bad, but Eagle, my brave black Eagle, we must gain the hills of Brandy-wine, or die! Soho, my boy! Hey! Eagle—hey! That's a brave Eagle—hurrah!"

He emerged into the open space, where the cross roads met, he was turning into the western road, leading to Brenton's Ford, when his black steed reared suddenly on his haunches, uttered a wild and piercing cry, and then fell heavily in the dust, while his rider saved himself by a sudden bound. The dying horse lay quivering on the earth, his long neck and head extended, while his eye rolled in its socket, and then glazed o'er with death. The blood streamed from his nostrils.

"Soho—Eagle—brave Eagle! Are you gone at last!" said the stout soldier, in a tone of ill-disguised emotion. "Gone at last, and you have borne me so long, old boy? Hah—what is this—my brain spins round, my eyes fail me ——" he shouted, as staggering in the hot sun, he pressed his hands to his forehead, while his mouth and nostrils streamed with his blood. "Hah! Devil-Dan you must not die thus. You've too much to do—You've ——"

He fell in the dust, and lay gasping with his head thrown on the heaving stomach of his steed.

"Oh God, to die thus, and so much to do!" he said, in tones husky with his blood. "Oh God—is there no one—no one to bear a message to Washington—no one ——"

The girls had seen the horse fall heavily in the road, and then beheld his rider sink down, with the blood streaming from his lips and nostrils. With one impulse they rushed from the windows, they threaded the passages of the Inn, and stood beside horse and rider, who stricken with death, grovel-led in the road-side dust.

"You see twenty minutes ago I was at Trimble's ford, ten miles above ——" gasped the dying man in a wandering tone—"Company of Britishers pursued —— one shot struck me, in the—back—one struck Black Eagle in the breast—ha! ha! Rode ten miles in twenty minutes—oh God—hah!"

"Can we aid you?" exclaimed Rose and Blanche, in a breath.

"Hah!" exclaimed the soldier, raising his head, and wiping the blood from his mouth and nostrils. "For the sake of God, away, away to Washington! Tell him, tell him, that the British have crossed the Brandy-wine at Trimble's ford—twelve thousand strong—away!"

He gathered his huge arms about Black Eagle's neck, and muttering "Brave old boy—Black Eagle—Devil-Dan Dabney," he lay insensible, with the blood still pouring from his mouth and nostrils.

"You remain here Blanche!" cried Rose, "I will run to Brenton's ford It is only two miles! God will aid me! This intelligence is most im-portant. This morning when I escaped from the farm house, there was some rumor of this kind, but now it is certain. The British would take Washington by surprise—Farewell Blanche, may God aid me!"

And ere Blanche could reply, the brave girl was darting along the side path of the western road, her long curls streaming in the wind. But in vain was all her generous devotion! She had not gone an hundred yards, in the full light of the hot noonday-sun, when she sank exhausted on the road side bank.

"Oh, my God," she said with a burst of tears—"I have not strength—they will surprise Washington! I have not strength to bear the message!"

"Maiden what troubles thee?" said a mild yet deep-toned voice. Rose looked up. The tall stranger, whose gaunt form, was robed in forest skins stood by her side, with the sun streaming over his aged face, and snow-white beard. There was a rifle in his hand; a knife in his belt.

"Away, away," shrieked Rose, "The British have crossed Trimble's ford, twelve thousand strong. I gained this news from a soldier, who lies dying yonder, a soldier who wears the uniform of Prince Randulph's troop. Away—for the Redeemer's sake—away!"

A few brief questions from the Forest-Stranger, a few brief answers from Rose, and the old man tightened the belt around his waist, slung his rifle over his shoulder, and rushed down the road, with immense strides.

"On, on, for the love of God! Brave old man! You bear the salvation of the American army!"

Rose shrieked these words, and then watched the aged stranger until he was out of sight. Then slowly returning, she found Blanche leaning over the dying soldier, who with his head supported on her knee, made a vain effort to drink from the cup, which she extended in her hand. The blood has ceased flowing from his mouth and nostrils; his eyes were wildly bright with death.

"There's no use, good gal," he said in a husky whisper. "I can't drink. I'm going. Can't you say a prayer for me, good gal? Tell God to have mercy upon me—I've killed men, in my time—my wife—my children—among the hills of the Santee—pray—God will listen to *you*—oh!"

"Behold this sign!" exclaimed Blanche, as she held a small cross of gold, before his glittering eyes. "This is the Cross of Christ! The Blessed Redeemer died for you; his mercy is fathomless as the sea! Kiss this cross, and give your soul to God!"

The dying man looked wildly at the cross; its glitter for a moment seemed to dazzle his eyes. Then with his dying hands he clutched it and pressed it to his white lips.

"Christ—died—for—me!" he said slowly, as if to stamp the truth on his soul. "Bless you gal—Ha! Brave Eagle—on, on!"

These last words fell from his lips, mingling with the death-rattle. His eyes grew glassy. His head fell from Blanche's knee, and lay upon the head of his noble steed. He was dead.

Blanche tne Catholic, stood over his dead body, with her beaming face and streaming eyes, uplifted to heaven. Rose the Catholic, stood by her side, her face and eye also raised. They joined their hands together; they chaunted a solemn prayer for the soul of the dead.*

An hour passed.

Blanche and Rose were gazing from the flower-decked window of the Inn. There was a cloud of dust, in the direction of Brenton's ford. Soon a gallant band, burst into sight, a gallant band arrayed in forest green, with the banner of the Eagle and the Oak, waving above their heads. They were led on by Randulph the Prince. They came dashing from the western road, while their gallant leader hurried them forward with deep-toned shouts.

"On, my brave men! On men of the Oak! This is the day to try your mettle! On, to the Birmingham Meeting House; we will secure that strong position, or die! Away men of the Oak!"

And his long brown hair waved on the wind, while with his gleaming sword, he pointed to the north. His noble band poured into the open space, where the cross-roads met, and at the same moment, the tramp of steeds was heard to the south. There came a gallant band, some three hundred told, a gallant band arrayed in white, with their leader, a man of stern brow and whiskered lip, riding at their head, mounted on a steed as black as death. It was the Count Pulaski, whose sword had drank the blood of his country's foes in an hundred battles; this day, for the first time, it would quench its fiery thirst in English blood. By his side, was the youthful General, the gallant La Fayette, his blue eye sparkling, as he rode forward to the battle-field.

"Hail to the Count Pulaski!" shouted Randulph the Prince, as his golden steed arched his proud neck, and tore the earth with his hoofs. "Hail to the Count Pulaski, my brave men! Hail to the Marquis De La Fayette! They fight with us to day, in the cause of freedom!"

One thunder shout arose from the brother bands.

"To day, the brave Washington will be the mark of British bullets,' said Pulaski, with his usual Polish accent. "Let us swear, my brothers,"

---

* The author of this work is a Protestant, but no Church-burner, or renegade Jew. This explanation is rendered necessary by the events of the year '44, when we saw, a Disciple of that good man, who burned Servetus, arouse his dupes and associates, to their work of sacrilege and murder, by his treasonable appeals.

Let the ruins of St. Michael and St. Augustine, rising in the light of day, tell the whole world, that the Religion of La Fayette, Pulaski, Koskciusko, and other mangods of our Revolution, was, during the brief reign of Protestant Bigotry, proscribed and hunted down, in the city of the Declaration of Independence. This book, will doubtless be proscribed by all the Renegade Jews, (who having forsworn their ancient Faith, are now, the guardian angels of Protestantism,) because the author has dared to introduce the Cross of Christ into its pages.

he continued looking from the troops of Randulph to his own, with a flash
ing eye, " Let us swear, that we will defend him with our lives ! Let us
swear that we will encircle him, with our hearts and swords—my brothers.
let us swear !"

" We swear ! We swear !" shouted the brother bands. That oath
from four hundred manly throats, went up to Heaven, with a sound like
thunder.

Then the black steed of Pulaski and the grey steed of La Fayette, advancing along the open space, formed a group, with the golden horse of
Randulph.

They crossed their swords these gallant leaders ; the sharp points glittered
in the light.

" We swear to defend George Washington to the death ! So help us
God ! Our hearts shall be his barrier, our swords his defence !"

And then with one fierce impulse, the brother bands swept on. Looking
back over his shoulder, Randulph waved a farewell to Blanche, while the
dashing Clerwoode Le Clere, now waving a Lieutenant's sword, flung a kiss
to her cousin Rose. The hearts of the brother bands beat high, with the
fever of carnage, yet there was many a rude cheek stained with tears, as
each eye beheld that touching sight ; the form of Devil Dan Dabney, and his
dead steed, resting together, in the light of the sun.

" Forwarts, Brüdern, Forwarts !" arose the deep-toned war shout of
Pulaski.

" Away Men of the Eagle and the Oak !" rung out the answering shout
of Randulph the Prince.

They dashed along the northern road ; the green trees soon received
them, in their cool and quiet shade.

How many passed into the shelter of those green trees, who ne'er came
back again !

" Look, Blanche, the fields are alive with bayonets and banners ! Listen ;
the terrible tread of armed men, echoes from earth to heaven ! See, how
they burst from the woods, toward the south ! Rank after rank, company
succeeding company, and regiment crowding on regiment ! They
come ——"

" They come," exclaimed Blanche, answering her cousin, with a flushed
cheek, and dilating eye. " They come, the legions of freedom ! They come
'o avenge wrong, to punish murder, to crush the hideous guilt of tyranny !
Hail to the legions of freedom ! See, Rose, they sweep by this house, they
overspread the fields as far as eye can see, they advance, they advance !
God go with them—the hosts of freedom ! Ha ! There ride the brave
chieftains, there is Sullivan on his noble steed, with Sterling and Stephens
by his side ; there are all the chieftains of the New World ! Look Rose,
how the Starry Banner comes in grandeur ! Its stars shine over the heads
if ten thousand brave men, who advance in the name of God ! Oh, is

there not a deep joy, in this battle strife, is there not a glory in this mad
dening battle music, is there not——is there not——Oh, God, go with
these hosts, a pillar of cloud, to victory !"

"Look, Blanche ! Observe that tall form bestriding that gallant grey
war-horse ! That form, speeding onward, surrounded by a circle of warriors—Know you his name ?"

"Ask the soldier the name he shouts in the vanguard of battle, ask the
dying patriot, the name he murmurs, when his voice is husky with the flow
of suffocating blood, and death is icing over his brow and freezing in his
veins, ask the mother, the name she murmurs when she presses her babe to
her breast, and bids him syllable a prayer for the father, far away amid the
ranks of battle ; ask Prophecy, for the name which shall live in future ages,
second only in sanctity, to the name of the Blessed Redeemer—the name
of GEORGE WASHINGTON !"

CHAPTER SIXTH.

THE CURTAIN RISES.

IT was the awful moment, when twenty-two thousand human beings
gazing in each others' faces from opposite hills, awaited the signal word
of fight.

Along the brow of the high hill facing to the south, and down in either
side, into the valley on the one hand, and the plain on the other, sweeps the
formidable front of the British army, with the glistening line of bayonets
above their heads, another gleaming line in the rear, while the arms of the
Brigade in Reserve, gleam still higher up the sloping hill-side, and yet
nearer the summit, another warrior band, a Regiment of horse, await the
bidding of their masters, to advance, or fall back as the fate of the day may
decree.

There are the long lines of glittering cannon, pointed towards the opposite hills, there are infantry, artillery and cavalry, a band of twelve thousand
men, officered by the flower of British chivalry, all awaiting the signal word.

On a clear space of green hill-side, between the Regiment of horse, and
the Brigade in Reserve, the British Generals rein their steeds, while around
them gather the chieftains of the host.

And from the trees along the opposite hills, pour the hurried bands of the
Continental army, at the very moment, that the British General, is about to
give the word which will scatter death among their ranks.

The Right Division of the American army, under the brave Sullivan, the gallant Sterling and the unfortunate Stephens, take their position in hurry and disorder, on the opposite hills, their line extending from the Quaker temple east and west.

The American soldiers come thronging in their coats of faded blue and buff, confronting the well-trained and well-clothed band of the British with firm hands and stout hearts. From one end of the Continental army, to the other, one stern determination was expressed, in each compressed lip, and steady eye, the resolve to strike one stout blow against an enemy, superior to the Americans in force, arms, in all that constitutes an army, save the Justice of their cause, and the daring recklessness of their courage.

The sunbeams shining through the chinks and crevices of yonder Meeting House, reveal the stout forms and battle-worn faces of Porterfield's brave riflemen. They await the word, with their rifles, whose every ball carries a death projecting into light, through the hastily hewn port-holes of the door and shutters. And there, in the centre of that dim Meeting House, scarcely visible in the twilight gloom of the place, five figures kneeling on the floor, await the signal word, in awful silence. These figures, are the Forest-Stranger in his robe of skins, the brave Pennsylvanian Gotlieb Hoff, the Inn Keeper, Hirpley Hawson, the stout blacksmith, Iron Tom o' Dilworth Corner, Black Sampson, and his white dog, " DEBBIL."

Woe to the Britisher, who encounters this small but desperate band! Their number is small, yet every one, from the noble white dog, to the Forest-Stranger, thirsts for British blood. They have burning wrongs to avenge. The sharpened scythe of Sampson, glimmers ominously in the light.

The graveyard is silent. Beneath the shelter of yonder wall, fronting to the British Host, crouch the Men of Brandywine, on hands and knees, their loaded rifles by their side. There too, kneels Norman Frazier, with the sun shining on his ancient Provincial uniform, blue faced with silver, and the sword of Lovat in his grasp.

The sun shines gaily on the graveyard grass. Back yonder, in the farther extreme of the enclosed space, in stern silence, cluster a band of horsemen, dressed in forest green. Their steeds stand ready for the chase of Death, their unsheathed swords gleam in the light, and in their midst, the golden hue of his brave barb, contrasting with the darker colors of the war-horses around, towers the form of Randulph the Prince, the eagle plume waving over his brow. His eye flashes with unnatural brightness—for—this is the day, when the Sanctity of his Mother's Name, shall be decided forever.

And down yonder in the valley, on the left of the British line, is the regiment of Lord Percy, with the green uniform of his own gallant company, contrasting with the blaze of scarlet all around. Captain Clarence Howard is at their head, awaiting the arrival of Colonel Percy, Lord of Monthermer.

In this awful moment of suspense, let us hasten yonder, up the hill, where

Lord Cornwallis, and his Excellency, Sir William Howe, survey the field of battle, from a rising mound. Their Generals are clustered round, while in front of Lord Cornwallis' war-steed, stand three contrasted figures, the miser, Philip Walford ; his burly son, the bravo David ; and quiet Gilbert Gates, arrayed in his Quaker garb, with his hawk-like eye, gleaming with a deep meaning.

" This man, Norman Frazier served His Majesty, in Braddock's War," said Cornwallis in a quick tone, as he turned to old Philip Walford.

" He held a commission as Captain, please your Excellency," replied Philip, in a cringing tone.

" And now, he serves in yon rebel crowd," exclaimed Cornwallis, as his blue eye flashed with a stern meaning. " Sir William, we have long sought an opportunity like this. It is necessary to make an example of these traitors, who hold commissions from his Majesty, and yet, raise their arms against his name and power ——"

" It is," replied Sir William Howe, and then turning to the bravo David he continued. " You command a troop of Royal Partizans ? Secure this man Frazier. and bring him safely to the British camp, and one hundred guineas shall be your reward. It is necessary that an example should be made. It is necessary that the royal name should be vindicated. This man Frazier is a rebel, and a —— *deserter.* He shall have a fair trial, by a court martial, constituted according to the proper form. If it is proven, that he holds a commission from his Majesty, then he shall die according to the laws of war. But mark ye, no violence ; bring him within the camp, alive, or you shall answer for it."

" I'll do my best, I warrant ye !" growled David Walford. " My boys the Ravens, ain't mighty apt to spare these rebel dogs, but if *you* want one, to pick to pieces, all alone by y'erself, we'll catch him for you !"

" No more words Sir, but away to your task !" exclaimed Howe, who like all the regulars of the Army, held the half-uniformed Partizans in un-disguised contempt. " Come hither my *pious* Quaker," he continued with a grim smile, turning to Gilbert Gates, " You state that the pacquet, which some days since was stolen from my tent, by a spy, is now in possession of Mr. Washington ?"

" In truth, is it !" whined Gilbert, smoothing his long hair behind his ears ; " In truth is it, Friend William ——"

" Bring me this pacquet, before the setting of the sun, and I will reward you with five hundred guineas !"

" In truth will I persuade Friend Washington, to yield the pacquet. In truth will I." Gilbert laid his hands on his heart, and with his hawk-eye flashing fire, looked meekly to the ground.

" Away then, and do it !" exclaimed Sir William Howe, " And gentle-men," he cried turning to the band of officers, blazing with the glory of scarlet and gold. " Away to your posts ! In a moment, the battle-signal will be given. Yet stay a moment, gentlemen. I am authorized by his Majesty to promise the highest honors in his gift, to any man, who may take this rebel leader, Mr. Washington prisoner. Remember this gentlemen, in the hour of battle !''

In a moment, the hill resounded with the tramp of the officers' steeds, as speeding to their various commands, they left the presence of the commander-in-chief.

" Colonel Percy," said Cornwallis, to a solitary officer, who was for a moment detained by his side. " You have the post of honor to day ! The rebels have entrenched themselves in yonder graveyard. Let the royal banner float over its grey walls, ere five minutes have passed !''

" I will take it," said Percy, as he gave his steed the spur, " I will take it, and then lay my dead body on its sward !''

His golden hued horse was speeding down the hill, and Lord Cornwallis and Sir William Howe, were alone. Their aids-de-camp clustered in group, somewhat further up the hill.

Sir William Howe raised his commanding form in the stirrups, and then, while his countenance betrayed his deep sense of the awful responsibility of the moment, he unsheathed his sword, and raised it over his head.

This was was the signal of battle.

An hundred bugles hailed that sign, with their maddening peals, an hundred drums rolled forth their deafening thunder, and then, the earth shook as though an earthquake heaved its grassy bosom.

Along the British line, streamed the blaze of musquetry, and then the roar of cannon, burst on the air. Around the hill-side curled the white smoke in vast and aëry folds ; the valley below was wrapt in clouds. A moment past ! The cloud was swept aside, by a breeze from the American line. That breeze bore the groans of dying men, to the very ears of Howe. That parting cloud disclosed the awful panorama of death, wounded men, falling to the earth, death-stricken soldiers, leaping in the air, with the blood streaming from their shattered limbs. Where solid ranks but a moment stood, now were the heaps of ghastly dead.

A single moment passed. The voice of Sullivan was heard along the Continental line, and from the southern heights a deafening report broke on the air—a blaze of sheeted flame burst over the British ranks. The piercing musquet shot, the sharp crack of the rifle, the roar of the cannon, these all went up to heaven, and then all was wrapt in smoke on the southern hills. Then the white pall was lifted once again ; the Quaker Meeting, House was alive with rifle-blaze and death-shot. Each window, each nook each crevice, poured death into the British ranks.

And then, a thousand cries and groans co-mingling in one infernal chorus went up to the smiling sky of azure blue.

Another moment passes. That loud shout yelling over the chorus of death ; what means it ? The order rings along the British line, Charge for

King George! The Continental columns give back the shout, with re-doubled echo, Charge in the name of God, Charge for Washington and the right!

And then, while the smoke gathers like a black vault, built by demon hands o'erhead, sweeping from either hill at the top of their horses speed, the troopers of the armies meet, sword to sword, with banners mingling and bugles pealing, fighting for life they meet. There is a crash, a fierce recoil, and then another charge!

Now the Red Cross of St. George, and the Starry Banner of the New World mingle their folds together, tossing and plunging to the impulse of the battle breeze. Hurrah! The fever of blood is in its worst and wildest delirium. Now are human faces trampled deep into the blood-drenched sod, now are glazing eyes torn out by bayonet thrusts, now are quivering hearts rent from the living bodies of the foemen! Hurrah!

How gallantly the Continentals meet the brunt of strife! Rushing forward on horse and foot, beneath the folds of the Banner, they seek the British foemen, they pour the death-hail into their ranks, they rend them with their bayonets, they throttle them with weaponless hands!

Talk not to me, of the Poetry of Love, or the sublimity of nature in repose, or the divine beauty of Religion!

Here is Poetry, Sublimity, Religion! Here are twenty thousand men, tearing each other's limbs to fragments, putting out eyes, crushing skulls, rending hearts, and trampling the faces of the dying under foot—Poetry!

Here are horses running wild, their saddles riderless, their nostrils streaming blood, here are wounded men gnashing their teeth, as they endeavor to crawl from beneath the horses' feet, here are a thousand little pools of blood, reddening the grass, filling the hollows which the hoofs have made, or coursing down the ruts of the cannon wheels—Sublimity!

Here are twelve thousand British hirelings seeking the throats of yon small band of freemen, and hewing them down in gory murder, because they would not kiss the feet of a good-humored Idiot, who even in this moment of horror, sate in his royal hall, three thousand miles away, combing the hairs of his little poodle dog, and catching flies upon the wall—Religion!

The valley is concealed beneath the shadow of a dark mass of heaving battle-clouds. Under this lurid canopy the Continentals advance, hewing their way in blood and smoke, with sword thrust and rifle-ball. They fight each man of them for life and freedom; each upraised sword bears a death, each bullet wings a doom.

The enemy come swarming to the encounter, rank after rank, column after column, they rush to the charge, superior in force, superior in arms, to the brave soldiers of the Continental host.

There is a moment of terrible suspense. The Banner of the Stars, tosses to and fro, it sinks amid the battle-cloud. Again the Continentals rush to the charge, again they breast the foe; the Starry Banner towers aloft. But now! It sinks again; the Red Cross gleams amid the dark clouds of smoke; the Continentals waver, they fall back. Sullivan, that man of noble port, speeding from line to line, with upraised sword, beholds his Right Wing in confusion; step by step, they retreat, and now the fight thickens around the graveyard, and around the meeting house.

They come rushing up the hill, the British troopers, swords raised and steeds ready for the charge, they come sweeping up the hill, while the shout of carnage echoes from lip to lip. The graveyard wall rises in their front.

All is silent there. Not a shot from the windows of the meeting house, not a rifle barrel glistening above the graveyard wall.

And on they come, the scarlet troopers, on and on, thundering in one solid phalanx, toward the graveyard wall. All is silent still.

Lord Percy of Monthermer, leads them on, surrounded by his chosen band, he lifts his sword on high, while his golden steed arches his proud neck, and thrusts his broad chest in the light. Lord Percy turns as he shouts to his men, he points to the graveyard wall.

All is silent still.

Here let us pause, for a single moment.

CHAPTER SEVENTH.

THE PERIL OF ISIDORE.

It was a picture, at once hideous and beautiful.

Above were the forest boughs, their broad green leaves shading the sward beneath from the light of the sun. And there on that green sward lay the form of a young and beautiful woman, with its voluptuous proportions, shown to advantage, by the manly attire, while on the budding bosom and red lips, were pressed the knees of the hideous wretch, whose sightless eyeballs rolled in mockery, upon the dark eyes of the awakening girl. There surveying the scene, with his bony hands placed on his knees, while his grey eye gleamed through the hanging locks of his blood-red hair, was the camp-follower Blood, quietly watching the progress of the murder. And the long dark hair of the Lady Isidore, streaming aside from her brow, down over her neck, and half-covered bosom in glossy waves, was sunken beneath the knee of the murderess, as its sharp bone pressed into the snowy globe. Her dark eyes unclosing with their flashing pupils, surrounded by the white surface of the eyeball, glared wildly in the skull-like face of Death, with the flaring red 'kerchief tied on her tawny brow

" Quick ! Quick ! One push Nan, and it's done," screamed Blood.

And the knee sunk deeper in the bosom. There was a groan—the other knee pressing down upon the lips, smothered its utterance. And then the arms of the beautiful girl were raised for a moment, with the grasp of despair she clutched the murderess ; she grappled her skinny arms with her slender fingers. There was another groan ; it died suddenly in the throat, while the dark eyes, projecting from the shadow of the brow, gave a hideous look of despair, to the face of the Lady Isidore.

Another moment and her heart would cease to beat, another moment, and then, with the shirt rent from her bosom, the buckskin hose from her limbs, the trooper's boots from her feet, the Lady Isidore would lay a corse. A corse, on whose fair proportion rude eyes would gaze, a lifeless body, whose voluptuous outlines, would be trampled under horses' hoofs, or whose young bosom, would be torn by the carrion vultures of the battle-field.

A hideous sound gurgled from the throat of the murderess ; it was her laugh of infernal malice. The Lady Isidore writhed beneath the pressure of that withered form ; she felt her heart throb and throb, until it seemed to fill all the avenues of her bosom, as with one fierce effort of despair, she grappled with the murderess. This effort was not in vain. Death was suddenly hurled aside, and as her hideous form rolled on the sward, the Lady Isidore sprang to her feet, and with her bosom all unbared, with her dark eye flashing and her raven hair streaming over her white shoulders, she confronted her foe. There was no fear in her eye. There was all the energy, which the approach of death imparts to bold and fearless natures, manifested in the tremulous quivering of her lip, the deadly flashing of her eyes, the long pulsation which heaved her white bosom, slowly into light.

" Now look 'ee Nan," said Blood, who in his quiet position had calmly surveyed the scene, " Buckle to she, or I'll have to do it myself! That's a Nan ! Hey to her ! To her, Nan !"

" These sharp nails, shall mark ye'r purty face," said Death, as crawling on hands and knees, by a strange instinct, which with her supplied the place of sight, she approached the Lady Isidore, and turned the glare of her sightless balls towards her face, " Look 'ee purty bird—he, he, he ! These claws shall twine in ye'r hair, these, these, shall clutch ye'r smooth throat, these, these, shall tear ye'r purty bosom !"

Quivering in every limb, yet firm as her soul was pure, the Lady Isidore beheld the camp-follower slowly creeping toward her, like a wild-cat preparing to spring on its victim. Nearer and nearer she came, rolling her sightless eyeballs in the light, and moving her discolored lips, until her toothless gums were laid bare.

" What will 'ee give for—life ? Hey ? Purty one ?" screeched Blood, as in his half-crouching attitude, with his hands on his knees, he surveyed the pale face of the proud girl. " Come, purty one ; what will 'ee give for life ?"

" Oh spare me, and take all my gold !" shrieked the Lady Isidore, turn ing to Blood, with her hands clasped over her bosom. And as she turned, and fixed her dark eyes on his face, Death came creeping like a reptile over the grass, all her ferocious instincts aroused, and her fingers quivering with the desire of revenge.

"Oh spare me—and take all!" shrieked Isidore, clasping her hands, as her eyes were turned beseechingly towards the sneering face of Blood. "Take my gold—take ——"

The word died in her throat. With one fierce bound, even as the panther darts on his unconscious prey, Death leaped from the sod, and with her skinny fingers clutched the Lady Isidore by the throat. There was a brief struggle. Those talon fingers writhed like serpents, around the smooth neck, and gathered its veins in a closer grasp. In a single moment all struggling was at an end. The Lady Isidore, with her hands dropping listlessly by her side hung motionless in the grasp of the camp-follower, while her dark eyes started from her livid face. The husky groan which betokens suffocation, gurgled in her throat.

"Do I clutch yo' proud wench?" said the deep guttural voice of Death. "Can 'ee struggle now?"

"Nan must ever play with her game, like cat with mouse," screeched Blood, quietly observing the scene.

At this moment, the green sward gave a softened echo, to the tread of a stealthy footstep. Death was hurled aside by a sudden blow from a clenched hand; she fell reeling on the earth, while Blood leaped backward, in surprise and affright.

Gasping for breath and quivering in every limb, the Lady Isidore, freed from the grasp of the camp-follower, stood gazing vacantly in the face of her deliverer.

A stout form, whose muscular proportions, were attired in a dark grey costume, stood before her. His dark visage, was shadowed by a slouching hat of coarse felt, while a broad belt, snow white in hue, slung over his brawny chest, supported a massive sword. There was a pistol and a hunting knife in his girdle. Leaning forward toward the fair girl, with one hand firmly clenched, while the other grasped a rifle, a strange expression came over the face of the stranger, as he gazed upon the blushing countenance of the disguised maiden. That expression mingled vacant astonishment, vulgar admiration, and brutal passion.

"So ho, my purty wench! I jist come in time, did I! So ho my purty gal, you must dress yourself in soldier clothes, must ye? and go about fighting duels, hey? I wonder what 'ud happened to yo' if one of ye'r brother *officers*, had 'n't told me of ye'r condition?"

And with that expression, mingling vague wonder and brutal passion, gleaming from his burly visage, David Walford advanced, and gazed upon the maiden. Her eyes downcast, her olive cheek crimsoned with blushes, Isidore tremblingly gathered the torn folds of the shirt, over her young bosom, and then stood silent and motionless ; a beautiful incarnation of maidenly innocence.

" In truth it is a pretty maiden," said a strange voice. " In truth it is a sweet young maiden !"

The tall, thin form of Gilbert Gates, stood beside the Bravo Walford, his long curling brown hair, swept back behind his ears, while his hawk-like eyes gleaming from his mild and saintly countenance, devoured the beauty of the trembling girl.

" My heart misgiveth me, sweet maiden, that thee parents are not aware of thee absence from home ?" said Gilbert Gates, with a mild tone sharpened by a sneer.

" Come gal, do'n't stand tremblin' and blushin' there !" cried David Walford, hastily advancing, " We Ravens o' th' Hollow, are quiet modest fellows to be sure, but still we know how to treat a purty gal ! Come with me, my lass ; do'n't be skittish now, and cut any capers. Come, I say !"

There was nothing doubtful in his tone or gesture. With that expression of brutal admiration, wreathing his thick lips, in a coarse smile, and gleaming from his dull grey eyes, he advanced to the shrinking maiden, he raised his hand to grasp her roughly by the shoulder.

At that instant, the whole nature of the girl was changed. Maidenly shame, modesty and fear, were gone. Towering in her full height, she threw her dark hair back on her shoulders, and fixed the gleam of her flashing eyes full upon the Bravo's face. There was scorn in her lips, compressed yet quivering ; there was defiance in her uplaised arm, with the hand extended, and the fingers trembling like autumn leaves.

" Back coward !" she cried, in a tone of proud defiance. " The Lady Isidore of Monthermer, perilled her life this day, to avenge the ruin of a peasant girl. She can defend her own honor, to the last gasp of life !"

There was a wild beauty in that scene. There, unarmed and weaponless stood the lovely girl, her form raised to its full stature, her dark hair streaming back from her pallid brow, there starting aside with involuntary awe, was the bravo Walford, with the sneering Gilbert Gates peering over his shoulder, and there, in the background, under the shade of the green boughs, cowered the twin shapes of grotesque ugliness, Blood and Death, their hideous faces gleaming with infernal malice, as they awaited the issue of this scene.

" Can thee tell a quiet friend, what means this wonder ?" exclaimed Gilbert Gates, turning to the camp-followers. " On our way hither we learned that a young soldier lay wounded, even unto death, far down in the wood. Lo ! The young soldier is alive, and turned into a lovely maid, withal ! Can thee tell me what was the cause of the duel ?"

Blood thrust his red hair aside from his grey eyes, and replied with his usual screech :

" Why ye sees, we, that is Nan and me, war' a watchin' the rumpus

from the bushes. This young hussy here, picked a quarrel with that brave
Soger, Cap'in Howard, 'bout a gal, wot the Cap'in had been a leetle too
kind-like to, at a farm 'us, 'way down somewhere. Let's see Nan, wot
whar she's name ?''

" Polly," spoke the deep bass voice of Death, " Lovely Polly—Polly
May—May—I do' know what else, Deek."

" Polly Mayland ? Was that the name ?" said the Quaker as his face
grew white as a sheet. " Does thee think that was the name ?"

" It wor, it wor !'' screeched Blood.

" And did the man of war, even Captain Howard, say that he had done
wrong unto this maid ?''

A rude laugh echoed from the camp-followers, and then came words, too
foul to speak, coupled with the name of Mary Mayland.

Gilbert Gates was lividly pale. His grey eyes seemed to burn in their
sockets. He slowly approached the side of David Walford. His voice
was unusually soft and subdued, as he spoke ——

" David, when I helped thee last night, to lure away Mary Mayland,
from the man Frazier's house, when I gave her into thee hands, say David,
did thee not promise that no harm should come unto her ? Did thee not
promise that she, even Mary, should stay at Rock Farm, until the battle
was over ?''

" W-a-l if I did ?'' said David, with a look of stolid indifference, as turning his head over his shoulder, he surveyed the agitated countenance of the
Quaker.

" David," said the Quaker, as his voice rose by degrees, " David thee did
not suffer harm to be done, unto this maiden ?''

" Why Mister Thee-and-thou, did'n't yo' hate old Jacob Mayland and
his darter ? Did'n't yo' swear revenge, and a sight more ag'inst 'em ?
Did'n't yo' burn the old rebel, alive ? Hey ?''

" David did thee suffer harm to come unto this maid ?'' The voice of
Gilbert Gates was deep-toned and sepulchral. His face grew whiter ; his
eye, more intensely bright.

" W-al if I did ? What's the use o' havin' words about it ? D'ye want
to know the fact, and no mistake ? W-a-l, then have it, and chaw-r it over,
like an old cow chaw-rs her fodder, if yo' like. Last night, at Rock Farm
Cap'in Howard was alone with the purty g-a-l, for an hour. I know, for I
held the door. There was some shrieks an' groans, an' other sorts o'
capers —— I'm afeerd o' talkin' much plainer, for fear o' hurtin' your delicate feelin's !''

And a brutal smile broke over the ruffian's face.

For a moment there was silence, as deep as death. Gilbert Gates stood
with his arms folded over his breast, while his lips tightly compressed,
worked with a tremulous movement, and his face turned from snow-white,
to livid blue. His grey eyes glared, from beneath his overhanging brows.

He was making a desperate effort to control his superhuman emotion. In another moment he advanced to the side of the Lady Isidore. He gazed intently in her beautiful face.

" Look thee maiden !" he said, drooping his head, and speaking in a husky whisper, "Did thee, peril life, to avenge the wrong of a poor girl, against a proud soldier-man ? Did thee stand fire, for the sake of Mary Mayland ?"

" I heard a soldier, speak of a peasant maid, in terms, such as no man with honor, in his breast, would ever utter. I listened to the story of her wrongs ; I would have avenged her !"

As in a calm yet modest and maidenly tone, the Lady Isidore spoke these words, the grey eye of Gilbert Gates, was riveted to her beautiful face.

" Look thee, maiden," he said in a quick tone, yet with a flashing eye. " For this—for this I would bless thee, only that my blessing would bring curses on thee head ! For this—for this I would kneel, to thee, and kiss thee feet, and ask thee to smite me dead, if my death, would give thee, but a moment's joy, for thee, maiden, for this——"

He paused. He stood silent as death, clenching his hands in the effort to retain his emotion.

" Get thee away, maiden, get thee away ! No one here, shall do thee wrong !" He cried, interposing his form, between the Lady Isidore and the Bravo Walford. " Nay frown not David ; thee knows that I am a Friend and a man of peace, and yet, thee knows, I would tear thee to pieces, when this mood is on me !"

He stood, trembling from head to foot, with his quivering hands extended toward the bravo.

" Stand back, or I'll cut yo' down !" shouted Walford. While he spoke, raising his hands, in a threatening gesture, the Lady Isidore stooping timidly to the ground, seized the coat and vest, which had been torn, rudely from 'her form, and with a nervous haste, essayed to robe her bosom, in warrior costume, yet once again. Like ravens, hovering over the field of battle, in the anticipation of their coming feast, Death and Blood, crouching on the sward, silently awaited the end of this strange scene.

" Get thee back, David," shrieked Gilbert Gates, " There is a fiend in these veins, David. Get thee back, I say ! He is tempting me, to work murder on thee body ! Get thee back—a worm that is trodden upon will turn, and even a man of peace, likeunto me, will battle, when there are fire-coals at his heart !"

David advanced, and raised his sword. At that instant the Lady Isidore stood at the back of the Quaker, attired yet again, in military costume. David advanced, and as he grasped his upraised sword, with a firmer clutch, Gilbert Gates, hurriedly thrust his hands into his bosom. In a moment he **drew** them forth again ; each trembling hand grasped a pistol

28

" Now David, advance, and I, yea, I, the man of peace, will shoot thee dead !"

David Walford started back thunderstruck. There was something terrible in this courage of the coward, Gilbert Gates.

" He, he, Nan, dost see it ?" screeched Blood to his amiable partner.

" Deek, I hears 'em, I hears 'em !" replied Death, with a fiendish chuckle.

As David Walford, stood stricken dumb with surprise, the Lady Isidore, oounded along the sod, and sprang upon her steed. Her motions were sudden as lightning.

One movement of her hand, and the bridle rein was free. Then there was the sound of horses hoofs, and the Lady Isidore and her steed, were lost to sight, among the forest boughs.

A horrid oath burst from Walford's lips.

" By * * * * Quaker you shall pay for this !" he cried, advancing fiercely upon his antagonist.

Without moving a step, or uttering a word, Gilbert Gates, placed the pistols in his bosom. All traces of agitation had vanished from his face.

" Put away thee sword, David," he said in his usual quiet tone. " There can be no quarrel between me and thee. What ! would thee mar all our peace, for the sake of a silly wench ? Mind thee—the man Frazier is to be taken; the pacquet about the person of Washington, is to be seized. Put away thee sword, David."

As he spoke the first thunder of the battle broke on the air.

That sound—the first note of the death hymn—acted like a spell. David Walford plunged his sword into its sheath, and darted away through the forest trees, bending his steps, along the winding road.

" Ravens o' th' hollow," he shouted, as he hurried along. " Hurra ! There's work for you yonder ?"

As that dread sound broke on the air, the camp followers leaped to their feet, with an instantaneous cry. Blood tossed his arms about his head, covered with shock red hair, and gave utterance to his screeching laugh. Death stood silent and motionless, with her skinny fingers placed on her discolored lips, and her head inclined to one side. She was listening for the death-groans. Her white eyeballs rolled wildly in their orbits.

" Deek, dont hear, dont hear ?" she shouted, as a breeze laden with the battle murmur, swept through the forest. " Dont hear the groans ? Ho, ho ! Drink, Deek, it's vale brandy—drink !"

She drew a flask from a pocket in her dress, and gave it to her partner. The fiery liquid gurgled down his throat. Then seizing the flask, Death, applied it to her lips, and drained the last drop, with a grunt of deep satis-faction. Her white eyeballs danced in their sockets ; her death's-head countenance was alive with an infernal joy. With his grey eyes flashing, and his freckled skin, reddening, with sudden intoxication, Blood seized her skinny hand, and pointed toward the battle field.

"There's plunder yon," he screeched, "Rich plunder, among the corpseses, gold to be got, in the pockets o' the dyin' sogers, and rich skins, all shinin' with spangles, from the bodies o' the dead!"

"Is yer knife sharp?" growled Death. "Come, Deek—Come!"

And joining hands, the hideous pair, rushed through the bushes, toward the field of battle, laughing wildly as they went.

Gilbert Gates was alone.

He stood with his face buried in his hands, and those hands, firmly clasped, were pressed against the trunk of a collossal oak. Look upon him as he stands there, with his tall form attired in the Quaker garb, with his brow shadowed by the broad brimmed hat, with his face buried in his clasped hands, look upon him, as he stands there, silent as death, yet trembling from hand to foot, and tell me, what are the emotions that shake his soul? That soul is a foul Chaos, where Love and Hate, Despair, and Remorse, meet and mingle in fierce combat.

The reader, in forming his estimate of the moral and intellectual character of this man, must remember, that both, were formed by an ardent perusal of the Bible. As the spider sucks venom from the sweetest flower, so the morbid soul of Gilbert Gates, turned the pure teachings of God's own book, into bitterness and gall. Hence his occasional elevation of language; hence his belief in a blind and implacable fate; hence, too, the solitary pure emotion, that lightened over his dark soul.

"I am alone in the wild wood," he muttered, "I stand beside his body, the cold body of my father! The setting sun falls over his face—ah, it is ashy pale! I take the OATH—yes, yes, THE OATH to slay his murderers, and all their kin! Not a drop of their blood, that shed my father's blood, shall beat in a living heart! That OATH is fulfilled! Mayland is dead— burned alive! Frazier shall die this day! Mary is not dead! Would to the fiend, that she were! What wrong had this soldier-man Howard to avenge, that he crushed her down, in such foul dishonor? He, yea HE, covered her lip with his kisses, he bared her bosom, that had never yet thrilled to the touch of man, he made her fair young form, but a dainty for his appetite! And he had no father to avenge! My doom I know; I am led on by hands that I cannot see to the work of revenge; and in the next world, these same hands, shall plunge me, in the lake of fire.

"This is my doom; I know it? But what shall be the doom of this man, who having no father to avenge, took the young girl, and bent her down, and crushed her into a foul wreck of innocence and bloom! Satan. Satan, I call on thee! Is there not a hell, that sinks beneath all other hells, where the monsters in sin, are doomed to gnash their teeth forever? Then to that hell, do I consign the soul of this tinselled wretch!"

CHAPTER EIGHTH.

THE GRAVEYARD WALL.

ALL is silent still.

All is silent still within the graveyard. Not a shot peals over the green sward, not an echo, awakes the deadly stillness of that place. That grave yard, that Quaker temple, rest amid the hurry and turmoil of battle, peaceful as some quiet cottage, whose sloping roof, covered with vines and flowers, smiles in the first glimpse of the summer dawn.

All is silent, silent still.—Around and afar, darkens the smoke of battle, and streams the sheeted blaze of musquetry, but in the graveyard, all is still. Yes, as if some spirit sent of God, had smiled upon the holy place, the dark clouds, roll back above the Quaker temple, and the beams of the declining day, stream richly over the green sward.

All is silent still.

Along the hill sloping down into the valley, from the nothern graveyard wall, thunders the desperate band, who have sworn to carry that wall, or die.

Dashing madly forward, toward the graveyard wall, Lord Percy, turns his head, and for a moment surveys, the glorious scene of battle strife. As the music cannon breaks on his ear, his lip curls, with battle scorn, his eye fires with battle hate. The fever of carnage burns in his veins. He casts one long look behind him. There, at his back, four abreast, ride the bold troopers of Monthermer, a chosen band of English peasants, whose broad chests are clothed in forest green, whose swarthy brows are veiled by long dark plumes, whose iron hands raise aloft four long lines of glittering swords. These men have tried their blades in many a desperate fray, and felt their eyes grow fiery with the fire of many a battle.

Lord Percy gazes upon these brave men, and smiles, and then with one eager glance, he surveys, the solid phalanx of crimson and steel, which thunders in their rear. There ride, the scarlet troopers of the British' host led on by Captain Howard, whose blue eyes, now blazes with deep excitement; there are seen gleaming swords and glittering uniforms.

And behind the steeds of this mingled band of red and green, the infantry come sweeping on in solid columns, with arms raised and bayonets fixed. This is no child's play! No! For that graveyard wall is to be passed, that Quaker temple won! And on, like some huge animal, with one vast heart, yet many limbs, thunders this phalanx of battle. The green riders of Monthermer form, the head of the Monster ; the chest is supplied by the scarlet troopers ; the columns of infantry, with their lines of gleaming bayonets, form the huge carcase of the mammoth.

Oh, it was a glorious sight to see that battle phalanx, sweeping on, with the thunder of horses' hoofs, and the clatter of arms, towards that Quaker graveyard, where all was still as an infant's sleep.

Raising his form in the stirrups, Lord Percy patted the neck of his golden hued steed, and cast one flashing glance before him. There over the dark grey wall, rising high as a man's breast, not thirty paces distant, there was the green grass, softened by the rays of the sun stream from the parted clouds above, and there, far back in the graveyard, under the shelter of trees, was ranged a warrior band, clad like his own, in uniform of green, with a golden steed and his chieftain rider in their midst.

Now was the moment of trial! The wall was somewhat high, and the way, toward its dark grey stones, was up a sloping hill. It would require all the energy of a warrior's steed, to clear that barrier. Lord Percy shouted to his brave steed, and then turning his head over his shoulder, seized the British banner from an officer who rode at his side, and flung its folds aloft.

" Men of Monthermer," his shout rung on the air, " You see that wall? One brave leap, and it is ours !"

There was an answering shout, and then, the solid phalanx thundered on.

Another moment and they will have gained the graveyard front—all is calm about the Meeting House—not a rifle blaze streams from the windows, not a musquet shot peals from the graveyard wall.

On sweep the British troopers, behind them follow the infantry with fixed bayonets, before them, is nothing but the peaceful graveyard sward. The roadside is gained; the gallant array are breasting the graveyard wall, they are rearing their horses for the leap. The hoofs of George Percy's golden steed rest upon the wall! The Red Cross gleams in the upraised arm of Lord Percy—another moment, and the barrier will be passed, when lo!

What means this miracle ?

Starting from the very earth, a long line of bold backwoodsman, spring up from behind the wall, their rifles poised at the shoulder, and the aim of death securely taken. The tall form of Colonel Norman Frazier, towers in the centre of that line, the sword of Lovat, waving in his grasp.

" Men of Brandywine, you see your enemy," he shouted in his deep tone voice—" Let them have it, in the name of Jacob Mayland, the murdered man of Chadd's Ford !"

The words had not parted from his lips, when a sheet of fire, gleamed over the graveyard wall, pouring full into the faces of the British soldiers. Clouds of pale blue smoke, went rolling up to heaven ; in an instant, as they took their way aloft, this horrid sight was seen.

Where thirty bold troopers, but a moment ago, rushed forward, breasting the wall, now were seen, thirty steeds their saddles dripping blood, rearing wildly aloft, and trampling their riders' faces in the dust. Lord Percy was left alone, the British banner in his hand, and his horse's hoofs upon the wall. Twenty of his troopers, were all that remained of the gallant fifty.

" On, on, and revenge your comrades !'' shouted Captain Howard from the rear.

" On, and revenge the bold Riders of Monthermer !'' shrieked George Percy, as his face, blackened by the powder blaze, was convulsed with a passion, like madness. " On, or ye are cowards by the Living * * * !''

And on they came, thrusting the riderless horses aside, and trampling the dead bodies of their comrades in the dust, on, with a fierce hurrah they came, their eyes flashing vengeance, and their arms nerved for the struggle.

They came on, in one impetuous line, they breasted the wall, when lo ! at a sign from Colonel Frazier the Men of Brandywine parted in the centre, and dividing into two bands retreated on either hand, to the side walls of the graveyard.

" Back, Men of Brandywine !'' shouted Norman Frazier, as he stood alone, with his broadsword gleaming in the light, " Back, your vengeance is not complete !''

The way was now clear for the British troopers. First Lord Percy breasted the wall, the Banner of England waving in his grasp, then his twenty green riders, and then Captain Howard and his scarlet men came on with gleaming swords. They were forming in the graveyard, forming over the green sward in the order of battle, when from the farther extreme of that place of graves, arose a deep-toned shout ——

" Riders of the Santee upon these British robbers ! Upon these robbers who redden our soil, with the blood of its children !''

And Randulph Waldemar tossed his long dark hair over his shoulders, and flung the eagle plume back from his brow. All the glory of his Indian fathers flashed in his dark hazel eye, and swelled his muscular form.

One word to his gallant band, one shout to his war-horse of golden hue, and then, the thunder of fifty horses' hoofs beating over the graves rose on the air. Four abreast with upraised swords the band came on. Four abreast with gleaming swords, and shout like a cannon's roar, the band came on, each foot of ground they passed, giving a terrible impetus to their speed.

They came on, they crashed against the half-formed Britons ; there was crossing of swords and waving of banners. Steeds mingled with steeds, green uniforms with green uniforms, and scarlet with green ; now right, now left, now backward, now forward, whirled the fiery whirlpool of that ight, with two forms seen clearly and distinctly amid all its roar and turmoil. Two forms, rising in the proud beauty of manhood, arrayed in forest green, mounted on golden hued steeds, and with a gallant band of sworn brothers all around them, fought their way to each other's hearts.

And as the bands of Monthermer and Santee met in battle, the British infantry came crowding over the graveyard wall, with long lines of bayonets gleaming in the light. Then the windows of the Quaker Meeting House gave forth their volleys of death, then the men of Brandywine, led on by

Colonel Frazier, closed with the Britons, then the bands of Randulph the Prince and George of Monthermer whirled round, in desperate fight. All was confusion, smoke, groans, shouts, and blood.

At this moment, the door of the Quaker temple, opening toward the east, was flung rudely aside, and rushing along the graveyard, came a small but desperate and death-devoted band. They were but five in number, five men, half armed, and but half clothed, yet with the energy of despair in their limbs. There was the stout Blacksmith, Iron Tom o' Dilworth Corner, his head and breast unbared, while his huge right arm swung aloft a ponderous hammer. There was Gotlieb Hoff, his blue eyes flashing vengeance, his golden hair streaming in the wind, while with both arms he grasped a clubbed rifle ; there was the Forest-Stranger, clad in white furs, his grey hair floating back from his aged face, and an upraised axe, a woodman's axe, gleaming in his grasp ; there was the Inn Keeper, Hirpley Hawson, transformed into a very devil, by the memory of dark wrongs, his lean form braced for the battle-strife, his only weapon a long sharp hunters's knife, which rose quivering in his clenched hand.

And there, striding forward with immense paces, foaming like some chafed tiger, suddenly let loose from his cage the Negro Sampson came on, and the white dog came yelling by his side. The negro's brawny arms, his feet, his iron chest, all were bare ; the glittering scythe swung aloft, guided by the impulse of his giant strength. He rushed forward, a Black Hercules, his aquiline nose with its quivering nostrils, his thick lips whitened with foam, his massive forehead topped by short wooly hair, all turned to lurid red by flashes of battle-light. He came on, looking in very truth like a demon from the fabled hell.

Dark and mysterious are the instincts of man, dark and foul is that instinct of lust, which grapples with womanly beauty, like a beast gorging his bleeding food ; dark and dread is that instinct of Hunger, which has put such fire in a Mother's veins, such agony in her heart, that she has devoured her own babe, tearing it to gory fragments as it hung smiling on her wasted bosom ; dark and horrible is that instinct of Life, which makes a man forget honor, forswear his own father, and give his dearest friend to death, in order that he, may prolong a few hours of ignominious existence ; but darker and more dread and most horrible of all, is the instinct of Carnage ! Yes, that Instinct which makes a man thirst for blood, which makes him mad with joy, when he steeps his arms to the elbows in his foeman's gore, which makes him shout and halloo, and laugh, as he goes murdering on over piles of dead !

This Instinct now burned in the veins of the Oath-Bound Five, who rushing from the door of the Quaker temple, sought to grapple with their foes. Oath Bound, yes ! For they had sworn to avenge the **murder of Jacob Mayland,** the ruin of his daughter.

Let us for a moment, while the bands of Randulph and Monthermer, meet and mingle in combat, watch the motions of this little band.

The British foot-soldiers leaping over the wall, crowd on crowd, uttered a simultaneous cry of surprise, as they beheld this strange band come rushing on! The bark of the Dog, mingled with the yell of the Negro. Then with infuriated zeal, the band rushed into the crowd of scarlet soldiers. The hammer of Iron Tom rose and fell. The scythe of Black Sampson, glittered aloft. The clubbed rifle of Gotlieb plyed its busy task. The axe of the Forest-Stranger whirled round and round, in sudden circles. The knife of Hirpley Hawson cut right and left, with unfailing vigor. The White Dog Debbil, leaped forward, seeking the red coated soldier, with open jaws and gnashing teeth.

In a moment this little band stood alone, with a heap of British dead all around. The bullets passed by them harmless ; the bayonets could not wound ; the arms of hundreds could not crush them down. They pursued their work in awful silence, only broken by a single word. Yes, dripping with blood, and begrimed by the blue smoke of the powder, these five men went on to their work, cheering their way by a single watch-word :

" *Remember the dead !*"   Such was the import of their cry of vengeance.

" *The dead !*" shrieked Gotlieb Hoff, crushing down his antagonist with his clubbed rifle.

" This for the dead !" shouted Iron Tom, burying his sledge-hammer in the skull of a Briton.

" Remember the dead !" spoke the deep-toned voice of the Forest-Stranger, as his woodman's axe sank deep in the chest of a falling soldier.

" Jacob Mayland !" yelled Hirpley Hawson, plying his deadly knife.

" This for Massa !" thundered the negro whirling his scythe around his head, and cutting down the red-coat soldiers, one by one, like wheat stubble in a harvested field.

The yell of the dog, and the fierce utterance of that fatal watch-word was the only sound that betokened the sword march of this Oath-bound band.

Gradually step by step, this company advanced toward the spot, where Captain Howard fought hand to hand, with Lieutenant Le Clere. Gotlieb Hoff descried the Captain, and shouting his war-cry, fought his way nearer to his side.

This all occurred in the western corner of the graveyard. In the centre, the fight between the Rangers of Santee and Monthermer, went on, with clash of swords and fiery shouts, and in the eastern corner of the graveyard progressed a combat as desperate and deadly.

The brave Colonel Frazier, attired in his Provincial uniform of blue and silver, with the sword, which the old Simon of Lovat, had flung him, from the scaffold, waving in his grasp, led the Men of Brandywine, a stout band of farmers, clad in their everyday attire, toward the graveyard wall, where a desperate band of British, came rushing on. That band, whose dark attire and slouching hats, made them look more like a company of trained assassins, than daring soldiers, were rearing their horses against the wall, and urging them to the leap, with blasphemies, too foul to name. A fierce brigand led them on. David Walford, with his tangled hair, flying about his burly face, dug his spurs into the sides of his black steed, and waved his broadsword over his head. Over his shoulder, encouraging the tory band, with shouts and oaths, was seen the mean face of his father, Philip Walford.

"On Ravens o' th' hollow," shouted David Walford, breasting his steed against the wall, "Remember the booty! Hurray! There's yer prize!"

"Men of Brandywine, the hour has come! Avenge yourselves on these trained assassins!"

As Norman Frazier spoke, the brave farmers around him, seized their rifles by the barrel, and leaped upon the wall. Their rifles mingled with the swords of the tory band. The contest was short and desperate. Many a brave farmer, measured his grave on the sward below, many a tory, bit the roadside dust, beyond the wall.

There stood Norman Frazier, the sword of Lovat rising and falling in his grasp, dealing a death at every stroke, there he stood with the memory of British wrong, giving a strange fire to his calm blue eye, there he stood, fearless and immovable amid the hurry of the battle, his war cry, raising above all other sounds.

"Death to the Englisher! Hah! Dog! Take that for my mother, outraged by her own hearthside; take that for the sake of good old Scotland, and hah! That for old Simon of Lovat? This, I give you, in the name of Washington! Hah! David Walford, have we met at last!"

As he spoke fighting his way along the wall, he approached the spot, where the hoofs of Walford's black horse, pawed the hard stones, while his rider dealt death all around. Philip Walford beheld the approach of Colonel Frazier, along the wall, and dropping silently from his steed, even amid the turmoil of that fight, stole quietly along with his deadly intent, visible in his cold grey eye.

Norman Frazier raised his sword. David Walford looked up and sought to parry the coming blow. It fell, but at the same moment, two hands grasped the old soldier by the feet, and dragged him from the wall. His blow was aimless. He fell over the neck of David Walford's steed, and ere an instant passed, a dozen tory hands, were extended to grasp him. A moment passed! He was a prisoner in the midst of the tory band. In vain were the efforts of the Farmers of Brandywine. The scarlet-uniformed infantry of the British army, came sweeping to the wall, in solid columns; they crowded with lines of glistening bayonets, between the Men of Brandywine, and their brave Colonel.

"Ha, ha!" shouted David Walford, as he turned the head of his steed towards Osborne's hill, while Colonel Frazier, stunned by a rude blow, lay

29

pinioned in his grasp, "It want two hours of sunset, and yet afore that sun goes down, your neck 'll stretch a rope my old boy!"

"I did it David, I did," chuckled his father, riding by his side, "I, I stole along the wall, I caught him by the feet, I—I—"

He was stricken down by a random shot that came from the British army. He toppled from his horse, and fell in the roadside dust.

With a brutal laugh, David Walford glanced at the bleeding form of his father, and then speeding through the advancing columns of the British army, followed by his troop, he sought the position occupied by the British commander-in-chief.

"Ho, ho, Ravens o' th' Hollow!" he laughed as he dashed along, "I hold the guineas in my grasp—hurray!"

CHAPTER NINTH.

THE LORD AND THE PRINCE.

WE will now return to the combat, between the Rangers of Santee, and the Riders of Monthermer.

After the first crash of steed against steed, after the first fierce clashing of sword against sword, after the first recoil of the charge, the fight had been, a wild and confused mellé, in which men and horses, green uniforms and red, went whirling round, over the ground sod, while their shouts broke on the air, mingling with the shrill report of the rifle, and the distant roar of cannon.

Two forms alone, were distinguishable, among the confused mass of green and scarlet and steel. Two forms, robed in forest green, and bestriding steeds, with skin all glossy with the hues of gold.

The form of Randulph the Prince, surrounded by the swords of his stout troopers, was seen amidst all the confusion of battle, separated by a wall of men and horses and steel, from the form of George of Monthermer.

They saw one another, above the heads of their soldiers, bending in conflict, their eyes met, in a glance of deep hatred, and a shout of defiance broke from each lip.

"At last"——shouted Lord Percy, as his dark eyes gleamed from the shadow of his interwoven brows.

"At last, we have met!" returned Randulph the Prince, waving his sword, as he measured the distance between him and his foe, with a flashing eye.

And then with one impulse, these young men, alike handsome, gallant and bold, rode madly toward each other, dashing friend and foe aside, with the impulse of desperation.

At last they met, each golden hued steed falling back on his haunches, while his rider contemplated the form of his antagonist.

For a moment, there was silence in the centre of that graveyard. The Rangers of Santee, fell back behind their leader ; the Riders of Monthermer, and the crimson-uniformed troopers, formed a crescent, in the rear of Lord Percy. Lieutenant Clerwoode Le Clere and Captain Howard, ceased their brief combat, by a spontaneous impulse. Every soldier, American or Briton, in the centre of that graveyard, felt that some wrong, deeper than a natural quarrel, some revenge, deadlier than a natural hate, had brought the twain together, on this graveyard battle field. For a moment, therefore, there was silence, while the contending foemen, ranging round, awaited the issue of this scene.

Reining their steeds back on their haunches, these young men, led to this graveyard by fate, contemplated each other. Their mutual gaze, was but for an instant, and yet there was a world of meaning in that gaze.

Randulph glanced over the form of Lord Percy, marking its manly proportions, clad in green and gold ; he looked in his pale face, shadowed by curling masses of jet black hair, and lightened by the gleam of eyes dark as midnight. Lord Percy gazed upon the form of his opponent, something more manly, something more muscular than his own, clad in a similar uniform of green and gold, strikingly relieved by massive locks of dark brown, and moulded in a wild beauty, that gave a decided character to the firm mouth, the aquiline nose, the broad brow, and the deep hazel eyes.

There was something strange and impressive in this scene. Alike young and handsome, alike mounted on golden hued steeds, they gazed in each other's face, these Representatives of two races of men.

The noblest race of the Indian, mingled with the Caucasian, found its type in the face and form of Randulph the Prince of Wyamoke. The Norman race, mingled with the Saxon, was typified in the slighter form, and striking, though less impressive face of Lord George of Monthermer.

Their eyes met. Their glances mingled with a strange magnetic sympathy. They gazed in each other's brightening eye, with a look of deep and absorbing fascination.

At that moment an awful memory rose to each soul.

Randulph stood beside the bed of a dying mother; his oath, and her last words rung in his ears :

‘ *In a quiet graveyard, where the mounds arise, without a tombstone or monument to mark the resting place of the dead, there, there, shall the Prophecy of betrayed mother, claim its terrible fulfilment !*’

Monthermer beheld the wan face of his aged father; again he heard the last words that fell from his quivering lips, as he hurried his son on shipboard.

‘ *Away my son to the hills of the Santee ; fulfil your solemn oath, fulfil the commission with which I have entrusted you ; when that is done, then, then, I can die in peace !*’

And now led on by Fate, he was come to die in the Quaker graveyard, with his father's last request unfulfilled ! He felt that some strange decree of the Unknown, linked his destiny, with that of Randulph the Prince.

"We have met at last !" shouted Randulph as his eye drank in the mag. netic gaze of Monthermer "Twice have I spared you ! We have met for the third time, and now you die !"

"It is the hour," replied the deep-toned voice of Lord Percy. "We have met in the peaceful presence of women, we have met amid burning rafters, we have met on the battlefield, and yet fate withheld you from my grasp. It is the hour ! Look well upon yonder sky—look well upon yonder sun, obscured by battle smoke, for never again shall you behold the rising of that sun. This hour you die ?"

The spectators, used as they were to scenes of blood, shrank with horror, at this scene of deep and deliberate hate.

With one impulse the antagonists backed their steeds, until a few paces of green turf, drenched with blood, lay between them.

"Let Blanche be the prize !" shouted Percy, and then, with upraised swords, they rushed together. Their steeds met breast to breast, and as though sharing the deep hate of their masters, pawed each other with their hoofs, and fixed their teeth in each other's necks, neighing wildly all the while. Leaning over the necks of their golden hued horses, the foeman fought their quarrel out, not according to the graceful rules of the fencing school, but with the blind fury of maddened hate. Once, twice, thrice their swords crossed, and then, one sweeping blow from Randulph's vigorous arm sent Percy's sword spinning over his head. Then leaning over his horse's neck, he seized his antagonist by the throat. Each horse uttered a wild howl, and then with their eyes starting from the sockets, tore the neck of its enemy with blood-dripping teeth. Randulph shortened his grasp of his sword, and in the fierce struggle, which ensued over their plunging horses' necks, while Percy's throat was in his frenzied grasp, sought to kill his an- tagonist, by one desperate thrust through the eyeball into the brain. Percy lay almost helpless in the stout grasp of Randulph ; his head fallen on his shoulder and his arms faintly grappling with his antagonist; he felt the hot breath of his foe on his cheek ; their hair mingled together.

"Die !" shouted Randulph, aiming the shortened sword point full upon the eyeball of Lord Percy.

At that moment, as if a musquet ball had stricken his arm, it fell stiffly to his side ; he relaxed his hold, and sate erect upon his steed, with a face livid as ashes.

"Go !" he said in a subdued voice, to Lord Percy, "Go ! And let us never meet again ! I cannot—cannot slay you ! There is a voice you cannot hear pleading for your life, when I attempt to dye my sword in your blood ! Go ! And let us never meet again !"

Lord Percy looked up in vacant wonder, which slowly vanished before a feeling of impassioned sympathy, that now stole gently over his heart. He felt himself drawn toward Randulph the Cassique of Wyamoke, by a tie, like brotherhood.

"Hold! Generous stranger——" he shouted, but his words were lost in the battle-shout which again resounded from every side. Again the bands of the Santee and of Monthermer, joined swords. Again living men fell stricken in sudden death. Still from the windows, from the nooks and crevices of the Quaker Temple, streamed the deadly rifle shot; still onward, strode the small band of Five, who had the death of the school-master, the ruin of his daughter to avenge; and faster and thicker gathered the infantry of the British army, crowding over the graveyard wall, with upraised sword and bayonet. Yet never again crossed the swords of Randulph and Percy. Borne hither and thither by the tide of battle, they each fought with desperation, the one for the cause of the King; the other for his country and his God.

In five brief minutes, that graveyard, was all one wild scene of tumult. All ranks, all military order were broken. The foemen fought with demoniac fury. Still Gotlieb Hoff pressed on to Captain Howard's side, and still the tide of battle rolled between. Still Black Sampson shouted the name of the murdered school-master, and urged his dog Debbil, onward. The graveyard was choked with the living, the wounded and the dead.

Suddenly Clerwoode Le Clere, streaming with blood, and separated from Captain Howard by a sudden recoil of the tide of battle, looked around for his brave friend and leader. Randulph the Prince, was gone. At the same moment Captain Howard, glanced over the ranks of battle for the form of Lord Percy. He also had disappeared. Randulph and Monthermer, were gone. Not a trace of their horses, or their forms was visible, through all the fiery tumult of that graveyard massacre.

In five minutes, the British were in possession of the Meeting House. The Red Cross banner, waved from its peaceful roof.

And now Sullivan speeding from column to column, covered with dust and smoke and blood, beheld his Right wing in confusion; he beheld, with horror that no words can tell, his men fall back before the superior numbers of the British Host. He saw the Banner of the Stars sink in clouds of smoke. Then, in a voice of anguish, he shouted to his soldiers, and prayed them to maintain their ground but five minutes longer. Washington, he said, was hurrying to their rescue, and La Fayette, and Greene. It was in vain.

On came the advancing legions of the British host. On came the Red Cross Banner. On and on, a mass of crimson and steel, swept the solid columns. Afar from the height of Osborne's hill, Cornwallis beheld the flying Continentals, and shouted to his brigade in reserve. Howe raised his hands in very glee, and cheered his men with shouts. And now stripping to the waist, whole lines of British soldiers, cast their clothes upon the ground, and grasp the musquet, and rush on.

Over the heaps of dead in the valley, over the ghastly corpses in the Quaker graveyard, up the hills of Birmingham, thunders the pursuing host.

It is now midway between four and five o'clock. But half an hour since the battle began, and yet such a world of carnage crowded in that space of thirty minutes !

Along the road, leading to Dilworth Corner, might be seen a tall soldier, clad in a uniform once white, but now reddened with the blood of his foe, riding a dark steed, whose breast was covered with dust and foam.

This soldier threw himself in the path of the fugitives; he wheeled his band across the road; with his mustachioed lip quivering with emotion, he besought the flying soldiers in broken English, to turn and face the enemy, he showed his sword, red with the blood of the British; he called them friends, brothers, but in vain !

The troops commanded by Sullivan rushed on. Then it was that the Count Pulaski shook with rage, and giving vent to his indignation in fiery oaths, called to his own band, and rode among the pursuing British like a war-horse, with the death wound in his heart, trampling them beneath the hoofs of his black steed, and cutting them down like sheep beneath the butcher's axe. Then Count Pulaski—whose memory may all the nations of America, bless for evermore—rioted in his battle joy, and as though sheathed in supernatural armour, rode madly on the bayonets and among the bullets of the British Host.

The Continental army were in full retreat for a thick wood, about a mile below the Meeting House. They had been attacked while forming in order of battle; they had performed miracles of courage, but the main body of the army was yet far from the field, and Sullivan's Division were forced to flee before superior numbers.

And now, onward from the south, came the Reserve under the brave Greene, headed by Washington, with La Fayette by his side. There is yet a hope for the starry banner.

Ere we take up the blood-stained thread of battle, and trace the movements of Washington, let us hasten once again to the summit of Osborne's Hill.

There, sheltered from the sun by the overarching boughs of a massive chesnut tree, sate the Lady Isidore of Monthermer, mounted on a dark bay steed, and attired in her warrior costume.

It was a quiet place, with the carpet of tufted moss, sheltered from the light by the circling trunks of beech and hickory and chesnut, with green shrubbering, growing thickly around their roots. Above was an impenetrable canopy of forest boughs, and toward the south, a small interval in the foliage of the chesnut tree, like an oriel window, gave to view a gorgeous panorama of the country, for long miles away.

And here, the Lady Isidore had silently watched the progress of the fight. With her dark eyes burning with an emotion too intense for utterance, she had seen afar, the tournament of the graveyard. One form, and one alone her eye had singled out from the ranks of battle. The charge on the graveyard wall, the rifle blaze and the smoke for a moment, overshadowing the foemen, the meeting of Randulph and Monthermer, and then the wild tumult of the fight, these all had broken on the gaze of Isidore, through the rifted battle clouds.

And now, as seated on her dark bay steed, in that sequestered nook of the forest wild, this strange girl for a moment gave her soul to deep memories of the past, her face and form disclosed in softened light with the greenery of the forest all around, furnished a picture of striking interest.

That slender yet full and voluptuons form, whose rounded limbs and womanly bust was clad in green velvet, faced with gold, that white hand laid absently on the dark neck of the steed, while the other pressed against the maiden's neck, seemed striving to subdue the emotions that swelled the veins, and heaved the breast; that face rich brown in hue, with deep vermillion reddening in the centre of each cheek; those eyes so full, so gleaming and so dark, showing all the passion and energy of the soul, from beneath the mingled shadow of pencilled brows and long jet lashes; those lips whose ripe red deepened into purple; that forehead pale as death, relieved by the hair, gathered beneath the military cap, and raven-like in its glossy blackness. O, beautiful was the face and form of the Lady Isidore, sitting alone in this forest nook, with the softened sunlight all around her and a glimpse of the distant battle visible through the interval of the forest boughs !

Suddenly a dark frown passed over her forehead; at that moment a desperate resolve took possession of her soul.

She gave her steed the spur, and advancing through the forest trees for a single moment paused on the brow of the hill, with the battle clouded sky above her.

One glance !

Like some fair map whose delicate outlines had been blotted with blood, and darkened with smoke and dust, the glorious landscape spread beneath. There was a world of dark smoke, through whose rifted intervals were seen banners and steeds, and mingling soldiers ; the living and the dead ; the pursuers and the pursued, all crowded together in seperate masses, extending over a tract of three miles. It was a dim and dusky and bloody map.

One glance, and the Lady Isidore gave the rein to her horse, and dashing madly down the hill, was lost in the clouds of battle-smoke.

CHAPTER TENTH.

THE WILDERNESS.

HALF-WAY between the Quaker Meeting House and the tenements of Dilworth Corner, there was a thick wood, darkening away from the northern road, toward the east, a dense mass of forest trees, with green fields and luxuriant farms on either side.

This wood has an important connection with our story. It was a strange old wood, with chesnut and beech and maple and oak and hickory trees, crowded together, while all around their massive trunks the thick underwood spread greenly, shutting the soft moss beneath, from the light of day.

A single road led into the recesses of this wood. A winding road, but a few feet wide, with its brown earth scarcely ever broken by the pressure of wheels, contrasting with the verdant arbor above. Deep into the hidden solitudes of this wood led this winding road, until turning the trunk of a gnarled oak it suddenly terminated, in a prospect of singular beauty. Singular beauty it is true, but a beauty that was strange and wild and almost supernatural.

Fancy an open circle, some fifty yards in diameter, whose circumference is described by a compact mass of forest trees, standing like battle legions, side by side, their arms enclasped and their foliage mingling in one green wall of leafy beauty.

In the northern quarter of this circle, a rugged mass of rocks tower rudely into light, lifting their collossal forms from the very border of the forest; and beneath the shadow of these granite piles, like a young girl sleeping in the embrace of a giant, a quiet cottage smiles in the occasional sunbeam. A quiet cottage, with a sloping roof, ornamented with fanciful carvings along the eves, with four pointed windows, two on either side of its rustic porch, overgrown with vines, and a lovely garden extending along its front, into the centre of the forest circle. Here in this garden, roses grow wildly amid beds of drowsy hoppies; here are masses of green vines, trailing over the neglected walks; and here, in the centre, beside a clear cold spring, which bubbles up from yellow sands, at the foot of an oaken tree, that stands like a grim and war-worn veteran, alone in the midst of that forest circle, here arises a cross of dark grey stone, with a wild vine, rich with untamed roses twining over its venerable form.

Believe me, that beside that clear cold spring, bubbling up from yellow sands, that cross of dark grey stone, looks like a holy thing, as the vagrant sunlight trembles over its loving roses. And then from the massy arms of oaken tree above, a sleepy voluptuary of a grape-vine hangs his cumbrous length, and lets down into light, purple clusters, that dangle lazily from among green leaves. O, let me tell you, that there is a strange wild beauty in that forest circle; with its cottage, its garden, its solitary oaken tree, its clear spring of cold water, and its holy cross!

This wood was called the Wilderness; this cottage with its bubbling spring and holy cross—the Hermitage.

This cottage at the time of my story, was the summer retreat of a retired Merchant, who had been scared from its peaceful roof by the din of arms, leaving it occupied by a solitary tenant, an aged and venerable woman.

Our way now lies deeper down, into the mysteries of the wood. Beyond the cottage, toward the east, until the forest terminated in a buckwheat field, there was one dense mass of forest trees, choked up with underwood and tangled vines. The centre of this wilderness was attainable by a rude foot-path, which winding under gnarled limbs, or diving down into occasional hollows, or brushing through thick vines, at last terminated in a wild and lonely retreat.

Deep sunken in the bosom of the earth, with a circular wall of entangled roots, covered with hanging moss, enclosing it on every side, a black pool of water rested in sluggish silence, with no visible outlet, for its sombre waves. Waves? Ah, it was waveless and motionless; silent as death, yet glittering as a mirror of polished steel. It lay there, in the midst of that wilderness, a deep well, enclosed by a wall of roots breaking from the sur-rounding earth, with forest trees girdling its banks on every side. Two stout hickory trees with trunks not more than half the thickness of the col-lossal forms around, bent over this pool, from opposing sides, and met and joined together in mid air. Originally these trees had grown in opposite directions, each trunk inclining from the pool, but now by the application of some tremendous force, they were drawn together, and confined by intri-cate cords of rope, which after encircling their bark some twelve or thirteen times, met in a firm knot. This was all the result of a whim, which in the first place, induced the retired Merchant to make a hermit's retreat of the space around the lonely well, and then, to shelter the dark waters from the beams of the summer sun, he had hired the aid of stout arms, and the hick-ory trees were forced together. It was evident that tremendous strength had been required to accomplish this feat. The earth was broken at the roots of the trees, and had not the rope, which bound them together been of strands like iron, it was plain, they would have sprung back to their origi-nal positions, with a terrific rebound.

Reader! Look well into the waters of that silent pool! Ere the setting ot yonder sun, which comes dimly through the branches, those black waters will give back the reflection of an awful tragedy!

Look well upon the cottage (separated from the pool by a distance of two hundred yards) and upon the rocks above, and the garden in front. Here will transpire, some of the darkest and yet loveliest scenes of our chronicle.

And while the sun gleams over the dark grey cross, beloved of roses, and the black pool resting silent and sullen, in the midst of the wilderness, we will away to the field of battle once more.

There was a spot in front of this wood, where the northern road emerging from thick boughs, was laid bare to the full light of day, for a few brief yards, and then lost again in the shadow of forest trees.

The sound of horses' hoofs resounded from either side of the unsheltered space, at the same moment.

And presently from the south, emerging from the forest boughs, there came a gallant band, whose steeds, covered with dust and flecked with foam, encircled a grey war-horse and his commanding rider.

That rider was Washington, and by his side was the calm-visaged Greene, and all around, were the brave chieftains of the Continental Host. Their uniforms of blue and buff, were soiled with the roadside dust, and every face was stamped with indications of anxiety and care. Breaking from the shelter of the green boughs, Washington glanced around, his head erect, and his dilating eye fixed steadily on the northern woods.

" On," he whispered, turning to the brave men around him. " On, we will yet carry the day ! The enemy attacked Sullivan, ere we had time to hurry to his assistance, but now, if stout hands and fearless hearts will work us triumph, we will drive the British from the field, Pulaski and La Fayette are *there!*"

He slowly extended his hand toward the north, and at that moment, there broke from the boughs in front of his path, a grey horse and his war-worn rider. It was the Marquis La Fayette. His face was covered with sweat and dust ; his uniform was rent in various places, and with his chapeau in hand and brow uncovered, he came dashing on.

" Mon dieu ! Mon dieu !" he shouted, " You come in time ! Sullivan is driven from the field ; the Continentals are in full retreat ! Pulaski is now endeavoring to stem the torrent, but in vain ! I have ridden at the peril of my life and steed, to hasten on the Division in Reserve ! Ah ! General Greene I salute you. Let us on—by one bold effort, we may yet carry the day !"

Washington turned hastily, and gazed for an instant, upon the advancing ranks of the Brigade in Reserve, which now came gallantly from the forest shade. Then with a deep toned voice, subdued to an impressive whisper, he turned to the officers by his side, and exclaimed :

" Greene, there is hard fighting for us yonder. But our men are true, and our cause holy in the eyes of Heaven. The British will know more of us, ere the setting of the sun. Colonel Hamilton bear a message for me to General Wayne, at Chadd's Ford. Away, as fast as your horse will carry you, and tell the General for me, that his brothers in arms look to him, this hour, for success and triumph ! Let him but maintain the ford till night, and we will take care of the British to the north ! Will we not gentlemen ?"

An involuntary shout burst from the band, as Colonel Hamilton turned his steed southward, and disappeared amid the advancing files of the Reserve.

Washington gazed in the faces of his officers. Not a lip but was firm, not an eye that did not fire with hope and rapture. The hope of victory, the rapture of the coming fight!

Then it was that the majestic form of Washington—and by the Cause for which he fought, his form was majestic! Then it was that the majestic form of Washington swelled to its full stature; his blue eye kindled; his face was sharpened in every outline, by the calm rigidity of a fixed determination.

He waved his sword, and pointed to the north!

And then with La Fayette and Greene, and the brave officers of his army ly his side, Washington gave the rein to his grey horse, and darted onward.

Then pouring along that wood-sheltered road, came the columns of the Reserve; the body guard of Washington, a band of gallant men, mounted on noble steeds; the infantry in solid masses with bayonets fixed; the artillery with heavy cannon of glittering brass; the cavalry with upraised swords gleaming in the light. The mingled mass arrayed in blue and buff, with a broad banner of stars waving above their heads, poured hastily along the narrow road.

There was the terrible tramp of horses' hoofs, there was the rattling of arms, there was a confused murmur, terrible from its very indistinctness, and ten minutes passed.

Ascending a gentle slope, Washington attained the summit of a wood crowned hill, and the glorious panorama of the battle broke like some scene of magic on his gaze.

One gaze, and all the stern realities of the fight rushed on his soul.

There was a mass of dark smoke clouding earth and heaven with heavy folds. From the bosom of this chaos, like lightning from a thunder cloud, poured the blaze of the cannon, and the sheeted flame of musquetry. Through the intervals of the huge cloud, Washington beheld a distant gleam of Osborne's hill, a glimpse of the Quaker Meeting House, and a short yet terrible view of the blood-drenched field, now crowded with the dying and the dead. From this very hill, but thirty minutes before, Washington had seen the American soldiers go bravely on to battle; and now he beheld them breaking in disorder, from beneath the thick cloud, and spreading over the hills and woods and fields, in broken columns.

One short and terrible glance at this scene, and Washington clenched his sword with a grasp that forced the veins on his hand into rigid prominence. A fearful change passed over him. His face, whose familiar expression was the very sublimity of calm courage, now was convulsed with fiery passion. You could see the white enamel making an ivory circle around the pupil of his flashing eye. His compressed lip quivered tremblingly. He turned to his officers; he gave one backward glance far down the road, over the advancing columns of the Continental Reserve.

"Now!" he shouted in a voice of thunder, as his broad chest swelled with emotion, "Now I will lead you to the charge! Now, face to face and foot to foot, we will fight these invaders, we will drive them back over the bodies of our comrades! Look! Soldiers! The eye of God is upon you, the arm of God will fight for you! Advance—advance!"

Oh how that voice of stern enthusiasm thrilled along the American columns! With one movement, the Brigade in Reserve rushed forward; Washington gave his horse the spur, and dashed on toward the battle cloud; but at the very moment, the hand of La Fayette was laid upon his right arm, while the hand of Greene gently yet firmly seized his bridle rein. Washington gazed around in wonder; the officers of his staff had thrown their horses in front of his path.

"We will go to battle, General!" cried La Fayette. "But your life is sacred!"

"Sacred!" echoed the band of officers,

"Aye General," exclaimed Greene, "we will go to battle, and if need be, leave our bodies on the field, but with your life, dies the liberty of our native land!"

"Back, gentlemen, back from my path!" shouted Washington with a flashing eye, "I *will* lead you to the field! Shall I remain an unconcerned spectator of the contest, while my men are bravely grappling with the foe? Shall I gaze quietly on, while whole ranks of American soldiers are trampled down beneath the feet of the advancing legions? Look yonder, gentlemen, I beseech ye, look! There are thousands calling on my name, as they charge, as they fall, as they die! I will answer that call! Yes, yes, there is the stern courage of despair in our veins, there is glory waiting for us on yonder field, there is the eye of God watching us from above! Onward then, in the name of God!"

There was majesty in that look, that deep tone, that extended arm.

"Nay, General, do not peril your life in this contest!" exclaimed General Greene, in a tone of deep emotion. "The American army needs all its brave soldiers, and this day it will lose many a stout arm, many a gallant heart on yonder field! These may be replaced, General, by other arms and other hearts, but where, where in all the hills and valleys of America, will you find another Washington?"

A deep murmur arose from the gallant band who encircled Washington.

"Look gentlemen! Yonder rides Count Pulaski, at the head of his brave soldiers. He is endeavoring to roll back the tide of retreat! Let us on, gentlemen, let us join our swords with the British and side by side with Pulaski, drive the invaders back!"

At this moment Washington looked like the Ideal image which all future time will delight to worship. He sat his grey war-horse with the dignity of a king; aye, with more than the dignity of an empurpled monarch; with the majesty of that manhood, which approaches in its impressive beauty, the sublimity of Godhead. His form so tall, so muscular, so well-proportioned, rose towering above the heads of his chieftains. That face, which once seen was never forgotten, now glowed with rapture, with scorn, with fierce indignation. All its calm composure had vanished. With a dilating eye he drank in the prospect of the battle ; with a beating heart he listened to the cannon's roar.

The chieftains were awed, but not silenced. They gathered round their leader ; with broken words and earnest tones, trembling with emotion, they besought Washington to listen to their request. They would fight, they would face the carnage of the field, but Washington must not peril his life in the bloody contest of that day. Heaven had reserved him for more glorious deeds.

As La Fayette and Greene, and all the brave officers who gathered round, poured these appeals into the ear of Washington a change came slowly over his visage. He was once more calm and immovable in all the quiet dignity of his commanding face.

At a sign from his sword, the Life Guard ranged their noble steeds and stout forms along the roadside. The American Leader, with La Fayette by his side, was in their midst. Another sign from the sword of Washing·ton, and the legions of Greene went thundering by.

And as the infantry swept on, in their torn apparel, as the artillery thun·dered past, as the horsemen of the army came rushing toward the battle-cloud, every eye was for a moment fixed upon the face of Washington, and his name leapt from lip to lip and from column to column. His name found its echo in every heart.

And then the Broad Banner of the Continent, waved high over the heads of its soldiers, and with the name of Washington echoing along the solid column, the army passed on to battle. Along the road, and down the hill, and over the green fields : the battle-cloud received them in its fiery bosom.

Washington and La Fayette were alone. There was dead silence along the bold front of the Life Guard. The eye of Washington beheld all the changing phases of the fight. He saw the retreating soldiers met in the blind hurry of their flight, by the legions of Greene ; he saw them turn with their brethren ; he saw them face the foe again. He heard them shout, as with infuriate hate, they turned upon the blood-hounds of the British army and drove them back, with merciless carnage. That shout came leaping from the battle-cloud, over the fields, and to the ear of the American chieftains.

One name mingled with that shout—his own—Washington.

"Thank God!" he exclaimed raising his hand solemnly to heaven. As his muscular chest swelled with emotion, he beheld Pulaski crashing on among the British ranks, with his long train of white uniformed troopers behind him. The fiery Polander was mad with joy.

La Fayette said not a word, but his deep-drawn breath came gasping through his clenched teeth.

" O, this is torture !" he at last exclaimed, while his blue eye flashed beneath his fair forehead. " Torture, torture ! Let me away, General, let me mingle in the fight ! I would strike one good blow in this battle, one good blow in the name of Washington !"

The French blood was up in his veins, that French blood which fires with instinctive hatred at the sight of a Briton ; that glorious French blood, which in after time, making one wide channel of the whole earth, flowed on in a mighty river, bearing on and on, to triumph and glory, the Napoleon of France. The blood of Charlemagne, and Henry of Navarre, and Conde and Turenne, burned in the veins of La Fayette at that dread moment, when from the summit of the hill, he surveyed the charges of the glorious battle.

" Away," whispered Washington, " Away, my brave comrade ! And with you take my gallant Life Guard ! Gentlemen, it may rest with you to drive the British from yon field !"

In a moment these splendid soldiers, were ranged along the road, four abreast, with La Fayette at their head.

" I cannot leave your excellency," exclaimed La Fayette. " You are without defence or guard. Pardon my thoughtless haste. I will remain with you !"

And the wild joy of battle, which flashed from the eyes of the soldiers, was in a moment succeeded by the calm look of mechanical obedience.

" We will not leave our General !" they said, with a deep murmur ; and every eye was fixed upon the form of Washington.

" Look ! The Continentals are again driven back ! Again Pulaski stems the torrent of the retreat ! On, on my brave fellows ; the glory of this victory is with you ! Away La Fayette—away ! Do not hesitate, for in this moment, hesitation is defeat !"

As Washington spoke with deep-toned utterance, and flashing eyes, the Life Guard raised their swords, their banner and their battle-shout ! La Fayette gave the word. They dashed onward to the battle

Washington was alone

CHAPTER ELEVENTH.

THE ROADSIDE.

Do you remember it?

That quiet nook in the forest, formed by a sudden angle of the road, in front of the wilderness, half-way between the Meeting House and Dilworth Corner?

Above the arching greenery of the forest boughs, beneath the brown dust of the road, on one side, the wood of the wilderness, on the other a tangled thicket and a winding fence. On the north and south, the view is shut in by the entwining branches that meet from either side, and form a tapestry of rustling leaves.

It is a quiet nook in the forest, and here we will recline on the soft moss, beneath the trunk of yonder beechen tree. We will watch beneath that tree, and while the din of battle brays afar to the north, we will look upon the travellers who may chance to pass our resting place. There is a cool breeze among the leaves overhead; there are gleams of sunlight embroidering the roadside dust, with leaves of light and shadow.

There is the sound of horses' hoofs to the south, mingled with the footsteps of a man. We lean forward, we listen! In a moment, emerging from the woods to the south, there comes a burly trooper, mounted on a jet-black horse, with a white belt drooping over his dark uniform. By the trooper's side, advances a man clad in Quaker costume, his immense strides, keeping pace, with the brisk canter of the horse.

David Walford—Gilbert Gates!

They are covered with dust, and their faces express hurry, and triumph and fear.

"Now to the battle, smooth-speech! I—to meet my men. You—to hurry on by yourself. While the Ravens o' th' Hollow surround this rebel Washington, you will have a little talk to him by yourself!"

"That is to say, David, thee will secure the person of Friend Washington, in case I should fail in persuading the man of war, to surrender to me a certain paper, which he carries about him?"

"That's it Gilbert. I say, was'n't it a capital move,—eh, Quaker?"

"To bring our prisoner to Dilworth Corner, through the rebel hosts?"

"Covered over with a long black cloak, so that his own mother would'nt know him?"

"Thee will leave him there, David, until the battle is past! Thee is a cunning one, in truth, David, were I not a man of peace, I should be afraid of thee! What does thee intend to do with *him*?"

"I've left him in the large room of the Inn, at Dilworth, but not alone. I

tell you! There's four of my ravens with him—stout fellers, who'll use
the knife if need be.   After the battle is over——"

"When our friends in the blue coats are beaten, when they are driven
far away to the south, then Friend Cornwallis will come to Dilworth Corner, and *try our friend in the black cloak.* Is it so David?"

"It is, my peaceful friend! What in the d——l makes you smile so,
Gilbert?   I don't like that smile—it's wicked.   It makes my blood run
cold—ugh!"

"Verily, I was thinking of the large buttonwood tree in front of the Inn,
yonder. I was thinking of one particular branch that seems just fitted for a
rope——"

"Ho, ho, ho!" laughed David.

"Thee is *such* a funny man. Thee really laughs at everything. A tree,
and a rope, and—does thee comprehend?   A man doing queer things with
his feet at the end of the rope.   Dancing, I think thee calls it?"

"Ho, ho, ho!" roared David, "Gilbert, do you know I did'nt believe in
the Bible, or any sich nonsense, fore five minutes ago; but now—since I've
heer'd you talk, and seen yo' smile,—I'm converted.   I believe in devils,
Gilbert—yes I do!"

"Forward David!"

"Forward Gilbert!"

And the worthy couple passed on. That quiet nook in front of the wilderness is vacant once more.

For some five minutes there is a dead pause.

Again the sound of horse's hoofs, and presently dashing into the quiet
recess of this quiet nook, there comes a gallant cavalier, mounted on a golden hued steed.   The rein is thrown loosely on the horse's neck, for the
arms of the cavalier enclose the form of a beautiful girl, who with her eyes
closed in a swoon, and her hair—so black, so glossy—showering over her
shoulders, rests in his embrace, like an image of death.

"Blanche, it is my last hour, but I swore to win thee, and—*I have
won!* Mine in life, Blanche, mine in death, mine now, mine only, mine
forever!"

The cavalier suddenly turned his head; the sound of horse's hoofs echoing from the south, struck his ear.

"Pursued?   But I will foil him yet!   Ho, ho, it was gallantly done!
To escape from the mellee in the Quaker graveyard, to ride southward, to
snatch this beauty from the arms of the twin-beauty at yonder roadside Inn
——this was but the work of a few brief minutes!"

The sound of hoofs grew nearer.

"He comes! Yes, yes, he beheld me in the very act of mounting my
horse, with the fainting girl in my arms.   He was but a hundred yards
distant but he could not rescue her!   Was not that a moment of triumph?

He has pursued me every inch of the way from the Quaker graveyard, and yet I will foil him, after all !"

The echo of horse's hoofs seemed now to resound from the other side of the trees, which enclosed the view to the south.

The cavalier reined his horse in the centre of the road.

Gathering the fainting girl closer in his arms, he silently perused her face. His pale countenance was convulsed with a strange and mingled expression —the fire of passion, the horror of despair. His dark eyes shone with deadly lustre ; his lips trembled.

That face, pale as marble, beautiful as some Madonna,—shining serenely in the twilight of a cathedral shrine—that face, relieved by the flowing hair, lay open to his gaze. The young form rested quiet as childhood's slumber, in his arms ; he could feel the low, faint throbbings of her maiden heart.

" Blanche," he whispered, bending gently down, " Awake—it is our Bridal hour !"

His horse moved gently toward the bye road, leading into the recesses of the wilderness. Slowly the horse, the cavalier, the fainting girl, passed from the sunlight of the roadside, into the shadows of the wood.

As the last gleam of sunlight fell over the pale face of Blanche, her lips moved, she opened her large dark eyes. She looked up into the face of her lover.

Then the branches closed around her form. She had gone with that lover, into the shadows of the wood. There was heard the sound of crashing branches, for a moment, and then all was still. The roadside was vacant again.

Meanwhile the sound of horse's hoofs echoing from the south, grew nearer and louder.

Another cavalier, mounted on a golden hued steed, turns the bend of the road, and dashes madly onward. It is Randulph the Prince.

He looks neither to the right, nor to the left, but bending over the neck of his gallant horse, with his dilating eye gazing steadily forward, he dashes on.

At this moment, when dashing over this quiet space of sheltered roadside, he is about to pursue the windings of the northern road, his path is suddenly intercepted.

There is the sound of horse's hoofs echoing all around him, the crashing of branches, mingled with the clanking of swords and the low-muttered words of armed men.

In a moment, as if by magic, the road is crowded with horses and men , the sunlight darting through the leaves above, reflects the gleam of arms.

At a glance, Randulph the Prince beholds his own comrades, the Riders of Santee !

A single trooper darting from this crowd who has so suddenly occupied the roadside, spurs his horse toward Randulph, and while the wild hurrah of the soldiers, thunders on the air, he whispers a hurried sentence—

" Welcome, Captain. Washington is in danger. Lead us on !"

" Clerwoode, I am glad to see you. In what direction have you come ?"

" From the north-east, from the Quaker graveyard. In the name of God, Captain ——"

" Washington in danger ?"

" Perhaps at this moment, a *Prisoner !*"

" A Prisoner ? Comrades, what say you to that ? Your Washington, our Washington a *Prisoner ?* What ! Are the Riders of Santee all dead ? Are their steeds tired, or their swords blunted ? Riders of Santee, did you hear ? Washington a prisoner, and we alive ! Shame !"

The air rung with a wild chorus of shouts.

" Captain, lead us to his rescue ! Away, away—Hurrah for the Eagle and the Oak ! Hurrah for the Prince !"

Randulph rose towering in all his pride of proportion, with his long dark hair falling back from his bronzed face. His black plume hung over his flushed brow, but did not conceal the gleam of his hazel eyes. His hand sought his sword ; the glittering blade rose in the light.

" Washington !" he shouted, his voice ringing like thunder through the still woods.

" Washington !" the gallant band gave back the echo. In a moment they were ranged at his back in battle array. Forty swords shone in the sun ; the bullet-riven banner fluttered above their heads. They were ready for the march of death.

" Clerwoode," said Randulph, bending over the neck of his steed, " Grant me a favor !"

" My life !"

" Away to Dilworth Corner. A band of British refugees, have entrapped a prisoner, to whom they intend mischief. Even as I speak to you, they watch this unknown prisoner in the large upper room of the roadside Inn. Be it your care to watch their movements, to save this prisoner at the hazard of your life ; to wait for me ! I will join you in half an hour. Will you go ?"

" Captain—not a word more—I am gone already !"

" And look you Clerwoode," said Randulph, in a deep whisper, with a meaning look ; " In another room of the roadside Inn, by the body of a dead girl, there watches a young and beautiful maiden ——"

" Rose !"

And dashing wildly through the trooper's band, Clerwoode Le Clerc was gone. Gone to the south, on a mission of danger—and death.

" Comrades, forward !" shouted Randulph.

" Forward ! For Washington !" was the thunder-echo of his band.

Randulph answered by two words ; one uttered with a shout, the other in a deep whisper.

" WASHINGTON—BLANCHE !"

And the Riders of Santee, thundered on.

CHAPTER TWELFTH.

THE MAN OF PEACE.

WASHINGTON was alone.

Alone by the roadside, his grey war-horse reined in, on the summit of a gentle knoll. The eye of that war-horse glared, his nostrils quivered, his sinews writhed—for the music of the bugle, the thunder of the cannon was in his ears ; he panted to share the fiery conflict of the battle.

The day was dying in the west : a single gleam of sunlight fell over the uncovered brow of Washington. His face was lighted up with an expression of convulsive agony. The compressed lips, the eyes that glared with strange fire, the brow, radiant with the desire of conflict ! Washington beheld the battle, and yet might not mingle in its fiery tumult. He heard the long pealing notes of the bugle, the cry of anguish, he heard his own men, calling fiercely on his name. Yet, he dared not peril his noble life in the fight. Mounted on his gallant steed, the panorama of the battle sweeping before his eyes, its terrible music ringing in his ears, he must remain, a statue-like spectator of the scene.

" I see Pulaski," he murmured—" There's a gallant soldier ! How magnificently he rides ! And then his charge—ha ! How it sweeps them down—how it crushes them into dust ! I see La Fayette, his brow bared, the uniform torn from his right arm ! That is a brave boy ! And Greene —there he rides ! And Sullivan, yes, brave Sullivan, rushing from column to column—and my men, my own men, *my brothers !* They are there ; they are there in the midst of the fight ! God be with them now, for they are brave, for they earn a victory by their gallant deeds !"

At this moment, echoing through the smoke and clamor of battle, there came a single cry, separated from all other sounds, by its terrible emphasis— " WASHINGTON !"

" They call on me, they shriek my name ! Hark ! Oh, God, is not this agony ? They call on me, they fight in my name, they echo with the last gasp, and yet I cannot hasten to their aid !"

Washington slowly lowered his head ; his clenched hands rested on the pommel of his saddle. The shrill, piercing neigh of his war-horse, rent the air.

"Friend Washington is it not a terrible sight?" spoke a calm and even-toned voice, at his side.

Washington turned, and beheld a mild-faced man, clad in the garb of the Quaker faith, standing near his horse's flanks, with his long curling hair falling behind his ears, and his hands crossed meekly on his breast.

"Is it not a terrible sight, to see men—brothers, butcher one another like dogs?"

That calm, even-toned voice, touched as it was with quiet pathos, thrilled through the heart of Washington.

"It is, my friend! It is! And yet I cannot strike a blow for my bro-thers, who are butchered in yonder plain!—But whence come you, my friend!"——The first part of this sentence, was uttered in a tone of agony; the last with a sidelong glance and hurried voice.——

"I come from my dreams!" said the Quaker, in a voice full of enthusi-asm, as slowly advancing he raised his right hand to Heaven. "And in my dreams, I beheld a warrior, riding on to conquest, over the bodies of the dead! I beheld a pillar of cloud and flame, going evermore before this war-rior, shadowing his enemies in darkness, while it bathed his face in glory! That pillar of cloud and flame, was the Presence of the Lord! For God, was with the warrior, and God is with thee, O, Washington! Thou art the warrior of my dreams, thou art the Chosen of God! Go forth and con-quer, Washington!"

The Chieftain gazed with wonder, upon the strange figure before him. The form, straight and erect, trembling with emotion, the simple Quaker garb, the eyes upraised, and the hand lifted on high, as if in solemn appeal to the God of hosts—it was a strange picture, contrasted with the horror of the battle, that now yelled afar. Washington felt an involuntary awe steal over his heart.

'Who are you?" said he gazing intently upon the Quaker's face.

"I am sent of God, to thee! To tell thee, to go forth and conquer! Does thee remember the pacquet, placed in thee hands, two nights ago? The pacquet in which was written down, the plans of this man of blood, whom men call William Howe? Who was it that reached forth his hand, and took this pacquet from the very couch of Howe? Who was it that faced death—yea, death by cord and steel—so that he might but have this pacquet delivered into thee hands? It was I, the Messenger of the Lord to thee!"

"Who are you—your name?" said Washington, as a sudden idea broke over him, that he might turn the frenzy of this strange man to the good of the cause

"Men call me Israel James," said the Quaker, mildly "but I know not

the names of men. I know one name, and one only, that which the Lord
hath given to me. I am the Man of Peace!"

"My friend," said Washington, kindly, "You had better hasten from this
field. There is danger here, perhaps death ——"

"There is no danger to those who are called by the Living God!" The
voice of the enthusiast was full of awe, as with uplifted hands, he uttered
this sentence. "Wherefore should I leave this field, before I have fulfilled
my mission to thee? Do I not bear about my breast another pacquet —"

"A pacquet —" said Washington, quickly—"a pacquet from Sir William Howe?"

"It is, even so! From the man Howe, but he sent it not. It comes to
thee, but not by his bidding! For! Lo! Is it not but another part of the
pacquet which thee has about thee? It speaks of his plans, it describes the
situation of his army, it proposes to crush thee by strategy and treason. But
God gives it to thee, O, Washington!"

The Quaker as he spoke, took from his breast the pacquet, enveloped in
thick folds of parchment.

Washington opened it with a gesture.

"This is indeed valuable!" he soliloquized—"Ha! You plan well, friend
Howe! Stay—let me compare it with the other pacquet."

Placing his gloved hand beneath his buff vest, he drew forth the pacquet
which had cost the one-armed schoolmaster his life. As he compared the
two, his face grew radiant. The Quaker had not spoken boastfully of their
importance.

While he read, his face almost buried amid letters and plans, there were
dim forms stealing silently through the brushwood at his back, and presently
red coats appeared among the green branches, and sharp arms glittered in
the sun. The crackling of brushwood, the tread of armed men, was lost in
the thunder of the battle, which now grew nearer and terribly distinct.

"These papers are **worth** their weight in gold—" said Washington, still
bending over the neck of his steed.

"So am I," said a strange voice, "For I have the honor of calling Mister
Washington, my prisoner!"

Washington looked up in wonder. Before him stood a tall soldier, clad
in the scarlet uniform of a British captain. Around him were the stalwart
forms of some fifty British soldiers, their swords gleaming, their blood-red
costume glaring in the light of the declining sun. Washington was encircled
by a wall of crimson and steel, and yet, not even an involuntary tremor shook
the firmness of his iron nerves.

With his blue eye flashing, he calmly surveyed the danger, and looked
the British captain fixedly in the face.

"You will observe Sir," said the Captain, whose fair complexion was
ruffled by a cool—almost insulting—smile,—"That you are my prisoner.
It would afford me the greatest imaginable pleasure to permit you to pursue

your way to the rebel army, but promotion is so d-a-y-v-l-i-sh slow. This is my only chance of a Colonelcy. Will you dismount?"

As he spoke, he approached the bridle rein of the Chieftain. At the same moment, the Quaker—who also was encircled by the dismounted troopers—leaned hastily forward, and with a sudden grasp, seized the papers which Washington held in his hand.

" Thee is a captive—" he muttered quickly, yet with a meaning look, " Give me the papers—I will convey them to General Greene!"

The action escaped the eye of the British captain, who still advanced toward the bridle rein.

" Give way friend broadbrim," he said. " You Quakers should never meddle in military matters. It's out of your line, and in—bad taste !"

He extended his hand to grasp the bridle rein of the grey war-horse.

" Will you stand from my path ? Or shall I ride you down ?"

Washington spoke in a tone, as cool and yet as contemptuous, as though he had but commanded a menial, to brush the dust from the flanks of his steed. His manner was perfectly calm ; he sate erect on his war-horse, and did not even draw his sword.

The British captain started back, as though appalled by the tone and look of Washington.

" This is in questionable taste," he said, after a moment, " You are my prisoner. You might escape, but the age of miracles is past. Will it please you, to dismount ?"

He extended his hand to grasp the bridle rein, but the hand never reached it. Even as the insulting smile was on his lip, even as he stood erect, his splendid form glittering with the scarlet uniform, he was stricken down by a sudden blow, that seemed to crush his iron chest.

He lay on the earth, quivering with agony, the blood spouting from the wound in his chest, over the roadside dust.

And over his prostrate form, stood the Quaker enthusiast, the bloody knife dripping in his hand, while his sharp features gleamed with an expression that chilled the very blood to behold.

" Washington, I have saved thee!" he shrieked, waving the bloody knife aloft.

" Oh God!" groaned the dying man, clutching the roadside dust by handfuls.

Washington started with horror. The action had been quick as a lightning flash—one moment, the British officer slowly advancing, while the Quaker looked calmly on—the next, the victim writhing in the roadside dust, while the Murderer shook his dripping knife in the air.

For a moment there was silence like death.

Then a frenzied yell shook the air— it was the cry of the British soldiers who now advanced to hew the murderer down.

Death to the Quaker ! Death to the assassin !"

Cooly wiping the dripping knife with a lappel of his coat, the Quaker gazed undismayed upon the frenzied faces, the gleaming swords, which encompassed him on every side.

"Back!" he shouted, "Back! On peril of the gibbet—the rcpe! Before ye strike me, learn the reason of this deed! Lieutenant Williams, does thee know the handwriting of Lord Cornwallis?"

The tone, the look of the Quaker for a moment held the troopers enchained in dumb wonder.

"Read this paper, Lieutenant Williams," said the Quaker, addressing a tall trooper, whose bushy whiskers half concealed his face. "Read that, and then strike, if thee dares!"

Washington gazed upon this scene in mute astonishment.

The British lieutenant took the paper, with a scowl and an oath; he read it; the scowl and the oath were succeeded by a look of wonder, an ejaculation of surprise.

"My * * * can it be possible!"

——"The bearer —— —— is connected with the British army in the most important manner. He is authorized to command the obedience of any soldier, or officer, while engaged in the execution of his trust. That trust is the punishment of a traitor, who, formerly a British officer, has betrayed the cause of His Majesty. The punishment hereby awarded by me, and for which I will be responsible, *is death*.

Sept. 11, 1777.   CORNWALLIS."

Such was the letter which the Quaker handed to the Lieutenant.

"Does thee understand? Lord Cornwallis received information but an hour ago, that this Captain Howard would betray his trust, by delivering Washington again into the hands of his rebel friends. There was but one way to avoid the evil. He wrote that note on the pommel of his saddle, not an hour ago. Does thee see how carefully the note is worded? He was fearful it might fall into other hands, and so defeat the punishment of this misguided man!"

He spurned the dying Howard with his foot, as he spoke.

It must be so," said the Lieutenant; "Comrades this is all right—stand back! Lay not a hand on this man if you value your lives. But look ye, Quaker,"—he said turning quickly round—"You must go with me to Lord Cornwallis, and answer to him for this deed?"

"In truth will I!" said the Quaker mildly. "I am not a man of blood. I loved this Captain Howard as a brother, verily did I! And now I will pray with him!"

He knelt beside the dying man.

The British soldiers murmured one to another, and grasped their swords. They evidently were dissatisfied with the letter of the Quaker. Their eyes gleamed with that terrible light—the hunger of revenge.

While their murmurs deepened, and their brows grew more ominous Lieutenant Williams approached the American chieftain.

"Sir your sword.   You are my prisoner!"

Washington answered him with a look of calm scorn, and then patting his hand gently on the neck of his steed, crashed through the wall of red-coats with a single bound.

A moment passed!   His gallant grey war-horse cleared the roadside fence with one bold leap, and he dashed up the green hillside toward his forest on its summit.

With a simultaneous hurrah, the British sprang to their horses in the neighboring thicket.   Some few moments passed ere they were mounted, and Washington was at least fifty yards ahead.   He rode his steed with the majesty of a king, urging him gently onward, toward the shadows of the wood.   The British pursued with mad shouts.   Washington neared the wood when a yell of triumph burst from the red-coat troopers.   They beheld a band of mounted riflemen burst from the woods on the summit, and while their leader waved them on with his sword, this strange company scattered around the person of Washington.

It was the band of David Walford, the Ravens o' th' Hollow.

With the red-coated troopers at his back, and this band of refugees in his front, Washington had no chance of escape.

Washington was a prisoner.

CHAPTER THIRTEENTH.

CLARENCE AND THE QUAKER.

The Quaker was alone with the dying man.

The gallant Captain Howard lay writhing in the dust which was crimsoned with his blood.   He gathered his arms together, and clutched the wound near his heart, as if to stay the flowing of his life-blood, and then with a groan, that shook his chest, he rolled over, and lay with face buried in the dust.

It was a hard death.

Young and vigorous and fond of pleasure—so much good wine to be drunken, and so many peasant girls to be loved—and now, to be forced to leave it all, the pleasure of wine and women, and the glare of this delightful world, to be forced to leave it all for the damp, unpleasant grave——ugh! It was a hard death.

He lay with his face in the dust. It might be seen that he was bleeding at the mouth, for that dust all around his head was purpled with blood.

Above the dying man stood the Quaker gazing upon him with folded arms. There was an icy smile on his thin lips as he watched the death struggle.

At last he slowly knelt; he turned the face of Howard to the sky again; he laid his head upon his knee. Then the Captain looked around, with a gleam of momentary consciousness.

" Does thee know me?" said the Quaker, bending down over his victim.

The blue eyes of poor Clarence, glared wildly in the face of his murderer. For a moment the blood ceased to flow from his mouth. He spoke with a rattling utterance.

" I burn—water—water!" he gasped.

" Thee is dry, is thee Captain?" Does thee hear the brook rippling in the woods yonder? Does it not seem to sing like a bird? Is thee very dry?"

He bent lower down, smiling all the while.

" Oh, God," gasped the dying man, as his lips became the color of blue clay—" I burn! Water!"

" Does thee know me, Captain? My name is Gilbert Gates! Did thee ever hear that name?"

" Gilbert Gates!" echoed Clarence Howard, as his mind wandered in the delirium of death.

" And her name ——" said Gilbert placing his lips against the ear of the dying man—" Does thee hear? *Her name?*"

By a sudden effort, the dying man raised himself in a sitting posture, while his blue eyes—Oh, they were unnaturally bright, nay even beautiful —glared fixedly in the Quaker's face.

" Her name?" he said in a choking voice, as he rested his hands against the breast of Gilbert, " You mean my sister—in England—Who will take care of her now? Who ——"

The blood gushed from his mouth.

" I mean——" said Gilbert, as his grey vest was turned to crimson, by the warm blood of Clarence Howard—" I mean ——"

" My sister——" was the last gasp of the dying man.

" MARY!" shrieked Gilbert, his hot breath streaming over the glassy eye balls of his victim.

The hands resting on Gilbert's shoulder tightened in a grasp of iron.

Clarence Howard was dead.

Ah, it was a ghastly spectacle!

That gallant soldier sitting in the crimson dust, his face white, his lips blue, his eyes glassy, the blood slowly dripping from the corners of his distorted mouth, his hands clenching the grey vest of his murderer in a vice like grasp—this was a terrible sight!

But the kneeling man, who attired in the Quaker costume, leaned forward his hawk-like features stamped with infernal malignity, as he hissed that solitary word in the freezing ear of his victim—that was in truth, a horrible sight.

It was a moment, ere Gilbert Gates could unwind the dead man's grasp. He arose. The dead man fell back into the bloody dust.

For a moment Gilbert stood gazing silently in the face of his victim. Then, as if seized by sudden frenzy, he bent down, and while his face was distorted with a hideous expression, he shook his clenched hands in the face of the corpse.

" Did Mary ever wrong thee? Speak, coward, speak? Had thee a father to avenge? Speak, or I'll crush thee with my boot! Coward, coward thou dost not answer! Her name ——"

And with a deliberate movement, he sank the heel of his boot into the dead man's face, crushing those chiseled features into one red mass.

" Her name was Mary !"

Again the boot sank ; again the hideous outrage was repeated.

" Now," said Gilbert, in a husky voice, as he wiped the thick drops from his brow ; " Now for Dilworth Corner !"

He went down the road into the hollow, with long and hurried strides.

As he disappeared, two hideous figures leaped over the thicket, and approached the corpse.

" I say Nan, here's the fine plunder ! Ho—ho ! Look at his toggery !"

" Yes, Deek, I feel his purse ! Here's the red goold !"

" Ho, ho, Nan, it's the brave Captain Howard !"

" Now 'ee do'n't zay ? The brave Cap'in, ho, ho !"

And Blood and Death proceeded to plunder and strip the body of the dead man.

CHAPTER FOURTEENTH.

PULASKI.

WASHINGTON was a Prisoner.

At his back followed the red-coated troopers under their Lieutenant, while in his very path, from the summit of the hill, David Walford and his band came thundering down. And now from thicket and hill, other bands of British begin to crowd over the scene, backing their comrades with a wall of crimson and steel.

Half-way up the hill, a solitary wall, the last fragment of a ruined mansion arose from the bosom of the green sod. It was some ten feet high and twenty long. Southward from this wall, stretched the hillside, for more than a hundred yards ; on the northern side was the cellar, filled up with earth and stones, and then green sward extended some twenty yards, until it was lost in the thick wood.

Near this solid wall, Washington reined his steed, and with uncovered brow calmly awaited the moment of his fate.

It was a magnificent scene.

The bravoes from the top of the hill and the troopers from the valley below, joined their bands, and sweeping over the hillside in the form of a crescent, began slowly to encircle the American chief. He was surrounded by this terrible semi-circle ; this crescent of men and horses and gleaming steel. The dark uniform of the bravoes was in deep contrast with the scarlet costume of the troopers, as reining the pace of their horses they came slowly over the green sward, that lay between them and their prisoner. Four hundred strong, they came sweeping on.

His brow uncovered, his face toward the distant battle, Washington sat his steed with calm grandeur. His enemies held their breath as they came on. There was something terrible in the repose of that majestic figure, with the sunshine streaming upon his uncovered brow.

But how could he escape them now ? Was he calling silently upon that God, who had saved him so often in the peril of battle ? Or was the earth to yawn and engulph his foes ? Where now was the trust of the rebel leader ? Strange legends were abroad in the British camp concerning this man ; soldiers who had been captive in the American army, when returning to their comrades, spoke of him with deep reverence, and said with rough but sincere emphasis that God fought for Washington.

But Washington was their prisoner ; already in grim fancy his head seemed to yawn above the gates of London, a warning to all traitors. The British came on with hushed breath, it is true, but with stout steeds and sharp swords ; slowly and silently but surely on.

At this moment the Eye of God in heaven beheld Washington !

At this moment the eye of Count Pulaski, gleaming through the battle-clouds beheld Washington.

Yes, from the summit of a hill, some three hundred yards distant, looming from the east, through encircling clouds of smoke, Pulaski looked forth and beheld the Chieftain and his danger.

The Polander turned to his troopers ; his whiskered lip wreathed with a grim smile ; he could speak but little English, so he spake to those iron men in his own fiery way, with his sword. He waved that sword ; he pointed to the Iron Grey and his rider ! He pointed to Washington, with the sunlight shining upon his brow.

There was but one movement.

With one impulse that iron band wheeled their war-horses, and then a

dark body solid and compact was speeding over the valley, like a thunderbolt, rent from the earth below—three hundred swords rose glistening in a
faint glimpse of sunlight—in front of this avalanche, with his form raised to
its full height, a frown on his brow, a smile on his lip, rode Pulaski!

Like a spirit roused into life by the battle-storm he rode, his eye was
fixed upon the iron grey and its rider, while his band had but one look, one
will, one shout—and all for Washington!

God of Battles! It was grand.

The British had encircled the American leader—already they felt secure
of their prey—Ah! how terribly the head of that Traitor, began to gloom
over the gates of London.

But that trembling of the earth yonder? What means it? That crashing of fences, that trampling of brushwood, now, now, that cloud of dust!
That terrible beat of hoofs—tramp, tramp, tramp? That ominous silence,
and now that shout, not of words or names, but that half yell, half hurrah,
which shrieks from the Iron Men as they scent their prey? What
means it?

" Pulaski! Pulaski!"

Yes, Pulaski is on your track, the terror of the British army is on your
wake!

Look down into the valley, nay into the road below—you can see the
white uniform of Pulaski's men, the dark skin of their horses, you can even
see their gleaming eyes!

And on he came, the Count Pulaski—he and his iron men! Washington beheld him, and smiled. He also beheld the narrowing circle of green
sward, that lay between him, and four hundred British swords. Then his
visage lighted up with a glorious battle-scorn.

" Gentlemen," said he, turning round with a magnificent wave of his arm,
" I regret to leave you! But I leave you to the care of the Count Pulaski!"

His expression—the very sublimity of cool scorn—roused their British
blood. With one sudden bound they cleared the space between them and
their victim. But that victim was gone, yes, gone with one tremendous
bound over the solitary wall. Was it not a magnificent sight to see? That
splendid war-horse, rising in the terrible leap, the form of his rider, in the
blue uniform, with the sun still shining upon his brow? For a moment he
seemed to hover in air above the wall, and then was gone.

Ah, how bitterly they cursed as they gazed upon the blank wall; for once
these good soldiers of King George indulged in terrible blasphemy. It
would have shocked the soul of their Good King; how nervously they
swore! Their eyes, their swords, the stars and sun; the God who made
the Saviour who redeemed them, all these they cursed with wringing em
phasis. But when they beheld Washington rising leisurely beyond the
wall, uninjured by his fearful leap, ah, then, they grew desperately wicked

Yet Washington halted his war-horse near the wood, and waited calmly for the vengeance of Count Pulaski.

And on he came, yes, as the British were in the very act of rushing forward, to secure the American chief, he came on, the Count Pulaski.

A moment! He had passed through the British, making a terrible lane right in their centre. He had passed on, leaving a ghastly furrow of dead men on either side, he had passed up the hill, he had passed the form of Washington. Crushed, mangled, dying, the British lay scattered along the green sod.

Another moment!

And the iron band have wheeled ; back in the same career of death they came ! Now they shout, now they yell ! Down red-coated troopers, down black-uniformed bravoes, for the Count Pulaski is among you ! Do you see the swords gleaming on every side, do you hear that deafening clang of steel against steel, as though the entire hill had been transformed into one vast blacksmith's forge ?

But this clanging steel is not half so terrible, as that which makes no sound ; that which cuts into faces, and through hearts. Your quiet steel, like still, deep water, is the most terrible after all. Not the sound of a pistol had been heard in all this brief but murderous conflict ! Sword against sword, dagger against dagger, pistol-barrel against pistol-barrel —— this was the only music of the combat.

Let us now take a hurried look at the scene.

Dispersed in some ten or eleven divisions, the British scattered over the hill. Where but a moment before, had been a solid crescent of men and horses and steel, now were only heaps of dead bodies, bands of scattered soldiers, green sod rent by horses' hoofs and stained with blood.

Then it was that the Count Pulaski and his men swept around the form of Washington, encircling him with their forms of oak, their swords of steel. Then their shout clove the air, and they came down the hill in solid phalanx, crushing the scattered foemen at every step of their terrible path.

The band of David Walford, drawn off to the south, alone maintained the show of fight. Their brave Captain, covered with blood, turned to the remnant of his men—they numbered but forty now—and with a curse, bade them secure the person of Washington, or die.

At this moment, while Pulaski was careering over the field, scattering and crushing the British as he went, the gleam of arms spread far over the valley below ; bands of Continentals and British engaged in fierce conflict came crowding up the hill.

In a few moments, Pulaski's troop became the centre of the sea of conflict, where banners rolled like waves, and long lines of bayonets gleamed like breakers, dashing on some rock-bound coast.

Suddenly a shout was heard to the south. The band of Randulph the Prince, came dashing up the hill, their leader in the van, and their banner

streaming over their plumes. The green sod flew behind their horses
flanks, and then at full speed, they came charging home upon the band of
refugees. Swords interlocked, steeds dashed against steeds, the green uni
form of the Riders mingled with the dark costume of the "Ravens," and
then David Walford looked around over the bodies of his men and gave the
word for flight.

"To Dilworth Corner?" he hoarsely shouted to the ten, who yet remained
alive. "Away—Ravens—we've work to do!"

Then Randulph—his brave band reduced to thirty—went crashing into
the very centre of the field, crashing through a wall of red-coats and steel.
You might see his sword gleaming far over the ranks of battle; you might
look upon his bronzed face, convulsed with the fire of strife. He fought as
the Last of a line of kings should fight; as though no bullet could wound his
breast, no sword could strike his arm.

Now might you see Greene and Sullivan, driven step by step from the
Meeting House, sweep up the hill and mingle in the fray, at the head of
their legions. Sullivan like a famished lion, ranged over the field, as if
seeking death at the points of the British bayonets. Greene, with his calm
face fired with battle rage, was hoarse with shouting, so he spake no more
with his voice, but made his sword do the work of his tongue.

There, O yes, he was there, the boy of nineteen, who had left the repose
of a young wife's bosom, to fight the battles of a strange people in a far land
—he was there!

His brow unbared, the uniform torn from his right arm, at the head of the
Life Guard, he went madly over the field, shouting his French war cry, and
fighting like a true child of France; as though these gay gentlemen in
red coats, were dear friends, whom he wished to embrace with the fierce
encounter of bullet and sword.

Ah, the gentlemen of the British army remembered long, the passionate
ardor of this boy of nineteen!

"Washington!" he shouted his war cry, as he dashed among the British
bayonets. Washington beheld the brave boy from afar, and followed his
path with gleaming eyes.

Meanwhile, the iron band of Pulaski, had gathered firm and immoveable
around the form of Washington, near the summit of the hill. The sun
shining upon his uncovered brow, Washington gazed over the rampart of
teel, that emcompassed his breast, and beheld that the day was lost.

You would not have wished to behold it—that silent agony which came
over his magnificent face, as this fatal consciousness possessed his soul,
—more than once in a life time.

He cast one look over the scene! O the banners, the bayonets, the
swords, that rose into the light of the setting sun, O the legions that wheeled
in solid phalanx over the hill,—steel and plumes above their heads, dead
men below—O, the dying men, who looked up amid the horror of that figh',

to catch a last glimpse of yonder sun, about to set forever, and then gave one prayer to God for their wives, their little ones, their homes !

Beyond this scene, all was clouds and gloom. A glimpse of Osborne's hill rose far away. The smoke moved like a curtain, around the Meeting House.

Washington uttered a single word—

" Pulaski !"

CHAPTER FIFTEENTH.

WASHINGTON'S FAREWELL.

" PULASKI !"

The noble countenance of the brave Pole, stood out in strong relief from the white smoke of battle. That massive brow surmounted by the dark fur cap and darker plume, the aquiline nose, the lip, concealed by a thick mustache, and the full square chin, the long black hair, sweeping to the shoulders—— this marked profile was drawn in bold relief, against the white smoke of battle. An expression of deep sadness stamped the face of the hero.

" I was thinking of Poland !" he exclaimed in broken accents, as he heard his name pronounced by Washington.

" Yes," said Washington, with a deep solemnity of tone, " Poland has many wrongs to avenge ! But God lives in heaven, yonder—" he pointed upward with his sword—" and he will right the innocent, at last !"

" He will !" echoed the Pole, as his gleaming eye reached beyond time and space, seemed to behold this glorious spectacle—— Poland free, the cross shining serenely over her age-worn shrines, the light of peace glowing in her million homes.

" Pulaski," said Washington, " look yonder !"

The Polander followed with his eye, the gesture of Washington's sword. Gazing down the hill, he beheld the last hope of the Continental army embosomed among British bayonets ; he saw the wreck of Sullivan's right army, yielding slowly before the invader, yet fighting for every inch of ground. He beheld the Reserve under Greene, locked in one solid mass, faces, hands, musquets, swords, all turned to the foe ; an island of heroes, encircled by a sea of British hirelings. The royal army extended far over the fields to the foot of Osborne's hill ; the Red Cross banner waved over the walls of the Quaker Temple. Far to the south, scattered bands of Continentals, were hurrying from the field, some bearing their wounded com-

rades, some grasping broken arms, some dragging their shattered forms
slowly along.

Still that brave Reserve of Greene, that wreck of Sullivan's right wing,
fought round the Banner of the Stars, while the Red Cross flag glared in
their faces, from every side.

The declining sun shone over the fight, lighting up the battle clouds with
its terrible glow. It was now five o'clock. But one hour since the conflict
began, and yet a thousand souls had gone from this field of blood, up to the
throne of God! The sky is blue and smiling yonder, as you see it through
the rifted clouds—look there, upon the serene azure, and tell me! Do you
not behold the ghosts of the dead, an awful and shadowy band, clustering
yonder,—ghastly with wounds—dripping with blood—clustering in one
solemn meeting, around that Impenetrable Bar?

At one glance, Pulaski took in the terrible details of the scene.

" Now," shouted Washington, " Let us go down!"

He pointed to the valley with his sword. All his reserve, all his calmness of manner was gone.

" Let us go down," he shouted again, " The day is lost, but we will give
these British gentlemen our last farewell! Pulaski—do you hear me—do
you echo me—do you feel as I feel? The day is lost, but we will go
down!"

" Down!" echoed Pulaski, as his eye caught the glow, flashing from the
eye of Washington—" Give way there! Down to the valley for our last
farewell!"

Washington quivered from head to foot. His eye glared with the fever
of strife. The sunlight shone over his bared brow, now radiant with an
immortal impulse. His hand gathered his sword in an iron grasp—he
spoke to his steed—the noble horse moved slowly on, through the ranks of
Pulaski's legion.

Those rough soldiers uttered a yell, as they beheld the magnificent form
of Washington, quivering with battle rage.

" Come, Pulaski! Our banner is there! *Now*—we will go down!"

And then, there was a sight, to see once—and die!

Rising in the stirrups, Washington pointed to the fight, and then he did
go down! Down that hill, followed by Pulaski's band, Pulaski himself,
vainly endeavoring to rival his pace, at the head of the iron men, Washington went down!

General Greene turning his head over his shoulder, in the thickest of the
fight, beheld with terror, with awe, the approach of Washington. He
would have thrown his horse in the path of the Chief, but the voice of
Washington—terrible in its calmness, irresistible in its rage—thundered
even amid the clamor of that fight.

" Greene—come on!"

Who could resist that look, the upraised sword, the voice? The band of Pulaski thundered by, and Greene followed, with horse and foot, with steed and bayonet! The fire blazing in Washington's eye, now spread like an electric flash, along the whole column. The soldiers were men no longer; no fear of bayonet, or bullet, now! The very horses caught the fever of that hour!

One cry burst like thunder on the British host: "Give way there! Washington comes down to battle!"

Far down the hill, La Fayette and the Life Guard were doing immortal deeds, for the banner of the stars. Brows bared, uniforms fluttering in rags, they followed the Boy of Nineteen, into the vortex of the fight, waving ever-more that banner overhead.

They saw Washington come. You should have heard them shout, you should have seen their swords; how dripping with blood, they glittered on high. La Fayette saw Washington come, yes the majestic form, the sun-lighted brow! That sight inflamed his blood ——

"Now La Fayette, *come on!*"

They were ranged beside the band of Pulaski, these children of Washington; the gallant Frenchman led them on. Thus Washington, Pulaski, Greene, La Fayette thundered down into the fight. It was terrible to hear the tramp of their horses' hoofs.

Randulph the Prince, with the last brave twenty of his Riders, was hold-ing a desperate fight, with thrice the number of British troopers. He, too, beheld Washington come, he too beheld the solid column at his back; with one bound, he dashed through the British band; in another moment he was by the side of La Fayette. Washington turned to him ——

"Waldemar, we go down to make our last farewell! Come on!"

And they went on, yes they did go down!

Washington at the head of the column—still there, the sunlight still upon his bared brow, the sword still gleaming in his upraised arm,—Washington led them on. With banners waving all along the column, with swords and bayonets mingling in one blaze of light, this iron column went down!

The British were in the valley and over the fields; you might count them by thousands.

There was one horrid crash, yes, a sound as though the earth had yawned to engulph the armies.

Then, oh then, you might see this bolt of battle, crashing into the British host, as a mighty river rushing into the sea, drives the ocean waves far be-fore it. Then might you see the bared brow of Washington, far over swords and spears, then might you hear the yell of the British, as this avalanche of steel burst on their ranks! Men, horses, all were levelled be-fore the path of this iron band. Follow the sword of Washington, yonder, two hundred yards, right into the heart of the British army, he is gone! Gone in terrible glory! On either side swell the British columns, but this

avalanche is so sudden, so unexpected, that these columns are for the moment paralyzed.

And now Washington turns again. He wheels, and his band wheels
with him. He comes back, and they come with him. His sword, rises
and falls, and a thousand swords follow its motion.

And down—shrieking, torn, crushed,—the foemen are trampled ; another
furrow of British dead strew the ground. Vain were the deeds of
all the heroes, in that moment of glory. Greene, La Fayette, Pulaski, Waldemar, the thousand soldiers, all seemed to have but one arm, one soul !
They struck at once, they shouted at once ; at once, they conquered.

" Now," he shouted, as his uniform covered with dust and blood, quivered with the glorious agitation, that shook his proud frame, " Now we can
afford to retreat !"

It was a magnificent scene.

Washington—his steed halted by the roadside, the men of Pulaski and
his own life guard ranged at his back—Washington gazed upon his legions
as they swept by.

They came, with dripping swords, with broken arms, horse and foot,
went hurrying by, spreading along the road to the south, while the banner
of the stars waved proudly overhead. First the legions of Greene, then the
band of Waldemar, with the gallant La Fayette riding in their midst. He
was ashy pale, that chivalrous boy, and the manly arm of a veteran trooper
held him in the saddle. His leg was shattered by a musquet ball. Yet, as
he went by, he raised his hand still grasping that well-used sword, and murmured faintly that word his French tongue pronounced so well ——

" Washington !"

Washington beheld the hero, and smiled.

" God be with you, my brave friend !"

Then came the wreck of Sullivan's division ; blood-stained their faces,
broken their arms, wild and wan their looks, sad and terrible their shattered
array. They swept by to the south, their gallant General still with his
band.

" Now," said Washington, while the Life Guard and Pulaski's men, encircled him with a wall of steel, " Now we will retreat !"

At this moment, while the British recovered from their late panic, were
rushing forward in solid columns, the face and form of Washington presented a spectacle of deep interest.

He sate erect upon his steed, gazing with mingled sadness and joy, now
upon the retreating Continentals, now upon the advancing British. Around
him were the stout troopers ; by his side the warrior-form of Pulaski ; far
away, hills and valleys, clouded with smoke, covered with marching
legions ; above the blue sky, seen in broken glimpses ; the blue sky and the
declining sun.

The blue and buff uniform of the Hero, was covered with dust and blood.

His sword lifted in his extended arm, was dyed with crimson drops   You
could see his chest heave again, and his eye glare once more :—

"On comrades, now we can afford to retreat !"

And the sunlight poured gladly over the uncovered brow of Washington.

CHAPTER SIXTEENTH.

THE RETREAT.

The Retreat of Brandywine !

History has not done it justice, this terrible retreat.   History has told us
of the manœuvre, by which Cornwallis turned the right wing of Washington ; she has pictured in almost contemptuous brevity the heroism of Wayne
at Chadd's Ford, where he held his post amid terrible bloodshed, from morning till sunset ; she has stated that there was a warmly contested battle, at
Birmingham Meeting House, followed by a retreat to Chester, but here, the
taciturn dame has held her breath.

She has not told us of the heroism, the glory, the splendid defeat of that
battle day.   Yes, splendid defeat, for General Howe gained but the field,
not the objects for which he grasped, the utter annihilation of the Continentals, the capture of Washington.   He paid for this crippled victory, with a
river of British blood.   Washington retreated to Chester, leaving his dead
and dying on the field.

This retreat was like a Parthian fight ; the Continentals faced and fought
the foe as they fled.   At every step of their way, they left their own bodies
and the corses of the British, as tokens of their bloody retreat.

Yet History, has done but little justice to this terrible retreat.

History has not told us of the columns of the Continental army extending
along the woods and falls, from Birmingham Meeting House, to the ancient
town of Chester, retreating, yet fighting every inch of the way.

She has not told us of those scattered bands of heroes, who in dim woods,
or shadowy glens turned upon their British pursuers, and grappled their
bayonets with weaponless hands.   Nor of those who dying by the roadside,
still maintained the conflict, shouting with their last breath, the name of
Washington.   Nor of the wounded men, who after tottering on, from the
field, for weary miles, at last fell, bleeding from their many gashes, and
crawled to the banks of Brandywine, to quench their burning thirst, but
could not, for the waves were red with blood.

History has not told us of those women, who like angels sent from God, came out from their homes in the twilight of the Eleventh of September, bearing bread and water to the famished and dying men.

History has not pictured one gleam of that beautiful Romance, which shines forever, like a halo around those hills of Brandywine. *

Nor has History pictured the magnificent view which broke upon the eye, from the summit of Osborne's Hill.

Ascending that hill in the hour of retreat, we might have seen the wide landscape over which the smoke moved like the curtain of some vast theatre, crowded with all the terrible pomp of battle.

Above, through the rolling smoke, the blue sky broke in glimpses on the eye ; far to the west, a gleam of the distant Brandywine came laughing into light, for a moment—a sheet of rippling water among green boughs,—and then was gone !

Beneath lay the wide spreading landscape, on which was seen pleasant orchards, embosoming quiet homes, legions of marching soldiers now gathered in one compact mass, now extending far over the hill and plain, heaps of dying and dead, the blaze of burning houses, the blue smoke of the rifle, rising from green woods ; plumes and banners, bayonets and swords, horses and cannon, all these were crowded together, in one glorious panorama of war

The gleam of arms, shone on every side, as far as eye could see. The distant horizon was shut in by a wall of dust and smoke, from which the flash of musquetry glared every second, like lightning from a white cloud.

Ever and anon, a far off hum, a distant murmur came suddenly up the hill. This was the music of the scene. For had that sullen murmur been analyzed, it would have separated itself into the mad hurrah, the yell of defiance, the cry of death.

Soon the breeze blew freshly from the south. Laden with the sweets of flowers and the smell of human blood, it came gently up the hill, making low music among the forest trees.

---

* Then what has she done ? Given our Pennsylvania battle-field but a line in her pages, where the most insignificant fray of the north, has been swelled into plethoric glory. We Pennsylvanians are a dull. plodding. quiet People ; we behold our own William Penn, almost crowded out of history, by the everlasting song of our northern brethren, about Plymouth rock and the Pilgrim fathers ; we read histories, written carefully for us by strangers, and when the battle-fields of our soil, are not treated with positive contempt, we thank these wandering historians for their kindness, in granting one ray of glory, one leaf of laurel. to poor, patient Pennsylvania.

God grant the time may come, when our battle-fields will find a chronicler. when a collection of accredited falsehoods, gathered by some vagrant L. L.D., or D. D. or other alphabetical notoriety, and thrust into prominence by their connection with a few facts, illustrated with pictures and bound in gilt and calf, will no longer be called "history ;" when, this eternal cant about Pilgrim fathers and Plymouth rock, will be succeeded by a healthy admiration of our own Apostle, William Penn.

For while flowing from Plymouth Rock, the bitter waters of Persecution and intolerance, deluged New England ; William Penn, under the Elm of Shackamaxon, founded a nation, without a priest, without an oath, without a blow.

The day slowly declined.

An hour passed—another!

The clouds rolled away from the west. The sun set calmly in all the beauty of azure, mellowed by flashes of gold.

The Brandywine rippled gaily in the purple light.

Night came down upon the battle-field.

All was dark and still.

Dark—save the occasional gleam of a lanthern, flashing for a moment like a falling star —— still, save the low-toned sound of human voices, heard from afar.

The moon slowly arose, and her first long gleam of light streamed over the pale, cold faces of the dead.

It now becomes our duty to chronicle the incidents which occurred, from the moment when Washington gave the word " Retreat," until the rising of the moon.

CHAPTER SEVENTEENTH.

" I COULD NOT DIE !"

THE silence which had brooded so long over the quiet walls of the Quaker Temple, was now broken by terrible groans.

The Prophecy uttered forty years before in that holy place—for it was holy, although the benches were rude, the plain railing which supplied the place of pulpit and altar, but a simple substitute for the marble shrine of a proud cathedral—the Prophecy of the Battle had met with an awful fulfilment.

The red beams of the sun, pouring through deep-silled windows, shone over the cold faces of dead men, piled up along the blood-clotted floor, and gave a ghastly glow to the writhing countenances of the living. The rude pulpit, the ruder benches, all were heaped with dying and dead. Shattered the windows, rent the doors, blood-stained the walls, groans and cries prayers and curses, breaking in one chorus on the air—Ah, sad and terrible was the fulfilment of the Prophecy, uttered long ago.

In the centre of that temple, yes, in the centre of the warm sunlight, an old man clad in the furs of wild beasts, with a long white beard sweeping over his breast, knelt beside a wounded man. The high brow, the clear grey eyes, the boldly chisselled features of the white-bearded stranger were in striking contrast with the low forehead, the small eye's prominent nose, thin lips and retreating chin of the wounded man.

The latter lay on his back, his face writhing in pain, resting in the steady gaze of those large grey eyes, which seemed as though they would glare into his soul. He was slowly bleeding to death ; his dark dress was crimsoned with his blood, which welled in a thick current from the wound near his heart.

The white-bearded stranger knelt by his side, never once removing his steady gaze. It was observable that his breast and arms, were concealed by a loose mantle of panther's skin, thrown lightly over the shoulders.

" Water—water—" moaned the wounded man, clutching the hard floor with his stiffened hands.

The Stranger gently laid the head of the wounded man upon his knee. Then, with his left hand he poured some water from a brown earthen jug, into a small tin cup, and held it near the lips of the supplicant.

The grey eyes of the wounded man glared with eagerness, when he heard the water rippling from the jug, but now, when the delicious liquid almost touched his lips, he madly extended his hands to grasp the cup. The Stranger slowly extended it beyond his reach.

" Philip Walford," said he in a low deep voice, as he bent slowly down, " Philip Walford dost thou know me ?"

The wounded man—his glance eagerly fixed upon the cup of water—shuddered at the sound of that voice, as though it woke some terrible memory within his soul. But when he looked up, and while the frenzy of pain burned in his veins, beheld for the first time the face of the Stranger, he gave utterance to a terrible cry, more like the yell of a wounded panther than a human being. Then he shuddered no more, but lay like a figure of stone, his eyes fixed upon the Stranger's face, in a wild glassy horror-stricken gaze.

While this strange scene is passing in the Quaker Temple, let us for a moment pause ; let us recall from the bosom of the past, a Legend which will throw some light upon the Mystery.

On the Eleventh of September A. D. 1759, just eighteen years before the day of battle, a beautiful woman was slumbering in one of the old chambers of Rock Farm. Reclining on her marriage bed, the young wife lay with her babe in her arms, while her lips moved gently in her sleep. The silence of the scene was disturbed by the footstep of her husband, a young and noble man. He stood by the bedside, silently contemplating the beauty of that sight—a young wife sleeping with her babe in her arms, while the breeze stirring gently through the windows lifted her dark tresses from her face, her robe from her young bosom. The husband beheld a letter laid against the alabaster skin of that bosom ; a carelessly folded letter rising and falling with every pulsation of the heart. Thinking it one of those letters which he had written to his wife, in the first dawn of their love, he gently removed it from her bosom, and—anxious to revive the hallowed memories of the past—he opened it and read.

That husband, so handsome in form, so noble in soul, so wrapt up in love for his wife, stood frozen to the floor with a sudden horror. The letter rattled like a dry leaf in his trembling hands. Thus it read :

MARY— September 11, 1759.

Have courage! In a few more brief days the persecutions of fate will be finished. Let it no longer madden you, when you think that your brother's will *alone*, forced you to marry my *rich* brother. Let this thought no longer madden you, for in a few brief days, all will be over. We will fly together, we will seek some calm retreat, where consoled by the smiles of *our child*, we can enjoy in security the love which hitherto has been hidden from all but God. Courage, Mary! Trust everything to me, and remember, the day when John visits Philadelphia, shall also be the day of our flight.

Yours in life or death,

PHILIP WALFORD.

John Walford read this letter, and went silently from the chamber of his wife. The agony of eternal despair was stamped on his livid face. The voice of his brother gaily singing, struck his ears. He hastily entered that brother's room—Philip stood before a mirror, arranging the broach which confined his shirt collar. As John entered the room, he saw his brother hastily hide within his vest a golden chain, to which was appended a medallion of peculiar shape. John saw the chain, the locket, but a moment and yet recognised it. He had given that chain to his wife on her bridal day ; the medallion contained her portrait and a lock of his hair.

The letter had filled the Husband with all the tortures of the damned, but this sight—the chain and medallion, in the hands of his brother—this was the crowning agony.

Still he approached his brother and spoke to him, in a quiet tone, yet with a burning eye and livid cheek.

" Brother, where did you obtain that chain ?"

Philip did not answer, but turned his face aside, and bit his lip, as though confused by the question.

" Brother," said that low-toned but hollow voice, " When did you write this letter ?"

Philip was on his knees. He clasped his brother by the hands.

" Kill me, John," he whispered, " Oh kill me, but hear, before you sacrifice me to your revenge. We loved before your marriage, but I was poor ; I found no favor in her brother's eyes. She married you, but still we loved ! Loved with a passion that trampled upon all vows, all obligations, in earth or heaven. We have been guilty ! Kill me John ; let me hide my guilt in the grave, but first, O first, let me obtain your pardon —"

" O God !" groaned John, terribly affected by the remorse of his brother.

"Let me obtain your pardon," shrieked Philip, "Let me behold Mary once more! Promise me that she shall not know, that I died by a bro-ther's hand! Promise me that you will make her happy, and then, then, let me die!"

John was silent and pale. The blood trickled from his lower lip, as he pressed it between his clenched teeth.

"Pardon! In the name of God, Pardon!" shrieked Philip.

John still was silent.

"Philip," he said at last, in a tone so terribly calm; "Swear to me by the God above us, that Mary loves you, and you only!"

"I swear!" shrieked Philip, clasping his hands.

"The child —" faltered the Husband.

"Is *ours!*" whispered Philip, veiling his face.

"Then Philip, be happy together!" said John in a choaking voice. "Tell Mary sometimes to think of me. Good-bye Philip: from this hour I am dead to the world. Rock Farm is yours —— Be happy——" his voice failed, his face was agitated by a frightful spasm.

He went forth from the room, from the house, that moment, and came back no more. Bareheaded, without a single dollar in the world, with noth-ing to call his own but the clothing which he wore, this noble heart, left his home that day, forever.

For eighteen years he was an outcast, a wanderer. Now in the icy deserts of the Arctic sea, now amid the lost cities of Mexico, now in the depths of Siberian wastes, now on the shores of the Ganges, he wandered on, not with the curse of Cain upon his brow! No! But, with a curse deeper than Cain's—the curse that withers a noble and magnanimous heart, when its first and fondest trust has been betrayed.

One day a young American sailor, who had landed with some comrades on a lonely island, which uprose from the waters of the Pacific, at least fifteen hundred miles from any habitable spot, was startled by the spectacle of an old man with a white beard, sitting by the waters of a spring, that gurgled forth at the foot of a bread-fruit tree. The features of this stranger, despite his strange costume of furs, designated him as an American. They entered into conversation—

"You come from the valley of the Brandywine?" said the Stranger, "Pray tell me, do you know a family named Walford?"

"I do," said the sailor surprised at the question.

"Did you ever hear of John Walford? Or of his wife Mary?" said the Stranger, eagerly grasping the sailor by the hand.

"Why, as for John he disappeared, some time ago, and haint been heered of since. But Mary ——"

"Mary!" shrieked the Stranger.

"Died some time ago ——" began the sailor, but he did not finish the sentence.

" Dead ! Oh, thank God, at last !"

The Stranger rushed into the thickest of the wood, with a wild howl of despair.

The sailor beheld him no more.

Other American sailors, who had voyaged to every quarter of the world, might also testify that in their wanderings they had met a strange man with a white beard, whose only questions were—" Do you come from the Brandywine ? Do you know Mary Walford ?"

The imagination shudders while contemplating the life of this self-exiled man ; the agony of this self-tortured heart.

The reader will now be prepared to understand the scene in the Quaker Temple.

. " Philip Walford dost thou know me ?" again repeated the Stranger, holding the cup of water extended in his left hand.

" My brother John ! The dead returned to life !"

This was said in an almost inaudible tone, yet with a look and accent of helpless despair.

" Then Philip, take this cup of water ! Drink—it is thy brother—it is John who gives it thee !"

Philip's extended arm dropped heavily by his side. He refused the cup, but his eyes were fixed upon his brother's face, with a vacant, glassy stare.

' Not from your hand John, not from your hand John !" he slowly murmured.

" Wherefore Philip ?" said John, in an accent of deep sadness. " How have I ever wronged thee ? Did I not give my bride to thy arms ? Did I not forgive thee ? Mary loved you, and I gave her to you. Drink, Philip, and pledge to me *a brother's love !*"

Philip writhed as though in mortal agony, but did not take the proffered cup.

" Did Mary ever speak of me, Philip ? Oh, tell me, tell me—— did she ever speak of her poor, forgiving husband, John ? Did she speak kindly Philip ? Many times in my lone wanderings, I have thought of her ; yes, Philip, in crowded cities, and on desert shores, I have thought of Mary— of you ! I have prayed God to bless you—bless your child !"

" Oh God," groaned Philip. " I am dying, dying when all my schemes were about to prosper ! And he has come back to haunt me—to damn my soul, ere it has parted from the body !"

No words can describe the low-toned emphasis of despair, which marked the utterance of these words.

" Yes, I do remember it !" said John, raising his head, while his eye was fixed dreamily upon the air. " That fatal day ! The letter—ah ! how

34

sweetly she smiled in her slumber, as I took that letter from her bosom! Then the chain which I had hung around her neck on our bridal day ——

A shriek thrilled through the Quaker Temple, a shriek so wild and terrible that it thrilled even the heart of John Walford. Philip had arisen into a sitting posture, his hands were nervously clasped, and his glaring eyeballs seemed to burn in their sockets. His face, lividly pale, was discolored by streaks of blue.

"Do you come from the dead to haunt me?" whispered Philip, as his mad gaze perused each feature of his brother's face. "Then do you not know, that I, I, Philip Walford lied to you?"

"*You* lie to me, Philip! *You!* Oh, this is frenzy!" said John, in an accent of pity.

"The letter—I placed it on her bosom! The chain—I stole it from her neck! The story which I told you—it was a lie, every word a lie! She hated me, she, Mary your wife hated me while living—she scorned me in her dying hour ——"

"Philip!" groaned John, as though he had not heard aright.

"You know this; you must know it! Arisen from the dead you come to claim my soul! Now crush me, if you dare—I am dying! Dying and I defy you!"

The pale face of John Walford, was flushed, from his beard to the roots of his hair with burning red. His eyes swam in a vertigo. For a moment his sight was gone, and with extended hands, he seemed to grope for the light. His chest writhed and shook, while a low moaning sound came from his white lips.

These were the external signs of his agony; the tortures which shook his soul, were seen by God alone.

Philip Walford, tortured as he was with mortal pain, gazed on his brother's face with a shudder of terror.

"Yes, crush me!" he fiercely shrieked, "You can but crush me! I am dying—I defy you!"

"No Philip, you shall live!" said John, in a quiet tone, while his face lost its burning flush, and his blood-shot eyes were fixed intently upon his brother's countenance. "You shall live—for—" he faintly smiled—"I would not have you die now, for the wealth of the world!"

Without another word, he laid bare the wound on his brother's heart. He then drew forth from his pouch, which was slung at his side, a small box, containing a valuable salve, renowned for its efficacy in healing wounds, or at all events, staunching the effusion of blood. This salve, procured at first in Hindoostan, and tested through the course of years, had served John a thousand times in his lonely marches, when without its aid, severe wounds received in pursuit of wild beasts, would have ended in death.

He now applied it to the wound which pierced his brother's breast. In a moment its influence ran through the veins of the dying man, like a spell.

He felt no more pain, but a healthy vigor spread over his whole frame. The delirium of agony was gone; he looked in his brother's face as though astonished at his presence.

"Do you feel strong brother?" said John.

"Yes," replied Philip, as a confused memory of what had passed flashed over his brain—"I feel strong—indeed, I think I could walk without assistance—"

"I am glad of it, Philip," said John with a smile of peculiar meaning.

Philip gazed in his brother's face with a look of anxious inquiry.

"There Philip—lean against my knee until you feel strong enough to walk. I must tell you a strange story Philip—a story of some interest. For eighteen years dear brother, I have been an outcast and a wanderer—"

"I'm sorry brother—" hesitated Philip.

"Yes, but before you pity, learn the true meaning of those words—*outcast—wanderer!* Let me paint you one or two scenes from my life.— Once in the midst of Siberian deserts, for five days, I held the entrance of an ice-bound cavern against a pack of famished wolves; for five days, without food or drink. Was it not terrible brother? I had this sharp knife brother—every minute I was tempted to plunge it in my breast, and *yet I could not die* ——"

"You must have suffered dreadfully, brother!"

"Once shipwrecked with five comrades, I floated for days on a rude raft —a burning sun above, the boundless sea around! We were without food or drink, for seven days. I longed—hungered for death. On the eighth day we cast lots who should die—do you understand Philip? Who should die to make food for the others? The lot fell on me. Though I longed for death, though this sharp knife would have ended my agonies in a second, yet, yet I could not die!"

These words, "I could not die!" were pronounced with a terrible emphasis.

"I fought with them, yes, over the raft, that cracked and quivered like a decayed branch, beneath our tread, I fought with them, one by one for my life! They rushed upon me with their weaponless hands, yet with horrid cries and awful blasphemies. I had this sharp knife—I killed them one by one. I was alone amid their mangled bodies—listen Philip, I ate their flesh, I drank their blood, for—*do you see—I could not die!*"

"Oh this is horrible!" murmured Philip.

"Wait a moment brother—spare your pity! Once taken captive, by savages who feast on human flesh—it was in the South Sea, brother.—I was nailed to a cross, with my head downwards. The blood rushed to my head, my eyes hung from their sockets; they pierced me with their arrows, they cut my flesh with knives. I lingered thus for a day; *I could not die!*"

Philip gazed in horror on his brother's face.

"At last they took me from the cross, as the sun was setting Crushed, torn, mangled, I was laid upon the ground. Next morning I was to be burned—do you hear—burned over a slow fire? A spark of life yet lingered in my veins—I was left alone on the sod, which to-morrow, was to cover my cindered bones. I crawled from my resting place towards a thicket; it was but twenty yards, and yet it took all night to do the deed. Can you picture my situation? My hands bled—my feet bled—my body was all one mass of gashes—the blood ran from my mouth and eyes. Oh, how I thirsted for death—and yet *I could not die!*"

"Brother, this is too horrible for belief!" ejaculated Philip.

"Hear me out, Philip. The next morning the savages found me; they deemed my escape a miracle, for do you see, they could not imagine how a mangled mass of flesh, like I was, could move an inch, much less crawl twenty yards. They gave me the choice, either to join their tribe, or be roasted over a slow fire. One hope alone remained—I beheld my knife, this sharp weapon in the hand of a savage; I grasped it; I resolved to die!"

"Thank God!" cried Philip, terribly interested by his brother's story.

"Yes, thank God when you've heard me out. The knife was in my hand—one blow, only one blow, and I would be free! The knife was raised —it dropped from my hand. *I could not die.*"

Philip groaned.

"I became one of their tribe. Yes, shudder Philip, I, John Walford, who had known the music of the church bells—the caresses of a wife—the smile of a babe—I the man, the Christian, became one of this infernal band. With them, I worshipped their brutal God—with them I fought and murdered—with them I ate of human flesh——For *I could not die!*"

Philip covered his face with his hands, and uttered a moan of agony. Even his base soul was rent by this recital of his brother's life.

"Now do you know what it is, to be an outcast, a wanderer? Now do you know what it is, to wish to die, to thirst for death, to ask God for it, as an innocent babe asks its mother's kiss, and yet, forever to hear a voice repeating slowly in your bosom, these words—' *You cannot die!*'"

"Brother," shrieked Philip. "I would have torn my heart out, ere I would have suffered thus!"

"Now would you know why it was, that *I could not die?* I will tell you Philip. On that day—the Eleventh of September—you remember it, Philip? On that day, when with hell in my bosom, I went forth from Rock Farm, a man accursed and doomed, went forth to come back no more, then I became conscious of my fate. It was to wander, to wander, oh yes, *to wander* for a certain period of years, and then, guided by the hand of Almighty God, to return to this valley, and watch over the life of Mary's child —"

"Blanche?" ejaculated Philip, his face manifesting the contest of opposing emotions.

"Blanche! Yes, that is her name! How shall I ever forget it? Do I not remember that day, when Mary, who had just passed through the agonies of a mother's travail, placed the babe in my hands, and whispered its name—*Blanche!* Now Philip you remember, that this *consciousness of fate*, which forever kept me back from Death, pressed most heavily upon my soul, at the time, when I believed your story Philip. *That Mary, false to me, loved you my brother.*"

" But why stir up these matters now John? It is so long ago—Mary is dead—Blanche grown up a fine girl —"

" And now after this terrible eighteen years of trial, I return to the valley of the Brandywine, guided by the awful hand of God, and discover that Mary loved me, that Blanche is my child. In short, Philip, that you, my brother, eighteen years ago, with a lie on your lip, drove me forth an outcast and a wanderer, with all the tortures of the damned in my bosom. Is it so, Philip answer me!"

"But John, you must remember, that we are all liable to err. Let bygones be by-gones. You have just saved my life; in return for your kindness, I will act with liberality toward you. After an absence of eighteen years, you will of course understand, that it will be difficult for you to recover Rock Farm. It will be no easy matter for you to prove your identity ——"

John was silent. His face was deadly pale.

Of what are you thinking my brother?" asked Philip.

" *Of your death*," said John, in a tone of terrible calmness.

" My death! Surely you do not mean it—you just saved my life —"

" I was thinking," exclaimed John, with icy coolness, " what manner of death you should die, my brother —"

" John—mercy !" shrieked Philip, as his livid features quivered like dry leaves.

" God has spoken it! Mary calls and I hear her! My own soul condemns you. You must die !"

" This is cowardly ! I am wounded—you are stronger than me —— "

" Am I ? Look there !"

With his left hand, John threw the panther's hide from his shoulder. A horrid spectacle was revealed. The stump of his right arm shattered by a cannon ball, the torn sinews still quivering at the shoulder, was disclosed in the light of the setting sun. With horror Philip beheld his brother, kneeling in his own blood, flowing freely yet silently from the shattered arm.

" Look there ! I am bleeding to death, do you understand my brother ? In ten minutes, I will be dead. For now—Oh * * * now, I can die ! The memory of eighteen years, alone keeps life in these veins, the sacred consciousness that now at last, *at last* I am about to execute the will of God, on you my brother : this consciousness fills me with supernatural vigor. Brother, prepare. Take that broad sword from the floor; clench it with both your hands.   You shall have a chance for your life.   I will fight with this knife."

Philip looked in his brother's eyes, and read his sentence there.   They slowly arose ; Philip with the sword, John with the knife.

They stood foot to foot, breast opposed to breast.

The light of the setting sun streaming through the western windows, gave a terrible glare to Philip's ashy features ; while it shone over the white beard of John, and illumined his face, radiant with an awful determination. His shattered right arm poured a stream of blood, down over his forest robes and along the floor.

Standing in his own blood, John Walford raised the knife in his left hand, and then, ere he gave the fatal word, gazed intently in his brother's face.

The sunlight glared in the faces of the dead and dying, who were scattered all around the Quaker Temple.   The cries of the wounded alone disturbed the silence of the scene.

" Now Philip, I will give you three chances for your life.   Strike once, twice, thrice with your broad-sword ; I will make no resistance.   But strike deep Philip, for when your last blow is stricken, I warn you !   This knife must drink your blood."

Philip grimly smiled.   The instinct of life fired his veins.   He saw he must either kill, or be killed.

" In three blows I can certainly kill him !" he muttered.

The broad-sword waved around his head, clutched in that nervous grasp —the grasp of a coward who is forced to fight.   John silently awaited the blow—it descended with terrible impulse, yet with an uncertain aim, inflicting a hideous wound over the right temple.

" *One!*" exclaimed John, as he lifted the torn flesh from his brow, and wiped the blood from his eye.   His grey hair was dabbled in blood

Trembling and pale Philip brandished the sword again.

It descended, striking John on the right leg, above the knee.   The blood poured from the wound, the sinews were severed—John sank to the floor, on his left knee.

" *Two!*" muttered John, looking up in his brother's face.

" Now," shrieked Philip, as the fever of bloodshed burned in his veins, " Now for the last blow !"

At this moment, while he prepared for the blow, two hideous figures came stealing through the shattered door of the Temple, along the shadows of the eastern walls.   Death—with her parchment skull and glassy eye-balls ; Blood with his thick red hair, covering his eyes and brow—these silently crouched in a corner, while the sun shone brightly over their hideous faces.   They watched the combat ; Death with her large quivering ears ; Blood with his small grey eyes : their low growling laughter mingled with the cries of the wounded.

" Now," said Philip with a smile of triumph, " Now for the last blow !"
His breast presented, his large grey eyes looking fixedly in his brother's
face, John calmly awaited the blow.

Grasping the broad-sword once more, with the point presented, he struck
firmly at his brother's breast. The blood spouted from the wound, mingling with the purple currents, flowing from the shattered arm and mangled
leg.

" *Three !*" shrieked John, as with the sword buried in his bosom, he
sprang towards his brother, inflicting three wounds in the space of a second.
These wounds were given by an arm already quivering in the death-agony.
The first, pierced the right eye, the second the left, the third gashed the face
from ear to ear.

John fell dead. Without a word, without a sound, the knife still clenched
in his left hand, he fell, his white beard dabbled in his blood.

Over him blinded, bleeding, dumb, stood Philip Walford, a horrid spectacle, the eyeballs and tongue protruding, blood pouring from the mouth and
eyes, there he stood, his hands extended grasping madly for the light.

As his crime had been, so his punishment was—infernal. He had de-
ceived his brother, with the malice of a fiend; the fiends themselves would
have pitied him now.

A horrible sound came from the cloven jaws of the wretch. He now
sought madly for a knife, a sword, with which to end his accursed existence.
But knife and sword were beyond his reach. He stumbled wildly along
the floor ; he fell over an obstacle that lay in his path, and gathering it to his
arms felt the cold body, the clammy face of a dead man.

Then his mad howl rang like the roar of a wild beast, through the Quaker
Temple. He now realized the awful words of his brother—' I could not
die !'

He lay quivering with intense agony, yet painfully conscious of life. He
heard the faintest sound, the slightest groan. He heard a stealthy footstep,
he felt rough hands at his breast, and then a screeching voice rang in his
ears ——

" No guineas Nan, but parchments, ho, ho, parchments !"

" Wall git zum un to read 'em Deek," spoke a hollow voice. " Who
knowz ? May be worth more nor gold ?"

Philip Walford then was conscious, that the parchments for which he had
perjured his soul, were passing from him forever. Those parchments, by
which under the name of Antony Denys, he held the broad lands of Randulph the Prince, had now gone from his grasp—he writhed with superhuman agony.

Then the memory of his crimes came slowly to his soul.

First came the remembrance of that day, when the pretended Waldemar,
in the moment of his flight, gave him those very parchments which

constituted him trustee for the estate of Wyamoke, in behalf of Adelé and her child.

That beautiful woman stood by his side, her large dark eyes gleaming with an expression of terrible meaning, as she murmured—" Perjurer, how have you fulfiled your trust?   Go, oppressor of the widow and the orphan, go to the bar of God, with their curse upon your head !"

Then came the broken-hearted Mary Walford, looking upon him with her eyes of unutterable woe; then George, his son, murdered by his father's hand ; and last of all, in terrible distinctinctness, he beheld the white-bearded Stranger, by his side, standing so silent and pale, his voice slowly muttering the fatal words—

" And yet, and yet *I could not die !*"

While these horrid visions crowded upon the brain of this miserable wretch, he could hear the horrible laughter of Death and Blood, ringing in his ears, like voices from the grave.

The sunlight shone redly upon his writhing form, and over his mangled face, with the eyeballs hanging from the socket and the tongue protruding from the gashed jaws.

On one side squatted Blood, his grey eyes twinkling with glee as he watched his struggles ; on the other side Death, her glassy balls shining in the light, listened intently to his groans.

Some few paces apart, in a pool of blood, lay the white-bearded stranger, his firm features, set eyes, and bleeding brow, disclosed in the sunshine.

Groans, prayers, curses, still arose on every side.

Philip Walford dying by inches, beheld written on a dark sky, these letters in words of fire——

" *I could not die !*"

Here let us draw the curtain over the slow agonies of that hour.   Let us leave the wretch to his Judgment; his soul to God.

CHAPTER EIGHTEENTH.

THE UNKNOWN.

BESIDE the body of the dead girl, the living knelt in prayer.

The sweet sad face of Mary, smiling as though she slept, the form, rigid and motionless, clad in flowing robes of white—these were in strong contrast with the kneeling form of Rose, her hands clasped her eye upraised, her young bosom trembling with life.

Bare were the walls of that lone room, rude its appearance, glaring the red sunshine, that came through the windows, and yet a sanctity seemed to hover about the place, as the young and beautiful girl lifted up her voice in prayer, while she knelt beside the dead.

Even as her prayer went up to God, even as her upraised eyes warming with devotion, fancied the spirit of poor Mary hovering there above her head, the sunshine of Eternity upon her brow, a smile of changeless love upon her lip, even in this moment of hallowed reverie, the solitary door of the room was slowly opened, and an intruder gazed in silent wonder on the scene.

Yes, his finger to his lip, his half-raised foot yet lingering on the threshold, Clerewoode Le Clere stood in the door-way, his dark hued face, with clustering brown hair and flashing eyes, presenting a picture of delight and wonder.

Still the low-whispered accents of the maiden's prayer, rose like gentle music, on the silence of that lonely room.

Clerwoode stealthily advanced ; Rose turned and beheld him with a half-uttered cry.

" Hist !" whispered the young trooper, as he hurriedly closed and bolted the door. " I come to watch over the life of this unknown captive. Tell me—where is he ? How many soldiers are there with him ?"

It was now the turn of Rose to beseech silence with a look, while she answered the questions with two signs.

First she pointed to the front room, and then upheld the four fingers of her small white hand.

" In the front room ? Guarded by four soldiers ? Well !" whispered Clerewoode, and then taking the hand of Rose, he led her gently aside, into an opposite corner. " Blanche ?" he murmured.

" Torn from my arms, not half an hour ago, by Lord Percy," returned Rose, in the same low tone. " Did you not meet Randulph ? He pursued this British lordling—"

Clerwoode's countenance manifested extreme surprise.

" How long ?" he whispered, " since this unknown captive was brought to Dilworth Corner ?"

" An hour ago ! I was looking from this window, when I beheld two horsemen approach, leading a prisoner, whose form was enveloped in the thick folds of a cloak.'

" Do you know the horsemen ?"

" Gilbert Gates—David Walford ! They dismounted at the side of the Inn, and were presently joined by four others, dressed like themselves, in farmer's attire. The four took charge of the prisoner—I heard them enter the Inn, ascend the stairway, and pass into the front room. There they have since remained. Hark ! Do you not hear them ?"

" Gates—Walford ? What became of them ?"

" Rode away to the north, again. Gates bade the others take good care of the prisoner for an hour, when he would return with Lord Cornwallis; 'He,' said Gates with a sneer, ' *will sentence the criminal.*' "

Clerewoode placed his hand upon his forehead. This mystery confused him. Who was the stranger, so strangely conveyed to the Inn of Dilworth Corner, his form concealed in a dark cloak, his life menaced by the smooth Gilbert Gates, whose smile was an omen; by the bravo Walford, who hesitated at no deed, provided it was treacherous and bloody.

This brave youth, Clerewoode Le Clere, whose green velvet uniform became his handsome figure so well, whose dark brown eyes were wont to melt so sweetly in the moments of love, to flash so brilliantly in the hour of battle, now found himself in a position of peculiar danger.

He would save the unknown from all persecutors, he would protect the honor of Rose from the touch of British violence, or lay his dead body beside the corse of Mary Mayland. This was his sworn determination.

Rose beheld the hand upraised, the look of anxious thought, and while her eyes gleamed and her cheek flushed, she read the chivalrous soul of Clerewoode, in his face.

" Her's was a terrible fate !" muttered Clerewoode, pointing to the body of the dead girl, and then as if a light from heaven had shone into his soul, he gazed upon the face of Rose, and shuddered.

" May not the fate of Mary, be also the fate of Rose before the setting of yonder sun ?"

This was a terrible thought.

" Rose," said he, in a whisper, deepened by his love, " We must await the course of events. In a little while Randulph the Prince will be here, with his gallant band. He will rescue the captive, or die. But in the meantime, Rose, should the British chance to enter this room, you will conceal yourself in this closet —"

" And you Clerwoode ?"

" Oh, never mind me, Rose. I will watch without the closet door. I am young, but I have killed more than one Briton this day."

Rose started as she beheld a sudden change pass over Clerwoode's face. His eye dilated, his lips compressed, his nostrils quivering, with his hand laid on the hilt of his sword and one foot advanced, he seemed about to spring on some unseen foe.

" Rose," said Clerwoode in a hollow voice. " Did you not give your love to me, in the moment when we escaped from these British bloodhounds ?"

Leaning her clasped hands against his breast, the young girl looked into his face, and answered him with her eyes. Ah, you may talk of the low-toned music of a beautiful woman's lips, but for me, I prefer the voice that speaks from her eyes. That voice, melting and beaming into your soul, has this great advantage over the voice of the lips ; it speaks in Hebrew,

Greek or Latin, with the same facility that the tongue speaks English. Therefore, Rose like a good girl spoke to her lover with her eyes.

" Rose," continued Clerwoode, in the same hollow tone, " Gaze upon the body of the dead girl, and take this dagger. I am young; they may kill me. When I am dead Rose, when the British spring forward to grasp you, then remember, that God lives in heaven, that I have gone before you, there! Say Rose, in that dread hour will you have courage *to strike, and follow me ?"*

Rose took the dagger. Splendid and sharp, with an ivory hilt and sheath of silver—the very thing to save a maiden from dishonor.

" Clerwoode, I will! The Virgin be my witness, I will!"

She looked magnificent, that young girl, as with a pale face and flashing eye she hid the dagger beneath the folds of her habit, close to her virgin bosom. To be sure, she prayed to the Virgin, to be sure her red lips murmured the gentle name of Mary, blessed Mother of Jesus ; a sad error in the eyes of those good Protestants, who manifest their love for God by burning his Church and trampling on his cross. Yet there is music in that name of Mary, when whispered by virgin lips, speaking to the Blessed Mother, who shines serenely in yonder heaven, her immortal face wreathing with love, as she looks down upon the sorrows of her child and sister, *woman.*

Ah yes, and those brave Catholics who in the bloody times of the Revolution fought side by side, with their Protestant brothers, for God and Washington, loved to repeat that name of Mary in the hour of battle, as with the sign of the cross upon their brows, they rushed to conflict. That was a happy time, when Protestant and Catholic fought side by side, and not a single burned Church darkened the soil of William Penn, when Bigotry lay slumbering in her accursed grave, beneath the gibbets of martyred Quakers, far away in the land of Plymouth Rock.

Friends who read this book, bear with me awhile. My heart is warm when I speak of this subject, for I am a Pennsylvanian. I love my state ; her soil contains the bones of my fathers. I love my state, for here in the olden time were stamped the footsteps of William Penn. I love my state, for here was first lifted the banner of toleration. I think of her Past, of the days when Catholic and Protestant fought side by side, for freedom ; even now, I see yon dying soldier lifting the cross with trembling hands, while his comrade of a different faith, places the cup of water to his lips. These were happy times. But now, yes the truth must be told now ; let us Pennsylvanians hide our blushes with our clasped hands. St. Augustine blackened and in ruins stares us in the face. This too, not on the soil of New England, where to burn Quakers and witches was but a pleasant pastime, for the good old Pilgrim fathers, but on our soil, on the holy ground of William Penn. This disgrace is scathing, withering.

There was a time when the love of Christ bloomed sweetly in our houses but *now!*

Now, our houses are polluted with obscene tracts, abusing men of different faith, in language unfit for a brothel, while they incite a brutal populace to deeds of murder. Now, our pulpits are too often filled by vagabonds, who escaped perhaps from some European galley, howl forth their ribald slander, for the greedy ears of bigotry and cant: Now, Ministers of the Gospel, forgetting to visit the sick, to cheer the wretched, to pray with the dying, surrender themselves body and soul to the influence of the same spirit, that deluged the old world with blood, for at least one thousand years. They take convicts to their homes and while the print of the prison chain, is fresh on their limbs, welcome them as converts from the Church of Rome, swallow their obscenities and circulate their lies. The name of Catholic, with them is a synonym of devil; to hate the Catholic is their religion; Persecution is their God.

It is against this blind rage my friends, that I, a Pennsylvanian, a Protestant appeal.

From this field of Brandywine I send forth my voice. I ask these bigots to pause—they stand on the soil of William Penn. To remember—that Catholic blood dyes our battle-fields, yes that Catholic blood was poured freely forth on the field of Brandywine, in the name of God and Washington. Remember the friends of Washington's bosom were Catholics, remember the names of La Fayette and Pulaski, and pollute our soil with persecution if you can.

By the memory of the dead, by the toleration which William Penn established, by the freedom for which Washington fought, by the honor of our state, by the awful name of God, who crushes persecution with the lightnings of his vengeance, I beseech these bigots to pause in their mad career. For the felon who stands on the gibbet, covered with the blood of murdered women and children, is a holy thing in the eyes of God and history and man, compared to the wretch who rears the banner of persecution on the soil of William Penn.

Pardon, my friends who are scattered through the states of this great union, pardon my warmth. But there are feelings that burn the heart, unless they are spoken, there are wrongs that gangrene the soul, unless rebuked, by all the power of word and pen and deed. The man who can be silent, when a burned Church and trampled cross stares him in the face, on the soil of William Penn, would also be silent were the fires of Puritan malevolence to blaze in Independence square.

"I will!" repeated the brave Catholic maiden, "God and the Virgin witness me, I will!"

Clerwoode gazed on the girl with a look of mingled love and **pride.**

"God bless you Rose," said he, "Now I can fight or die, as fate may decree!"

Then approaching the northern window, he silently lifted the sash, and half-closed the shutters. The light, subdued to a twilight dimness, fell over the faces of the lovers, and softened the pale features of the dead girl.

"From this window we can command a view of the northern road, without being seen," said Clerwoode, "Now we must wait for Randulph and his band."

They drew near to the darkened window, and conversed in low tones. The sound of voices resounded through the thick walls from the front room. From afar, a freshening breeze ever and anon whirled the clamor of the distant battle.

Half an hour passed.

Still Randulph did not come.

All sounds, save the voices from the front room had now died away. A strange silence rested upon the atmosphere.

Clerwoode was about to utter a cry of impatience, when all at once, a terrible sound, louder than a thunder peal, seemed to dart from the bosom of the earth into the cloudless sky.

The tramp of ten thousand footsteps, the cries of conflict, the hurrahs of charging legions, these all were mingled in that sound.

"Look from the window, Rose; I dare not!" whispered Clerewoode. He was ashy pale as he spoke. The Continental army is defeated—it was this terrible fear that paled his cheek.

"I see a cloud of dust," whispered Rose, "A cloud of dust and smoke; through its folds I behold men and horses; I see the gleam of swords and bayonets—two banners, one red, the other blue; one emblazoned with a cross, and the other with thirteen stars!"

She uttered an involuntary shriek. That terrible sound grew nearer, it reached the Inn, it whirled by like a mighty hurricane.

Clenching his sword, Clerwoode looked forth, and beheld the fearful retreat of the American army. For ten minutes or more, the tramp of their legions, shook the earth, and thundered into the sky. Washington, Sullivan, Pulaski, Greene, wounded La Fayette, he saw them all pass on, cheering the Continentals with looks and words; the roadside stained with blood, the terrible array of broken arms and torn banners. But Randulph the Prince and his gallant band, were not seen in all the columns of the retreating host.

Pressing on the heels of the Continentals, the British army burst into view, far over the fields, far along the road. Then the stragglers were ridden down without mercy, then the cry for quarter, was answered by the death-blow, then the dying were trampled into the dust by the horses' hoofs.

The declining sun pouring through the intervals of smoke and dust, shone over the wide array of arms and banners.

For half an hour, this hurricane of crimson and steel thundered on, and passing the Inn, was heard echoing far to the south.

A gallant officer, arrayed in a splendid scarlet uniform, reined in his steed, beneath the window. In the commanding form, brilliant with epaullettes on each shoulder, and a star on the left breast, in the manly face, now quivering with the fever of battle, Clerwoode recognized the Lord Cornwallis. Beside his war-steed were two men, whom our young soldier had cause to know—the bravo Walford and the smooth Gilbert Gates.

With a low-muttered word, Cornwallis dismounted.

Clerwoode beheld him enter the side of the Inn; followed by the bravo and his comrade. In a moment their steps were heard on the stairs; they seemed to pause before the door of the back room. Clerewoode grasped his sword; Rose held her breath, but in a moment, the footsteps were heard in the front room.

"*Let me behold the prisoner!*" the sonorous voice of Cornwallis resounded through the thick walls.

Then a confused sound, followed by indistinct voices was heard.

Clerwoode and Rose listened with parted lips and hushed breath, for the slightest sound, but not a word was distinguishable through the massy wall.

After the lapse of five minutes footsteps were heard again on the stairs.

"Cornwallis has sentenced the prisoner!" whispered Clerwoode, "Hark! They are passing from the room—Cornwallis, the prisoner, Gates, Walford, the guards—all, all are passing down stairs——they are leading the prisoner to execution!"

Clerwoode leaned forward and gazed from the window, while Rose retired a pace or two apart, awaited the result of his gaze.

In a second, the young soldier drew back from the window, and turned his face to the maiden. That face was distorted by an expression of overwhelming horror. He spoke not, but stood with his eyes glaring in her face.

Rose sprang forward, urged by an involuntary wish to behold the sight which covered her lover's face with such unutterable horror, but with extended arms he held her back.

"In the name of God, do not advance to the window!" he said in a husky voice.

"Have you seen the prisoner?" asked Rose, as a dark presentiment overshadowed her soul.

"I have!" answered Clerwoode, still holding her back from the window.

Again Rose sprang forward, but Clerwoode grasped her by the wrists and fell on his knees.

"In the name of God," he murmured, fixing his eyes upon her face, "do not look from the window!"

There was something in the manner of Clerwoode, in his earnest voice and flashing eyes, and trembling grasp that thrilled her heart with awe. She stood quivering with emotion, while that dark presentiment gloomed more terribly over her soul.

Thus a moment passed, while the tread of footsteps was heard without, mingled with suppressed voices. Then the sound of horses' hoofs broke the silence of the air, and then as if gurgling from the depths of the grave, a low deep groan prolonged with all the emphasis of mortal agony, thrilled on the listener's ears.

"Cornwallis is gone," muttered Clerwoode. "He has left the victim to the murderers, Oh * * * that groan!—Rose I beseech you remain here for a moment, for a moment only, until I return!"

He rose, and while his face was stamped with the hues of death, hurried from the room.

Her heart torn by contending emotions, Rose remained standing in the centre of the apartment, her outstretched hands trembling with the same horror that swelled her bosom and dilated her eye.

Thus she stood for a moment, and then as though led by unseen hands, she passed from the room along the entry, into the front chamber. It was quiet as death. The sun shone over the unruffled coverlet of the bed, and revealed the old-fashioned furniture carefully arranged along the snow-white walls. All was the same as in the morning, when gathered in the arms of Blanche, Rose had looked forth from the vine-hidden window. Yet now, her dilating eyes was not fixed upon the quaint furniture of the chamber, nor yet upon the cool leaves or fragrant flowers of the wild vine.

She beheld a youthful form, half-concealed among the white curtains of the western window, and in an instant recognised Clerwoode Le Clere. He was gazing from the window, while his deep drawn breath attested the interest of the spectacle which enchained his eye.

Rose approached on tip-toe, with extended arms. Without touching the young soldier she looked over his sholder, and beheld a sight that turned her heart to ice.

Yes, looking through the folds of that snow-white curtain, she beheld the tall buttonwood tree, that arose in quiet grandeur in front of the Inn. There was one massive limb which tossed and plunged as though shaken by a thunder storm.

Rose beheld that limb, she beheld a human form writhing and quivering in the air, she beheld a manly face convulsed with mortal agony. And as she looked that face turned to livid purple, those blue eyes hung from the sockets, the tongue blackened and hideous, protruded from the fallen jaw.

Rose beheld the writhing form, the hideous face, and then the rope which doubling like a whip-cord, shook the massy limb of the buttonwood tree.

An involuntary ejaculation escaped from her lips ——

"Oh God! My father!"

She fell to the floor, as though a sword had torn her heart in twain.

CHAPTER NINETEENTH.

HIRPLEY'S FESTIVAL.

Two men were threading their way through the windings of a forest path, while the rays of the declining sun fell through the canopy of leaves overhead, and along the mossy sod below.

It was a tangled path, leading among the trunks of aged trees or through the interlacing boughs of slender saplings, now open to the sunlight, and now buried in shadows thick as night. Now its course was stopped by some grey rock rising up from the very bosom of the sod, and again thickly woven vines hanging from the trees above, wounded our wayfarers in the eyes, and cut their faces like so many knives.

It cannot be denied, that the appearance of our friends was rather singular.

The man who ran, or leaped or stumbled first, was clad in a long grey coat, which fell about his slender limbs like a Roman tunic hung on a bean pole. His eyes resembled oysters, his nose a lighted coal, while his mouth every now and then assumed the tremulous appearance of an untied shoe string. His left hand grasped an enormous sack which hung over his shoulder, while his right clutched a thick cord.

Following the undulations of this cord with your eye, you might see that it was fastened to the wrists of the other wayfarer, who walked some few paces in the rear. His person, face, in fact his entire appearance was in violent contrast with the gentleman in the grey coat.

Picture a stout burly fellow, six feet some inches high, with immense chest and shoulders, enormous arms and ponderous legs. His red round face appears beneath the shadow of a grim Hessian cap, which black as midnight bears on its front this cheerful device, a death's head and cross bones. He wears a jet-black uniform, relieved by gold facings, and his collossal legs are enveloped in boots of dark leather. His wrists are corded together by the same string which grasped by the gentleman in the grey coat, leads him through the devious windings of the forest path, gently as a vagrant dog follows the footsteps of his master.

The gentleman in the grey coat was no other than Mr. Hirpley Hawson, of Chadd's Ford ; the stout trooper in the handsome black uniform, with the corded hands was a Hessian soldier, whom he had taken prisoner of war.

This had been the history of the capture.

The Hessian, somewhat fatigued with the adventures of the day, had laid his enormous bulk at the foot of a tree by the road-side. He was indulging in fragrant draughts of rum, from the canteen of a dead soldier, when a blow from a clubbed rifle flung him prostrate on the sod. The blow was administered by Hirpley, whose lean figure greeted the unclosing eyes of the Hessian. He tried to rise, but Hirpley's knee was on his chest. He endeavored to throttle Hirpley but his hands were tied. He then swore elaborately in High Dutch, but Hirpley silently replied by a hideous contortion of his not altogether handsome face. Then our Hessian friend grew furious, and gave utterance to a number of beautiful sentiments, which were altogether lost on Hirpley, whose collegiate course in German had been limited.

Still Hirpley's knee pressed harder on the Hessian's chest, and his red face began to lose its lively hues, while his fat, round eyes projected in a manner more picturesque than classically beautiful. Then the imprisoned trooper was seized with a happy fancy; he had sworn all his German oaths, without creating a sensation; he would now turn the tables and swear in stout English.

Pursing up his lip, he gave utterance to this beautiful remark :

" Cot-tam !"

" Cot-tam your own self," was the apostolical injunction of Hirpley ;
" You haint got a right to ' cot-tam' anybody else !"

Still keeping his knee on the Hessian's breast, he proceeded to transfer an elegant pair of silver mounted pistols from the belt of his prisoner, to his own, and then drawing forth a thick cord from a sack at his side, wound it around the wrists of the gentleman in black, with an intricacy of knotting and tying, quite wonderful to behold.

" Now," said he, brandishing a sharp knife across the Hessian's eyes, " You're my prisoner ! You need not wink—I tell you it's a fact. Haint I as good a right to take a prisoner, as anybody else ? Hey ?"

The Hessian by this time, began to believe himself not in the power of a human being, but a devil. The wonderful dexterity with which Hirpley had knocked him down, tied him, abstracted his pistols, and brandished the sharp knife over his eyes, struck him with a feeling of awe. For Hirpley was his inferior in height, uniform and grandeur of appearance. He was thick, Hirpley thin ; he, was gifted with immense strength, Hirpley, apparently weak as a child. And yet this thin, poorly clad individual, with the pale face and red nose, had made him prisoner. The Hessian began to believe that the devil himself fought for the Continentals. So as he was familiar with but three phrases applicable to all questions in English—' Yah,' ' Nah,' and ' Cot-tam',—he replied with the first.

" Y-a-h !"

" Very good my friend. Now please get up, and foller me. I'm a girn to cut up yer black soldier clothes, and make a good Amerykin of you. D'ye hear ?"

" Yah !"

" You shall mix toddies for me at the Green Tree Inn. Yes you shall.

Then you shall dig garden and do arran's, and make yerself generally use ful—d'ye understand, or shall I explain it to you ?"

He flourished the knife across the Hessian's eyes.

" Yah—Nah !" growled the prostrate soldier, using two of his stock of answers in the same breath.

" Then git up and foller me !"

In a moment with the sack on his shoulder, Hirpley led the Hessian into the woods, holding his prisoner by the thick cord.

The vanquished trooper followed, submissive as a lamb. His large eyes rolled as he looked upon his strange captor, who, sack on shoulder and string in hand, led him swiftly through the woods. He had not understood a single word of Hirpley's discourse, and was now wrapt in deep thought with regard to the intentions of his captor.

Thus they had advanced into the devious path where we first discovered them, Hirpley, ever and anon, turning round to make a hideous face at his prisoner, who replied, by rolling his eyes and muttering in a deep tone :

" Yah—Nah—Cot-tam !"

" I say you-sir, what's your name !" exclaimed Hirpley, suddenly turn-ing round, as their path was blocked up by an immense rock.

" Yah !"

" No I'll be darned if it is !"

" Nah !"

" That's wuss than the fust. Try again, Mister?"

" Cot-tam !" emphatically rejoined the Hessian.

" Now look here," cried Hirpley, drawing his knife and advancing to the prisoner, " I haint what they call a pious man,—though my grandmother had an uncle, who was purty well acquainted with a deacon—yet still it's enough to make won's blood bile, to hear you take on so. D'ye know you're a-swearin' like a rale privateer ? What d'ye expec' 'ill become of you ? For the last time I axes you, *what's yer name ?*"

The Hessian was in despair. He could see that his mysterious captor was enraged ; that was evident by his oyster-like eyes and red nose ; he had exhausted all his stock of answers, and now stood with his cheeks puffed out, as though he had taken a couple of oranges in his mouth, for a wager.

" What's yer name ?"

" Fotz yer n-a-a-m !" roared the Hessian, in complete agony. He fancied that this strange being was endeavoring to instruct him in English, and therefore earnestly repeated his words.

" Now is'n't it enough to puzzle the patience of old Satten himself !" ejaculated Hirpley.

This sentence was too long for the prisoner to remember.

" Nah !" he ejaculated in a voice of thunder.

It was now Hirpley's turn to despair. He stood threatening the Hessian with the knife, while his nose grew frightfully red. At last by signs, threats and broken morsels of German, he gained the desired information.

" Hon-Adam Spichelweizer !" exclaimed the Hessian.

" Mr. Swingletree ? Very good ? Why could not you answer at fust ? Very purty name, though it might be a morsel shorter without hurtin' you any. Now look here ! You've got to foller me up that rock ; d'ye mind ? If you try to escape, I'll ——"

He pointed to the knife and pistols.

" Nah—Yah !" cried the Hessian.

Silently Hirpley led the way over the rock. On the other side was a quiet spot, sheltered from the sun by the surrounding foliage, and carpeted by a soft thick moss. Through the bushes, the gleam and music of a brooklet broke on the ear.

" Now sit down at the foot of that tree, Mr. Spinklesprinkle," said Hirpley in a quiet tone.

The Hessian sat down.

Then Hirpley gathered some dry leaves and withered branches, in the centre of the glade, while the captive watched his movements with wondering eyes. Next with his knife, he cut two pieces of stout hickory, pointed at one end and forked at the other. He inserted the pointed ends in the sod, while the forked ends rose on either side of the withered leaves and dry sticks, with about three feet between.

The Hessian groaned. He began to see the object of these preparations.

Hirpley drew a flint, steel and tindex-box from his sack. Some dry powder from his horn was poured on the stick and leaves. In a moment the sharp clink of flint and steel startled the Hessian's ears ; in another moment the sticks and leaves, placed between the upright pieces of hickory were in a blaze.

The Hessian groaned again. All the terrible legends which the British had carefully circulated among their superstitious allies, came home to his mind. The devil fought for the Americans ; their generals were his Prime Ministers, and inferior officers his imps ; their women were witches, their men wizards—all these fearful legends passed through the thick brain of our Hessian friend.

But when the merry blaze of the fire illumined the leaves, and the cheerful crackling of the dry wood mingled with the ripple of the brook, then the Hessian shuddered.

He was to be killed, roasted, eaten. This was to be his doom. Had not the British told him that the Continentals were addicted to the use of human flesh ? Poor Hon-Adam Spichelweizer thought of his native cottage, nestling far away yonder, under the shadow of a wood, with a green meadow spreading down from the door to a clear laughing brook, he thought of his round faced brothers who were now drinking beer and smoking pipes, while he was about to be roasted and eaten in a foreign land. Then came the

vision of his sweetheart Katrine, whose voluptuous form was as broad as it
was long, whose ancles were so beautifully thick, whose face was like the
full moon. Hon-Adam sighed, shuddered, and turned pale.

Meanwhile Hirpley retired among the trees, with his sack before him
was engaged in an operation of deep mystery. Hon-Adam saw his long
thin arms rising and falling, he saw the glimmer of his sharp knife, but saw
nothing more than the red nose of his enemy shining in an occasional ray
of the setting sun.

Moments of deep agony passed.

Hirpley appeared with a strange object in his hand—a pair of corpulent
chickens, transfixed with a cleanly peeled strip of hickory. This strip was
placed across the fire ; the forked ends of the upright pieces supported the
chickens and their extemporaneous spit.

For a moment a vision of festival joys illumined the fat face of the Hessian, but this vision soon gave place to the deplorable reality. The wizard
who sat on the turf, his legs crossed and his red nose shining in the light of
the fire, was preparing some infernal spell, with which to abstract the soul
of his prisoner, before he killed his body. Here was a terrible fate for Hon-
Adam Spichelweizer, whose brothers were now smoking their pipes in a
distant land, while his sweet Katrine perched on a stool, was milking the
brindled cow.

The fire began to blaze more fiercely. Hirpley piled on the wood. The
chickens began to roast. The fat trickled down into the flame. That
sound so full of music to the ears of corpulent Hunger, for a moment
aroused Hon-Adam from his lethargy. He opened his round eyes and
moved his lips. It might be a feast after all, he thought, but that strange
figure squatting by the fire with his red nose glaring in the light ? Hon-
Adam's pleasant delusion vanished. It was a charm, a spell, or some other
deviltry. Hon-Adam was in despair.

Time passed on, and the chickens were turned. Still the fat hissed down
into the fire, still Hirpley piled on the wood. Hon-Adam sat with his eyes
half closed, gazing in apathetic terror on the scene.

Hirpley turned round, and made a face at his prisoner. He drew one
side of his mouth up to the eye, while the other sank down somewhere
under the chin. It was a hideous face.

Hon-Adam swore quietly in Dutch.

Now Hirpley divesting his limbs of that elegant grey coat, spread it carefully on the grass. Then he drew from the depths of that dismal sack a
mysterious looking platter of dark pewter. He laid it silently on the out
spread coat. The spell approached completion ; Hon-Adam closed his eyes
in utter despair.

When he opened them again he beheld the chickens elegantly done, laid
on the pewter platter, while the air was filled with a delicious fragrance.
There was a lump of golden butter peeping from the folds of a large green

leaf, sundry slices of snow-white bread, and a mysterious brown jug, all spread forth on the grey coat. Hon-Adam strained his eyes. This looked very much like witchcraft.

The wizard still squatted on the grass, his wide mouth distorted by a horrible grin, as he surveyed the chickens, the butter, and the brown jug. He rubbed his red nose and smacked his lips.

Hon-Adam's fat face now expressed desire, horror, wonder. Hirpley brandished the knife. Two or three flourishes in the air, and he had severed one of the chickens into luscious sections. Sticking his knife into a piece of snow-white meat from the breast, he held it before the lips of the Hessian, with an emphatic word ——

" Eat !"

Hon-Adam looked at the delicious morsel, snuffed its fragrance, opened his lips. He was a lost man. He had swallowed the charm. O, those fat brothers smoking their pipes, that voluptuous sweetheart milking the brindled cow ! Hon-Adam uttered an incoherent prayer.

Hirpley now presented the brown jug to his lips.

" Drink !"

Ah, that delicious smell, that insinuating fragrance ! Hon-Adam smelled, tasted, drank. The unknown liquid gurgled down his throat, smooth and thick as oil, penetrating as an invisible flame.

Then Hon-Adam rolled his eyes, opened his mouth, forgot his brothers, his sweetheart and the brindled cow, while a single ejaculation escaped from his lips —

" Cot-tam !"

" Did you ever taste sich whiskey ? It's the rale old rye, mind I tell you ! How d'ye like the chicken—hey ? You want more do you. Well, I should'n't wonder. Eat—drink, I say ! That's it ! Now what I want to axe you is this, haint you ashamed of yourself, to come over the sea, to fight against decent civil people, who raise sich chickens and make sich whiskey ?"

Hon-Adam uttered an incoherent sound, which bore a distant resemblance to the word 'whiskey !'

" Good ; that's sensible," said Hirpley, supplying his captive with chicken and whiskey. "You're comin' to, I guess !"

It were vain to attempt a description of the Hessian's delight. His eyes winked, his lips smacked, his fat cheeks were alternately drawn in and puffed out, while he gazed upon Hirpley with a look of maudlin affection.

" Yah—Nah—Cot-tam !" he shouted, raising his corded hands with inexpressible joy.

" Now look here," said Hirpley, " You need'n't think I'm goin' to feed and drink you for nothing'—"

" Nah !" happily answered the Hessian.

" I'm goin' to convert you. You must repent, you ornery villi'n. You must leave the Britishers, and jine Gineral Washington's army.—"

" Yah !" felicitously replied the soldier, brandishing the brown jug.

Hirpley drew from his vest a dingy brown pamphlet, which he spread open on his knees.

Then in a drawling voice he read these words :

——" These are the times that try men's souls.

" The summer soldier and the sunshine patriot will, in this crisis, shrink from the service of his country ; but he that stands it *now*, deserves the thanks of man and woman. Tyranny like hell, is not easily conquered ; yet we have this consolation with us, that the harder the conflict, the more glorious the triumph.——"

Noble words are these ! Written in the dark days of '76. They had been scattered through the Continental army for two years, carried by every soldier, next to his heart, and grasped by the hands of dying men, as words of hope and life. Our rude patriot had witnessed their effect on others, and now in his sincere devotion to the cause, imagined that the stout Hessian, who did not understand a word of English, could be converted from King George to George Washington, by these earnest words. But there was this difficulty in the conversion of the Hessian ; he did not know what he was fighting for, under the King, and therefore could not easily change his opinions, as he hadn't any to change. His bread and butter seemed the only thing at stake ; but now, when in addition to bread and butter, roast chicken and old rye whiskey were conjoined with the rebel cause, Hon-Adam would have been very eager to change sides, had he understood but five words of homely English.

" What d'ye think of them words ?" asked Hirpley, " Good—aint they ? Shall I read you more ? Would like to hear about the British King ?"

" Cot-tam !" emphatically responded Hon-Adam.

" Oh, you swear at the name o' th' varmint do you ? That's right ! Let's take another pull at the chicken and whiskey."

Soon the Hessian leaned against the tree, his eyes rolling in the stupid glare of convivial excitement.

In plain words, he was drunk. Hirpley gazed on him with a grim smile, and without the least symptoms of intoxication, proceeded to finish the chicken and the brown jug.

Leaning against the tree, our Hessian friend murmured in German, the names of his brothers, his sweetheart and the brindled cow.

Hirpley now produced two clay pipes, filled with fragrant tobacco. The delight of the Hessian was beyond all bounds. As Hirpley was about placing the pipe in his mouth, he leaned forward and inflicted a hearty kiss on the lank cheeks of the Inn-keeper.

" Yah—Nah—Cot-tam !" he shrieked, tears of drunken joy rolling down his fat cheeks.

" My friend, it seems to me your pork is purty well corned," sententiously remarked Hirpley, lighting both pipes with a coal from the fire.

Then the Hessian puffed for his life, gazing lovingly in Hirpley's face, between the wreaths of smoke. The Inn-keeper, with the brown pamphlet on his knees, read and spelled his way through its exciting pages.

Above their heads, undulated the white wreaths of smoke, glistening in the light of the sun.

——'Every tory is a coward; for servile, slavish, self-interested fear is the foundation of toryism; and a man under such influence though he may be cruel, never can be brave.'——

"Now that's what I call gospel!" ejaculated Hirpley, "Every tory is a coward! That's what I always say! Who burnt old Mayland alive? Who ravished and murdered his daughter? Who plunders our houses in the dead of night, and who kicks and cuffs innocent women, when they haint the spunk to look a man in the eyes? Tories, every rascal of 'em, tories, by hokey? I wonder what Sattin 'll do with sich cattle in tother world? Fryin' live frogs on a hot bake iron, or stickin' pins through grasshoppers' ribs—that would suit 'em to all eternity.—Hey—hallo! What's that?"

The wood echoed with the sound of footsteps, and presently the dusky form of Black Sampson came through the branches, his scythe on his shoulder, his white dog by his side, while the face of Gotlieb Hoff peered over his shoulder.

Hirpley gazed upon their faces, and then upon the face of a third person, who entered the glade with them.

His eyes distended with surprise, his lips dropped apart; he sprang to his feet, as though a keg of powder had exploded beneath him.

"At last!" he shouted, "Now we'll have the fun!"

CHAPTER TWENTIETH.

THE DEAD FATHER AVENGED.

GILBERT GATES stood in the road-side, his face and slender form bathed in the light of the declining sun, as he gazed upon that sight so pleasant to his soul:

A dying man suspended from the buttonwood tree, his form writhing in agony, while his eyes hung from their sockets, and his tongue protruded from his fallen jaw.

That man long years ago, had given his father the Spy, to death, far away in the wild wood. By the side of the dead man's corse, a boy of twelve years had sworn an oath of vengeance. That boy grown to manhood, had witnessed the agonies of an old man burned to death; had seen that old man's innocent daughter torn from her home, and surrendered to the shame too deep for words to tell; and now he stood gazing upon the death-struggles of Norman Frazier, by whose word his father had been executed.

Gilbert Gates stood alone by the road-side gazing silently upon the dying man. His grey eye gleamed with the fulfilment of his awful revenge, his lips were firmly set over his locked teeth, while his clenched hands were laid upon his heaving chest.

On the porch of the Inn stood David Walford and his four bravoes, dressed in dark uniform, relieved by white belts, rifles in each hand, knives and pistols by each side. They were silent; the death-groans of Norman Frazier, thrilled wretches like these with horror.

Somewhat apart leaning against a pillar of the porch, was a man dressed in a flowing black robe, his face concealed in his hands, as he veiled his eyes from that terrible spectacle. This was a Preacher of the Gospel.

Above, from the midst of the green leaves that half enclosed the window, the face of Clerwoode was visible, as in speechless horror he gazed upon the dying man.

The declining sun shone over all.

Sounds of battle roared and thundered far away to the south, but here, in front of Dilworth Inn all was still.

The groans of Norman Frazier broke terribly on the air.

We will return for a moment to the scene of his condemnation. Taken prisoner in the heart of the American army, hurried through the country with a cloak thrown over his form, he had been left in the spacious cup-board of the front room in the tavern, for an hour or more, while the four bravoes guarded the door.

For an hour or more he laid in silence, his limbs cramped by the confine-ment, while the tightly drawn cords cut into his wrists and ancles.

During this hour, his daughter Rose was separated from him by a slen-der partition, for the cupboard opened into the closet of the next room.

The hour past, he heard the sound of footsteps, was dragged forth from the closet. The cloak was thrown from his face. He stood erect, with his sight and senses for a moment confused, by the strange incidents of the day.

At last, looking around he beheld that chamber occupied by the four bra-voes He recognized the repulsive visage of David Walford. The hawk-eye of Gilbert Gates gleamed in his face, from a farther corner of the room. In his hand he grasped the order for the execution of Frazier, which he had used with such terrible effect, in the death of Clarence Howard.

Before him stood a man of splendid appearance, clad in a scarlet uniform, with an epaulette on each shoulder, a star on his left breast.

" Your name is Norman Frazier ?" said this British officer, in a deep voice.

" It is," answered the brave Scot, his blue eye lighting up with a look of fierce resolution.

"**You** held a commission from his Majesty, in Braddock's war!"

"I did!"

"You never resigned that commission?"

"Never; unless you will accept my deeds this day as a resignation. It seems to me, that my resignation has been carved upon the faces of your soldiers to-day, with all the sincerity in my power."

"You then acknowledge that you held a commission from his Majesty, in Braddock's war. That commission you never resigned. To-day you are found in arms against the King. Can you tell me, Sir, what is now your proper designation?"

"An honest man, by the grace of God!"

"These fine words will not serve you now. You stand before me as a rebel, a deserter, a traitor!"

"You stand before your God, even worse than this, as the assassin who murders in a tyrant's name for hire."

"Come Sir," exclaimed Cornwallis reddening with rage, "What have you to say in your defence?"

"You are determined to murder me; wherefore a defence? You know Sir, that I accepted a commission in Braddock's war, not to serve your Elector of Hanover, but to rescue myself and neighbors from the tomahawk, That service done, the war over, my commission expired, with the accomplishment of its object. If I am a traitor, then is George Washington a traitor. He served in the same war, held a commission either from your Elector, or from those who governed under him; he is now in arms against your boor of a tyrant. Therefore he is a traitor!"

"You have spoken truth Sir. He is a traitor. Once in the hands of his Majesty, he will be made an example, for the terror of rebel mob. In the meantime, Sir, it is a part of the policy of General Sir William Howe, to do justice upon all inferior traitors. If you have any requests to make, or prayer to offer, I would advise you to hasten both requests and prayers. For in five minutes you will die."

"Sir, you cannot condemn me thus. This looks like an assassination—"

"It was our original intention to try you by the formalities of a court martial. But you may escape, in the meantime, and it is necessary to make an example for the terror of those mistaken men, who, with royal commissions in their hands, fight against their King. Besides you admit your offence, what need of further formality? I take the responsibility; you must die. I am very sorry for you Sir. Gentlemen, look to your prisoner."

The amiable Cornwallis moved toward the door. Gilbert Gates advanced from a dark corner, while David Walford came from the other side of the room. The bravoes gathered round.

"One word General—"

Cornwallis turned round.

"When I was a child, I beheld the dead bodies of my parents laid across

their own hearthstone. They both were laid in a pool of blood; both murdered, and by British soldiers, in the name of a British King. General, I
have seen the axe drink the blood of my dearest friends, in the name of that
King. I have seen that name sanction outrages, too foul even for the fiends
of darkness to look upon without remorse. As the last link in the long chain
of British murders, upon which I have looked with a bleeding heart, you
now tell me, an old man, that I must die, by the hands of assassins. I
accept my death : with my mother, with my father, with the long train of
British victims, I will meet you and your kings, before the throne of God !"

Cornwallis gazed with involuntary awe, upon that old man, who stood
with his corded hands upraised, and his blue eye gleaming with a prophetic
fire, which sometimes heralds approaching death. The cold, icy tones of
Norman Frazier thrilled him with a feeling of uncomfortable solemnity.
However, after a slight pause, without speaking a word, he left the room.

He was followed by the Tories, with their prisoner. As Cornwallis was
seen riding down the southern road, they stood beneath the buttonwood
tree.

"How are you to kill me, assassins?" said the old man, turning fiercely
around.

David Walford retreated before the glare of those eyes. Gilbert Gates
advanced with a smile.

"Thee is in a bad way, friend Frazier. In truth is thee. It was the
General's order, that thee should be shot, but my friends are out of powder.
Verily, they will have to put thee to death by hanging—"

"Come hither, ruffian," said Norman Frazier, turning to David Walford,
"You are a brute, a coward, and a murderer. You know it, as well as I.
But you are my nephew, and therefore, I ask you to do me a small kindness,
Kick me, this hypocritical Quaker out of sight, and then stab me with your
hunting knife. Come, David, if you are a murderer, be manly for once in
your life !"

The four bravoes, with the Quaker, turned their eyes toward David's face.
He stood, with his head drooped on one side, looking upon Norman Frazier
with a sidelong glance.

"Curnel," said he with a brutal laugh, "I'm afeered you must hang.
Fellers rig the rope on that limb. Be quick will you?"

The Tories obeyed, and in a moment the rope hung dangling from the
limb.

Gilbert Gates advanced, and loosened the neckcloth of the old man. Then
with that infernal sneer on his face, he wound the rope around his neck,
whispering in the ear of the prisoner all the while——

"Does thee remember the hunter, whom thee shot in the wild wood so
many years ago ? At the hour of sunset—does thee ? The paper that
thee pinned on his breast, kindly informing the son, who were his father's
murderers ?"

Colonel Frazier gazed in the face of this strange being with a wondering look, as though he endeavored to recall some vague memory of the past.

"I do!" said he at last, "What then?"

"Only I am the son of that hunter; I fit the cord around thee neck, I will trample over thee dead body. That is all my friend."

In a low whisper he hissed these words in his victim's ear.

At this moment a cry of surprise ran through the group. A wayfarer, dressed in a long dark robe, with a plain black chapeau upon his brow, approached the Inn. As he drew nigh, David Walford eyeing him intently beheld his tall, straight form, his firm features, illuminated by the light of two deep dark eyes. His hair, worn in thick masses, which unbound by "que" or "tie" fell to the shoulders, was dark and glossy. He was altogether a man of striking appearance; his step indicated the vigor of early manhood.

"Who are you?" roughly asked Walford.

"A Preacher of the Gospel," calmly responded the stranger; "I perceive that I am just in time to pray with a dying man."

He passed through the bravoes with an even step, and took Colonel Frazier by the hand.

"My friend," said he, "I will pray with you!"

"What—you here! Breckenridge!" gasped Frazier in surprise, for he beheld before him, one of those brave Ministers, who preached the Continentals on to battle, prayed with them in the death hour, shared their rude fare, made their bed with them upon the hard earth; in short faced all the perils of war, in the name of God.

"I am here," said the Preacher. "I am afraid all hope is over, my friend. . Let us pray!"

He knelt down and gave utterance to a short and impressive prayer. The light shone over his manly features, over the bared brow and grey hairs of Colonel Frazier, while the bravoes stood aside stilled into silence by the words of that earnest prayer. Gilbert Gates alone, stood with a mocking smile upon his lip.

The Preacher arose, and shook the old man warmly by the hand.

"Give my blessing to Rose—to Blanche," said Norman, in a tone tremulous with emotion. Tell them I died like a man. Do this for me Breckenridge, and the blessing of God be on you. Farewell!"

The Preacher retired toward the porch deeply affected by this scene.

"I am ready, assassins!" said Colonel Frazier, in a firm voice.

David Walford whispered to one of his men. The bravo knelt in the road, placing his hands in the thick dust.

"Now get on this feller's back will you?" said David with a brutal sneer.

Norman Frazier stepped silently upon the back of the prostrate Tory. Gilbert Gates advanced and shortened the rope. At this moment a vision of Rose and Blanche came over the soul of the doomed man, while the sun-light fell warmly over his face.   For a moment traces of deep emotion were written on that wrinkled brow, in those clear blue eyes, but that moment passed, all was calm again.

Gilbert Gates stood before him, folding his arms as with a quiet smile he gazed steadily in his face.

" Remember my father and die !"

The kneeling Tory was thrown aside by a sudden movement of David Walford.

Norman Frazier was hanging in the air, with his feet scarce six inches from the ground.

It was a horrid death.

The slowly purpling face, the eyes bulging, the tongue protruding, the writhing form, touching the ground at every plunge with the extended feet, the thick gurgling groan !   Hanging in any form, is a hideous death for one of God's children to die, but this hideous mockery of a mockery this hang-ing a man, whose feet stirred the road-side dust at every fatal plunge—the devil himself, would have turned aside from such a sight.

David Walford and his comrades retreated to the porch.   The Preacher hid his eyes in his hands.   Gilbert Gates with his clasped hands pressed against his chest, drank in the agonies of the dying man.

At this moment Clerwoode and Rose, looking from the upper window be-held the blackened face of Norman Frazier, writhing in the light of the de-clining sun.

The Preacher at the same moment raised his face from his hands, gazing in vacant horror upon the struggles of the brave old man.   He advanced into the road-side, and stood with his brow bared and hand uplifted, in the full glow of the sun.

" In the name of God," he said in a choking voice, " I forbid this murder !"

As he spoke a form was seen, twining around the quivering branch of the tree, a knife shone in the sun for a single instant, and then the body of Nor-man Frazier fell in the road-side dust.   The severed rope dangled in the air.

When the Tories recovered from their surprise—and this incident burst upon them, like the deed of a supernatural hand—they beheld the form of a young soldier, arrayed in a green uniform, bending over the prostrate body, with a gleaming knife in his hand.   In a moment the cord was severed from the throat ; the young soldier looked up, advanced the right foot and glared upon the bravoes, with a knife in one hand, a pistol in the other.

" That was a brave deed my boy !" said the Preacher, looking upon the young soldier with as much surprise, as though he had dropt from the skies.

" Why my friends ye are very polite !" sneered Gilbert Gates, turning from David to his bravoes.   " Here is a strip of a boy cuts down the crim-mal and defies ye, and yet ye do'n't say a word. But he has a pistol—a knife—in truth has he !''

David Walford made a sign to his men. The five advanced with drawn swords, their separate curses sounding as one.

" Cut the rebel down," growled David, " Stand aside preacher, or you mought come to harm !''

Yet the Preacher did not stand aside. With a sudden gesture he seized the pistol in Clerwoode's belt, and clenching it with an iron grasp while his brow flushed, and his nostrils quivered with the excitement of the scene, he took his position by the young soldier's side.

" I pray with repentant sinners," said he, in a tone of cool scorn, " But here is my prayer for *assassins !*''

He covered the body of David with the aim of his pistol, as he spoke. It was a noble sight ; the tall form of the Preacher with the bared brow and flashing eye, contrasted with the more youthful figure of Clerwoode, who stood by his side, near the body of Norman Frazier, their arms clutched with the same iron grasp ; while with presented breasts they awaited the attack of the bravoes.

Gilbert Gates smilingly surveyed the scene, the fore finger of his right hand laid upon his thin lip, while his grey eyes shone with a wild deep light.

David Walford and his bravoes sprang forward, but at the same moment a shout and howl echoed from the north. They started back in the very impulse of their leap, and gazed in the direction from where these sounds had echoed.

They beheld three figures hurrying from the northern road along the open space ; a man with light golden hair floating on the wind, a giant negro, and a snow-white dog. The man with golden hair, bore a blood-stained rifle in his grasp, the negro a dripping scythe ; the dog, with dilating jaws, exposed his white teeth, crimsoned with human gore.

With involuntary terror, David Walford heard the howl of that dog, the wild hurrah of that negro, the mad yell of the man whose golden hair floated on the wind.

" Hah-a-whah ! At 'em trote Debbil !''

With that shout they came on, Gotlieb with his rifle clubbed, Sampson with his scythe gleaming, Debbil with his jaws expanded and his white teeth glittering in the sun.

Then occurred a brief but terrible combat.

Ere a moment passed, those two brave men and the dog, had plunged into the midst of the bravoes. Three times the sharp scythe encircled Sampson's head, three times the clubbed rifle rose and fell. Like an enraged tiger, the Giant Negro dashed the Tories to the ground ; knife and rifle were no defence against the sweep of that terrible scythe. As they fell, the rifle of Gotlieb crushed them deeper in the earth ; as they writhed upon the ground, the teeth of Debbil sunken deep in the neck, tore their flesh into ribbands.

Gilbert Gates, the Preacher, Clerwoode Le Clere, all gazed in silence upon this scene. When the first rush of the conflict was over, they looked around and beheld three tories weltering in their blood, amid the roadside dust; the fourth gazed with a mad yell upon the gleaming scythe, and then fled down the road, without once looking back.

For a moment there was a pause,

Gotlieb stood with his blue eye fixed upon the Quaker, while Sampson, his scythe half-lowered, silently advanced toward David Walford.

" You've murdered my comrades, you ugly nigger," roared David, " But you'd better leave me alone. Move one step toward me, and I'll blow your brains out with this pistol!"

The negro showed his white teeth. This was always a dangerous sign with Sampson.

" Look heah Debbil, do yah see dat ar man ? He burn Massa Mayland alive ! Hah-ah-whah ! At 'em trote Debbil !"

The white dog sprang—David fired. The bullet whistled by Sampson's ear, but David Walford plunged to and fro, with the teeth of the white dog in his throat. Right and left, backward and forward, David Walford leaped and plunged, while the dog uttered a low growl as his teeth were stained with the Tory's blood. David extended his weaponless arms—for he had dropped his knife and pistol in the contest—and concentrating his immense strength, grasped the throat of the dog with his iron fingers.

Debbil howled, his teeth loosened their hold ; David Walford held him aloft, with his tongue protruding and his large eyes starting from their sockets.

" Debbil !" shrieked Sampson. The dog heard him, and gave one terrific bound, and was free. Crouching on the earth, his eyes fixed on the face of the Tory, he awaited the signal of his master.

Sampson now presented a terrible picture of rage. His parting lips disclosed his ivory teeth, clenched together like a vice, his eyes rolled until their whites stood out against the dark skin, his broad chest heaved with choking gasps. He spat on his hands and grasped his scythe afresh.

David Walford was fairly warned that the most terrible moment of the conflict had now come. He seized a rifle from the dust, and grasping the barrel, stood on his guard.

The negro silently advanced a step, his huge black form scarcely burdened by one article of apparel, glistening in the sun. David prepared for the blow, but the next movement of Sampson struck him with surprise.

The negro silently retreated, one, two, and three steps. His eyes were deously blood-shotten, and now the white foam hissed around his lips.

He sank for a moment in a crouching position, and then with one tremendous bound, sprang over six feet of earth, his scythe glimmering around his head as he sprang.

That bound was the work of a second; the second passed, a body fell heavily to the earth, while a head rolled bleeding in the dust. The body lay quivering for a moment or more with life; the head lay covered with dust, while the face was still stamped with the conflict of hideous passions. The eyes wide open glaring on the sky, the brow glooming, the lip compressed; it was a loathsome spectacle, that face of David Walford, now forever cold in death.

"Massa Mayland," cried the negro, wiping his scythe with some green leaves; "Dat ar counts anoder for you! Hah-ah-whah! How you like dat, Debbil!"

The dog uttered a long deep howl.

Sampson turned around and beheld the awe-stricken faces of the Preacher and Clerwoode, who, during the conflict had guarded the prostrate form of Norman Frazier. Then looking for Gotlieb, he saw him standing beside Gilbert Gates, with a pistol presented to his breast.

"Gilbert te must come mit me," exclaimed Gotlieb, as it might be seen, that he struggled with emotions, which to speak would have strangled him; "If te tries to run off, Sampson will cut cut your head into pieces mit his scythe. Come Gilbert!"

Silently Gilbert followed Gotlieb into the Inn, and up the stairs. They paused before the door of the back room.

"Go in Gilbert and pray," said Gotlieb, pushing his golden hair, damp with sweat and blood, away from his forehead. "Pray Gilbert, for you must tie in a fery few minutes!"

It was broken English, but Gilbert felt it was sincere. What Gotlieb's tongue lacked in clearness of accent, was more than made up by the steady glare of his blue eyes.

Gilbert silently entered the room.

He beheld for the first time the corse of Mary Mayland.

As though a snake had charmed him, he stood glaring upon that pale face, with his eyes fixed, like the glassy stare of death. Then a low moan escaped him, and like a dead man, he fell beside the corse. He lay for a moment with his face pressed against the hard floor, but soon raised himself into a kneeling posture. His hands dropped stiffly by his side. His stony eyes were fixed upon the face of the dead girl.

At length large tears rolled down his cheeks.

Gilbert Gates had never wept before but once, and that was when he gazed upon the corse of his father.

Gotlieb advanced, starting backward as he beheld these tears.

"Yes Gilbert it was padt," he said, resting his hand upon the shoulder of the kneeling man: "Oh it was fery padt! How didt Polly May ever harm you Gilbert? I never heardt her speak a cross wordt, even to a cat.

How couldt ye do it, Gilbert? To murder poor Polly May—oh Gott!
Gott! It was too padt! Ant look ye, how purty she lays tere, mit her
hands crost, and her lips smilin'! Oh Polly May, Polly May, I shall never
see you ag'in. Tont she look jist like as if she vos asleep Gilbert?"

Gilbert did not answer. His stony eyes were still fixed upon the face
of the dead girl. The only thing he ever loved; he might have been happy with her, but for that terrible oath in the wild wood. He looked upon
the dead girl in silence; he scorned to tell Gotlieb how the ravisher had fallen
by his own hand.

At last startled by the sound of footsteps, Gilbert raised his eyes. Colonel Frazier stood before him, leaning for support on the arm of the brave
Preacher Breckenridge, while in the background near the window, the black
form of Sampson, was thrown in bold relief by the light of the setting sun.
The white dog also was there, licking his master's hand.

As Gilbert looked up stricken with awe, by the steady gaze of Norman
Frazier, whom he had given to a terrible death, but a few moments since,
there was the sound of footsteps; Clerwoode entered the room, and then a
light form came bounding to the soldier's arms.

Rose lay panting and weeping upon her father's breast, while Clerwoode
and the Preacher turned their faces aside to conceal their tears.

The negro advanced.

"Massa Frazier," he said in his rude accent. "T'ree nights ago we
swore to kill all de murderers ob poor Massa Mayland. Hamsdorff am
dead, sar. My dog Debbil lap him darn Hessian blood. Dave Walford,
am dead sar. My scythe cut off him head. Dis is de only one left, sar.
What you s'pose we do wid him?"

"Gilbert Gates," said Norman Frazier, as unwinding the arms of Rose
from his neck, he clasped her hands within his own, and thus held her
gently back from his bosom. "Three nights ago, the freemen of Brandywine sentenced the murderers of Jacob Mayland to death. Hamsdorff,
Walford—these have met their doom. You alone remain. Gilbert, ere
the setting of the sun, you must die!"

Gilbert meekly bowed his head, while a fiendish smile stole over his lip.
In that moment an awful resolution took possession of his soul. He was
resigned to death; his heart was torn by the sight of Mary's corse, but the
sight of Norman Frazier, *who had executed his father*, awoke the devil in
his soul.

"It is just," he meekly said, rising to his feet. "I deserve to die. Yet
before I go hence to another world, my friends, I beseech ye pardon me for
my crimes. I have been a sinful man; in truth have I. Norman Frazier,
I ask thee to pardon me! And thee Sampson, Gotlieb thee also!"

Clasping his hands he now approached the maiden. "Friend Rose, a
dying man asks pardon of thee!"

" May God pardon you, as I do !" said Rose, looking up from her father's bosom, with a sad sweet smile.

The words yet lingered on her lips, when Gilbert Gates tore a knife from the folds of his vest—raised it—and struck with all the vigor of his arm.

" This for my father's death ! The last sacrifice I offer to his Ghost !" he shrieked, aiming the blade at the maiden's heart.

The blow descended ; Colonel Frazier started back with horror as he beheld the rushing blood. Yet the blood came not from his daughter's bosom, but from the arm of Clerwoode Le Clere. The gallant soldier had been watching the movements of the Quaker ; one bold leap, a brave extension of his arm, and the maiden was saved. The knife sank deeply into his right arm.

" Black Sampson moved forward——

" Debbil !" he said, and raised his scythe.

" Not yet Sampson," exclaimed Gotlieb, " for as Mary Mayland is teadt on that floor, dis wretch shall tie by inches."

Gilbert Gates folded his arms, his thin lips trembled a smile of scorn.

" You can but kill !" he said. " When I am dead, I will feel no more !"

As the setting sun fell over his face, illumining the sharp features, relieved by long curling hair, his grey eyes gleamed with a look that bore more resemblance to the glare of a hyena, than the gaze of a creature made in the image of God.

CHAPTER TWENTY-FIRST.

THE HOME OF THE WILDERNESS.

THE fountain bubbled brightly in the sun, and the wild roses scattered their perfume over its clear waters, and around the cross of dark grey stone.

The long beams of the declining day, like threads of gold floating in the air came gleaming ever and anon through the tops of the forest trees, while a milder light lay like a holy spell upon the cottage roof, with its pointed windows and vine-embowered porch. The dark rocks, rising above the peaceful home of the Wilderness, were for the moment changed to living gold, by the rich lustre of the declining sun.

A twilight quietude sank down upon that wood-hidden glade, surrounded by forest trees, adorned by the cottage and neglected garden, beautiful with the bubbling fountain and hallowed by the cross of dark grey stone.

Around were the giant trees, above the clear blue sky ; for here the sky

was clear and bright and blue, without a battle-cloud to mar its surface, but
with a golden glow caught from the declining sun, mellowing warmly over
its deep azure.

The breeze came freshly through the trees, untainted with the smell of
blood.   Yes, rich with the sweets of wild flowers, the breeze sung its low
toned hymn through the tops of the trees, and whispered its music around
the cross beloved of roses.

The hour was still and solemn, as though the trees, the flowers, the sky,
nay the very air that flung its fragrance round, were conscious that the forest glade was soon to be the scene of solemn words and sad and fatal deeds.

The garden fence was rent and trampled to the earth ; the print of hoofs
had crushed the wild flowers and beat down the vines, across that neglected
garden, even to the cottage porch.

A horse stood panting near that porch, his golden skin marred with
bloody spots and whitened with foam.   The rein hung loosely on his
neck ; the saddle was vacant.   The rich caparison fluttered down his
streaming flanks, torn by swords, red with gore.

The windows of the cottage were open, and the porch-door hung ajar.

That door led into a quiet room, lighted by a single pointed window.   It
was furnished with high-backed mahogany chairs, a book-case, stored with
massive volumes stood in one corner, and a picture of the Saviour smiled
from the wainscotted walls.   The wainscot of dark walnut imparted a deep
gloom to the quiet chamber, while the floor of polished mahogany reflected
the walls and furniture as in a mirror.

In the full glow of the sunlight, which came pouring through the pointed
window, sat a young man, dressed in rich green velvet, his elbows resting
on the arms of the walnut chair, his pale cheeks buried in his clenched
hands.   His bared brow, relieved by long black hair, was distorted by a
swollen vein, that shot upward from the eyebrows.   His dark eyes sunken
far in their sockets glared with glassy lustre.   His entire face, moulded in
the outline of manly beauty, was now livid in its hues, and impressed with
the traces of a terrible agony.

Thus had Lord Percy, sat for half an hour, never raising his head save
once or twice, and then his gaze wandered to the door of the next chamber.

That chamber contained his all in life or death, his fate, his love, or per-
chance his doom.

——Arriving half an hour ago at the lonely cottage, he had laid the fainting
girl on the bed in the next chamber, and then turning from the room he be
held an aged woman, who attired in black with a high lace cap, watched his
movements with her wondering eyes.   A brief conversation then took
place, between Percy and the white-haired dame.

" This is my sister.   She is wounded—perhaps bleeding to death.   Is
there no physician near this place ?"

" Alack-a-day Sir !   Bleeding to death and so young too !   Wait here

Sir—I will run across the woods and over the fields. Doctor Smith lives not more than a mile from here. Wait here with the lady, Sir—I will bring the Doctor, right away."

"Thanks Madam," said Percy with a bow, as contemplating the withered form of the old lady he muttered to himself, " She is old ; it will take her at least an hour, to go and return. One hour is sufficient for all my schemes."

The aged woman hurried away from the cottage, leaving Percy alone with the fainting girl.——

He locked the door of the chamber, and then sat down in the walnut chair near the window. Here he remained, fixed as a block of marble, for half an hour, while his face betrayed the agony that shook his soul.

Ah his thoughts were dark and terrible !

The sunlight how gaily it streamed over his corrugated brow, yet that sunshine he was about to leave, forever. The last sun that ever could shine upon his forehead, was now sinking in the western sky. To-morrow he would be dead ; to-morrow his young form, trampled beneath the hoofs of the war-horse, or tumbled into the rude grave of the battle-field would think and feel no more.

His dream on the ocean, that fatal valley, with its quiet temple and grassy graveyard, that form flung over the rising mound, with death in the streaming wound and glazing eye—these terrible thoughts passed one by one over his soul.

Could he but die in this cottage, die in the wild wood, or in some world-hidden dell, with the music of rippling streams in his ears ! But that fatal valley of his dream, with its rustic temple and grassy graves ; his soul shuddered within him at the memory.

And he must die !

Condemned by no human power, but by the awful voice that spoke from the other world to his soul, he must die ! The fragrance of the flowers, the glory of the sun, the summer breeze, the blue sky—these were present with him *now*. To-morrow, he would feed the Raven of the battle-field, or sink into the loathsome corruption of the grave. He must die. The voice spoke in his soul ; he tried to drown it by memories of the past, by the vision of his grey haired father, or the dark-eyed Isidore, who now prayed for him three thousand miles away, but still that voice whispered its unceasing chaunt —— Death, before the setting of the sun, death in the graveyard of the Quaker Temple !

At last he arose, and silently approached the door of the next chamber. Inclining his head, he listened intently for a moment ; all was still as the grave.

" I must die," he said, slowly pacing the floor of the lonely room, " Yes, it is in vain, that I attempt to drown the voice, speaking forever to my soul —I must die ! Yet shall my last hour go out in glory ! Not the glory of battle, not the hollow echo of human fame, but that glory which is priceless —the glory of a woman's eye and lip and bosom! I must go down to the grave, but thou shalt tread the dark path with me, Blanche. Thy round arms about my neck, thy sweet kiss upon my lips, thy heart mingling its pulsations with mine own—ha, ha Blanche! This were a merry death! This death shall be thine and mine!"

His voice was wild and hollow, while his dark eye, no longer glassy in its lustre, emitted a clear and flashing glance. With a mocking smile on his lip, he seized a goblet of glass, shapen like one of those golden goblets, which in the olden time glowed with the fire of deep red wine, he seized a goblet of glass, from the table by his side, and hurried towards the fountain.

In a moment he knelt there, and dipt the glittering vessel in the cool waters. The freshing breeze tossed his dark curls aside from his pale brow, and a solitary sunbeam lighted up his face. That face now glowed with an excitement, like the frenzy which heralds the approach of death. His lips were burning red, his cheek flushed, his eye full of wild delirious light.

He drew a slender phial from his vest, and for a single instant, his hand was suspended over the goblet of clear cold water. A solitary drop from the phial, another and another, fell gently into the cup, mingling with the stainless liquid, without producing any perceptible change in its color.

" I will die, but not by bullet or steel!" he gaily murmured. " Ho, ho! This is a rare poison. It mingles with this cold water and dissolves, without the slightest change of hue; a rare medicine by my soul! Was it a presentiment, that induced me, three years ago, when I was but young in this gay world, to procure this poison, and hug it to my heart as a miser hugs his gold? Little did I think, then, that it would one day, slide George Percy gently into his unknown, unwept grave! Blanche will awake from her swoon—what so pleasant to her lips, as a cup of clear cold water? She will drink—I will drink—hurrah! Down together into the dark valley, down together, wrapt in each other's arms, gathered in the embrace of death and love, down together into the unwept grave?"

His language was wild and frenzied, his tone hollow with shuddering gaiety, yet his voice sunk to a whisper of deep and wringing agony, when it came to that word—the unwept grave! *The unwept grave*—that was the horror that parlyzed his soul. His father's commission unfulfiled, no kind hand to smooth his dark hair back from his clammy brow, or plant a single flower over his grave—this was the fear that wrung his heart strings, and sunk like eternal night upon his soul.

He arose with the goblet in his hand, and was hurrying toward the cottage porch, when his eye was enhanced by a spectacle of strange loveliness.

He beheld the cross of dark grey stone, with its entwining roses now tossing to and fro, to the impulse of the breeze, he beheld that cross and its roses mirror in the bubbling spring.

There was something in this sight that touched his soul. He had seen the cross full many time, shining in hues of gold, through the gloom of proud cathedral shrines, he had been in the land where Religion is Romance and Beauty, he had trod the marble floor of princely domes, where the triumphs of art were offered up to God, and yet never felt as he did now, when contemplating that simple cross of dark grey stone.

He knelt down on the mossy sod again, and endeavored to breathe a prayer to God, but the half-formed accents died on his lips.

In place of the sweet revelations of prayer, came a vision of his home. He beheld the towers of Monthermer rising from among the tops of massive oaks, the green lawn stretching away from the hall-door, with its statues and its fountains, the wide park, dotted with the brown deer, who wandered among the trees, the broad lake, rippling gently in the light of the sun, the distant hills gleaming far above the shadows of many a vale; this vision came like a revelation from heaven to his soul. His countenance suddenly assumed an expression of tender regret, his lips parted, his eyes grew dim, his soul was far away amid the scenes of his home.

This tender memory held possession of his soul for a moment, and a moment only.

Suddenly he arose, and goblet in hand, with a flushed cheek and ominous brow, strode toward the cottage porch. His gallant horse beheld him, and uttered a low sound of recognition. Percy started. The large rolling eye of that war-steed, the quivering nostrils extended towards his face, the head rubbed gently against his arm—ah, the brave horse was speaking to his master in his own way, as though he would have said, Mount, Master of mine, mount, and let us go forth to the battle once more!

Percy turned his head away and hastily entered the cottage. He stood for a moment beside the door of the next chamber, the goblet sparkling in his hand, while his face half-covered in shadow, assumed an expression full of dark and fatal meaning.

" Shall I ever forget the gleam of her full dark eyes, as when awaking from her swoon, she found herself encircled in these arms ? Then her hurried ejaculation, ' Save me now, O God!'—it rings even yet in my ears. Then the blood forsook her face, she lay fainting in my arms again. She passed through this cottage door, wrapt in unconsciousness. Hark! She murmurs in her swoon—she whispers a prayer to God. Her voice thrills my blood, and yet she must be mine, she must die !''

He stood listening beside the chamber door with the goblet in his hand.

Let us enter that chamber, half an hour before this moment.

The sunlight shone smilingly through the windows, over the bed with its snow-white counterpane, and tinged the silver hangings with a ruddy glow. One window, with the sunlight softened by snow-white curtains looked out upon the neglected garden, the other faced the rude rocks which rose from the sod, in the rear of the cottage. The sash of this window opening like a door, was thrust aside, disclosing the huge mass of granite, relieved by the thick, green leaves of a solitary vine, which twined around its rugged brow. Between this rock and the back window, intervened a space of green sod, a yard or more in extent.

It was a gem of a chamber, with silken hangings, impressed with the hues of the lilac, a carpet of luxurious softness, an elegant bed with snow-white counterpane, and three chairs, of dark mahogany, intricately carved with a thousand fantastic shapes. It was a gem of a chamber, and a holy quietude was there, broken only by the faint sound of a woman's sigh; it was a quiet home, and a twilight shadow was there, relieved only by the sunshine pouring with softened lustre through the curtained window.

Reclining on the bed in the careless posture of slumber, her cheek resting on her bent arm, while her long black tresses fell negligently over the white counterpane, Blanche laid with eyes closed, lips gently parted, and bosom throbbing almost imperceptibly under the folds of her snowy robe.

Her face pale as death, was only relieved in its alabaster whiteness, by the intense darkness of her eyelashes, resting softly on the clear skin, her crescent shaped brows, and flowing black hair. A single ray of sunlight shone over her white neck, just where it deepened into the virgin bosom.

She laid there, unconscious as the babe that sleeps upon its mother's bosom, her senses wrapt in the oblivion of a swoon. The events of the day crowding on each other, in terrible accumulation, had well-nigh frozen the life in her young veins.

She had not lain there but a few brief moments, when a shadow darkened the back window, and a young form came stepping stealthily along the carpet. A young form whose voluptuous proportions were clad in warrior costume, deep green velvet faced with gold, stood beside the bed, and a young face, rich and ripe and lovely, with its olive hues and vermillion lips, gazed in the maiden's face with full dark eyes.

The Lady Isidore of Monthermer gazed long and sadly in the face of Blanche of Brandywine!

"At last I behold her! It is she who has torn his heart from my love—this peasant girl!"

Her heart smote her for that contemptuous word, as her gaze rested upon that face so beautifully pale, with its long black hair.

"Not peasant girl, but angel!"

Her face was shadowed by a deep sadness. She stood with her fingers joined across her full bosom, concealed in its masculine garmenture. She stood perusing the face of her rival, with burning eyes.

"Ah, she is beautiful, but it is with the beauty of a dream! He could not but love her! Her face is so fair, her form so light and etherial, the smile on her lip speaks of innocence and faith and hope! He could not but love her! But me—me! Ah my cheek is bronzed with fiery blood, my eyes kindle into light, only amid scenes of darkness and gloom, my soul may exist in the quietude of home, but it lives and burns amid the terror of the storm, the clamor of battle! I see how it is, now; now I know why he loves her! So young, so delicate, so gentle!"

A tear stole gently down the cheek of Isidore, as bending over the bed, she took her rival softly in her arms, and whispered in a tone of tremulous love—" Sister awake! Awake and fear not, for it is I—I—your sister!"

Starting from that blank unconsciousness, Blanche raised herself in the bed, and gazed wildly in the face of Isidore.

" Who are you?" she said, as the soft gleam of those full dark eyes, shone like a mother's love into her soul.

" A woman! A sister!"

" But this disguise?"

" Yes, this disguise! Speak it out, this disguise is a shame to my woman's nature! Ah, hear my friend—my sister, before you condemn! It was in this disguise I left my princely home, now gleaming on yonder sun, three thousand miles away, it was in this disguise, I dared the storm of the ocean, in this disguise I faced to day, the terror of the battle, and the shame of dishonor!"

" Your motive? For courage like this must have a motive, yes, a high and hallowed purpose—"

" Was it high and hallowed? Come closer to my heart, and speak lower, for there is danger in the air. You believe then, that my motive was a holy one? I thank you for that belief, from my heart! I know you, as though we had mingled our hearts together from childhood. My motive—"

" Your motive! Yes, I listen!"

" Was that which is the life of woman's life, the soul of her soul! That which the world names but to scoff, which man knows but to trample under foot! That which is at once the immortality and the hell of woman's destiny——her love!"

" This led you from your princely home—over the waters—into the terrible battle?"

" My sister, come nearer! My heart is full, and mine eyes are dim. Hear me, oh hear and love me! For I have none but you to love me now. When I say that my love was the impulse of this unwomanly daring, let me also tell you, what I mean by love—"

" That which is truth—purity—heaven on earth?"

" By love, I mean that which stamps the soul in a thousand ways, with *his image* , who is *to be loved*, long, long before the eyes, behold him. I mean that which comes to us in dreams, which speaks to us in the moonlight, the flowers, the sky! I mean that silent voice, which in the hurry of our most worldly thoughts, is evermore, whispering gently in our souls. When I speak of this love, sister, my heart burns, my blood is fire! For this love is but a memory of the world we lived in, before our souls came

to the present world, but a hope of the world which shall come, when this
has passed away !"

"Thus do I love him !" whispered Blanche, her eye drinking in the wild
light that glowed over the face of Isidore.

"Him ?   Percy ?   Is it he whom you love ?" gasped Isidore, starting
from the bed, with Blanche's hands within her own.

"Can I love this man, who defies God and man, in his mad attempts to
conquer my soul ?   No, no, no !   When he plead. I pitied, but now that
he uses force, I scorn him !"

"Speak not harshly of him, Blanche ——"

"Blanche ?   You know my name ?"

"Has he not whispered it in his dreams, in the march by day, the watch
by night, at the camp fire amid the pale corses of the dead, he has whispered that name !   Yes a thousand times ?   Has he not spoken to me, his
poor Ensign De Lorme, of the beauty of this proud girl Blanche, the wild
charm of her eyes, the soft music of her voice ?   Speak not harshly of him,
Blanche, for he is my betrothed husband !   Yes, he Lord Percy was betrothed from childhood to the Lady Isidore of Monthermer.   For him, I put
on this unmaidenly disguise, dared the shame of the world, the peril of the
battle and the storm !   And yet—God pity me—he knows me not !"

"Knows you not ?"

"We had not met for four years, when he left England.   In the poor
Ensign, who followed like a shadow by his side, he never dreamed to behold his betrothed wife, in whose veins flowed the blood of a royal line !"

"Ah, it makes my heart grow cold, when I think of the perils you have
faced for the love of this man, noble lady !"

"Call me sister friend, but do not call me by any name which revives the
memory of the home I never shall see again."

"But he will love you !   He cannot help but love you !   You, so true,
so trusting, so generous !   His passion for me will pass away, when he sees
and knows you.   Yes, yes, at his feet I will plead with him for you, I will
tell him of your devotion, I will paint to his trembling soul this heroism
t..at passes belief."

"It is now, it is only now, that I perceive the terrible error of my life.
Reared afar from the world, I have made my dreams reality, and reality itself a dream.   Yes, in the solitude of the old dim halls of my ancestral
home, I have taken to my heart a love which can never be realized.   Yes,
a love that must be crushed by the palpable and bitter truths of this everyday world ——"

She bowed her head low on her breast and was silent.   Blanche gazed
upon her with tearful eyes, gleaming with wonder, love, and awe.

Thus imperfectly have I endeavored to picture this strange communion
between two young and trusting hearts.   The words are written down but
the looks of deep anguish, the broken accents of sympathy, the blushing

cheeks so soon again pale as death, the breasts now heaving with agony and then tremulous with hope, these cannot be written down in human words, but must be left to your hearts.

—For this book is written for that old fashisned class of people, who pleading guilty to a heart, are not ashamed to acknowledge that there is such a thing as pure love, such a being as a holy God, such a life as the immortality of the soul.

You that instead of a heart and a God and a soul, have a sneer for all that is good or holy, and an absorbing adoration for the Dollar, will please close this book, and attend to the flounce of your dress, the tie of your cravat, the ink of your ledger or the price of dry goods. You were never designed by Divine Providence. to think or feel any more than a grub-worm was intended to fly. Therefore close the book and eat your good dinners, drink your rich wines and sleep your leaden sleep ; for these at least are substantial.

But God—immortality—the pure love of woman, which is a part of both ? Pshaw ! these are the flimsy fancies of a sick brain ; eating and drinking and the dollar, these are the substantials, the realities, the Gods of this life, after all. Therefore shut the book and count your pennies.——

For a moment deep silence, reigned in that cottage chamber.

At last Isidore raised her head, and while the sun shone over her radiant brow stood with a smile of delight, wreathing her lips.

" Blanche," she whispered, " Blanche when the heart trusts and is betrayed, when the first glowing dream of youth is crushed by the bitter awakening into life and its despair, then, thank God, there is still a remedy for the bruised spirit, still a home for the weary soul !"

" That remedy, that home ?"

" Death and the grave !"

Isidore upraised her hands, and her form dilated as though she stood on air. Her eyes shone with holy rapture, her face glowed like a face already immortal.

Yes, beautiful girl, with the olive cheek and full dark eyes, it is true ! Death is a glorious remedy, the grave a quiet home !

" The world may crush us, our love betray us, our hopes which we have cherished in joy and tears—like the gold of the fairy tale—prove but withered leaves, poverty may starve and persecution hunt us, yet there is a remedy for us, and a home ! A blow with a knife, a bullet, a drop from a phial, the delirium of a fever, or at most a few brief months of lingering decay, and then poverty, blighted love, persecution and despair, are but idle words. Then we go home. Then there is but another mound in the graveyard ; perhaps some kind hand plants it all over with lilies and roses. Or if there is no heart left in all the world to love us then wild grass grows greenly over our graves, and the feet of children at play, bound merrily over the sod, which encloses our bones.

"Then those who scorned us, or visited us with persecution, or gave us betrayal for our blind confidence, will come at times to look upon our graves and shed a tear. Or it may be in the silence of night, our phantoms will glide noiselessly into their homes, and scare sleep from their burning eyes."

As in a deep whisper, with dilating stature and radiant brow, the noble girl gave utterance to these words, she seemed to Blanche like a beautiful Prophetess, who felt in her own bosom all the wrong which the world inflicts on trusting hearts, all the scorn, poverty, persecution with which it repays the martyrdom of genius ; she seemed to speak not only for herself, but for that innumerable host of young or gifted and beautiful, whose fate is written in three brief words—to trust, to be betrayed, to die !

"Yes, there is a pillow for the weary head of despair ! Yes, there is a home for the broken heart ! When we have suffered long enough, *God* smooths the pillow and prepares the Home !"

These words spoken in a tone of deep sadness, had scarce passed her lips, when the sound of a stealthy footstep was heard without the door.

"Wait—endure—trust !" hurriedly whispered Isidore. And in a moment she was gone. Blanche looked around the apartment with a frightened glance, and beheld the thick curtains what veiled a closet in the corner near the back window, stirring with a quick rustling movement.

There was deep silence for a single instant. Blanche felt that the crisis of her fate was now at hand. She arose in a sitting posture, with her small feet projecting from the folds of her robe over the side of the bed. As she hurriedly gathered her dark hair in her white fingers, and raised her arms to wreathe it around the faultless outline of her head, there was a faint and stealthy sound echoing through the room. It was the noise of the opening door. She turned her face over her shoulder, she looked toward the door with a frightened glance, while her arms uplifted, as if paralyzed in the action, were half-concealed by the flowing tresses of her hair.

The door opened, and Percy entered, holding the glittering goblet in his hand.

Blanche was strangely impressed by his singular manner, as he came on.

His head was drooped low on his breast, while his dark eyes glaring from a face lividly pale, were upraised toward the maiden's countenance. His dark hair fell wild and disordered about his brow. His steps were leaden ; the hand grasping the goblet quivered with a tremulous motion.

He advanced and stood beside the bed.

"Blanche," said he, "You are faint and weary. Here is water, yes water from the spring yonder. Look—it is like yourself, brilliant and beautiful, but cold. Drink, Blanche, it will refresh you !"

" Thanks Sir; this is kind!" answered Blanche, eagerly extending her hand.

The curtains behind the back of Percy stirred tremulously and a white hand was thrust warningly through the folds. Blanche beheld this hand and it was gone again. A strange tremor shook her frame. She extended her hand to grasp the goblet, but Percy drew it suddenly aside.

" Blanche do you remember my dream on the ocean ? The dream of the fatal valley, the graveyard, the form thrown over the mound, with death on the cheek and brow ?"

" This is the third time that you have spoken to me of this wild fancy," answered Blanche, gazing with an unknown feeling of awe, on the pale face of Percy.

" Yes Bianche, it is the third time, but it shall be the last! Since I beheld you this morning, I have seen the valley, yes I have seen the mound ! My dream is no vain fancy ; my dream is but the voice of fate !"

" O, Sir, you are brave, you are a soldier. You do not fear the terror of battle ! Come then, be yourself, be a man ! Scorn these idle dreams —"

" Blanche, do you remember the fair form that came stealing through the clouds of battle, towards that dying man ? Do you remember the beautiful face, that looked down upon his agonies, and smiled away the death pain ? O, Blanche, do you remember how that sweet voice thrilled through the soul of the doomed man, stretched there in death, thrilled through his soul, and called him back to life ? The film of death fell from his eyes, the blood poured no longer from his heart ; he arose, he beheld those beautiful eyes, gleaming so gently into his own, yes, he the doomed and dying, recalled by that voice to life, gathered the angel-form to his heart, and blessed her name between his kisses ! Do you remember the dream ?"

' It was thus you told it to me," and Blanche smiled, but the smile was artificial, for the deep voice and earnest eyes of that strange man, sent a thrill of awe through her heart.

" You are that form, Blanche ! It was you that I beheld in my dream, so beautiful, so blessed, so like an angel sent from God ! It is to you I kneel ! It is you, and you only who can save me ! Behold me at your feet, pleading for love, and not only for love, but life ! For life, Blanche, speak but the word, and I am saved ! I do not fear death, believe me, but to die when a word from you, may turn back the hand of fate, and avert this fear-ful doom —— oh * * * this is terrible ! This I confess makes me a cow-ard ! Speak, Blanche, and sentence me to death, or let me live !"

As he knelt on the floor, the goblet still grasped in his trembling right hand, the large, thick drops of moisture stood out on his forehead, like the death-sweat. His voice, his look, his quivering features, all impressed Blanche with pity and horror; she bowed her head between her hands, while her long black hair fell in showering masses over her white neck and bosom.

"Speak Blanche! I do not ask you to say, ' *I love you George of Mon-*
thermer !' no, no! But if you will save me, if you will be mine, whisper
but a single word, a single name, and I will bless you for that word! O,
speak in that voice whose music rung in my ears, when covered with wounds,
I laid in your father's house; whisper but your own name, whisper only
' BLANCHE !'"

Blanche raised her head. With a start she beheld that white hand again
thrust forth into light. A terrible purpose, at that moment took possession
of her soul. Urged by an undefinable impulse, she slowly bent down her
head, and fixing her full dark eyes on Percy's face, whispered a single
word——

" ISIDORE !"

As though a thunder stroke had blasted his reason, he cowered back upon
the floor, one hand madly clutching the carpet, with a mechanical gesture,
while the other clenched the goblet in an iron grasp. The glare of his dark
eyes was terrible to behold. A hideous contortion darkened his brow and
convulsed his features.

Blanche recoiled on the bed, affrighted and appalled at the effect of that
single word.

This agitation lasted for a moment and a moment only. It came and
went, like a solitary lightning flash from a blue sky.

" Ha, ha !" lightly laughed Percy, springing to his feet with a joyous
bound. " You are disposed to jest with me! However you are merry
Blanche. In my love scene—ha, ha, ha! Don't I act these things clever-
ly? In my love scene I quite forget two things, the goblet and your thirst.
Drink Blanche, the water is clear and cold. It will refresh you."

Startled by this sudden change of manner, Blanche took the goblet with
a trembling hand. She raised it to her lips.

Percy with his dark eyes, intently gleaming upon her beautiful face, muttered a sentence in a tone that seemed wrung from his very soul——

" Death is a kind Priest, my Blanche! He unites us now beside the
grave—our hymeneal torch will be lit in a skull—this couch at once our
death-bed and our marriage altar !"

She raised the goblet to her lips. Percy's eye glared with ravenous
delight.

At this moment a light footstep pressed the carpet, and a fair white hand
thrust over his shoulder, tore the goblet from the lips of Blanche.

Percy turned with an oath on his lips.

" Frank De Lorme !" he shouted, eyeing the intruder with a look of
browing indignation.

Yes, there stood Frank De Lorme, his olive cheek crimsoned by a single
browing flush, his lips parted, his breast heaving, her dark eye dilating with
a frenzied glare. There he stood, his jet-black hair gathered carelessly beneath his trooper's cap of glossy fur, while his form quivered in every inch

of its stature, as his right hand grasped with a firm embrace, the goblet of limpid poison.

"George of Monthermer"—he began in a low and choaking voice, "Sir, what means this insult, this intrusion?" cried Percy his brow reddening with anger. "You shall rue this Sir, by my soul, I swear——"

The words died on his lips.

All at once, as he spoke, the trooper's cap fell from the head of Frank De Lorme, and the gold buttons that gathered the velvet coat about his neck flew apart, torn from their fastenings, by the fiery pulsation of that throbbing chest. That long dark hair, falling in such glossy waves about the shoulders ; that snowy bosom, heaving so rich and full into light, between the parting folds of the trooper's coat, even as a rose bursts into bloom amid its encircling leaves !

Percy stood as if suddenly frozen to marble.

"Who are you?" he gasped in a voice of agony.

Freer and more glossy waved the dark hair, in the evening breeze, higher and more beautiful arose the virgin bosom, urged all at once by terrible pulsations into the golden sunshine of that hour.

The hand grasping the goblet was upraised—the sparkling liquid touched the red lips.

Then the veil fell from Percy's eyes. As though fate had lifted the cloud from his path he beheld that face, those full dark eyes, the womanly outlines of that form.

He beheld, he recognized, he trembled from head to foot, but dared not speak. For the goblet was raised, the limped poison touched her lips.

"Isidore !" he faintly gasped.

She replied with a glance and a smile. O, that glance beaming with terrible beauty fired his brain, that smile, so sad, so despairing, so awfully resigned, convulsed his soul—yet still the cup was raised, the poison moistened her red lips.

The warm sunlight poured over the glittering goblet, and over the calm majestic face of the Lady Isidore.

CHAPTER TWENTY-SECOND.

THE BLACK POOL

The Avengers led the Quaker through the woods.

It was a difficult and winding path, leading through the thickest under-wood of the Wilderness. Above, the thick foliage lay like a cloud, covering the shrubbery beneath in a twilight gloom. Around, the trunks of massive trees, the forms of slender saplings, the luxuriant tracery of wild vines, were confounded in one mass of shade, broken ever and anon by a red gleam of sunlight.

The Avengers walked one by one, bearing the criminal to his doom. As they passed along an open space, which like an oasis of sunlit turf, intervened among the shadows of the forest, their forms were revealed in glaring light.

First breaking from the boughs, came Gotlieb Hoff, his curling hair floating in locks of gold, around his brow. His right hand clutched a loaded rifle. While his blue eyes glared steadily forward, he passed hastily over the patch of green sward.

Then came Gilbert Gates, his spare form arranged in his grey Quaker garb, his face lividly pale, his hawk-like eye glancing nervously on either side. There was a mocking smile about his thin lips, as with his unpinioned hands carelessly placed within the arm-holes of his waistcoat, he followed the footsteps of Gotlieb Hoff.

Hirpley Hawson followed next, making strange faces as he went, while each of his extended hands, presented a loaded pistol at the back of the prisoner.

Last of all came Black Sampson, his enormous form bared to the waist, while his right arm encircled the handle of the blood-dripping scythe. The veins on his broad chest writhed like serpents, beneath his dark skin. His thick lips were clenched together, and the nostrils of his aquiline nose dilated with pent-up rage. By his side, the white dog, with the glaring eye and distended jaw, leaped silently along, snuffing the air, with his head thrown back and his ears erect.

For some moments deep silence, only broken by the crashing of branches, or the heavy sound of footsteps on the mossy sod, rested upon each member of this strange procession like a spell. At last Hirpley Hawson spoke, with a low chuckling sound of half-suppressed laughter:

"It seems to me, we're doing somebody's funeral? Hey Sampson? If sich is the case, you're the only decent man among us for you're in black, as chief mourner? He, he—nigger!"

" Hirpley tont joke," muttered Gotlieb, without looking back, "Remember Mary ——"

" Yes, 'member Massa Mayland," growled Sampson. " An' den laff am you kin ! Say—Debbil—am yo' dar ?"

" My friend, thee seems to put theeself to a great deal of trouble about a peaceful man like me ?   Friend Gotlieb thee will not harm thee friend Gilbert ?   Thee would'n't do such a wicked deed ?"

Gotlieb was silent, but he drew from his pocket the thick coils of a stout rope, and extending his left hand behind his back, held it before Gilbert's eyes.

The frame of that strange man shook with a convulsive tremor. You could hear his teeth chatter, as with an ague-fit. At this moment, however, a hope of escape broke upon his soul, and his grey eyes emitted a flashing glance.

Not a word more was said, until the party emerging from the boughs, stood beside the black pool of the wilderness.

The sunlight fell warmly over the green sod, encircling that well-like pool, and the dark waters gleamed in light as they quivered to and fro, with a sullen motion.

Over the pool arose the hickory trees, distorted from their original positions, and confined together by thick strands of rope, terminating in a single knot.   Around, the thickly interwoven foliage formed a wall of leaves, impenetrable to sunlight, but through the apertures above, the blue sky flung the reflection of the setting sun down over the hickory trees, and over the waters of the pool.

While Hirpley and Sampson took their positions, one on either side of the prisoner, Gotlieb advanced toward the pool.   He gazed down upon the mass of roots, which encircling that singular spring, enclosed its waters like a wall.   Then he beheld his face reflected in the dark water, as in a mirror. They could see him veiling his face in his hands ; they could see his chest writhing under his folded arms, but they could not see the tears, which fell drop by drop in the waters below.

" Mary !" he muttered in a choking voice.

Then stepping back he raised his head and examined the hickory trees with a keen and searching glance.   Those coils of rope were strong as iron bands, that single knot, a knot of steel.   For the rope once broken, the knot once severed, the hickory trees young, fresh, vigorous, with healthy sap in their veins, would spring apart with a terrible rebound.   Gotlieb examined the rope, the vigor of the trees, even bent down and gazed upon the earth, which was broken around their roots.

" Hirpley, Sampson !   Come here !"

They advanced, while the white dog stood with his eye fixed upon the prisoner.

"Hirpley, turn your face. towards Gilbert, ant let me whisper a word in yer ear. Sampson, come close, I want to talk mit you!"

Gilbert Gates beheld Gotlieb and Sampson inclining their heads together, behind the back of Hirpley, who, with his face turned towards him, listened to their words. Suddenly Gilbert beheld the grotesque face of the Inn keeper change to a livid paleness.

"No!" shouted Hirpley, with a tremendous oath, "I wont consent to that by * * * !"

Even Black Sampson started aside, as the words of Gotlieb fell whispering on his ear. He started aside, thrust the handle of his scythe in the sod, seemed to think deeply for a moment, and then extending his hand, grasped Gotlieb by the wrist.

"It am right, Massa Gotlieb!"

Then Gilbert beheld Hirpley turn hurriedly round, and converse with his comrades, in a low tone, but with violent gestures.

It is in vain to deny that these mysterious movements, the sudden horror manifested in Hirpley's face, the start of Sampson, his deeply muttered words, in reply to Gotlieb, all thrilled the heart of Gilbert Gates, with a strange and uncomfortable sensation.

"My friend if thee is a-going to hang me, had'n't thee better do afore sundown?"

He said this with a desperate attempt to revive his accustomed sneer.

Gotlieb Hoff left his companions and advanced. His large blue eyes gleamed with a glance that Gilbert had never seen before; a strange glassy glare, freezing the blood in his veins. His face had become suddenly pale; Gilbert beheld thick drops of sweat upon his brow. Even as he spoke, his voice was changed from its usual bold tones, to deep and husky whisper, which invested with terrible interest, these words marked by mingled Quaker phrase and German accent.

"Gilbert, if thee has any prayer to say, thee hadt petter say it now!"

He then turned away, while Gilbert listened to the slightest word in quivering suspense.

"Hirpley you will pleaz cut that rope into four pieces mit your knife!"

Gilbert watched the movements of Hirpley with straining eyes. The Inn-keeper knelt down, took the rope in his hands, and slowly severed it into four parts, measuring three yards or more. As he did this, the tears streamed down his cheeks, and his hands trembled. Gilbert Gates could not believe his eyesight.

"Friend Hirpley," said he, as if to assure himself of the fact, "Wherefore does thee cry?"

Hirpley did not answer, but rose with the pieces of rope in his hands, and turned his face away.

"Sampson," continued Gotlieb, in the same unnatural voice. "Does te rememper when Misder Johnson hired us, mit some of the napors, to tie

ese trees tcgeter ? He was goin' to pild an' arpor by tis spring—you rememper Sampson ? Well, we hadt a latter, Sampson, to help us to fasten
tat rope, when the men, pulling each way, mit all their might, drawed the
trees togeter. Look in the pushes for the latter Sampson !''

Sampson laid down his scythe and searched among the bushes. Presently he drew forth the ladder from its hiding place, and lifted it against the
hickory trees. His giant frame quivered as he ascended the ladder, and
placed himself astride of a stout limb, near the place were the trees were
joined together.

"Go up the latter Gilbert !" said Gotlieb, in a low tone. Pressing his
lips between his teeth until the blood came, Gilbert advanced and prepared
for death by hanging, as the least terrible of all deaths, ascended the ladder.

"It will soon be over—eh ? Gotlieb ?" he sneered turning his face over
his shoulder.

The words lingered on his lips, when strong arms from above seized him
by the shoulder, and lifted him into air. Then an iron hand wound its fingers around his throat, his brain swam in a terrible vertigo ; he saw nothing
but blood before his eyes. Yet while that strange dizziness, that choaking
at the throat, that sound of a waterfall in his ears continued, he had also a
dim consciousness of hands busy about his form, of cords tightening about
his legs and arms. He felt a painful compression about his ancles and
wrists.

The vertigo passed away : Gilbert Gates looked around with clear eyes.
Then a terrible howl, yes a howl of despair escaped from his chest. The
reality burst all at once upon him. He was suspended in the air, one arm
and leg tied to the tree on his right, the other arm and leg corded in the
same manner, to the hickory on his left.

He quivered, he struggled, but the cords were like iron ; he could not
move an inch. His head alone was free. He bent it on his breast, and
with a creeping horror, that no words may paint, beheld the thick cords
wound around each leg, in intricate folds, half-way from the knee to the
thigh. He turned his head to the right and left ; each arm was bound to a
tree, with cords reaching from the wrist, above the elbow.

Gilbert looked below. There silently watching his movements, stood
Gotlieb, Sampson and the dog. Hirpley Hawson leaned against a tree,
veiling his face from the sight.

Gotlieb looked up and met the glare of Gilbert's eyes. He beheld the
agony of his look, the quivering of his white lips, and then right over the
head of the doomed man the fatal knot, which bound the trees together
stared him in the face.

" Gilbert Gates, may Gott have mercy on y'er soul, put you must tie !'
the voice of Gotlieb thrilled on the ear of the Quaker. " T''at olt man, Jacob Mayland, was a goot man. You purnt him alive at teadt of night.
T'at oldt man's d'arter was goot—yes, as an angel. You stole her from

her home, gave her up, to the British offizer. You know t'e rest. She is teadt now. Gilbert in the sight of Gott you have committed murter and worse than murder! In the name of Gott, Gilbert you must die!"

He raised his hands solemnly to heaven.

"You mus' die!" exclaimed Sampson, also raising his hands.

The white dog uttered a low howl.

"Hirpley," screamed Gilbert in agony, "Thee will not see me killed in this terrible way. Thee is an old friend o' mine Hirpley. Does thee hear?"

The rude Inn-keeper turned round with clenched hands. His eyes showered tears over his quivering features

"It tain't any affair o' mine Gilbert!" he exclaimed, "It is Gotlieb's business, not mine. It was his gal. you murdered, his father-in-law you burnt. Gilbert, I'm sorry for you, but you must die!"

He turned his face away again.

"Yet thee will not leave me here, to be starved to death in this way?"

A wild laugh shook Black Sampson's chest.

"Starved to death! Hah-yah! Debbil do you hear 'um talk?"

"Gilbert thee burnt oldt Mayland alive! Does tee hear? T'at oldt man standts afore me, he speaks in mine ears, he tells me kill the murterer, in a way as horriple as he kilt me! Thee sha'n't starve to death! This rifle will put an endt to you!"

"Thee is kind, friend Gotlieb?" sneered Gilbert. "One rifle ball in my head, and it is over!"

"But the rifle ball will not strike y'er headt, nor y'er heart! Murterer, tuyfel as you ar' it will only strike that knot above your head!"

The full horror of the coming death was now palpable to Gilbert's brain. He said not a word, but dropped his head on his chest, while a cold sweat oozed from every pore.

Gotlieb made a significant gesture to Sampson, and drew Hirpley from his resting place by the tree. Then placing three blades of grass in his worn hat he exclaimed ——

"The one as traws the shortest, fires the rifle!"

Hirpley was livid in the face; Sampson even he the giant negro trembled; Gotlieb alone was firm, although his blue eye flashed with a glance like madness.

Hirpley drew first, then Sampson, and last Gotlieb. With his head drooped on his breast, Gilbert Gates beheld this fearful lottery. With gasping breath, the three compared the blades of grass. Hirpley uttered a scream of joy, Sampson shouted a wild laugh; Gotlieb pale, yet firm, his blue eye glaring with death-like lustre, silently grasped the rifle.

"Go!" he said, waving his hand. He had drawn the shortest of the three. The lot of the executioner was his.

Silently they left that fatal spot, leaving Gotlieb alone with the doomed man. Pushing through the bushes for some thirty yards, they reached a green space, where the light of the declining day gleaming through a long forest arcade, fell warmly over the turf.

Sampson grasped his dog by the neck, and looked intently in Hirpley's face, while they both listened for the echo of that fatal shot.

Not a sound. All was terribly still.

A moment—two—three! Each moment an age of tortured suspense. All still; not even a moan or prayer was heard.

Hirpley fell on his face. This suspense was too horrible. The dog uttered a low growl. Sampson choked him, with a grasp of his iron hand, and then knelt down, and in his rude way sent up a prayer to God.

The light fell over his dark face convulsed with agony, over the dog, whose moaning were stilled by his fierce grasp, and over the writhing form of the Inn-Keeper.

All at once a horrid sound came echoing on the air.

The echo of a rifle, branches crashing one by one, the groan of a human being, a noise like thunder bursting from the earth ; these all were mingled in that horrid sound. Then separated from all other sounds by its emphasis of supernatural agony, there came one long and solitary cry, deepening and re-echoing far through the woods. Black Sampson heard that cry, and fell on his face ; Hirpley thrust grass in his ears ; the dog sprang in the air, with a mad howl.

Still for a minute or more, that solitary cry quivering in one long-drawn note of agony, yelled through the woods.

Then all was still.

Hirpley and Sampson still lay with their faces buried in the sod, while the dog leapt over their heads, howling as though by some strange instinct, he smelt human blood upon the air.

There was a rustling sound among the leaves, a footstep ; Hirpley and Sampson raised their heads.

Gotlieb Hoff stood before them, fixed and erect as marble, his golden hair hanging in damp flakes about his brow. His face was hideous, the cheeks pale, stained beneath the eyes with streaks of blue, the lips parting in a silly smile, the glassy eyes projecting from their sockets. His face, so pale, so hideous in its awful transformation, was spotted with innumerable drops of blood.

"Come boys," said he, with that silly smile, "Let us go! To night I'm to be married—to Mary!"

CHAPTER TWENTY-THIRD.

THE MECHANIC HERO OF BRANDYWINE.

THE Blacksmith was returning home.

As he went through the dim old forest, the light shone over his broad chest, now throbbing beneath the rude vest, stained with the blood of battle while his muscular right arm, bared to the shoulder, grasped the massive hammer. crimsoned to the very handle which he clutched, with the life current of the slain.

The Blacksmith was returning home, and a smile lighted up his bluff face, a beam of joy shone from his clear grey eye.

He was returning home, but not to the home of Dilworth Corner––ah no !

Let me tell you a secret of that rude Blacksmith's heart.   One year ago he married a young wife, and took her to the rented cottage of Dilworth Corner.   But since the last spring, he had been strangely absent from home, for an hour or more each day.   Nay, his occasional holidays were spent away from his wife ; he would leave his cottage early in the morning, and not return until the dusk of evening.   When he returned his brow was flushed, his frame wearied.   He then replied to the anxious queries of his wife, with a smile, and while she gathered her arms about his neck, and in that soft, persuasive voice, which a young woman and a young wife knows how to use so well, ask the cause of these mysterious departures from home, the hale blacksmith would laugh quietly to himself, and close her mouth with a kiss.

This mystery, these strange departures from home, had continued until last night, when the secret was explained in the most remarkable manner. The wife had been on a visit to one of her relations, and it was almost night when her husband came to bring her home.

They were passing along the forest road together—a babe prattling all the while in the mother's arms—when suddenly emerging from the shade of the trees, their eyes were delighted with a sight of singular beauty.

It was a quiet cottage, nestling away there, in a dim nook of the forest road, a quiet cottage, overshadowed by a stout chesnut tree, with a small garden in front, a well-pole rising into light on one side, while on the other through the thickly gathered foliage, was seen the rude outlines of a blacksmith's shop.

There was something so beautiful in this sight, that the young wife uttered a cry of delight, nay even the babe, attracted by the mother's voice, clapped its little hands and laughed aloud.

That garden, planted with beautiful flowers, and divided by a gravelled walk, the cottage with its casement half hidden among vines, the roof overshadowed by a giant chesnut tree, its broad green leaves shining in the last ray of the setting sun—ah, it was a quiet cottage, a dear home in the wilderness, where a man might toil hard for a whole life, and toil with pleasure, love his wife, and seek no joy but that which shone from her blue eyes, and die at last with children's faces around his head.

It was a lovely sight, and the young wife sighed as she whispered, what a pretty home it would make for a new married pair! Then she pointed to the trees that gathered around it, on every side, and drawing near the neatly-whitewashed fence, which separated the garden from the road, she uttered a new exclamation of delight. There, in the midst of the flowers, a clean spring bubbled forth, and sparkled along the garden until it was lost in the shade of the wood.

The wife sighed again! It was like a fairy tale, this cottage springing up so unexpectedly, in the centre of the wood. Who were the tenants of the quiet home? Happy people no doubt, for it were a kind of blasphemy to imagine that a single care might enter that cottage door. Happy people no doubt, who prayed to God every night and morning, loved their neighbors, and never cared a throb for death.

The young wife sighed, the babe catching gloom from its mother's face began to cry. The stout blacksmith said not a word, but leading his wife along the brown walk, pushed open the cottage door, and in a thick voice, bade her look upon her home!

Her home? Yes her new home! He had purchased a piece of ground, hoarded his earnings for a year, to employ the carpenter and mason; worked himself full many an hour, there in the garden and about the cottage, and now his arduous task was done. That very day he had removed the furniture from Dilworth Corner thither; the wife sat down in her new home, with her babe reflecting back again the smile of joy, which came over her young face, as she kissed the brown face of the blacksmith from his forehead to his chin.

There was a Joy, born there in that cottage, in the moment when the wife sat down in her new home, such as never crossed the doors of all the marble palaces, built in the sweat and blood of millions, since the world began.

It was their home, their *own!* Ah that was the charm! Never to leave that home, until the reverent hands of neighbors bore them to the Quaker graveyard, and laid them gently under the green sod. That was a thought to swell the heart of the young wife, and make the stout blacksmith turn aside and look into a closet to hide his tears.

In the moment of their joy, Iron Tom arose, and told his young wife that he must away to the camp of Washington. It was true he cared but little for battle, or war, so long as his stout arm, plying the hammer or the anvil, might gain bread for his wife and child, but he had overheard the plot of some Tory refugees, for the surprise and capture of Washington. Now careing but little for the panic which shook the valley, our stout blacksmith had a sneaking kindness for this man Washington, whose name rung on the lips of all men.   He was resolved to hurry to Chadd's Ford, and there tell the Rebel Chief the plots of his enemies.

So bidding his wife a hasty good-bye and kissing the babe, that slept on her bosom, smiling as it slept, he hurried away.   He reached the camp, but event crowding on event detained him till morning.   Then the fight of the Ford gloomed over the valley ; the brave blacksmith, as we have seen, could not resist the impulse of his heart.   He joined the conflict, and fought in the bloody waters of the Brandywine.   That conflict over, he was returning home, when the corse of Mary Mayland calling for vengeance awoke the devil in his heart, and sent him madly over the battle-field, offering many a bloody sacrifice to her ghost, with the fatal hammer in his hand.

That hammer red with British blood, his face and garments also stained, now that the first fiery tumult of the fight was past, he was at last returning home.

The sun half way down the western sky, shot his beams along the forest path, illumining his honest face with its kindly glow, as he hurried fast along.

Some few paces beyond, the bye-road took a sudden turn, around a stout oak, hoary with the honors of three hundred years.

The Blacksmith beheld the venerable tree, and felt his heart grow warm, for right beyond that oak was *his home!*

With this thought warming his heart, he hurried onward ; thinking all the while of the calm young face and mild blue eyes of that wife, who the night before had stood at the cottage door, waving him out of sight, with a beckoned good-bye—thinking all the while of the babe, who hung sleeping on her bosom, smiling in its sleep, he hurried on, he reached the oak, he looked upon his home ——

Ah, what a sight was there !

There, where the night before, he had left a peaceful cottage, smiling under a chesnut tree, in the light of the setting sun, there was now only a heap of black and smoking ruins, and a burnt and blasted tree !

This was his home !

For a moment the Blacksmith stood with folded arms surveying the ruins of his home, but that moment past a smile broke over his face.

He saw it all !   In the night his home had taken fire and been burnt to inders, but his wife, his child had escaped.   For that he thanked God !

He did not despair—not he !   With the toil of his stout arm, he could build another and a better home for wife and child.   He would plant a love lier garden there ; fairer flowers should bloom around the casement, the chesnut tree might flourish again, or a luxuriant vine gay with blossoms, would twine over the cottage roof ——

As he stood there, in the glow of the declining sun, with this resolve kindling over his face, a hand was laid upon his shoulder—a cold, stiff hand, that chilled his blood——

He turned and gazed upon the face of a neighbor.   It was a neighbor's face, but there was an awful agony wreathing over those plain features and flashing from those dilating eyes—there was a supernatural woe, heaving in that farmer's bosom, and speaking in the convulsive motion of those lips, that moved and moved, but made no sound.

The farmer tried to speak the horror which convulsed his features, but in vain.   Still that convulsive motion of the lips, without a sound !   At last urging the blacksmith along the brown walk of the garden, in silence he pointed to the smoking embers.

There, amid the ashes of his home, the blacksmith beheld a dark object flung over the wreck of his hearthstone—a dark mass of burnt flesh and blackened bones.

——" Your wife !" shrieked the farmer, as his agony found words, " Your wife—" and he pointed to that hideous thing.   " The British, they came in the night, they ——"

——He spoke the outrage which heart grows cold to think upon, which the tongue is palsied, but to name ——

" They burned your house.   They flung the dead body of your wife into the flames.   They dashed her babe against the hearthstone."

This was the farmer's story.

And there stood the Husband, the Father, gazing upon that mass of burnt flesh and blackened bones—all that was once his wife !

Last night, only last night, he had brought her to her new home, the babe smiling on her bosom, and now ——

Do you ask me for the words that quivered from his white lips ?   Do you ask me, whether a light like the glare of a Lost Soul, blazed from his eye ?

I cannot tell you.

But I can tell you, that there was a hand upraised to heaven, that a vow went up to God !

Yes, as the warm sunshine streamed over the peeled skull of that fair young wife—she was that only last night,—up to the blue sky there went a vow, the last groan of a maddened heart.

Do the spirits of the VAST UNKNOWN ever look down upon the scenes of this world ?   Then was that vow written down by the angels of God !

How was it kept, this awful vow, thrilling through the still air, up to God ?

Go there to the battle of the Brandywine, in its last and bloodiest hour ! Wherever the fight is thickest, wherever the carnage is most bloody, there, may you see a stout form, striding madly on, there may you see a strong arm, lifting a huge hammer into light.   It is the blacksmith's form.   Where that hammer falls it kills, where that hammer strikes it crushes.

And the war-cry he shrieks as he goes on in his terrible career !   Is it a

bois erous shout, a wild hurrah ? Is it but a mad cry of vengeance, heaving upward from his breaking heart?

Ah, no, ah no !

It is the name of MARY.

It is the name of his young wife.

Mary ! Thou mild-faced Mother of Jesus, beaming upon me now, even
in the darkness of this midnight gloom, beaming upon me, with those large
full eyes, divine as the eyes of a mother, loving as those of a sister, Mary !
That name of thine is musical at all times, for it stirs the heart with its twin
syllables of rippling melody, for its calls up the forms of loved ones, now
dead and gone home, for it speaks of the dim long ago, when the tears of
the Virgin Mother watered the paths of the Redeemer, for it speaks of all
that is like God, in our love for woman ! Mary ! That name is full of
deep, low-toned music at all times, amid all memories, but it never rang on
the air, with such startling emphasis, as when it quivered from the white
lips of the Blacksmith of Brandywine !

"Mary !" he shouts, as he strikes yon red-coated Britain down—"Mary !"
he shrieks, as with one blow he hurls yon tinselled soldier from his steed—
"Mary !" quivers from his lips, as that fatal hammer sinks into the skull of
yondering cowering wretch—"Mary," still Mary ! as his form is last in the
clouds of battle !

Thus like a man possessed by a demon, his breast bared, his arm rising
and falling with a terrible impulse, he fought his way back to the Quaker
graveyard, until he was encircled by a wall of dead, still rushing on the
British with glaring eyes, and shouting Mary as the hammer fell.

Look yonder—in the centre of the combat—amid heaps of dying and
dead—look yonder and behold a terrible scene.

A young officer, with floating locks of golden hair, kneels on the blood-
stained sod, and clasps the blacksmith by the knees.

"Spare me !" he shrieks, "Quarter ! I have a wife—a child in England
—spare me !"

Then a tear stood in the eye of the frenzied blacksmith ; the hammer
hung suspended in the air.

"A wife—a child," he muttered, wiping the blood from his eyes. "I had
a wife and child once, and ——" he could not speak the outrage, but his
wife, his child were there before his burning eyes—"And I could spare you,
but d'ye see ? The form of that wife has gone before me all day—she is
there, now, there ! She calls on me to strike ! Mary !"

And the hammer fell. There was a mangled body on the sod of the
Quaker graveyard ; the wife and child in England, never beheld that gallant
soldier again.

Then as if this deed had fired his veins with new energy, the Blacksmith rushed on again, and the hammer rose and fell, as though at every blow it struck an echoing anvil, instead of a human skull.

At last, sinking down in the centre of that graveyard, the blood streaming from his many wounds, his face, his hands, his hammer red, he wiped the blood from his eyes, and as though speaking to some one by his side, faintly muttered " Mary !"

In the terrible hour of the retreat, when the din of battle brayed far away to the south, he was found sitting by the roadside, his leg broken, his head sunken on his breast, the blood streaming from his many wounds.

It was in a dark pass, where the narrow road was fenced in by high banks on either side ; a dark pass, now growing darker with the gloom of twilight.

Here he was found by a waggoner, who had at least shouldered a cart whip in his country's service. The good-hearted fellow would have placed him in his wagon and borne him from the field, but the stout blacksmith refused. All he asked was to be placed at the foot of a cherry tree, that rose above the roadside.

" Yo' see my neighbor—" said the Blacksmith in that voice husky with death, " I never meddled with the British 'till they began to burn our houses and murder old men like dogs ! and last night, they, they ——" he could not speak that foul outrage, but his wife and her babe were there before his dying eyes—" And now I've but five minutes life in me, and all I ask is a rifle, a powder horn, and three balls. And d'ye see that ar' cherry tree ? D'ye think you could lift a man of my build up thar ?"

The waggoner placed him there, and placed a rifle in his grasp, with the powder horn and balls by his side. Then whipping his horses through the narrow pass, he reached the summit of the hill into which it rose, and looked down upon the last scene of the blacksmith's life.

There lay the stout man, at the foot of the cherry tree, his head sunken on his breast, the rifle in his grasp, his broken leg hanging over the bank, pattering its warm blood upon the brown earth below.

The shades of night began to fall. The sun was setting, but the woods were thick and dark.

There he lay with the life-blood welling from his many wounds—he was dying.

Suddenly a strange sound reached his ear ! It was the wild hurrah of British soldiers ; that sound called him back to life. He raised his head, he grasped his rifle. Soon breaking into view, one glittering array of crimson and steel, a band of British thronged the pass, mad with carnage and thirsting for blood. They pursued a scattered band of Continentals, who turning in their flight, fought their pursuers with weaponless hands. On came the British ; an old man with grey hair, a veteran officer hastened them with shouts, and waved the way with his sword.

41

The Blacksmith raised his rifle—with an eye bright with death, he took the aim, he fired !

" That's for Washington !" he shrieked, as the grey-haired officer fell dead among his men.

Again with that eye brightening, with that hand stiffening in death, he loaded, he fired his rifle.

" That," he shrieked in his husky voice, " that is for Mad Antony Wayne !" And the pursuing British rode over another officer, trampling his face with their horses' hoofs.

On swept the scattered Continentals, on came the British, now turning their eyes and swords toward the wreck of a man, who placed at the foot of yonder tree, dealt death among their ranks. They rushed toward the bank, with shouts and curses. While the Continentals swept on their way. a fair-visaged Briton spurred his steed toward the cherry tree, his brown hair waving back from his brow

As he came, the blacksmith looked upon his young face, with glazing eyes. As he came, with that hand strong with the feeling of coming death, the sturdy freeman sitting under yonder cherry tree, again loaded, again raised his rifle.

He fired his last shot. The young officer swayed to and fro, and then with the blood spouting from the wound between his eyes, lay writhing on the sand.

A tear quivered in the eye of the dying blacksmith.

At that moment the last gleam of the setting sun, poured over his face, lighting up his fearful eyes.

" And that ——" he cried in a husky voice, that strengthened into a shout—" And that's for ——"

The shout died on his white lips. His voice was gone. His head sunk ; his rifle fell.

A single word bubbled up with his dying groan.

——Even now, methinks I hear that word, that last sigh of a broken heart, echoing and trembling there, amid the woods of Brandywine !——

That word was—" MARY !"

CHAPTER TWENTY-FOURTH.

THE GOBLET.

THE Lady Isidore stood with the goblet raised to her lips, while Percy with one foot advanced and hands half raised, gazed in her face, with a look of blank despair.

Blanche looked from one face to the other, with an expression of wonder and fear. Now she beheld the beautiful girl, with her olive cheek and full dark eyes, standing motionless as marble, the goblet raised to her lip, while her black hair fell in glossy waves over her virgin bosom—this was a strange yet lovely picture. Then turning her gaze, she beheld the livid face of the young Lord, his form cowering back, as though stricken by an unseen hand, yet with one foot advanced, and half upraised hands, trembling with a gesture of horror—this was a dark, yes, a terrible picture.

A sweet sad smile stole over the face of Isidore.

Percy gasped for breath.

" Give me the goblet—do not, do not drink !"

" Is it not beautiful, this sparkling water ?" Isidore replied, with a gentle inclination of her head. " This water from the fountain yonder, is it not beautiful ?"

Percy shuddered. He shuddered and covered his face with his trembling hands.

" Do not drink," he gasped, his livid face now covered with burning blushes. " It is poison !"

Blanche felt a cold shudder pervade her frame. " Poison !" she echoed, turning from one face to the other. Isidore replied with a light laugh that chilled her blood.

" Poison ?" And her long black hair waved in glossy undulations about her neck and bosom. " Oh, no—not poison ! This is a sorry jest, my lord.

Her dark eyes pierced his inmost soul, as looking up between his trembling hands, he saw the goblet gleaming in the sun.

Then those dark eyes were raised to heaven, her lips murmured as if in prayer. While the breeze bore her long hair back from her bosom, she placed the goblet once more to her lips.

" I am athirst, my lord," she said, " Methinks there is strange virtue in this goblet, not only for the fever of the blood, that burns the veins, but for the agony that tears the life-chords of the soul ! Look, my lord, is it not beautiful—I drink !"

She drank, and dashed the empty goblet on the floor.

Percy fell on his knees.

Blanche felt a horror worse than death, glooming darkly over her soul.

Isidore stood, her dark eyes glaring with new lustre, as she crossed her hands upon her bosom, and looked up to heaven.

The sunshine poured over the scene, lighting up the pale face of Blanche, mellowing the dark locks of the kneeling man with a golden glow, and gathering like a halo around the floating tresses of Isidore.

A deep silence rested on the air, for a single moment.

Percy raised his head, and in a tone of wringing agony, shrieked the name of Jesus.

"O, Christ, Saviour of sinners, let me die!" he groaned. "For I have murdered this angel,—this angel, who followed my path for three thousand miles—who endured the storm and battle for my sake—who loved me with a love, fathomless as Eternity!"

Blanche looked still, from one face to the other, with dilating eyes. This scene was too horrible for belief.

"Blessed Mary, awake me from this hideous dream!" she whispered, clasping her hands.

Isidore slowly advanced. Her brow was radiant, but her face had become pale as death, while her dark eyes larger and brighter every moment.

"George, arise!" she said, in a voice whose deep music rung like the accents of a spirit, on the air, "Arise, and behold your bride!"

She took his hand within her own, and placed it within the hand of Blanche. Blanche and Percy started with the same shudder, for the hand of Isidore was cold as death.

"Arise, George and behold your bride! Love him Blanche, for he is young, and gallant and brave! Swear to me Blanche,—to me, who will soon be dead and cold—that you will love him, that you will be his bride?"

She bent over the bed; her eyes now glaring with a terrible lustre, shone into the soul of Blanche.

"Swear that you will be his bride?"

Blanche beheld those glaring eyes fixed on her face, she felt the hot breath of Isidore upon her cheek, her cold hand laid upon her own, and then shrank cowering back upon the bed, her brain whirling in mad confusion.

"I cannot, cannot love him!" she gasped.

Meanwhile, Percy kneeling on the floor, one hand mechanically extended toward Blanche, the other veiled his eyes from the light, listened to the words of Isidore, with all the apathy of despair.

"Not love him," exclaimed Isidore, "And he so gallant, so brave? Oh, Blanche, listen to the prayer of a dying woman! With my last breath, I beseech you, love him. Love him through life, be near him in sorrow and in joy, let your hand minister to his wants in sickness, and when death comes, gathered in each other's arms, sink gently in the grave. Then Blanche, O, then I will await you yonder!"

She pressed their hands together to her breast and looked up to heaven. Blanche gazed in her face and shuddered. The poison had commenced its fearful work, That face so deathy pale, the eyes dilating with a burning glare, the cheek crimsoned by a single spot of livid purple, the lips changing to a deep unnatural red, the moisture starting from the brow, the bosom quivering with short, tremulous pulsations——ah, Death, had touched that beautiful face, that young bosom with his icy fingers.

Isidore sank on her knees, and took the hands of Percy within her own.

"Do you remember George, the olden time? When we were children together, when hand clasped in hand, we wandered through the halls of Monthermer? Ah, was it not a dear and happy time?"

Percy uttered a groan of agony. That voice of low deep music, that look of immortal love, took his soul by storm.

"Tell me George, do you remember the winding walk, that lead through the park, down to the fountain? And then the fountain, how often in the deep hush of a summertwilight, we sat by its waters, and talked of the dim future? The waters of that fountain were sweet, George, but sweeter far, the waters of yonder spring!"

"And I have murdered you!" groaned Percy, with a livid face, and starting eyeballs.

"Do you remember the old hall, hung with armour, George, where together we sat for long, long hours, our eyes fixed upon the moth-eaten page of some old-time Romance? Together, we drank in the legends of brave deeds, courage that dared not only the shock of war, but the dungeon-cell, and the unwept grave? Deathless love too, George, we read of it, there! Love that lifted poor mortal things into immortality, and made the heart swell with the rapture of eternal life—oh, George, do you remember?"

"I do—I do! Yes, Isidore the Past comes home to me now, but that Past is terrible, for it is armed with a lash of serpent tongues! Then Isidore we loved, we were happy, for we knew not the world——"

"Knew not the world? Ah, that is the secret after all! For the world is cold and dreary George, for the world crushes in us all that is holy, while it nourishes the demon, *self!* I will leave the dark, drear world, George, but you will live! O, promise me, when fair arms twine about your neck, and the kiss of Blanche is on your lip, promise me, that you will sometimes think of me. That you will plant one flower above my grave, in memory of the past?"

"Eternal Father, have mercy!" shrieked Percy, tearing his hands from the grasp of Isidore. "This torture is worse than death, more terrible than the damnation beyond the grave!"

He sprang to his feet, and grasped his sword.

"I am a murderer! Yes Isidore, your murderer! In return for that love, which reached its arms through space, to grasp my soul, I gave you neglect, indifference, heartless wrong. And now I have murdered you. Yet will I redeem my life of folly and crime, by one good deed. You will die Isidore, but I only ask that my life-blood may be poured out at your feet !"

His sword gleamed in the sunshine. The point was at his heart, while his hand clutched the blade, half-way from the hilt.

" Come Isidore—we die !"

With the last impulse of life, she sprang to her feet, she seized the sword, she dashed it to the floor.

At this moment she looked divine !

The breeze wafted her long black hair aside from her pale face ; the sunshine streamed in softened light, over her snowy bosom. Her dark eyes shone with the light of death. Her form, so magnificent in its voluptuous beauty, seemed about to rise hovering in the air, for every nerve quivered, every pulse throbbed with strange life ; her small delicate feet, did not appear to touch the floor.

" George," she said taking his hands to her bosom, " Live ! Be happy ! Blanche will be your bride !"

And the breeze tossed her long black hair over his hands, and along her bosom. That bosom was cold as ice. Percy shuddered, as the dying girl in her last phrenzy, passed his trembling hands along its snowy surface.

" Blanche—George ! In death, I unite you ?"

With low sad tones, she said these words, and sank gently on the floor.

She lay in an attitude of slumber, her cheek resting on her arm, while her glassy eyes, half closed, were like the eyes of one awaking from a pleasant dream. Not a throb disturbed the marble stillness of that bosom. Her lips gently parted, disclosed the ivory whiteness of her teeth. Her long hair, as black and beautiful as ever, lay in glossy waves about her face and over her form.

She was dead.

The Lady Isidore of Monthermer, for whom rank, power, and wealth, were waiting far away, now lay a corse, in the unknown cottage of Brandywine.

Beauty and tenderness and truth had *gone home.*

Blanche did not shriek, nor sob, nor even groan. Silently she sank on the floor, and cast her form upon the bosom of the dead girl, kissing her cold lips, and closing her glassy eyes.

Percy gazed upon this scene, with eyes as fixed and death-like as those of the corse. His stiffened arms dropt by his side. He stood like a figure of stone, half warmed into life, by some terrible spell. No groan came from his lips, not a tear moistened his dark eye. An awful change was passing over his soul.

Meanwhile the tears of Blanche, showered down over the pale face of the dead.

" O, she is not dead !" she murmured, kissing the cold lips, " Death could not touch a form like this, a heart like hers ! So young, so beauti fu.; her voice, I hear it yet; she is not dead! Isidore—awake! I will love you! Did you not call me sister?"

A wild, dread laugh, echoed through the chamber. Blanche sprang to her feet. She beheld Percy, standing before her with his sword in his hand, while his dark eyes glared on her, from the paleness of his livid face.

Again that wild laugh thrilled through the room.

"Come," he said in a mocking whisper, "She has said it! You are my bride! Death will unite us!"

"God save me now!" murmured Blanche, stricken with horror, as she retreated slowly from the madman.

"You are her murderer! Your eyes, lured me to ruin. Your voice made me forget honor, faith, love. You have been my evil angel. By the soul of Isidore, you must die!"

He slowly advanced, while his sword gleamed in the sunshine. Blanche beheld his glaring eyes, his white lips, quivering over his set teeth, and felt that her hour was come. Beside the body of the dead girl, she fell on her knees. With upraised eyes, and clasped hands, she awaited the blow.

Percy advanced, he raised his sword, the keen point glittered above her breast!

At this moment as he stood, with clenched lips and nerving his arm for the blow, his eye attracted by a faint sound, wandered with a side-long glance to the door.

A mad howl rang through the room, as with his sword upraised, he sprang toward that door.

"At last!" he shrieked, "At last the hour has come!"

There, in the door-way, with his dark plume drooping over his brow, stood Randulph Waldemar, gazing in mute surprise, upon the strange scene before him. That gaze of fixed wonder, lasted but for a moment. His sword, gleaming in his hand, he sprang forward, and stood face to face with Percy.

"Thrice I have spared your life. Thrice I have warned you. Now we meet for the last time!"

"Come on! I am ready for you, now! You have been a shadow in my path, a doom upon my life. Now one of us must die!"

Not a word more, but swords gleamed in the light, arms rose and fell, two forms moved hurriedly over the floor. Now beside the body of the dead girl, now by the wall, now in shadow, and now in light, that terrible, combat was maintained.

Blanche shrank affrighted, into a dim corner of the room. Veiling her eyes from the sight, she prayed to God.

At last the clashing of swords was succeeded by a sudden silence. Blanche looked up and beheld Randulph standing over the prostrate form of Percy, his sword presented to his throat. The long hair of Randulph swept aside from his brow, disclosed the outlines of his face, stamped with all the energy of revenge. Slowly, as if concentrating his soul for that blow, he raised his sword. Percy looked upward, with rolling eyes.

"Spare me!" he shrieked, "I will die, but not by your hand!"

"No! I have sworn it, by my mother's name! That oath cannot be broken. You must die!"

He struck, but his blow was aimless, for a young form lay panting on his breast, a woman's arms were round his neck. The sword swayed aside from its aim, sunk in the floor.

"Spare his life!" said Blanche, looking upward into Randulph's face, "For my sake spare him!"

It was hard to resist that pleading voice, that eloquent look, but Randulph slowly unwound her arms from his neck, thrust her gently aside, and clutched his sword with a firmer grasp.

"The voice of God has spoken, Blanche! He must die!"

He advanced, but Percy with one bound, sprang from the floor, and through the open door. With a terrible oath, Randulph pursued him. In a moment, Blanche heard the sound of horse's hoofs echoing through the forest. She looked from the window, and by the light of the setting sun, beheld two golden hued horses dashing madly, not for the forest road, but for the thick shadow of the interwoven boughs. She beheld the forms of their riders, their green velvet uniform, their long hair waving on the wind. One, with his face turned over his shoulder, looked mockingly in his pursuer's face, while a pistol rose in his clenched hand. Blanche saw this but for an instant, for that instant passed, the horses with their riders crashed through the thickly woven boughs, and were gone.

Blanche again sank on her knees beside the form of Isidore. She was about to press her lips to the cold cheek of the dead, when her eyes were riveted to an object by her side. It was a pacquet of dark parchment, fastened with a massive red seal. That seal was broken by a sword-thrust and stained with blood.

"It fell from Percy's breast in the moment of the combat," whispered Blanche, and then guided, not by chance, but by the same awful hand which from the invisible world, had governed the course of this fatal day, she opened the pacquet and read. Many papers were there, enclosed in that parchment, with its broken seal, and Blanche read with gasping breath and dilating eyes. At last, a word written there in bold characters, fired her soul; she sprang to her feet, with an exclamation of horror.

"May God have mercy upon me, in this hour." she shrieked, rushing toward the door, "I will yet turn aside the hand of fate!"

She stood in the cottage door, her hands pressed to her forehead, while her pale face glowed in the light of the declining sun. Her very soul was rent by the pangs of an agony, more terrible than death, when she remembered the contents of that fatal pacquet.

As she stood there, her pale face glowing in the light of the setting sun, a traveller mounted on a grey horse, came riding from the shadows of the forest road. By his horse's side, an aged woman, dressed in the old-time costume, her white hairs covered by a high cap, walked hastily along.

"Hurry Sir, hurry, I beg o' you,"—Blanche heard the old woman scream at the top of her voice. "Dr. Smith, you see is sick, and the poor girl is wounded. I left her more than an' hour ago. Though you aint a doctor, you may be of help. Here we are—hey, what's this? The wounded girl standing at the cottage door?"

The traveller came slowly through the garden, and reined his steed beside the porch. Blanche beheld a mild-faced man, whose brow was shadowed by a broad-rimmed hat. His tall form, moulded in all the imposing proportion of mature manhood, was enveloped in a loose-fitting grey overcoat, which descended below his boot-tops.

Blanche sprang forward and grasped the stirrup of the stranger. In a low voice, with a hurried utterance, she poured forth the broken details of a dark history. The stranger bent down, his mild face manifesting a deep interest in her words, and gently lifted the maiden from the ground. Blanche, grasping the pacquet with her right hand, while the stranger's arm, held her firmly in the saddle, pointed to the north.

"Come, Sir—in the name of God! We must lose no time! Even now it may be too late to save them! O, Sir, let us away!"

The stranger gathered his arm around the form of the frenzied girl, and spurred his steed toward the wood. In a moment, the thick boughs received them in their shadow.

"Well," exclaimed the old lady, gazing upon the boughs which rustled and shook as they disappeared, "If that aint clever! To think that sich a fine-looking gentleman would run away with a girl in that style! And she wounded too! Well, well, this world aint what it was, when I was a girl! No more it aint!"

With this consolatory remark, the aged dame entered the cottage, and looked through the doorway of the northern chamber. She stood spell-bound with horror.

The mild light of the setting sun fell over the pale face and white bosom of the dead girl. The attitude of unconscious slumber, which her form assumed in the death struggle, displayed in striking loveliness, its beautiful proportions; the fulness of the bust, the roundness of the limbs and arms, the faultless elegance of that voluptuous shape, now cold in death forever. Her eyes half closed as if awakening from some pleasant dream, the parted lips revealing a glimpse of the ivory teeth, the showering black hair, ah, she was beautiful in life, but in death, magnificently beautiful, the brave and loving Isidore.

Come, let us bid her farewell. Come let us kneel in the softened light

43

and twine our hands in the glossy waves of her da.k hair, and close her
eyes and lips, with kisses, let us gently dispose those faultless limbs in the
quiet attitude of death—for to-morrow, ah, the coffin, the grave, the falling
clod! Let us smooth the black hair in lengthened waves, but do not close that
bosom from the light. Let it gleam in the sun, until the very last moment;
for it is pure, for thoughts born of God and eternal as heaven, once found a
home, within those globes of snow. Farewell, Isidore, we leave you now
forever. Farewell Isidore, we leave your face to the grave-worm, your
bosom to the clod, your soul to its home. Farewell, brave and beautiful,
on your cold brow we drop no tear, for since the world began, it has been
the fate of hearts like yours, to love and break and die. And when the
flowers bloom over your grave, the breezes of God will kiss them, and
fling their fragrance like blessings upon the summer air.

Crashing through the forest, the grey horse of the stranger, at last
emerged into open day. From the verge of the Wilderness, a field of snow-
white buckwheat, sloped down into a dim valley, through whose shadows
gleamed a quiet brook.

" Look, yonder they ride! Yonder far down the hill, those two soldiers,
mounted on golden-hued steeds! The one who rides first, is Percy : the
other, Randulph! Look, Percy turns, a pistol in his hand, ah, that sound,
that smoke; he fires! Randulph—Father in heaven—does he fall! No,
no! He spurs on, he nears Percy's side, ha! They cross the brook and
enter the wood!"

The stranger made no reply to these frenzied exclamations, but gathering
the form of Blanche closer in his arms, spurred his grey horse, swiftly over
the field. His clear blue eye shone with a fire, as deep and wild as the
dark eye of the maiden. A terrible stake hung on this race, a stake of life
and death, aye, more than life or death.

" On my brave horse, on : we must overtake these men, at every hazard !
A moment's interview, but a word and they are saved ! But should a combat take place, should one fall by the other's sword—then God pity the sur-
vivor ! His remorse will be a thousand times more terrible than death."

The gallant steed dashed over the field, trampling down the white buckwheat, and flinging the brown earth against his flanks at every spring. It
was magnificent to see that manly stranger, girdling the white-robed girl in
his muscular arm, as they dashed down the hill. For a few moments the
sun shone warmly over his wild countenance, now lit up with a feverish ex
citement, over the pale face of Blanche her upraised hand grasping the pacquet, and then they passed into the deep shadows of the valley.

Down into the valley, over the brook, up through the thick wood, and
forth again, upon a wide-stretcl.ing field of summer green ; Blanche leaned
over the horse's neck with starting eyes, and beheld the two horses and
their riders !

They entered a wood, which cast its deep shadows from the opposite extremity of the field, ere Blanche had time to turn to the stranger's face, and with her eyes beseech him to hurry on.

Over the field, another wood, a valley, on and on! Those two golden-hued steeds, their riders still in sight! On and on! The white foam hangs round the nostrils of the grey horses, and flecks his heaving flanks. Still the stranger urges him on, still Blanche with upraised hand grasps the pacquet, and bids him hasten for the love of God.

At last the summit of a gentle hill is gained, and the stranger halts his steed for an instant, and gazes on the magnificent view before him.

Like the creation of some fairy dream, that beautiful valley, that rude Quaker temple, those far stretching plains, the massive hill overlooking valley and plain, the distant Brandywine, seen only in broken glimpses, burst on their eyes.

"Look, they near the Quaker graveyard! Randulph leans over his horse's neck and fires! Ha! Percy's horse falls, and now he is down! On, on, for the sake of heaven—oh, * * * we will be too late! Now Percy rises again; he fires, Randulph's horse totters, falls! Percy leaps the graveyard wall—Waldemar pursues him, with his sword gleaming in the sun!"

"It is but two hundred yards to the Quaker graveyard—we will be there in time!"

The stranger dug his spurs into the flanks of his steed. The gallant horse bounded forward like an arrow. The earth seemed to glide under his feet. Blanche started forward on his neck, and fixed her eyes upon the Quaker graveyard. She beheld two forms, standing erect amid dead bodies, their swords gleaming in the setting sun.

Then her shriek rang like the voice of madness, far upon the air, she raised the pacquet in the light, and with starting eyes and gasping breath beheld the distant swords, gleam brightly in the sun.

CHAPTER TWENTY-FIFTH.

THE LAST OF THE RIDERS.

LET me tell you the Legend of the Last of the Riders of Santee.

The scene was a rude hut, in the centre of thick wood. The time was the sunset hour, when broad belts of sunshine broke the shadows of twilight. Where are the gallant men who went forth to battle this morning?

A hundred bold riders went forth in the first gleam of the morning sun; brave men, with warm hearts throbbing beneath their velvet coats. Brave men with gallant steeds and gleaming swords! Where are they now? Arise Rangers of Santee, and speak to us; arise and shout your battle-cry once more; arise, for the Flag is forth upon the breeze, the sword gleams in the sun, arise, for the Eagle is yonder, sailing grandly in the blaze of the sunset sky. Ah—it is still, and sad and dead, this thick green wood. Ninety Riders are clay upon the battle field; ninety faces are frozen in death.

Hither to the shadows of this wood, came five men, the last of Randulph's gallant band. They throw themselves into yonder hut—hark! The shouts of the British are on the air. In this hut they await their hour. —Yes these brave men, in their coats of forest green, now rent by bullet and sword, and stained with blood, prepared to make a desperate defence against the pursuing British, when they were joined by two soldiers in the blue Continental uniform. One of these soldiers, with a bronzed visage, dark hair and eyes, was attired in the uniform of a Captain; his comrade, a man of muscular figure, with a ruddy face, sandy whiskers and light brown hair, wore the costume of a Major, in the Continental host.

Scarcely had the two strangers thrown themselves in the hut, already occupied by the five Rangers of Santee, when the sounds of pursuit thundered through the wood. In a moment, the hut was surrounded by British, some on horse, some on foot, some with gleaming swords, others with glittering bayonets, all thirsting for the blood of the gallant seven.

Yells, shouts, curses, arose from the British band, as they gazed upon the door of the hut, now bolted and secured, or glancing towards the logs, beheld a rifle projecting from every crevice. The Riders of Santee, the two Continental officers were destined for a sudden and merciless death.

" No Quarter to the —— rebels!" growled the British without.

" Let us die together!" was echoed from within.

For a long time, there was a dead pause. The British held their heads together, and took counsel, ere they began their work of murder. They passed to and fro along the green sward, under the shadow of the leaves, and yet the rebels did not fire. Their rifles peeped from every crevice, and yet not a single Briton bit the dust.

This strange silence awed the British. They had not perceived those projecting rifles, until the moment when they surrounded the hut. To retreat now, was dishonor to all, and death to many. But one course remained; to carry the log hut by storm.

Meanwhile, within the hut, long streaks of light flung through the crevices, dimly revealed the faces of the five Riders, the two Continental officers. The Riders were ashy pale; the officers regarded them with surprise.

"Why do you mutter together?" said the Captain, "Why look pale and tremble? Are you afraid?"

"Afraid!" echoed the Riders, in a tone of menace. "Do you say that to us?"

"But why all this whispering and muttering?" exclaimed the Major. "You don't seem to be at your ease anyhow."

The coolness of that stout Major was delightful.

"Let me ask you a question," said one of the Rangers, in a whisper. "How much powder have you?"

"One charge and that is in my rifle."

"And you?"

"But one charge, and that is in my rifle. Well?"

"We have not a single charge," said the Ranger, cooly, "And all we have to do, is to grasp our knives and fight like dogs."

"No powder!" echoed the Major.

"And there are at least fifty of those British devils, yelling on the outside!" exclaimed the Captain.

Here was a terrible prospect. But two charges of powder in the whole band, and fifty British yelling without the hut. This would have made the stoutest heart quiver.

"We will have to await our fate!" said the Captain, calmly. "When the lance begins, we will cut a few throats, anyhow!" cried the Major.

"We have liquor, at all events," said one of the Riders, and in the uncertain light which illumined the place, you might see the flask passing from lip to lip. The health of Prince Randulph, success to Washington, joy to their wives and little ones far away; these were the toasts of the Last five Rangers of Santee. The Captain and Major would not drink.

"I don't mind drinking at home," said the Captain, "But when it comes to dying, faith I'd prefer to die sober."

"Yes, its rascally to die drunk," responded the Major.

They both gazed through the crevices, watching the movements of the British. A confused noise was heard without, a crackling sound like dry wood flung suddenly on the earth, and then the trampling of many feet to and fro.

"What is it?" asked the Major.

"I don't know. The hole through which I am looking, is half-way between the floor and the roof. I can hear a noise around the walls, but I can't see."

" I'll tell you what it is," whispered the Major.

" Well —" exclaimed the Captain. The Riders of Santee listened. " They are placing dry wood around this hut. They are going to burn us out. That's what it is !"

The Riders uttered a spontaneous groan. The Captain placed his hand to his brow, and felt it cold with a sweat, clammy as the moisture on the brows of the dying.

Meanwhile, those ominous sounds grew louder, without the hut.

The dry wood crackled as it was thrown down, the British muttered together, as they hurried to and fro, and now and then a laugh was heard.

Meanwhile, within the hut, all was silent.

The Captain was thinking to himself. The Major was swearing in an almost inaudible tone. The five Rangers were grouped together, pale as death, their unloaded rifles in their hands.

Presently the crevices were clouded by a dark and heavy smoke. The sound of light wood crackling under the influence of a brisk fire, was heard.

" Now burn the —— rebels in their den !"

" That is complimentary !" growled the Major.

The Riders, rough veterans that they were, with torn coats and scared faces, said nothing. Those dear vallies of the Santee, where their wives and little ones were now waiting for them—ah, that was a thought to sadden any man, even a brave Ranger of Santee.

At last the Captain spoke.

" I have it !" he said. As he spoke, the flames flashed up between the crevices and the light of day. In a few moments the hut would be one mass of flame.

" There is a door to this place, a trap-door through the floor, and a chimney."

" Well," gasped the Major. The Riders gathered round.

" Two of us can dash through the door, into the midst of our foes, and, perhaps, mind I only say perhaps, win their lives by one bold effort. Two of us can climb the chimney ——"

" And then ?" whispered the Major.

" There is a stout oaken tree that hangs over the roof. From this tree, to the other trees is but a jump. It is not so difficult as the dash from the door, — and can be done."

" Well, the other three ?" faltered a veteran Ranger.

" I have been in this hut before," cooly replied the Captain. " That trap-door in the centre of the floor, descends into an under-ground passage. Follow that passage ten yards, and you will find yourself in a spring-house Rather cool, compared to this hot place, eh ?"

A murmur of delight was heard. That Captain was a jewel. Meanwhile the flames began to make themselves felt, as they flashed into the crevices, and twined among the rude logs. The place began to grow uncomfortably warm. In fact, it soon bore an unpleasant similarity to an oven

The perspiration rolled down the Major's cheeks; he puffed and blowed like a cow, who has innocently been eating nightshade with her clover.

"Come, it is time," said the Captain, "Who will dash out of the door?"

There was silence. It was a delicate question. Flames, troopers, swords, bayonets; these were unpleasant things to stare you in the face, when opening the front door of a forest hut.

"I and the Captain," said the Major, whose coolness was delightful. "Well. Who the chimney?"

"I and Jacob," replied one of the troopers, "Peter and Charles and Harry will take to the trap-door."

"Begin, for these flames are growing unpleasant," said the Captain. One by one, the troopers shook the hands of these brave officers, and then went to their tasks. The sound of the opening trap-door, and a noise in the chimney echoed around the room for a few moments, mingling with the roaring of the flames.

At last all was still. The flames roaring around the hut, flashed through each crevice, making the interior light as sunshine. The Captain saw the Major's ruddy face, with the blue eyes and light brown hair: the Major beheld the Captain's bronzed visage, with dark eyes and jet-black locks. Each face was bathed in the light of the flame.

"Hot?" said the Captain.

"Dev'lish!" responded the Major.

"Now," a shout resounded without, breaking the silence which had reigned for the last five minutes, "we'll burn these rebels in their nest."

"They have not discovered our comrades," whispered the Major.

"Good," said the Captain, "It is now time to act."

He walked toward the door, and applied his eye to a crevice. Through that crevice, between the undulating clouds of smoke, he beheld that wall of crimson and steel. The British, some on horse, some on foot, were ranged around the hut. All chance of escape was gone.

The Captain walked again to the Major.

You have a mother?"

"Yes, near Ephrata, in Lancaster county. A pretty place, too, with its monks and nuns and Monastery. Dev'lish cool too. Wish we had a little of it here—eh, Captain?"

"You'd better pray God to bless your mother, and be a comfort to her in her old days. I'm thinking of my sweetheart. How sorry she'll be?"

"What do you mean? Pray for my mother, thinkin' o' your sweetheart! Why you talk as if we were goin' to die!"

"Not to die exactly. But to be roasted alive."

The tone in which the Captain spoke, chilled the Major's blood. They sat down on the floor, looking in each other's faces. The smoke rolled in through the crevices; the air was suffocating.

All at once, a terrible cry thundered through the woods.

" They are escaping !" shouted a British soldier. Then there was the sound of men, hurrying to and fro, the trampling of horses' hoofs. One, two, three, hurrah ! Three shouts and a yell.

" Now Major !" The Captain put his foot against the door, and drew the bolt. " Are you ready ? Is your rifle in your grasp ?"

" Aye, aye." The Major stood ready by the door. As the Captain let go the bolt that door flew open, and a volume of flame rushed in the hut.

One bound, a hurrah, another spring ; the flames were passed. The Captain and Major stood on the green sward, beside the burning hut. At one glance, they looked around, and took in the details of their danger. Five British soldiers were watching there, while the others pursued the fly-ing Riders. Three stood with their musquets in their hands, the others stood watching two magnificent black horses, who were ranged beneath the trees, all ready for the march, an elegant saddle on each back, grim pistols in each holster.

" Two horses and five lobsters ! Fire !" shrieked the Major. They fired, and leaped, with knives in their hands. It was a noble fire, a magni-ficent leap ! Two Britons lay writhing on the sod ; our Captain and Major were seated each of them, in an easy saddle, striking right and left at the astonished soldiers who grasped each bridle-rein.

The Britons swore. The Captain cut with his knife, and spurred the black horse. The Major thrust with his blade, and sunk his boots into the ribs of his steed. Another moment, and away through the wood, away from the burning hut. One—two—three ! Hurrah, did you hear those shots ? One shaved a piece off the Captain's plume, another grazed the Major's nose, the third tipped his horse's ear. Hurrah, hurrah, they come ! Down this dark road, it is a winding road, with thick shade above, and a gravelled path below, down this dark road toward yonder shadowy glen ! Then our troopers laughed, then they yelled, then they rent the air with songs. Down into the dell, then along a winding road, then across the dim valley of the Brandywine, and then came another thick wood, into which their horses plunged, as though they were possessed of devils.

At last by a cool spring, not many miles beyond Chadd's Ford, they halted their steeds, and while the last rays of the setting sun stole through the trees, fastened their bridle-reins to neighboring trees, and sat down be-side the cool waters.

Then these gallant comrades took breath, and looked in each other's faces.

" How are you, Diller ?" asked the Captain.

" How are you, Lippard ?" responded the Major.

It was pleasant to see the glance which shot from their gleaming eyes, as they grasped each other's hands.

Presently the Captain drew forth from the portmanteau, which was hung behind his saddle, two bottles bearing this suspicious label—" Brandy !"

The Major replied by investigating his portmanteau, carefully suspended behind his saddle. He drew forth first some bread, in a white cloth, then some butter nicely folded between huge cabbage leaves, and then two chickens, cold, well roasted and delightful to look upon. Other dainties were also there, such as cold ham, delicately sliced, a box of anchovies, and a neat luncheon of crackers and cheese. In fact, it was the very jewel of a portmanteau. The Captain opened his wondering eyes, as the Major drew forth his treasures. The Major himself, was ready to cry for joy.

It was a festival, yes, a merry festival. The man that would condemn the wild wood feast of these brave men, who were hungry and athirst from the fiery toil of battle, would run like a whipt cur from the face of his country's foe, or sell the graveyard of his fathers' for building lots.

It was a festival, a joyous, heart-warm festival. The cloth was spread beside that clear cold spring, the chickens, the ham and anchovies were exposed to view ; the bottles shone grimly in the light, and our soldiers began their feast, beneath the shade of those grand old trees.

" Pretty well Captain John ?"

" Tolerable, Major Enos ?"

Many a toast was drunken, but at last as the shades of night sunk down, they gave—The memory of the brave Riders of Santee !

The words had not died on their lips, when a dim figure advanced from the shadows, toward the spring. A dim figure with a blood-stained visage, and uniform fluttering in rags.

"What! One of the Riders! Welcome comrade! Where's the others?"

" Here's Jacob and Peter. Charles and Harry will be here presently !"

Ten minutes passed.

There were seven happy men, seated beside that clear cold spring, filling the air with merry songs and hearty shouts, while their breakers sparkled gaily in the light.

And thus endeth this *Legend of the last of the Riders, and their brother's in arms. They are all gone now.—Their bones are scattered over the battle-fields of this great empire ; their souls are with the heroes of the Past.

This page alone, shall rescue their names, their deeds, from the silence of the grave which encloses their dust !

---

* The Captain named in this tradition, was John Frederick Lippard, grand-uncle of the author. The Major, Enos Diller, (a relative of General Diller, formerly Adjudant General of this State) was a brave soldier of the Revolution. Both these men distinguished themselves at the Battle of Brandywine. The other heroes of the legend, were members of Lee's partizan legion.—It may be as well to mention here, the fact, that the brave Preacher, whom I have introduced in the preceding pages, was none other than Hugh Henry Breckenridge, a sincere Christain and a pure patriot, who afterwards was the author of " Modern Chivalry," a work celebrated for its original humor and deep philosophy. He preached to the Continentals on the evening before the fight, and went with them to battle, the next day. After the war, he filled various posts of honor, with dignity and justice.

CHAPTER TWENTY-SIXTH.

A WORD TO YOU!

A WORD TO YOU!

Yes, ere we part, let me speak a word to you, my reader, from the silence of this room.—Yet do not read this word, until you have finished the last chapter.—

It is night, and I am about to close my task.   Soon the curtain will fall and the play be over.   But before we part, let me speak a word to you. Are you yet young with the bloom of life upon your cheek, the warm hope yet burning in your heart?   Or old with grey hairs, and one foot on the threshold of the grave?   Rich, with gold to lap your form in purple, or poor, with but a hard crust on the table, a flickering light to illuminate the gloom of your lonely home !

To you—rich or poor, young or old—with the same warm throb that swells the mother's heart, when she presses the last kiss on the forehead of her boy, as he stands upon the threshold of his native home—about to leave that home for the untried danger of the world—to you, do I dismiss this child of my soul.

It has been with me three years.   It was commenced in that golden time, when Honor is not a Romance, when Truth is not a bubble.   The time of illusions—hopes—air-built fancies of the future, the time when the heart is young, and the hand warm.   Amid joy and pain, love and sorrow, the loss of friends, the persecution of enemies, in every fluctuation of this great panorama—life—this book has been with me.   Now it must go forth, to kindle a throb in other hearts, or die neglected by the way.   Will you blame me then, if I crave to speak a parting word with you ?

Gleaming upon me, from the shadows of this room, a strange picture stares me in the face.   A strange picture full of light and gloom, pregnant with a mournful moral.

Here is the picture :

An artist has sunk to sleep, weary from labor, heart-broken from neglect, amid the darkness of his chamber, whose walls are hidden by thick shadows.   His head rests on his bent arm, and the arm upon a rude table.   A feeble light placed on that table, struggles with the shadows, and reveals the broken pitcher—the crust of bread.   On one side, near the sleeping artist, you see the canvass, already glowing with a divine Thought.   Farther back, deeper in the gloom, the white form of a statue, an Eve kneeling in lonely loveliness, glares on your eye, an image of beauty in that silent cell.   The artist sleeps, yet is he not alone.   He dreams.   Around him, breaking from the gloom, one by one, a long and solemn train, come the Masters of his

art, from the silence of ages. They gather round the able, the pitcher, the
flickering lamp and crust of bread ; dim, vague and shadowy, they smile
upon the sleeping artist. You see them stand in awful grandeur there ; and
as you look, a love for the sleeping Genius steals over you. The picture
fills you with a deep awe. You follow that spectral band, as they extend
into darkness and space, with a trembling eye. You look with pity on the
tired head, resting on the bent arm, with the flowing hair tinted by the faint
light. You would not awake that artist for the world, to the reality—the
hard crust, the broken pitcher. With a sigh, you bid him sleep on.

Such is the picture. It is before me now, as it has been for years. It
is connected with a painful story of a strong young heart, who painted this
picture, and then—neglected, heart-broken,—went sadly to the madman's
cell. There he has been for years, a ghastly wreck of genius. While I
write, he is slowly recovering his intellect, but at the same time, dying by
inches. Life and death shake hands with him at once ! It is a mournful
history ; a mournful picture.

Perhaps you ask me, why I speak of it now. I will tell you.

That picture, gleaming from the darkness of my room, forces painfully
upon my soul, the fate of Genius in every age.

The crust—the bowed head—the flickering lamp.

So reads the terrible Litany of Intellect in the every day world. To coin
its soul into glowing thoughts, and then stretch forth its hands and die. To
toil by night for man, and be trampled upon by day. To feel the agony
and not moan: to speak out certain brave words, which will never die, and
then creep quietly home—into the grave.

Is it not true ? Is it not enough to make the heart despair ?

Ah, sad and dark and bitter is the fate of the American Author.

He flashes for a moment, there—a falling meteor above the horizon of
life—and then hisses down into night, and is dark forever !

Or is he successful ? Then malice hunts and envy stabs him. Hideous
lizards, that crawl into a slimy eminence, hiss at him as he goes by. The
mercenary Press—the Libel—the Lie ; these are the bloodhounds tracking
every footstep of his way.

It is this consciousness my friends, that makes me sad. It is this painful reality that tells me now, that the labor and the love, which I have bestowed upon this work of the past, may all be in vain. Not that I fear
your critic with his microscopic soul, ah, no ! For I am familiar with the
truth of the homely reward—' when little dogs bark, they are hungry for a
bone.' The narrow-souled critic is not angry with you, when he assails
you with falsehood and darkens your path with slander. No. He is only
hungry. ' Your purse or your life !' He is a gentlemanly brigand, armed
with a pen instead of a stilletto.

It may be that this book will kindle a throb of joy in ten thousand hearts,
or sink unnoticed into oblivion.

If the former is the case, if it cheers one weary heart, or soothes the sadness of a single sick-bed, then am I rewarded.

If the latter—then be it so.

Then perhaps when I am dead and gone, some child of Genius, groping his way to fame, by the flickering lamp, his head bowed down, with but a crust to cheer his toil may chance to look upon this page, and read the record I have written here.

Then, if that child of Genius reads—and feels—and greets me as a Brother, then I will not have lived in vain.

My word to you is said.

CHAPTER LAST.

FATE, THE EXECUTIONER.

It was the sunset hour.

They met in the centre of the graveyard, amid the pale faces of the dead, illumined by the glow of the setting sun; they met for the last time, Randulph of Wyamoke, and George of Monthermer.

Percy stood with his right foot placed upon the breast of a dead man, awaiting the approach of Waldemar. His sword was clenched in his hand, while the breeze tossed his dark curls, softly aside from his pale brow. His dark eye glared with a fire like that which for a moment, ere the last struggle, gleams from the eye of a dying man.

"Come on Sir! It is the place and the hour. For the last time we meet. I have been driven to this accursed spot by the hand of fate, but here, on this doomed place of graves, will I battle for my life against you, and ——"

He paused, and looked shudderingly over his shoulder. The Phantom was there, the terrible shadow, that had glided by his side for days, scared sleep from his couch, and planted in his heart the undying agony of hell—dim and terrible, it stood between him and the sunset sky.

Randulph came on, slowly on, over the bodies of the dead. His sword was grasped in his right hand. The sunset streamed warmly over his bronzed visage, with its every lineament compressed like a face of marble, His long brown hair tossing on the evening breeze, disclosed the massive outlines of his forehead, darkened by a single swollen vein, that shot upward between the brows. The light in his clear hazel eyes was even more strange and brilliant than the wild glare of Percy. He came slowly on; he confronted Percy, with a single exclamation :

" You must die !" he said in a husky voice. A husky voice, but calm and cold, as a voice from the grave.

Percy replied by a glance of deep hatred, and then placed himself upon his guard.

They stood face to face, in the centre of the graveyard, their drawn swords gleaming in the sun.

The hour was terribly still.

The armies, pursuers and pursued, had swept far away to the south. The sun pouring his full glory from the western sky, shone along the sloping breast of Osborne's hill, over the graveyard wall, and the rude roof of the Quaker temple.

All was silent there, save the groan of anguish, the prayer of mortal agony, the low-toned mutterings of madness. From that temple, the dying strown around in heaps, sent up their fearful voices to God.

The graveyard, that place of green mounds, mellowed by the last glow of the setting sun, ah, here was indeed a ghastly sight. Pale faces, with glassy eyes and fallen jaws, mangled bodies with bleeding arms and shattered limbs, skulls rent and crushed, eyes scooped from the sockets, the image of God cut and carved, as a sculptor carves his marble, or a butcher his oxen—this was the vision illumined by the last ray of the setting sun.

That graveyard was crowded with dead bodies. The grass was rank and wet with blood. The very walls were reddened by the clotted blood, nay.—shudder if you will, but it is true—the brains of men who two hours ago, felt the joy of life bound in their veins, were scattered over the dark grey stones.

Old men with grey hairs, boys with brown locks and beardless cheeks, gay scarlet uniforms and the farmer's russet costume, wretches who had died a death of agony after a long life of bloody deeds ; and brave men, who had never done a dishonest act in all their days—these were there, mingled in the hideous confusion of the battle-field.

And the setting sun shone over all. Yes, the blue sky with not a cloud to mar its beauty, looked smilingly down upon the scene. Far away the Brandywine, sweet and beautiful as a sinless girl, came laughing into light, amid green boughs, its clear waves dancing in the sun.

Percy and Waldemar stood gazing in each other's faces. The proud form of Randulph swelling with the excitement of the hour, presented a strong contrast to the agile, but more effeminate figure of Monthermer. Their eyes met with the same deep gaze ; their lips compressed, their brows woven, their long hair streaming in the breeze and sun, they stood prepared for the last struggle.

Each soldier murmured wildly to himself, in that moment of suspense.

" I see my mother's form ; her face so pale, so ghastly, lighted up by those burning eyes ! I hear her voice again—' *In a lonely graveyard, beside a rustic temple, unblessed by cross or altar, amid the din of battle and the smoke of war, there shall your mother's fame be avenged, there shall the prophecy of a wronged and betrayed woman, claim its terrible fulfilment!'* I know not why it is, but a voice within my soul whispers, 'the hour has come!' "

" My father's form stands before me ! Ah, that pleading look, that snow-white hair ! *' Hasten to the wilds of Carolina, to the hills of Santee, fulfil the commission with which I have charged you, and I will bless you ! Fail, and the curse of an old man, a father, rest upon you forever !'* And here I am, the commission unfulfilled, but the death certain. My father's curse will rest upon my soul, and haunt my last hour !''

These were the fearful memories of Randulph and Percy, as gazing in each other's face, they waited for the signal.

The sun was setting. His broad disc was already sinking behind the distant woods.

" Come !" cried Randulph, placing himself on his guard.

" I await you !" exclaimed Percy, also placing himself in the graceful attitude of defence.

For a moment they stood with their swords presented, after the elegant rules of the fencing school, but that moment passed, with one wild bound, they sprang together, as if seeking for each other's heart.

Now gleaming on high, now right, now left, now circling in the air, now darting forward, their swords shone like writhing serpents in the sun. They fought amid the bodies of the dead, their eyes mingling in one steady gaze.

As Randulph was advancing, his sword levelled for a fatal thrust, a wild shriek quivered through the air from the south.

He turned, he beheld the form of Blanche, encircled by the arm of the stranger, and then felt the sword of Percy piercing his left arm, with one sharp, sudden pang.

He turned with his left arm wounded, but with his right arm free. He sprang forward ; his eyes gleamed with deadly fire ; he grasped his sword, and with terrible thrust, bounded toward Lord Percy's heart.

That sword pierced his breast, his body, and came out at his back, the red point gleaming in the sun.

Randulph held a death-stricken man suspended by his sword, for his hand still grasped the hilt, with a clutch of iron. Randulph gazed upon those livid features, the white lips and starting eyes, and felt his rage glide from him, like ice before the summer snow.

Lord Percy fell, and lay across a rising mound, pierced through and through by Randulph's sword, the hilt protruding from his breast, the red point projecting from his back, He did not bleed, but his eyes grew glassy ; his lips were like ashes.

Randulph gazed upon the dying man in silence. His rage was gone, but a strange apathy, a leaden stupefaction paralyzed his soul.

The tread of footsteps crushed the grass, and two forms stood beside

Randulph and the dying man; the form of the tall stranger, whose calm face was shadowed by a farmer's hat, the figure of Blanche, clad in snowy white, her face pale as her attire, her right hand lifting a massive parchment into light. Randulph gazed vacantly in their faces. The stranger looked upon the dying man, and turned his face away and groaned; Blanche laid her hands, one still clutching the pacquet, upon Randulph's arms, and looked up in his face.

She uttered two words, and then fell on her knees.

"Your brother!" she whispered, forcing the pacquet into his grasp.

With a wild stare, Randulph seized the parchment, opened it with trembling hands and read. Yes, read the testimonial of his mother's marriage with Waldemar, afterwards Earl of Monthermer, yes, read the offers of favor and patronage from that proud Earl to the Indian woman's son.

He tore those offers in rags, but placed that testimonial of his mother's honor close to his heart.

Then kneeling on the sod, he gathered his arms about the form of Percy, and clasped his brother to the heart, while the tears fell from his deep dark eyes.

"My brother!" he said, "Look up, and know me!"

The dying man unclosed his eyes, no longer glassy but flashing with supernatural lustre. How is it that the approach of death gives such strange powers to the soul? How is it, that things long dark, then become clear, dim shadowings of truth, then are bright day, the hand of fate, before uncertain and indistinct, then is plain and palpable? These mysteries we must leave with God our father, with Eternity our home. We have now but to tell the plain facts, not to explain them.

But certain it is, when Percy unclosed his dying eyes, and looked up in Randulph's face, certain it is, he also stretched forth his arms, and murmured:

"My brother!"

Certain it is, that—while Blanche was kneeling, the stranger standing near, both frozen with the same awe—certain it is, that their arms were interlocked, their breasts placed together, while their cheeks touched and their hair mingled.

And each murmured the words—"My brother!"

The stranger turned aside to hide his tears; Blanche wept like a babe.

At that moment perhaps, as the brothers embraced in the light of the setting sun, from the shadows of the unseen world, the beautiful face of Adele Waldemar, looked out and wept and smiled. That is, if angels weep or smile, or know a single throb of human bliss or woe. Wept for the death of the child of the proud English Countess, in whose veins flowed the blood of Norman kings—Smiled for the triumph of her child, in whose breast flowed and burned the blood of a long race of forest kings.

Percy slowly unwound his arms from his brother's neck, and then looked in his face with those dark eyes.

"Good-night, brother," he said, with a sad smile and wandering look, "We will meet again!"

He fell back on the grassy mound; the blood gushed in one thick torrent from his mouth. With that torrent his life gushed forth; he never spake a word more, but as the red stream spouted over his breast and upon the grave, he cast his eyes upward toward his brother.

Randulph arose. He drew the sword from his brother's breast. With one vigorous grasp he drew forth the dripping blade, and confronted the stranger.

"Washington!" he exclaimed, with a start of wonder.

"Yes," said the stranger uncovering his brow, "It is I, your friend. I rode northward, seeking for a pacquet which was taken from my grasp, some two hours ago, on yonder hill, when the British endeavored to make me their captive. On my way northward, I encountered this lady; she told me that Waldemar my friend, and the English lord were brothers. We pursued you, but arrived—it wrings my heart to say it—*too late!*—Have no fear for me; I will reach the American camp in safety. But this scene, Captain Waldemar, ah, it is sad and terrible!"

An expression of deep feeling, shadowed the face of the American leader, as he spoke.

"Congratulate me, General," said Randulph with a mocking smile. "For I am now, *Lord Percy.* When my father—that good old man, who left my mother to shame, some years ago—when my father dies my title will be, *Randulph, Earl of Monthermer!*"

"This is indeed a fearful history," said Washington, in a tone of deep sadness.

Randulph took the sword, dripping with his brother's blood, and bent it over his knee, with all the force of his muscular arms. It snapt in two, like a withered reed.

"There, General is my sword," he cried, flinging the pieces at the feet of Washington. "It is stained with my brother's blood. It shall never again shed blood, in any cause. Never again will my hand unsheath the sword in the cause of the white man. With that broken sword, every tie that bound me to your race, is rent asunder!"

"In the cause of the white man?" echoed Washington, with a look of surprise.

"Yes, accursed be my hand, if I ever draw a sword in your quarrels again!"

"Your quarrels?" again echoed Washington, with another wondering look. "Do you not belong to the white race? Are you not an American?"

"I am an Indian!"

The proud form of Randulph dilated to its full stature, while his bronzed visage flushed with deep excitement, glowed in the beams of the setting sun.

"I am an Indian! Yes, I am one of that race whom it has been the policy of your European adventurers, to despoil of their lands, to trample under foot, to kill by nations at a blow! I am an Indian, aye, my fathers dwelt in this land two thousand years ago. I am a king, standing upon mine own ground, for here, my fathers reigned among their people, when this European race were but a horde of savages, bending beneath the Roman yoke! If there is a drop of white blood in my veins, I disown and curse it, from this hour! For that white blood to me, brings no memory, but one brooding horror—my father's treachery, my brother's shame, my brother's murder!"

"Randulph," said Washington, whom the frenzy of this man touched with deep confusion; "Have I ever done you wrong?"

"Never, for your heart is noble, as your hand is true! But what are you? A giant among pigmies, a god among these things of clay! You will fight for them, spend your life and soul for them, and what will be your reward? They may make you a king, if success alights upon your sword, but if defeat perches there, they will nail your head to the door-post of Independence Hall!"

"Randulph ——" began Washington, in a pleading tone.

"Call me not Randulph! Nor any of these names, by which I am connected with your race. Randulph—Waldemar—Percy—Monthermer—I disown them all! My name is Wyamoke!"

He raised his hand to heaven, while his chest swelled with irrepressible emotion. At that moment as with a flushed brow and burning eye, he stood with his proud form disclosed in all its majesty by the light of the setting sun, he looked like a king, with millions at his word.

As he stood there, beside his brother's corse, two hideous forms came gliding between him and Washington; a man and woman; Death, with her parchment skull and sightless eyeballs; Blood, with his tangled red hair falling about his hideous face.

"Look 'ee stranger, will 'ee read these parchments for me?" said Blood in his screeching voice. "I got um from a dead man, in the meetin' 'ous', yander."

Randulph took the parchments, glanced at the super-scription, and then tore the envelope with an eager grasp. He read with wonder, joy, scorn and hate, flashing over his bronzed face by turns.

"Ho! Here is rare intelligence for me! Rare at any time, but now beside the dead body of my brother—ah, it is priceless! Philip Walford and Antony Denys, one—the juggle by which he held my broad lands—ah, ha, it is written here. Now I hold the deeds of my estate in my hands. Now I possess again the home of my fathers. Now—by my soul—I am Lord of Wyamoke!"

He clutched the parchments, with a frenzied grasp.

44

"Look ye fellow, here is gold for you. These papers are mine. Take the gold, and if you would gain more, bring me a spade !"

Washington's face manifested extreme surprise.

"Yes, a spade, to dig my brother's grave !"

Washington turned away from that flushed brow and glaring eye. Randulph turned, and beheld Blanche, kneeling beside the dead.

As Washington turned, he saw a massive figure advancing hastily along the graveyard. In that half-clad form, with the ebony skin glistening in the sun, he recognized the negro, whom he had seen going through the smoke of battle, his scythe in hand, and a white dog leaping by his side. The scythe still gleamed above his head ; the white dog still leapt by his side.

"Massa Wash'unton, I hab follor you for two mile," said the negro, as he stood before the rebel chief. "Look heah—I take dese papers from a dam Quaker, dat we kill in de wood yander ! 'Spose dey b'long to you ?"

Washington with a look of delight, beheld the pacquet, which Gilbert Gates had taken from his grasp, two hours ago.

"You shall be rewarded for this service, my good fellow. But this blood upon the pacquet ——"

"Dat is de scoun'rel's own blood. He murder my massa. I and Debbil help to kill him. Did'n't we, hey, Debbil ?"

The dog uttered a howl, loud, long and piercing.

"Come, my good fellow, follow me to the Continental army. I will reward you for this deed."

Washington mounted his steed, and cast one look backward, towards Randulph. He saw that it were better to leave the fate-stricken man alone with his despair, than to attempt the poor consolation of human words. He put spurs to his steed, and soon was lost among the trees to the south.

"Look heah, Debbil," shouted Sampson, as scythe on shoulder with his dog by his side, he followed the footsteps of Washington, "Do you see dat man a-hors'-back ? Eh ? Dat de gen'ul—dat Wash'unton ? 'Spose any dam red-coat lay a hand on him ? D'ye hear Debbil ! Den you mus' lap 'um blood, den I will cut him head off, wid dis scythe ! Hey Debbil— dars a debbil for you !"

Randulph stood beside the dead body of Lord Percy, gazing in silence upon the kneeling form of Blanche. She knelt in prayer, veiling in her eyes from the light, with her clasped hands.

There was deep silence for a moment, only broken by a stealthy footfall. Blood stood by the side of Randulph with a rude spade in his hand. He took the spade and waved the camp-follower from the scene. He was then alone, with Blanche and the dead.

"Blanche !" he said.

She looked up. Her dark hair escaping from its slender cincture, fell in waving masses down over her white robes. The sunlight streamed over

her pale face, while her eyes lighted up with an expression of ineffable tenderness.

"Blanche," he said, his bronzed visage softening in a look of deep and
mingled emotion, "You will help me to bury my dead brother? Will you
not?"

The sun went down.

His last beam streaming over the cold faces of the battle-field, lighted up
this strange scene.

In the centre of the graveyard, lay the corse of a young man, whose
graceful form, was clad in velvet and gold. His pale face, relieved by curls
of jet, was upturned to the blue sky; a strange smile lingered about his
cold lips.

On one side of the grassy mound on which his corse was thrown, knelt
a man in the prime of early manhood, his kingly form also clad in velvet
and gold, his bronzed visage bearing a striking resemblance to the face of
the dead. Grasping a spade in his manly arm, he knelt there, and with
tears in his dark eyes perused his brother's face.

On the other side of the mound knelt a young and beautiful girl, clad in
robes of white, with her raven hair falling over her shoulders, her hands
clasped, her pale face turned toward the blue sky.

The sun went down.

The voice of that maiden murmuring the earnest accents of prayer, arose
in sweet music, from the silence of that place of graves.

The moon arose.

Her first long gleam shone over the cold face of the **dead**, and lighted up
the darkness of that new-made grave.

"Come, Blanche, we will bury our brother!"

Randulph bent down and took the body of Percy in his arms. He was
about to lower that corse into its last nome. when a deep sob shook his
chest. Bending down by the cold light of the moon, yes, kneeling on the
upturned earth, he gazed long and earnestly upon his brother's face. So
pale and yet so beautiful, with its dark curls and manly brow! He gathered that cold form to his heart; his tears, the scalding tears of man's despair, fell pattering over the closed eyelids of the dead.

At last he lowered the body into the grave. He placed the hat, the sword
of the soldier beside his corse. Then gathering up the pieces of his brother's
sword, Randulph flung the hilt into the grave, but placed the point, stained
with his brother's blood within his vest, next to his heart. A meaning
smile lighted up his face as he placed it there.

"Blanche," said Randulph in a choking voice, "He is my brother. Cover
his face. I cannot!"

The maiden advanced, and took the white 'kerchief from her breast.

That 'kerchief was pure, for it was warm with the pulsations of that virgin bosom, which now rose gently into light. What holier offering than this, to the corse of the dead ? She stood over the grave ; the white 'kerchief floated down, and rested upon his face.

Then murmuring a prayer, she took the fresh earth in her hands, and scattered gently over the 'kerchief which veiled the brow of George, Lord Percy of Monthermer.

She knelt on the graveyard sod. Randulph grasped the spade, and then with a hollow sound, the cold clods rattled down upon the form of the dead. His bosom heaved with sobs ; his tears fell all the while. At last the work was done. Then the green sod was smoothed over the mound again ; the moonbeams shone gently over the blood-stained grass. George, Lord Percy of Monthermer was left alone in his grave, with the 'kerchief from a virgin's bosom, veiling his face from the death-worm and the clod.

They joined hands above the grave, the maiden and the Prince of Wyamoke, and while the moon shone over her upraised face, over his magnificant form, this vow was recorded by those good angels who watch over woman's love —

" Thou art all that is left to me, Blanche ! By the form of my mother, who now hovers above us, by the corse of my brother, who rests beneath this sod, I swear to love thee, in life, in death, forever !"

END OF BOOK FOURTH.

EPILOGUE.

THE Fourteenth of November, darkest night of all, came at last.

Within the confines of the third chamber, knelt the old man. That room, was hung with black velvet, drooping in heavy folds to the floor. The floor and vaulted roof, were all of the same dead hue. On a small table, standing near the centre of the room, stood a tall wax candle, flinging a brilliant light around.

All was silent there. Without the storm was heard, bursting in all its fury above the towers of Monthermer. The thunder mourned, ever and anon from the ravines of distant hills.

The old man, the proudest of the English nobility, the ruler of broad domains, where revenues might have purchased the life-blood of thousands, knelt there alone, in the last extremity of despair.

At last he arose, he drew aside the hangings, in one corner of the room, and then started back with clasped hands.

The picture of a beautiful woman, in the blush of maidenhood, gleamed in the light. Beautiful she was, as the shadows of the hangings, gathering darkly around, made that painted canvass, seem a living woman, beautiful she was with one small foot advanced, from the white dress, the fair hand uplifted twining among her flowing dark hair, but it was a strange, a wild, almost a supernatural loveliness.

The face, clear and white as alabaster, reddened by a solitary flush in the centre of each cheek, the large dilating eyes, fringed by long lashes, the small mouth curving in a smile, the young form, with limbs and bosom, just starting into the bloom of womanhood ; it was a picture to love and look upon, the whole day long. The contour of these features, was not European, but moulded in a beauty, that was at once, original and indescribable. A loveliness that seemed born of deep forests, nursed into bloom, by the music of mighty cataracts, under the blush of stainless skies.

The old man advanced, and fell on his knees before the picture, calling on God for mercy.

"Adele, my wife, for twenty-three years, have I borne in my breast the agonies of the damned. Now hear my last confession—forgive me—pray to God that I may die. Twenty-four years ago, we were married, in the wild forest of Wyamoke. You know that I loved you ; that I never loved, but you. But a letter from my father called me home—I was to marry a proud lady, a Countess, who would give a new lustre to the House of Monthermer. My father bade me, to return. I struggled—agonized—yielded, and was a villain !

"I returned, married my noble bride, and an eternal remorse. When I gathered her to my breast I thought of you. You were my soul, my dream ; at last the agony warmed my very blood and—One morning my wife, the Countess, was found dead on her couch, with a mark about her throat. I murdered her because she slept on the bosom, which was *your's.*

(349)

"Then the hell of my life began. Then I built these rooms, eacn consecrated to an awful memory. One, to the Seventeenth of July, when I fled from your side—one, to the Eleventh of September, the anniversary of my wife's marriage and death—and the last, O God be merciful—to the Fourteenth of November, the day when we joined hands and heart, in the dim woods of Wyamoke. Then I began the awful penance, which has endured for twenty years. In one room, the lash, in the other, the dead body of my murdered wife, in the last your picture; these awaited me. Say, Adele, have I not suffered, enough? Is not the cup full? Can one more drop of agony, be wrung from my withered heart?

"Old before my time, my name the proudest among the proud, but an eternal memorial of my guilt; the meanest peasant who digs for his bread, is my superior. Now Adele, may I not die? Speak—tell me that I have suffered enough!

"Yes, Adele, you know it; wrung by the memories of twenty-four years, I have sent my son, heir to the broad lands of Monthermer, across the wide waters, to search out and bless your child, *our* child, with the testimonial of his mother's honor! I learned the story of your death, the fraud of the villain who usurped your lands, the existence of our son, but three months ago, by a wanderer from Wyamoke. Tell me, have the brother's met? A fearful dream flashed over my brain, on the night of the Eleventh of November, but it was but a dream! Tell me have the brothers met, have they embraced?"

"They have met," a voice rang through the chamber, like a knell, "They have embraced!"

The old man, turned his head over his shoulder. With a shudder, he beheld that proud form, rising like a shadow from the other world, the bronzed face with its waving locks of dark brown, the gleaming eyes, shining steadily into his soul.

"They have met in battle, they have embraced in death!"

The stranger drew from his breast. a piece of steel, and flung it at the old man's feet.

"That steel is red with his blood! My brother—your son!"

"Who art thou?" shrieked the old man.

"Thine heir. The Earl of Monthermer when thou art dead,—but that I scorn your race, your title and your blood now coursing in my veins!"

The Earl rose tremblingly to his feet.

He gazed in the bronzed face of that strange man, now glooming with unutterable woe, and then sprang forward, with outstretched arms:

"Child of Adele, be merciful to thy father!"

"Back," shrieked the stranger, "Back. by the memory of my mother's shame, by the cold corse of my brother. I warn ye! Touch me not! My name is Wyamoke."

He folded his arms, and gazed in the face of his father, with glaring eyes. His frown, his look were terrible. His deep voice thrilled the blood of the old man.

For a moment they stood regarding each other, the father and the son. Deep silence reigned throughout that chamber.

"I come to visit your last hour, with a curse," said the stranger, "The curse of the widow, who died broken-hearted, from her shame, the curse of the orphan who became a fratricide for you! Go old man, go to your God, this curse upon your soul!"

The Earl looked upon his son, for a moment, and then sunk to the floor, with the blood spouting from his mouth.

At the moment the child of the Indian woman looked up and beheld his mother. That face, the smile, came over his soul like a spell, driving the gloom from his brow, the phrenzy from his heart. He knelt beside the Earl, with outstretched hands:

"Father," he groaned in a husky voice, "It is a dark world—what are we all, but the playthings of a merciless fate? Father—I have endured much, but I forgive! Father, my mother's fate was dark, but she smiles forgiveness on you now!"

The old man raised his pale face—smiled faintly—and was dead.

"Now," said he, whom we have called Randulph the Prince, as he arose, Now I am *Earl of Monthermer!*"

A mocking smile quivered on his compressed lips.

"And now, the rude Indian, the Earl of Monthermer, trampling this pomp and power beneath his feet, will seek his forest home. Wyamoke! I long to breathe your air again, for now my mother's face shines serenely on my soul, Blanche! For you, the Earl of Monthermer forsakes his princely home, his lands, the smile of Royalty, the pomp of **power—Blanche I come!**"

THE END.